List of

Lancelot, a woman in disguise.

Guinevere, queen of Britain as the wife of King Arthur, Lancelot's lover

King Arthur, king of Britain

King Arthur's relatives and close connections:

Mordred, King Arthur's bastard son, born to a prostitute and raised cruelly in a brothel. Arthur doesn't know of his existence.

Queen Morgause, Arthur's aunt, the sister of the mother he never knew. Morgause has ruled Lothian and Orkney since the death of her husband, King Lot.

Gawaine, Morgause's eldest son, King Arthur's cousin, and Lancelot's closest friend. He knows Lancelot's secret but doesn't disclose it.

Agravaine, Gawaine's younger brother.

Gaheris, Gawaine's brother. He's younger than Agravaine.

Gareth, Gawaine's youngest brother.

Morgan, Arthur's half-sister and one-time lover

Elaine, Morgan's daughter by Arthur. Arthur doesn't know of her existence.

Galahad, a girl disguised as a boy and raised in a convent. Morgan's daughter by Gawaine, but she has been told she's Arthur's child. No one outside the convent knows of her existence.

Cai, Arthur's foster brother, the seneschal in charge of managing Camelot, including the kitchen and the servants.

Merlin, the man who raised Arthur. Merlin was schooled in the old religion at Avalon, which no longer belongs to Old Believers but now to monks. Old Believers are fading away.

Women at Camelot:
Lionors, Bors's wife and Guinevere's friend
Fencha, Guinevere's old serving woman
Ragnal, a serving woman and Gawaine's favorite mistress
Luned, Guinevere's serving woman
Creirwy, a serving woman
Talwyn, a girl whom Guinevere is fostering
Gwyl, a mistress of Arthur's
Nimue, a girl at Camelot
Felicia, Gwyl's daughter, a girl at Camelot
Gralla, a girl at Camelot
Lavinia, a girl at Camelot
Lysanda, a lady at Camelot
Gwynhwyfach, Guinevere's bastard sister, who was captured by the Saxons when she was a girl. Guinevere believed she was dead.

Warriors at Camelot:
Bedwyr, Arthur's first follower, a warrior
Bors, one of Arthur's long-time warriors
Peredur, a long-time warrior of Arthur's
Gereint, a warrior
Sangremore, a warrior
Bellangere, a warrior
Tristram, a warrior

LANCELOT AND GUINEVERE

CAROL ANNE DOUGLAS

Hermione Books
WASHINGTON, DC

Lancelot and Guinevere/ Carol Anne Douglas
ISBN 978-0-9967722-2-8

Dinadan, a warrior who is Cai's lover
Patricius, a warrior
Mador, a warrior and Patricius's cousin
Galihodin, who trains the young warriors

Younger warriors:
Percival (Percy)
Lionel
Camlach, he's been told he's Gawaine's son, but he isn't
Cildydd, he's also been told he's Gawaine's son, but isn't
Clegis
Colles, Gwyl's son
Blioberis
Gillimer
Accolon

Other men at Camelot:
Father Donatus, the chief priest at Camelot
Catwal, Lancelot's blind serving man
Hywel, Gawaine's servant
Tewdar, Arthur's servant
*Gryffyd, a warrior who went mad during Arthur's war
with the Saxons and is now confined to a room. He thinks
all the men he sees are Saxons and enemies. He's
Talwyn's father.*
Huw, Gryffd's attendant
Cuall, the stable master
Cathbad, a stablehand

Convent of the Holy Mother:
Abbess Perpetua
Mother Ninian, a nun who earlier was a leader of the Old
Believers
Sister Darerca, Ninian's special friend
Sister Valeria, Guinevere's childhood friend
Sister Fidelma, Valeria's special friend

Monastery:
Father Paulus
Abbot Ulfin
Infirmarian

Saxons:
Aldwulf, a thane
Hilda, his daughter

Other characters:
Drian, a harper who is a woman disguised as a man,
a friend of Lancelot's
Iseult, Tristram's lover and the wife of King Mark of
Cornwall
Enid, Gereint's wife
Antonius, an old friend of Lancelot's
Branwen, Antonius's mistress, who left the convent to be
with him
Cecilia, a wealthy lady
Bagdemagus, a lord in the Southwest of England, who is
raising Elaine as his daughter at Morgan's request. His
dead wife was Morgan's cousin.

Aglovale, a former warrior of Arthur's now living quietly at his home in Dyfed. He doesn't want to fight anymore. He's Peredur's brother, Percy's father, and Lancelot's friend. He knows Lancelot's secret.

Olwen, Aglovale's wife, who also knows Lancelot's secret

Illtud, Aglovale and Olwen's younger son

King Maelgon of Gwynedd

Keri, Maelgon's daughter

Royce, her betrothed

Uwaine, son of King Uriens of Rheged

Dunaut, Coan, and Tudy, panderers who raised Mordred brutally

1 CAMELOT

The great hall at Camelot blazed with torches and the fires in its huge firepits. Lancelot felt her face blaze even more as Gawaine said, "So, Lancelot, how is Etaine? Why don't you visit her before she gives birth? I look forward to drinking a toast to your son or daughter. What did she say she was going to name a boy? Galahad, was it?"

Lancelot cast an angry look at red-bearded Gawaine, who was clearly the tallest man in the hall even when they were all seated at the spokes of the round table. The gold torque around Gawaine's neck showed that he was highborn, son of the late King Lot of Lothian and Orkney and Queen Morgause, who had succeeded her husband. The torque was only a little less grand than the one King Arthur wore, but the difference was enough to be noticeable.

"I have no intention of seeing Etaine, now or ever." Lancelot thumped her goblet on the table. As Gawaine knew well, Etaine had pretended to be Guinevere so she could lie with Lancelot and claim that Lancelot was the father of the child she was carrying. Gawaine had lain with the lady instead, and guessed that she was already with child, but had persuaded Lancelot to refrain from denying paternity. That was his idea of protecting Lancelot, now that he had discovered she was a woman. Lancelot thought she had been right not to tell Guinevere that Gawaine knew, for Guinevere would have cringed at his jests even more than Lancelot did.

"As you won't marry the lady and have no wife to fatten you up, I must do what I can to keep you from starving," Gawaine replied, cutting off a shank of mutton and throwing it onto Lancelot's plate.

She made an angry gesture with her knife and looked pointedly at the weapons and shields hanging on the walls, as if suggesting she wanted to fight him if he didn't stop talking about her supposed fatherhood. Would Gawaine's love for teasing and jesting lead him to reveal her secret unwittingly? Lancelot shuddered inwardly, remembering how recently the king's exiled sister, Morgan, had threatened to reveal her sex. The thought of losing her place at Camelot made Lancelot's stomach muscles tighten. She did not want to eat the meat that Gawaine had tossed to her, but it smelled so appealing that she began to slice it.

Some warriors laughed with disbelief at Lancelot's denial of attachment to Etaine. "No doubt Lancelot has good reasons for refusing to see the lady," King Arthur said. The slightly graying red-haired king, who knew that Lancelot had not lain with Etaine but not that Lancelot was a woman, cast a sympthetic look at his queen, Guinevere.

If only Guinevere were not Arthur's wife, Lancelot wished, as she had wished every day for many years. Guinevere was her own true love, and it still pained them that they could not acknowledge that fact.

The king was not the only one looking at Guinevere, Lancelot noticed. Half the hall was staring at Lancelot, while the other half watched Guinevere to see her reaction to the talk of Lancelot being the father of another woman's child. Although almost no one knew that Guinevere and Lancelot were lovers, people constantly watched them for signs of love for each other. How difficult it was to try to hide their love.

Lancelot made a slight sign with her fingers to communicate her sympathy to Guinevere. At least Guinevere knew that she never looked at any other women.

Then Bedwyr, a thin-lipped man with a left arm that had lacked its hand since the Saxon War, chimed in, "Lancelot says that he has no call for congratulations, but Bors does. His wife just gave birth to their twelfth child, the eighth boy! Let's toast him."

The warriors bellowed their congratulations and swilled their mead in Bors's honor. The gray-mustached warrior who was their object beamed, nodded his thanks, and said, "Another gift from God."

Gawaine added, "You helped, Bors," and the hall was filled with such loud laughter that the harper, who was playing a song about Arthur's defeat of the Saxons, paused.

While the warriors' attention was focused on Bors, Guinevere made unobtrusive hand signals to Lancelot indicating her extreme annoyance over Gawaine's remark. Guinevere's blue eyes showed displeasure. Lancelot signaled back that she could do nothing about Gawaine's tales and jests.

The sage Merlin, whose once-gray beard had turned white, did not join in the warriors' laughter. Instead, he sighed. "Such merriment," he said to the king. "I hope it will last."

"Why, of course it will. Let the hall be filled with joy," Arthur replied heartily, then took a swig of mead.

"Have some mead, Merlin. You've been looking a little pale."

The old man took only a sip.

One of the king's wolfhounds, padding about in the rushes on the floor, approached Lancelot and thrust her head in Lancelot's lap. Lancelot cut off a bit of the mutton and gave it to her.

Later in the night, Lancelot went as usual to the queen's bed chamber. Guinevere thrilled at the sight of her. Lancelot's advent always felt like a celebration.

"Our room awaits you. Here is our enchanted bed," Guinevere said, indicating the bed draped with the finest green cloth.

Guinevere enjoyed the warm fire in the brazier and the scent of her beeswax candles. But she scarcely saw the hangings on the wall that depicted women picking apples and gathering wheat, or her gray cat, Grayse, sleeping on a chair heaped with cushions.

Lancelot's beauty outshone everything else, Guinevere thought. Lancelot's long, angular face framed by wavy black hair led many of the ladies to cast glances her way. Of course they believed that Lancelot was a man. Her large brown eyes, touched as ever with a hint of sadness, looked at Guinevere as if she were the fairest woman in the world. Lancelot's movements when she first entered Guinevere's room were always tense, as if she feared being sent away, though she never had been. After a while, she seemed to relax.

"I don't like this tale about your being the father of a child." Guinevere sighed. She also had been displeased by the way Arthur had looked at her when everyone talked about Lancelot fathering a child. Must she worry about keeping him at bay? She had stopped lying with Arthur before she began with

Lancelot, and she liked her husband much better now than when she had been required to go to his bed. Arthur knew that she and Lancelot loved each other, and did not mind overmuch. He imagined that it had been his idea, so Guinevere would conceive a child, but Lancelot had been her lover well before Arthur had suggested the affair.

"Gawaine's just jesting, as he likes to do. What does it matter? I love none but you," Lancelot said soothingly. "Be not angry, my queen, for you are my forest as well as my love. Let me comb your hair and visit my trees," she said, brushing a stray strand of Guinevere's black hair from her forehead.

"If I may visit your water-meadow later," Guinevere teased, removing from her neck the golden torque that showed she was queen.

"Water-meadow? Is that a swamp? Oh, lovely. Your compliments are not so sweet, my lady." Lancelot laughed, undoing Guinevere's black braids, which were dark as her own hair.

"Fair, indeed. A water-meadow in which an orchid grows. I prefer moors to mountains."

Lancelot kissed her neck. "What, do you think of mountains as men? No, they surely are breasts. And here is my forest," she said, pressing her face into Guinevere's hair. "Here are the oaks, the alders, the hazel, and the rowan. I am jealous of anyone else who has ever combed your hair."

Guinevere laughed. That, at least, Arthur had never done. "Including my old nurse Macha, who always complained about the tangles?"

"Including her, of course. I wish I had seen you as a child."

Guinevere swished her head back and forth so the hair flopped across her warrior's face. "You would have seen many tempers if you had."

"Stay still, or I cannot comb your hair," Lancelot complained, trying to pull a silver comb gently through the long strands.

"I can't enjoy it while your poor breasts are bound." Evading the comb, Guinevere turned to her. "Let me unbind them."

Lancelot surrendered the comb. She raised her arms and let Guinevere help her take off her crimson tunic, then stood while Guinevere unwrapped the thick cloth that held down her breasts.

Guinevere pressed her lips to the breasts and Lancelot held her tightly.

"Bind me to your bosom," Guinevere teased, and Lancelot, who was much taller, kissed the top of her head.

"Would that I could. How soft your cheeks are. If only mine could be soft for you." As Guinevere knew, Lancelot rubbed them with pumice every morning so it would look as if she had shaved.

"If they were any softer, I would faint when I touch them, so it is well that they are not." Guinevere reached up and caressed Lancelot's cheek. It was far softer than Arthur's cheeks ever had been. Now he wore a beard, and the hair in it was stiff, like a boar's. She was glad that she could just brush her husband's cheek with her lips and be done with it.

She had wanted Lancelot ever since the day they met, but it had taken years to win the sweet warrior to her bed. Lancelot hadn't realized that Guinevere could see that she was a woman, and even when she learned that Guinevere knew the truth, had feared the sin of adultery. The sin didn't worry Guinevere greatly, though perhaps it should. She suspected that Lancelot, who had not received the sacraments since the day they first embraced, said prayers that were haunted with guilt. But how could such a deep love be wrong? Rather, it had been wrong to lie loveless with Arthur.

The night passed all too quickly, and at a dark, early hour, Lancelot had to bind her breasts and clothe herself again. Dawn was the one time that they could not see each other. Guinevere imagined how the rosy light would look illuminating Lancelot's face.

Guinevere called her back to the bed and pressed her lips one more time. She gently touched Lancelot's left hand, which had lost two fingers in the Saxon War. It was amazing that Lancelot could use that hand for many things, fighting included.

"'Til tonight," Guinevere murmured.

"A thousand things will happen before we can be together again in the dark," Lancelot said, sighing.

She walked to the largest tapestry, the scene of women gathering fruit, and pulled it back, revealing the hidden panel to the passageway she used.

Guinevere returned to sleep. When dawn had passed and sunlight streamed into the room, her white-haired serving woman, Fencha, who had the only key to the queen's room other than Guinevere's, entered and greeted her.

"Did you sleep well, Lady Guinevere?"

"Indeed. And you, Fencha?"

"Tolerably well, my lady." She smiled because Guinevere had asked her.

Guinevere slid out of bed and took the damp cloth Fencha handed her to wash her face.

A series of mews, increasingly desperate, startled Guinevere.

"Here, Grayse," she called, looking about the room. The cat was not under the table or the bed, nor was she hidden among Guinevere's gowns.

The mews became louder.

"She's in the secret passage,"Fencha said, moving to free her.

Grayse bounded over to Guinevere, who reached down to pat her. "God's eyebrows, what if someone else had heard her and discovered the hidden door--and the fact that I was using it!" Guinevere exclaimed. Fencha had always known about the door--had in fact told Guinevere about it when she came to Camelot--and about Lancelot. "Such a simple thing. How near we come to being discovered." Guinevere gritted her teeth and tried to dismiss the thought. Arthur did not object to their love, but he would care very much if anyone else learned that his wife was unfaithful to him. Indeed, he would have to punish them. Guinevere did not want to contemplate just what that punishment might be.

Mordred crept through the darkened brothel. He knew what door Dunaut, the owner, slept behind. With a whore, of course. Sometimes when Mordred was younger, he had been the one who was forced to lie with Dunaut. Raped. Now was the time for his revenge.

He wished he could torture the panderer, but that would rouse the others. Mordred clutched the sharpest kitchen knife, the only weapon he was allowed to touch. He was sorry that Dunaut would die in his sleep and would never know that Mordred had killed him, but there was no time for the luxury of confronting him. It was necessary to act as quickly as possible, and Mordred understood necessity.

Mordred knew every inch of the brothel, for he had been raised there. He was ignorant of the rest of the world, but he would remedy that.

Mordred wedged his knife through the crack in the door, springing the latch noiselessly. He stole his way to the bed.

Dunaut lay far enough away from the girl so that Mordred could probably kill him without killing her, too--not that he cared. Not when every scar on his back had come from Dunaut's beating.

For an instant, he regarded the sleeping panderer. Then he slashed Dunaut's throat neatly.

The girl opened her eyes.

"Make a sound and I'll kill you, too," Mordred whispered.

She cowered, and shrank to the furtherest corner of the small bed.

There were two other panderers to kill, though Dunaut had been the chief one. All of them had mocked Mordred for being a king's son, born to a whore. If his so-called mother, who was only a whore, hadn't died when he was a small child, he would have killed her too, Mordred thought.

Drunk with elation, he moved to the second panderer's room. His bloody knife was ready for more work. Now for Tudy, who had liked to kick Mordred when he was a boy and watch him fall on the floor. And then kick him again. Tudy was heavier, and might require a deeper thrust of Mordred's blade.

This latch also opened easily--Mordred had of course tried them earlier. He entered. Tudy stirred in his sleep, so Mordred bounded across the floor and stabbed him. The girl beside him screamed before Mordred could warn her not to and leapt from the bed.

"Shut up, fool! I'll be the owner now, and you dare not disobey me," Mordred said, checking to make sure that his knife had gone home and Tudy was dead.

"What's up?" came a shout from outside the door. Coan, the third and youngest panderer, not so many years older than Mordred, was on his way. Coan had liked to shame Mordred by throwing the food Mordred served in Mordred's face.

Mordred waited. The girl shivered in a corner.

Bearing a rushlight, the panderer peered cautiously through the open door. His other hand held a club.

Mordred grabbed a chair and threw it at him.

Dropping both torch and club, Coan fell. Mordred was on him in an instant, holding down the thrashing man until he could slash his throat. Coan screamed and tried to get away, but Mordred kept slashing until he fell silent.

Kicking the corpse, Mordred grabbed the chamber pot and doused the fallen torch. The brothel was his now, and he didn't want it damaged.

Emerging from the doorway, he yelled, "Here, every one of you! Come here. I'm the master now."

He had waited for a night when there were no customers. Only the whores and assorted rough men who worked at the brothel were there.

"Light the rushlights," Mordred commanded.

Men and women scurried to obey him.

Mordred held his bloodied knife before the assembled throng. "I've killed all three of the masters, and I'm the master here. Obey me, and you'll live as you did before. Disobey, and you'll follow them. Which will it be?"

Several cracking voices called out, "We'll obey."

"You'd better. Now clean up their rooms and throw their bodies to the pigs. And bring me some mead."

Mordred took a seat at one of the tables in the front room and waited to be served, for a change, instead of serving. He did not wipe off the blood that had splattered on him. It pleased him.

This was only the first step. He would have money now, plenty of money. And he would find a man to teach him sword-fighting and the ways of the High King's court. He would go to his father, the king, someday, but only when he was prepared.

He was young, strong, and clever, Mordred told himself. His whole life was ahead of him. King Mordred had a good sound to it. Mordred Rex.

2 IDYLLS of CAMELOT

Guinevere's morning had started out fair, but just as she set out rain began to pour down. She pulled the hood of her fine blue wool cloak over her head and dashed over the cobblestones to the house where Bors and his wife Lionors lived.

Lionors was Guinevere's favorite of the court ladies, so she wanted to see how Lionors fared after childbed. Much as she liked Lionors, Guinevere was glad no one expected the queen to attend women when they gave birth. The sights, sounds, and smells of a birthing room reminded her too vividly of the night that she had watched her mother die, trying to bear a son for Guinevere's father, King Leodegran of Powys. The mere thought of being so torn apart made Guinevere shudder. Convinced that she would have died if she had borne a child, Guinevere had taken a potion to prevent conception when she was lying with Arthur. But she was willing to pay her respects to Lionors the day after the birth.

Guinevere thought of the other reason that she had never born a child. Arthur had had dreams that an infant son would rise up and kill him. He therefore had also sometimes tried to prevent conception. She still shuddered at the memory of his dreams, and his belief in them. He had hoped that if she bore another man's child he would escape the fate foretold in his dreams.

A serving woman opened the door to Bors's house, bowed her head to Guinevere, and took her dripping cloak.

The first thing Guinevere saw on entering the house was a cross on the wall, and the first thing she heard was the children. Two small boys were squabbling over the rules of a board game and a little girl was talking to her wooden doll. Guinevere thought she would go mad if she had to listen to such chatter all day, but of course if she had borne children they would not have had to live in such close quarters.

The older of the boys bowed to the queen, but the other two children were too young to know court manners. She nodded to them all and followed the serving woman into the room where Lionors lay in bed.

Lionors was pale, but her gray hair was neatly braided. A red and wrinkled baby lay sleeping beside her, and Guinevere was grateful that it was not awake and crying. She silently castigated Bors for fathering a child on a gray-haired woman. Would Lionors never have a chance to rest? Bearing twelve children--not to mention the miscarriages and stillbirths Lionors had endured--was enough to kill any woman.

Lionors tried to prop herself up. "Lady Guinevere, how kind of you to come."

"Rest, rest," Guinevere said, making a gesture indicating that Lionors shouldn't try to rise. "How are you faring? Was it a difficult birth?"

"Not as easy as some, but I'll be fine presently." Lionors lay back against her pillow, which showed that she must be fatigued. "Here is my dear little one." She regarded her infant tenderly, for Lionors seemed to have all the proper sentiments. "He is well, God be praised. We are naming him Ban, after Bors's father."

"How nice. I am glad that you are recovering." Guinevere was overjoyed that Lionors had survived. She never fully expected that women would. Bors's father was King Ban of Lesser Britain, and Bors lived modestly for a king's son, even one of the youngest sons. But Bors had always been humble, which made him far different from the other kings' sons at Camelot. No one could call Gawaine of Lothian and Orkney modest or humble.

"We are fortunate that the Lord has seen fit to give us so many children," Lionors said. "But the Lord's ways are mysterious." She appeared to be apologizing to Guinevere because she assumed that Guinevere must grieve over her childless state.

Guinevere wished she could say that she had been terrified at the thought of bearing children, indeed had taken a potion to prevent bearing any, but she could not confide in anyone but Fencha.

The baby woke and began to wail. Lionors took him to her breast, and Guinevere made her excuses to depart.

As Guinevere left the room, her skirt swept too close to the fire in the brazier that heated the room. She suppressed a gasp and pulled her skirt away.

"Are you all right, Lady Guinevere?" Lionors asked.

"Yes, of course." Guinevere flushed. She was afraid of fire, and anyone close to her knew that, but the fear embarrassed her. She did not want to fear anything, certainly nothing so ordinary. She hastened away.

The rain had ended, at least for the moment, but Guinevere had to pass Gawaine in the courtyard. She might have preferred a downpour. She had little liking for Gawaine, a man of many mistresses, both highborn and lowborn, and moreover, he bragged about his prowess.

"Good-day, Lady Guinevere," he said, nodding to her but not smiling. His red hair and beard were thoroughly soaked from the rain.

"God grant you good day, Lord Gawaine," Guinevere replied in a cold tone, and walked past him. They were always polite, of course, despite their lack of fondness for each other, but she thought that as a queen she could be cooler to him than he was to her. And why should she be cordial to a man who had pretended to be Lancelot when he bedded a woman--that shameless Etaine? And Lancelot was supposed to be his friend, and they had saved each other's lives. Thank all the angels he did not know that Lancelot was a woman.

There was only an occasional drizzle on a fine spring day. Tiny green leaves heralded the coming of the new world.

Lancelot might have preferred to ride through the forest alone, but she blended into the group of warriors surrounding the king as if she were one of the pack of hounds that had been brought on the boar hunt.

The forest was her home, dearer to her than walls, save those of the room where she lay with her sweet queen. Yet the forest saddened as well as delighting her, for it was in a wood in Lesser Britain, across the sea, that a brigand had raped and murdered her mother when Lancelot was only a child. The smell of pines reminded her of that day. She had grabbed a stick and put out the murderer's eye, but not being able to save her mother had seemed unbearable. Her pious father, horrified by the rape, had raised her as a boy so that she would be safe from all men forever.

She might be safe from rape as long as men believed she was a man, but she certainly had her share of battles with them, and had slain too many.

The warriors on their horses galloped through the trees. The sight of the men, their eyes bright with the thought of killing, and the sound of their horses' hoofbeats reminded her of the times when she had fought beside them, hunting Saxons and burning Saxon towns.

She closed her eyes at the memory of battlefields littered with corpses, but a wren's song lifted her spirits.

Barking drowned out the music of the wren. The master of hounds and the men who accompanied him had found a boar and were driving it towards the king and the warriors. Dismounting, they held their spears in readiness. Arthur's face and some of the others' were red with an excitement that Lancelot did not share. She smelled the damp spring forest and noticed new fronds curling out of the earth. A few hepaticas and crocuses grew where patches of light shone through the trees.

Spring was not the proper time for a boar hunt, but the king wanted one, and everyone must do as he wished. They would not kill a sow in the spring, of course, only a male.

The boar burst into sight. His tusks were larger than most and his eyes blazed with fury at those who harried him. Like a warrior determined not to die without killing a foe, he lunged at Arthur. Arthur, usually steady and swift with a spear, slipped in the damp earth and fell to his knees.

Lancelot threw herself in front of the king, as she always had when he seemed to be in danger. Saying her usual brief prayer to the spirit of the creature she expected to kill, she readied her spear.

Thrusting himself between Lancelot and the boar, Gawaine impaled it. Startled, Lancelot barely managed to hold back her own blow to avoid injuring Gawaine. The boar grunted with rage, trying to turn to strike his attacker, but Gawaine forced the spear further in, pushing the beast to the earth.

Warriors shouted with exaltation at the boar's death. Gawaine pulled out his spear, and the huntsmen rushed in to cut off the bits of the kill that would be thrown to the dogs and to bind up the body to carry on a pole to the caer.

Smirking as if he had slain all the boars in the forest, Gawaine turned away from the boar.

Lancelot glared at him. A warrior never took another man's kill, unless he lost his footing as Arthur had. "How dare you do that."

"Pardon. It was your kill, but I know you don't much like slaying the beasts and I wanted to particularly." Gawaine grinned broadly, as if he had proved himself a better hunter than Lancelot.

Arthur put a hand on Lancelot's shoulder. "What you did was very odd, Gawaine. I'd think you had killed enough boars not to care much about being the one to kill this one. Lance, be your good and gentle self and don't quarrel. Certes, I am the best protected king in the world with both of you great men to guard me."

The king turned away.

Glancing from the boar to Gawaine, Lancelot said, "You're a swine yourself."

"How not, since the goddess Cerridwen has come to me many times as a swine, and I have pleased her," Gawaine said.

"May you have many more sows," Lancelot retorted.

"Thank you," he said graciously, as if she had wished him good health.

The warriors who had heard them laughed.

Lancelot knew that if Gawaine had still believed she was a man, he would have left the boar to her. If he persisted in such foolishness, he not only insulted her but also jeopardized her position. Surely the other warriors would think it strange if Gawaine always threw himself between Lancelot and danger.

The king's party rode back full of good cheer. Several talked about the taste of roast boar.

Harpers who had come to lighten the journey sang heroic hunting songs, but Dinadan, a handsome blue-eyed warrior whose sardonic smile matched his friend Cai's, sang a different tune. Dinadan's words told of a warrior who boasted of slaying a great bear (and everyone winced because Arthur was called the Bear), but then admitted that he had really killed an old wolf. Then he acknowledged that his prey was indeed a fox. Reluctantly, he was forced to admit that it was a hound. No, truly, it was a very fierce weasel. The warrior who listened to him looked behind a bush and saw that the boastful hunter had killed a mouse. But, the first warrior insisted, it was a mouse with a rare streak of ferocity.

Arthur and the warriors all roared. Gawaine laughed most of all. Lancelot knew that not even Dinadan would have dared to sing such verses if any warrior other than cheerful Gawaine had slain the boar.

The hunting party passed by a peasant's hut. Half a dozen thin children ran out to watch them.

"Lucky nobles'll eat that boar tonight," piped up one in a reedy voice.

Arthur stopped his horse. "Are you hungry, boy?" he called.

"Yes, lord," the boy stuttered.

"We killed our last pig at Samhain because it was too weak to last the winter. We finished the salt pork long ago."

"Cut off a leg for them," Arthur commanded the huntsmen.

Most of the warriors smiled, proud of their king's generosity.

A gaunt woman who must have been younger than she looked if she was the children's mother came out of the mud-daub hut and scolded, "Children, don't bother these nobles. Why, 'tis the king himself!" She bowed her head.

"Please accept some meat, good woman," Arthur said. "I know that spring is the starving time, before the crops come, but I don't want my people to go hungry."

"Bless you, majesty," she cried, raising her arms in a gesture of praise.

Lancelot told herself for the ten thousandth time that she had sinned greatly by lying with her kind lord's wife. And by wishing that she didn't have to see his face every day.

Lancelot found that the tunic she wanted to wear at supper had a slight tear. She therefore searched for Catwal, her servant, who was blind and liked men, both of which made her comfortable with him. Not finding him, she went down the stairs to the cellars, for she knew that the serving people liked to gossip there. It was the time of day when Cai the seneschal, Arthur's foster brother, was generally in his office working on accounts, not watching over the servants.

Sure enough, as Lancelot descended she heard the sound of voices and laughter. But the voices were only one voice. Someone was imitating the voices of the king, the queen, and Lancelot, and doing so perfectly. The words were innocent enough, "My dear Lady Guinevere," "my dear wife," "my dear Lancelot," but the way they were said suggested that Lancelot and Guinevere were lovers and the king was complicit in it. She descended a few steps further and saw that Ragnal, a buxom, gray-haired serving woman, was the one who produced this near perfect mimicry, much to the amusement of a group of serving men and women.

"If you had been a man, you would have been a fine jester," Lancelot said to a sea of suddenly upturned faces. "But you should not mock the king and queen. Jest only about poor Lancelot, who cannot possibly be half as good as people claim." Then she sat on the step and sang the song that Dinadan had sung on the return from the hunt, only she made Lancelot the warrior who had slain the mouse.

The little group laughed, and Ragnal remarked, "You're twice as good as people say, my lord." She smiled at the gentleness of Lancelot's scolding.

"But you don't say Lancelot's the best warrior in the world," one fat serving man--Lancelot was, as always, glad that the serving people at Camelot were well fed--chided Ragnal. "We all know who you think that is," and the company laughed at that.

"I say only what I know, and I know nothing about fighting," Ragnal retorted.

Lancelot joined in the laughter, for she knew as well as they did that Ragnal was Gawaine's favorite mistress and doted on him. Hearing Ragnal's wit, she could see why Gawaine would like her so.

"Why, Lancelot of the Lightning Arm often bests him in fighting, so who knows but what he's a better lover, too?" a red-haired serving woman called out. "What do you say, Lord Lancelot?"

Lancelot shook her head and tried to suppress her laughter. "No lady has ever been with us both, nor is any likely to be, so that will have to remain a mystery. I make no contest. Yet surely good lovers exist not singly, but in pairs." She let herself muse as she would have been embarrassed to do with the company of warriors. "How can one take the words and gestures that please one beloved and simply use them with another? I think there are no good lovers, but only lovers who are good for one another, and might not be pleasing with someone else. But I know my views on love are quaint." So saying, she rose and climbed back up the stairs, before the conversation took any bawdier turn. She hoped she did not show too plainly that she was Guinevere's lover and had never been with anyone else, nor did she want to be.

She had forgotten her errand, but Catwal followed her. His dark hair was graying, but his face still was handsome.

As they climbed out of the cellars and walked back through the kitchens, Lancelot smiled a greeting at Handsome Hands, a tall, clean-shaven young man who was turning a haunch of mutton on a spit. Sweat dripped from his forehead and the red hair surrounding it also was damp. Lancelot was not surprised to see him apart from the other servants, because he generally was. As anyone could see from the hands that turned the spit, he had not grown up as a scullion.

"Tomorrow morning," Lancelot promised, and the young man nodded with delight. For on some early mornings, instead of going off to the forest as usual, Lancelot privately taught fighting to Handsome Hands, who had been given this name by Cai the seneschal. The youth clearly had much training already. Why he had appeared in the kitchen rather than the training quarters for noble lads was a mystery, but Lancelot was not disposed to pry into other people's secrets. Perhaps the lad was taking on a penance, although surely he was too young to have committed any great sin.

3 THE RED WARRIOR AND THE BLACK WARRIOR

Handsome Hands rode through the forest of oaks and beeches on his way to Camelot. The beginning of rain dampened his spirits only slightly. He was full of pride because the king had sent him out to help a lady save her sister from an evil warrior. Angry at being delegated only a kitchen hand, the lady had insulted him the whole way, but he had saved her sister nonetheless. Perhaps the king would accept him as one of his warriors now.

As his horse cantered down a hill, Handsome Hands heard men on the path below talking.

"It's a fine day despite the rain, noble Black Warrior. Shall we spend it besieging some caer?" said one loud voice.

"No, let us rob some travelers instead, noble Red Warrior," was the reply, which was accompanied by much laughter.

The louder voice pealed with laughter also.

Horrified, Handsome Hands rode straight towards them, as if charging at the mouth of hell. Here was another evil for him to battle. "Stop, foul demons!" he yelled, as he came in sight of the two warriors, whose visors were closed against the wet weather, as his was also. Straight away he aimed his horse at the larger man.

"Are you the Red Warrior?" he demanded.

"I suppose I am," the voice began.

"Named for the blood of all those you have murdered, no doubt. Stand and fight!" Handsome Hands aimed his spear at the warrior almost before the other man had time to put up his shield. Handsome Hands knocked the man from his horse.

Immediately, Handsome Hands was on the ground beside him, raining blows with his sword. The Red Warrior fought back, but one blow hit his helmet, and he reeled, falling to the earth.

"Stop!" yelled the Black Warrior, leaping from horse to ground. "Would you murder him for no reason? You must fight me."

Handsome Hands turned to face the new opponent. "Evil Black Warrior, named for darkest night and all that is cruel and foul!" he screamed, attacking.

The Black Warrior struck out, and Handsome Hands replied with a mighty blow. They both dealt strong hits, then the Black Warrior exclaimed, "Handsome Hands! Isn't it you? Cease fighting, this is Lancelot."

"Lord Lancelot!" Handsome Hands stopped in mid-strike and put down his sword.

The warrior lifted a visor, revealing Lancelot's face, and Handsome Hands opened his visor as well.

"Why are you here with this evil companion?" Handsome Hands asked, gasping in bewilderment.

The large warrior on the ground opened his visor.

"Gareth! Little brother! I thought you were in Lothian. What are you doing here?"

"Gawaine!" Handsome Hands, now truly named as Gareth, shuddered with horror and hastened to him. "My brother! And I have hurt you. Forgive me."

Lancelot stared wide-eyed at him. "You're of the House of Lothian? I should have known it, with that height, red hair, and northern accent. But why hide it?"

"I wanted to make my way on my own," replied Gareth.

Gawaine's face was pale as the flour in the royal kitchen. He raised himself on his elbow and shook his head. "How is it that you know Lancelot? And why do you attack any traveler you meet on the road?"

Gareth went down on his knees beside his favorite brother. "I deserve to be driven away from Camelot forever for striking you," he said, beating his breast. "I worked in the kitchen at Camelot, and asked good Lancelot of the Lake to help me practice fighting. Of course I do not attack travelers. You called yourselves such evil names, the Red Warrior and the Black, and you said you were going to besiege people or attack them."

"Why, there is nothing evil about red or black," Lancelot said in an angry voice. "Since your brother's adventure with the Green Warrior, we at times have called each other after the colors of our hair. We were only jesting about the attacks. In your haste, you could have killed your brother, and I think you have hurt him. Are you injured, Gawaine? You look much shaken," the great warrior asked in a tone of concern.

"I am hurt, it is true. Hold me, Lance. It is said that your touch can work miracles." His voice quavered, but there was a hint of a smile in his blue eyes that perplexed Gareth.

"Far better that you should let your brother minister to you and allow him to make up for the injury. Help him, Gareth,"

Lancelot said kindly, all of his alarm gone. Gareth put an arm around Gawaine, who stood readily and brushed himself off.

"Is it true that you can work miracles?" Gareth asked Lancelot.

Lancelot shook his head. "Indeed not. It is just one of Gawaine's tales."

Gareth kept trying to explain himself and insisted that red and black were of course the colors of the devil, but Lancelot maintained that they were not.

Agravaine and Gaheris, brothers much older than Gareth but younger than Gawaine, showed their pleasure at having Gareth at the court. He basked in their attention, for it had been many years since he had been with them. He had caught only glimpses of them when he hid in the kitchens.

"It will be a proud morning when Gawaine receives you as a warrior," Agravaine said, slapping Gareth on the back. "We have a ceremony when a man is admitted into Arthur's company." They stood in Gawaine's small house, which was cluttered with swords and spears and smelled of ale.

The house seemed modest for the heir to the throne of Lothian and Orkney, Gareth thought with approval. He found it strange that Agravaine and Gaheris did not live in Gawaine's house, but had a small house of their own.

Agravaine looked rather like Gawaine, but his expression was less pleasant, sourer than Gareth had remembered. "Who'd have thought you'd grow so tall, Little Skinned Knees?" Agravaine said.

"Little Puffin Eater," Gaheris said, poking Gareth in the ribs. "I miss eating puffins in Orkney," added Gaheris, whose beard was shorter than his older brothers'. His eyes were gray, not blue like the others', and while he was tall compared with most men, he was short compared with his brothers. Gareth was surprised, for he had remembered all of his brothers as tall. Now he was the only one as tall as Gawaine.

Gareth pulled himself up straight, as if he were already participating in a ceremony. He gloried in the thought of kneeling in a candlelit chapel. "I have asked Lancelot of the Lake to receive me, for he is the best and kindest warrior in the world, and he has graciously agreed."

"What, asked Lancelot when you have three older brothers at the round table? So you've imbibed those tales about him like these boys raised in the South?" Frowning, Agravaine pulled back from Gareth.

"True, we aren't good enough for him. Don't let it bother you," Gawaine jested, but Agravaine and Gaheris left the house shortly.

Gareth sighed. He didn't understand why anyone would mind being seen as lesser than Lancelot. That was like admitting one was lesser than King Arthur. He turned to his eldest brother.

"I shall pray all night before the ceremony. I suppose you didn't pray all night before you became one of the king's warriors," Gareth said with some distaste. Gawaine seemed lacking in zeal for virtue. Gareth little liked the smell of ale and mead that hung about the room. The many weapons that were strewn around pleased him, though. He examined his brother's swords, which were better than the one he had possessed until Gawaine recently had given him a good one.

"On the contrary, I was most devout," Gawaine replied with a twinkle in his eyes. "I celebrated the holy means through which I was brought into the world."

Gareth grimaced. It was foolish to expect Gawaine to be serious about holy matters. He could never refrain from making bawdy jests. "You mean that you sinned, as you came into the world with a soul already tainted with sin."

"How not, considering all of the lives that I have led? At least I acknowledge that women had some part in the process, which your priests do not," Gawaine teased him.

"No one is truly born until he has been baptized," Gareth affirmed in pious tones. If only Gawaine would care more about his own baptism and stop mentioning false gods. How sad it was that their mother had raised her sons to believe in them, and that she herself had never been baptized and was therefore damned. His older brothers had been baptized only to please King Arthur, who in turn had wanted to please the bishops.

"You were sucking at our mother's breasts long before the water was splashed on you," his elder brother insisted, pouring himself some ale.

Gareth felt his face grow hot. "How dare you talk about our mother that way! It's indecent."

"It's not, and you should be grateful. Most ladies of high station don't nurse their own babes, but she did, except for Gaheris, because she was sick after his birth." He had left off teasing and sounded exasperated.

"This is no fit subject for discussion," Gareth objected, setting his drinking horn in its stand. "Why must you always think of women carnally? Why can't you be pure like Lancelot?"

Oddly, Gawaine chuckled. "Lancelot and I were not made the same."

"What foolishness is that? God made us all with the same chance to follow the path of virtue or not," Gareth insisted, but Gawaine only laughed.

"Let's wrestle." Gawaine grabbed Gareth's arm, but Gareth wrested it away from him and moved halfway across the room.

"Are you too good to wrestle with your brother?" Gawaine complained.

Gareth turned away from him, went into another room, slammed the door and knelt down and prayed. Touching Gawaine was torture, but he could never let his brother know that.

When Gareth returned, Gawaine smiled in a conciliatory manner. "That's my sleeping room," he said. "You can share my bed. You'll have it much to yourself, because I'm hardly ever in it." He winked. "I'm sorry you had to live in the servants' quarters. Why did you ever pretend to be a servant?"

"To quell my pride," Gareth said, as if that should be obvious, "and I thought I could better avoid temptation that way than if I lived with the young men studying to be the king's warriors."

Gawaine shook his head and laughed. "Are the kitchen wenches so virtuous? No doubt many of the young warriors are no better than they should be, but I doubt that the servants are purer."

No, they were no purer, Gareth thought, but the young warriors' well-muscled bodies tempted him more than most serving men's.

Gawaine offered him ale, and Gareth did not turn him down. It was good ale, of course, far better than any he had sampled in the kitchen.

They sat at Gawaine's table, and his older brother leaned towards him. "Don't follow Agravaine and Gaheris too closely. I hate to say it of my brothers, but they are not among the best men at court."

Gareth spilled some of his ale. "I fail to see how they could sin more than you do. If my brothers go astray, I must try to help them."

Gawaine sighed.

It was nearly dawn when Gawaine returned to his room, whistling as he usually did, then stopping so as not to wake Gareth. He threw himself on the bed and went to sleep almost instantly. A little later he abruptly wakened as Gareth jumped out of the bed.

"What's the matter?" Gawaine asked without bothering to open his eyes.

"Nothing!" snapped his younger brother. "I'm just getting up to pray."

Gawaine groaned and went back to sleep.

Gawaine was gone for the next few nights, but then Ragnal had the ague and he didn't particularly want another woman, so he prepared to sleep in his own bed. Although nearly every noble was dressed and undressed by servants, Gawaine had never had the patience for such niceties when undressing. He tore off his clothes and flung them onto the floor for his serving man, Hywel, to pick up in the morning.

Gareth's face reddened. "You're messy as a pig," he exclaimed. "How can I bear to share a room with you?" He turned away so that he wasn't looking at Gawaine.

"You're awfully particular for one who not long ago slept in the hall with the servants," Gawaine grumbled, and went to bed. He forbore saying that he was the one who was used to having the room to himself.

He had scarcely fallen asleep when Gareth leapt out of the bed.

"What now?" mumbled Gawaine.

"I can't share a bed with you. Let Hywel go and sleep in the servants' quarters, and I'll take the pallet in the other room," Gareth said.

"What foolishness is this? Hywel has served me for years, and he will take it very ill," said Gawaine, thoroughly awake now, and noticing that Gareth oddly enough was still wearing his breeches and tunic and apparently had gone to bed so. "Why can't you sleep in my bed? I'm hardly ever here anyway."

"Your smell is unbearable." Gareth threw the words at him and rushed out of the room.

Those words stung Gawaine. The next morning he asked Hywel to move to the servants' quarters because Gareth was so odd that he insisted on sleeping alone, and he gave Hywel some fine leather for new boots to appease him.

Gawaine asked a lady who had once been his mistress--he was afraid that the current ones might not feel they could tell the truth--whether his smell was bad, and she told him that it was not.

But still he was afraid that she might not have told the truth, so he jokingly asked his fellow warrior Bedwyr, who laughed and said that he had never noticed, so Gawaine must smell much like other men.

Then Gawaine decided that Gareth's words came from meanness, and he felt aggrieved.

Nevertheless, he tried to be friendly with Gareth, and asked him to go hunting with him and practice with him, because his youngest brother was a better man than Agravaine or Gaheris and Gawaine had become somewhat estranged from them. He also arranged for a room for Gareth to be added to his house.

But no matter how pleasant Gawaine was, Gareth was always a bit cool with him.

Gareth sparred with Lancelot, now in the practice room like a true warrior. Lancelot defeated him as usual, but Gareth hoped that there would be a day when he might win. Or would that be a sad day, rather than a happy one? It was good to have a hero.

"You did well, Gareth." Lancelot was always generous with praise. "Your days in the kitchens did you no harm." Lancelot toweled his face. Although Lancelot sweated as much as most other warriors, he never had an enticing smell like Gawaine's. Neither did his muscles bulge as much as Gawaine's.

Lancelot had never married, and never flirted with the ladies, but never looked particularly at Gareth or any of the other men. Gareth thought that Lancelot might have the same inclination to sin that he did, but through virtue had conquered it, and therefore was a good example.

Gareth saw how easily Cai jested with his foster brother, King Arthur, and guessed that Cai had never had criminal thoughts like Gareth's. Gareth was sure that he was the greatest sinner of all, combining Cai's sin of desiring men with the king's youthful sin of desiring one born of the same mother. For Gareth, like many others, had heard that when Arthur was a young man he had been with his sister, Morgan, whom he later called a witch and exiled to Cornwall.

4 PENTECOST

Lancelot, Gawaine, Bedwyr, and Peredur sat drinking wine in Arthur's room. Lancelot as usual drank less than the others. The king liked to have his favored few in his room after he left the grand table for the night. Lancelot felt honored to be included but always longed for the moment when she could leave and go to Guinevere.

Arthur imbibed some expensive wine--the wine at this table was always finer than that served at the large one. "Gawaine, tell us the tale you once told about bedding two women."

Lancelot's clenched her hands, which were under the table.

Gawaine choked. "That was just a foolish story that I told when I was young. I think it is more common for men to tell tales about such things than actually to do them. I never really did anything like that." His face reddened to the shade of his beard.

Arthur set his winecup on the table. "What difference does it make whether you really did that or not? No one cares. Tell the tale."

Gawaine regarded his winecup. "Rather, I shall tell about the time that I met the goddess Cerridwen in a forest glade . . ."

"Lying with Cerridwen? That's foolish." Arthur grumbled. "Why not tell the other story?"

"Of course I have been intimate with Cerridwen. She was supremely fair. Her hair looked sometimes gold as the sun, sometimes red as fire, sometimes black as a raven's wing. Her eyes were sometimes deep blue, sometimes green, and yet also brown..."

Lancelot quietly rose from the table, inclined her head to the king, and departed. She tried to keep herself from shaking with anger at the thought of a man lying with two women at once, or even telling a tale about it. That seemed to profane a love like hers.

When Lancelot woke the next morning, Guinevere touched her cheek. Her hand thrilled to the touch, as always. "Can you go riding with me today?" she asked, looking into Lancelot's eyes. "I long to go to the forest with you. I don't care what the weather is."

Lancelot sighed. "I need to work with the young men to prepare them for the Pentecost contests. I wish I could go with you. Could you go with another escort?"

Guinevere looked at the wall. "I want to go with you. I understand that I cannot. But Bors is the only other one I would want to ride with, and he will also be busy. How I wish I could go to the woods without an escort. But I know that is not your fault."

Lancelot kissed Guinevere's hand. "I'm sorry that you cannot go without an escort. But I think Arthur's right that it would be too dangerous."

"Perhaps. But I wish I could decide that for myself rather than being ordered." Guinevere tried to pull herself together. She understood the rules that she must follow as a queen. "Please enjoy your day."

"I would enjoy it more if I could be with you." Lancelot embraced her, then rose from the bed and dressed.

It was always the same. It would always be the same. Guinevere told herself she must be grateful for all she had. Perhaps it would have been better if she had not grown up loving to ride so much.

In fighting practice, Lancelot avoided being partnered with Gawaine. But when she left the great hall after supper, he followed her into the darkened courtyard. The night was clouded, hiding the stars.

"Don't be angry over a foolish story I told years ago, when I didn't know about you," Gawaine said in an unusually contrite voice--or was it cajoling, not contrite? "I wouldn't make up one like that now because I don't want to offend you."

"I'm not angry, just disgusted." Without saying anything further, Lancelot strode away. She would have to speak with him in the future, of course, but she didn't need to do so at the moment.

The older warriors had been teaching the younger ones, who seemed nearly mad with enthusiasm as they practiced for the coming Pentecost contest, a first for some of them. The new spring grass had quickly been worn to dust on the practice field.

Gawaine casually walked up to Lancelot and said, "I'd like a word with you."

Lancelot did not smile, but she could not refuse to talk with him. "Very well." Wiping the sweat from her brow, she handed her horse to a stablehand and put down her spear.

Camelot rang with the clatter of blacksmiths sharpening swords and fixing chain mail in preparation for the contest. Lancelot was more used to the tumult than she had been when she first came, but it still made her long for the quiet forest.

They walked away from the noise, towards the tilled fields where farmers tried to grow enough for the permanent army and the livestock that it needed. A blackbird sang.

"Pentecost is coming," Gawaine observed.

"Do you want me to pray for your soul?" She didn't look him in the eye. "I doubt that would help much."

"Probably not," he said cheerfully, as if he hadn't noticed the lack of warmth in her tone. "Of course I'm referring to the fighting contests. We'll defeat everyone else, so we'll have to fight each other as usual."

"Yes, for the first time you'll have fight me knowing I'm a woman." Lancelot couldn't help smiling at that prospect. She was the same warrior he'd always fought, but she knew he wouldn't feel the same about it.

"Fighting a woman goes against everything in me, but of course I'll have to do it." His forehead wrinkled. "But I'm not going to try to knock you off your horse. I've told Arthur that it's undignified for such senior warriors to knock each other about. We'll fight standing on the ground."

Understanding that he wouldn't want to knock a woman off her horse, she nodded. "Agreed. But if I win, you'll have to learn to live with it."

"Yes, it's likely enough that you'll win." He grinned. The sunlight shone on his red hair.

"What do you mean by that?" Lancelot stared at him.

"Nothing." Gawaine shrugged his shoulders.

"If people ever find out I'm a woman, won't you mind if I've defeated you?"

Gawaine grunted. "If people ever find out, there will be a great deal more to worry about than how I fought at the last Pentecost contest."

"That's true," Lancelot conceded. Then she changed the subject because the thought of what might happen if more men found out that she was a woman was not pleasant. She had long feared rape, perhaps even from her brother warriors. Perhaps none of them would attack her, but she did not want to put them to the test. "Do you think the young warriors have practiced the jousts enough? I think we should make them practice more on horses these next few weeks."

On Pentecost, the warriors prayed--or some did--then fought. Lancelot was not so eager to don her chain mail. It seemed to shine less brightly than it had when she was young, though Catwal had polished it almost to silver. The long-vanished bloodstains of war still seemed to cling to it. How much she had wanted glory when she was young! Now she no longer believed that fighting was glorious.

She did not smile when she picked up her sword. Was it a friend? Many a time it had saved her life, but had it led her to lose her soul? Arthur claimed that his sword was enchanted, a gift from a lady who emerged from a lake. Perhaps, Lancelot thought, all swords were enchanted objects that drew the souls from their owners' breasts and, in exchange for might, left them shells, with no substance beneath their chain mail.

Sighing, she sheathed her sword and went out to the contests.

Sangremore and Bellangere, two of her less preferred companions of the round table, stopped her before she got to the field. Sangremore's appearance was distinguished only by a long scar on his cheek, and Bellangere was a burly man with a brown beard.

"I know you'll win," Sangremore said. "We're betting on you. Agravaine and Gaheris always bet on Gawaine, but I don't think he's in as good shape as he used to be."

"None of us are, me included." Lancelot shook her head. "You know I don't like placing wagers on these contests."

Bellangere chuckled. "We know you won't disappoint us. Bedwyr is betting on you, and that's a good sign."

Lancelot didn't like the sound of that. Bedwyr usually bet on Gawaine. Had Gawaine told him that Lancelot would be the winner? Perhaps because Bedwyr had let Gawaine know in advance about the plan to deceive Lancelot with a woman who pretended to be Guinevere? Was Gawaine planning to throw the fight? It was bad enough if the winner of the fight was predetermined, but much worse if people wagered on a predetermined winner.

Lancelot proceeded to the field. The crowd shouted her name, but she glanced neither to the left nor to the right. Although she was proud of her fame, she thought that it was fleeting.

When Lancelot faced Gawaine, on the ground, she sensed that he had changed. His moves were technically perfect, but there was no force behind them. He would not fight his best against her. For a time, she fought fiercely, trying to compel him to attack her, but he would not. She saw that he was determined to let her win. Finally, when she struck his shield, he let the blow knock him down, and she won.

Gawaine rose quickly and clapped her on the back.

"Why did you do that?" she whispered as they walked away.

"You can't afford not to be the greatest warrior in the world," he told her.

She saw that it would always be that way. She would never again have a chance to contend with his full strength and cunning. They would be watered down, like a young girl's wine. He would never let her defeat him honestly, but would pretend that he was letting her win, and tell himself that it was for her protection. She sighed, then shrugged. The most tiresome thing about men was their endless contests to see who was best.

When she re-entered her small house, Lancelot saw a man-- one she had killed in the Saxon War--his guts spilling out of him as he lay on the floor. She covered her face with her hands. When she uncovered her eyes, the dead Saxon was gone. She saw such sights at times, but she told no one. It seemed to be the price she must pay for killing so many.

The contests were over. Half the warriors had gone off and the others milled around. The horses had been led off, but the contest field was pungent with their wastes. Dinadan laughed at the thought of the comments Cai would make about the smell.

The spectators had dispersed, but lost flasks and cloaks and crumbled bits of food littered the ground where they had stood. Some poor people were scavenging the lost objects, and dogs wolfed down meat pies that had been dropped.

Dinadan had done well that day, but his muscles ached. Humming a tune, he strolled to the stands to look for Cai. A tall, veiled lady walked up to him. Strangely, she wore a scabbard.

But this was no she. The height and the muscles showed that it was a man. Why was he wearing a gown?

Stepping up close, this strange man pulled a sword from his scabbard in an unmistakable gesture of challenge.

Dinadan just stared at him. He had no desire to strike at this strangely disguised challenger, but the he-lady's sword cut his cheek and Dinadan found that he really did have to fight. Dinadan drew his sword, but the other slashed at him mercilessly. Blows came before Dinadan could parry them. The sword danced around him so that he tripped and fell. The pretended lady laughed a guttural male laugh, like those that might be heard in a tavern, jumped on a horse, and rode off.

Several hooting warriors grabbed Dinadan and pulled a gown that they had obtained who knows where over his head and his chain mail, beat him, and knocked him back onto the ground. He fought back, but fighting one against four was more than he could manage.

That night, he sat on Cai's bed, in a room that had one of the caer's best hangings on the wall. Cai muttered over Dinadan's bruises and cursed his assailants roundly. "That was the young warrior Tristram wearing the gown, wasn't it? Many men were saying it was Lancelot because the fighting was so fine, but of course Lancelot would never have done such a thing."

"Aye, it was Tristram. I recognized the blows," Dinadan said, holding his aching head in his hands.

"If he had hurt you worse, I'd challenge him myself," Cai asserted, stroking Dinadan's hair.

Dinadan groaned. "It's a good thing he didn't. Then I'd have to patch you up. You're the worst fighter in the kingdom--but the best lover," he added, as Cai grumbled.

"Tried them all, have you? Sit still, and move that arm." He ran his hands over it. "Are you sure it isn't sprained?"

"It isn't. Only in my imagination, of course, fair seneschal."

Cai stroked his forehead and Dinadan leaned on his shoulder and sighed with contentment. "It's good to have you looking after me for a change."

"What is that supposed to mean?" Cai grumbled. "You don't have to look after me."

"Only to soothe you in your bad moods, dear seneschal, which are of course rare," Dinadan teased. "Ow, don't touch that bruise on my shoulder."

"Why you have to go to the trouble of helping that ungrateful Tristram in his foolish passion for King Marcus of Dumnonia's wife, Iseult, I don't know, unless perhaps you lust after him secretly."

Cai's grumble was as constant as ever. He poured some wine--the best Falernian--into a silver goblet and gave it to Dinadan.

"Muscles he has--all too many," Dinadan said with a grin. "No, I am not overly fond of him. I help him because of the lady. Barely a girl, she is, queen or not. She begged for my aid, 'I don't know why,' she said, 'but I trust you more than other men, Dinadan. Would you help us? If I have to stay with Marcus much longer, I'll kill myself, I swear it.' Now, how could I not help her after that?"

"God's elbow, will you become another Lancelot, rescuing every unhappy woman in the land? You'll never be at home then," Cai muttered, pouring another goblet of wine for himself. "I'm glad that I'll never be a hero, and I hope you won't be one either"

Although Guinevere's fosterling Talwyn had long since learned to read, still she took lessons from Guinevere. She sat in the queen's room and read a heavy tome. The queen gave her ever more complex books.

Guinevere was the only one who cared about her, Talwyn thought. Her mother had died in childbed and her father, the warrior Gryffyd, was mad, hidden off in a room in the caer. The king ignored Talwyn except to smile at her occasionally, when he remembered her, and Lancelot, who had playfully sparred with wooden swords with her when she was younger, was formal with her now that she was becoming a young lady.

Talwyn glanced through the window at the courtyard, which was full of puddles from an earlier rain. Now the sky was still gray, but the air smelled fresh.

"Did Helen really want to go to Troy?" Talwyn asked, pausing in reading the vellum pages of the Aeneid. "Or was she dragged off?"

"She might have gone for love," Guinevere replied, a strange expression on her face. She stared off into the distance.

"If Cassandra had so much insight, why couldn't she use it to save herself?"

"Seeing what will happen does not always give one the means to avoid it." The queen frowned slightly as if she were not entirely confident about the future.

Talwyn sighed, as she always did when she thought about the future. What man would she be required to marry? Some of the young warriors were handsome, but she wasn't so sure she wanted a husband. She would rather stay forever at the queen's side and read books. Every girl married except those who entered the convent, a fate that didn't much appeal to her. But the Amazons in her story didn't marry.

"Why did the Amazons fight for Priam?"

Turning back towards Talwyn, Guinevere beamed at her. "You ask good questions, my scholar. They had no one better to fight for. And they wanted to defend their homeland."

Talwyn looked out of the window. Swaggering as if they owned the world, warriors strode across the courtyard. How good it would feel to swagger. Did one have to know how to use a sword to be that proud?

Then Talwyn asked, "If the Amazons could learn to fight, why can't I? Every time I see the fighting contests, I imagine that I am riding with the warriors."

Guinevere shook her head. "You know that you never can do that."

The Amazons captured Talwyn's imagination. She moved her arm as if she were holding a sword. "Could women fight? Then why do they not? What happened to the fighting women?"

Frowning, Guinevere spoke curtly. "There are some such women in Ireland, and some wild Saxon women fight, but it's foolish to imagine that you could. No woman in Britain has fought since the days of Boadicea. Pray concentrate on your reading. That will help you far more than such fancies." The queen took up her scroll as if ending the conversation.

But still Talwyn dreamed, twisting her brown hair around her finger. The Amazons must have been strong, much stronger than she was, if they could fight men and defeat them. She tried to imagine what an Amazon might look like. Perhaps some were a trifle plump and buxom like herself. They could not all have been thin. Could she ever be as strong as an Amazon?

Pentecost came, and Talwyn sat in the stands with the other girls her age. The girls exclaimed over which warrior was strongest or handsomest or rode a horse best, and teased each other about the ones they liked.

The crowd yelled at the sight of the warriors walking out to the field.

"There's Bors, the pious warrior!" A group of monks cheered, and so did Bors's many children.

"There's Bedwyr, who lost a hand in the Saxon war. Yay, Bedwyr!" called out the crowd.

"Here's Gawaine! Gawaine! Gawaine of the Matchless Strength!" A great yell surged from the crowd.

Another cheer went up. "Lancelot! Lancelot of the Lightning Arm! Hurray, Lancelot!"

The crowd smelled powerfully of sweat, ale, and meat pies brought to stave off hunger during the long matches. Talwyn covered her nose as often as she could.

"Lancelot is so handsome," trilled fair-haired Gralla in the stand where the girls watched. "If only he would look at me!"

"There's Gareth! I think his looks are even finer, and he's young, too," exclaimed Felicia, who almost fell off the stand. Felicia tripped often, but she was sweet, Talwyn thought.

"I wish Gawaine would look at me, but of course I'd be careful not to let him do any more," said dark-haired Lavinia.

Talwyn scarcely heard them, for she was watching the start of the fighting and wondering how a woman might fight. What would it be like to be knocked off your horse? If you couldn't win a fight through superior strength, how would you win? Perhaps you would have to be very fast.

"It's not fair, Talwyn," Felicia complained. "All of us have said which warrior we like best, but you haven't. You have to say."

To quiet her, Talwyn gave what she believed was a mysterious smile and said, "I'm saving myself for the best and bravest warrior of all." In truth, she had never before had such a thought.

The girls all giggled.

"Do you think the king will marry you to Lancelot?" Felicia asked, choking with laughter. "What a dreamer you are!"

"The queen wouldn't care much for that," Gralla said with a sly smile. "You think well of yourself to want the most eligible man at Camelot."

"Gawaine is the most eligible man!" exclaimed Lavinia, patting her hair. "And I'm sure he's better at what we're not supposed to talk about." She giggled.

"When I was a young girl, I dreamed of marrying Gawaine, but I haven't in a while," Talwyn admitted. "He's awfully old now. Besides, I realized that even if he wanted me, Queen Guinevere would never permit him to marry me because she dislikes him."

"And he wouldn't be faithful," Felicia objected. "Lancelot would."

"What difference does that make?" Lavinia demanded. "Gawaine will probably be king of Lothian and Orkney, and his wife will be a queen. He is by far the best catch at Camelot."

But Talwyn stopped listening. What would an Amazon look like? She stared at Lancelot and Gawaine, who were commencing their match. An Amazon would have to be tall for a woman, but surely not as tall as the tallest men. She would have to be sturdy, though she might be thin. She couldn't let herself be struck often, so her blows would have to be better aimed than the men's blows.

An Amazon's face would be weathered, but of course she wouldn't have any hair or stubble on it. She would have impressive muscles, although not as large as those of a man like Gawaine.

Talwyn watched Lancelot fight Gawaine. How fast Lancelot was! How justly called Lightning Arm!

Lancelot evaded all of Gawaine's blows, and Lancelot's own blows were so well aimed.

Talwyn gasped. It couldn't be. Lancelot had no stubble, never any stubble on those weathered cheeks. Lancelot had never married, and did not carouse or flirt with anyone except-- except that Lancelot seemed closer to the queen than anyone else. But the queen didn't much like the other warriors.

Talwyn stared at Lancelot. Talwyn's vision was hazy, as always, but the features that she could not see clearly, she remembered.

An Amazon might look like Lancelot. Talwyn caught her breath. Many others in the crowd stared at Lancelot and Gawaine, so Talwyn's scrutiny would go unnoticed.

Lancelot defeated Gawaine. He and Lancelot clapped each other on the back, and, because the fighting was done for the day, all of the warriors were clapping each other on the back and trading jests and mild insults. Talwyn's gaze followed Lancelot. Then, as the warriors approached the royal stand and were given their prizes, Talwyn looked up at Guinevere, whose eyes were fixed on Lancelot. Guinevere leaned towards Lancelot, as if she wanted to leap out of the stand and embrace the warrior. The queen moved her fingers in an odd gesture. For an instant, Lancelot returned the queen's gaze, and also made a strange move with her fingers, as if she were returning a signal from Guinevere.

Talwyn realized that she had learned much more from Guinevere's lessons than the queen had intended to impart. Lancelot was a woman, and yet the queen looked at her the way women look at men they love. Strange, especially since they both seemed old to be in love.

Some days later, when she had brought Guinevere a little essay on Ceres and Persephone, Talwyn made bold to begin, "Lady Guinevere..."

"One moment, Talwyn." The queen raised her eyes from the essay. Her jeweled hand pointed at a word. "Your use of the past tense in this sentence is not correct. And you shouldn't use the ablative here." Guinevere pored over the wax tablet on which the words were written. "But your idea that Persephone missed her mother even more than her mother missed her is plausible." She smiled with pride at Talwyn.

The queen's cat appeared and dropped a mouse at her feet.

Talwyn jumped back slightly, but Guinevere did not flinch. She patted the cat's head. "Good Grayse. Luned!"

The serving woman, who had been mending one of the queen's gowns, jumped up, swept up the mouse with a broom, and carried it out of the queen's room.

Talwyn decided to seize the moment while Luned was gone. "Could I write my next essay about the Amazons? They interest me the most." How could she be bold, but not so bold as to irritate the queen?

"Mmmm." Guinevere lowered her eyes and mumbled. Such a signal of displeasure would usually be enough to deter those who disagreed with her, but it did not deter Talwyn.

Talwyn leaned closer to the queen. "Could there be Amazons in the present day? I mean, outside Ireland?"

"I hardly think so." Guinevere's tone was cool. Holding the tablet before her face, she said, "You must take more care with your sentences."

"I suppose there aren't any. Except for Lancelot of the Lake."

Talwyn had made her feint, and now she held her breath while she awaited the response.

Guinevere turned pale. "What nonsense is this?" she snapped, but the tablet in her hand shook as if it were vellum.

"I'll never tell, I swear it," Talwyn averred. "I spoke only because I want so much to learn just a little about sword-fighting. Do you think she'd teach me?"

Guinevere glared like a wild creature whose cub was threatened. Talwyn had never seen so little tenderness in her face nor heard so little in her voice. "Do you know what men would do if they learned about her? Never speak of this, not even to me."

"Oh, Lady Guinevere, you can't think I'd tell." She backed off as if struck.

"I can't think it, and you can't think of it either." Guinevere slammed the tablet down on the table.

"I don't want to hurt her, I just want to be like her. Just a little bit. Just to know how."

But Guinevere put her off. "Not just now. Perhaps at some future time. Now read your Virgil." She gestured towards the large book.

Talwyn scanned it more reluctantly than usual. Tales were all very well, but discoveries about the people you knew were better.

Luned returned and took up her needle. There would be no more dangerous discussions that day.

The shyness Talwyn had felt toward Lancelot in recent years vanished. She plotted her course.

One morning Talwyn required herself to rise early for Mass, one place where it was quite decent for a girl to go alone. As luck would have it, Lancelot also attended the Mass, and no one else did. It was raining heavily, so Talwyn had gambled that the warrior would not be off in the forest. The Mass was short, as it tended to be when there were so few in attendance.

Talwyn barely listened to the Latin words. The incense made her want to sneeze as it always did, but she tried to hold back.

Before Lancelot could leave the nearly deserted lime-whitened chapel, Talwyn met her at the door.

Even as Lancelot murmured her usual, "God grant you good morning," Talwyn was ready with her words. She stood directly in front of Lancelot, blocking her retreat.

"It would be a better day if you would speak with me as you used to, Lord Lancelot. You played at swords with me when I was a child. I would that we could renew those exercises."

Cornered, Lancelot had to answer, not without coloring. Yes, Lancelot blushed much too often for a man. "I am sorry to say it, Talwyn, but it is not considered proper for you to do such things with a man, even one who sees you almost as a daughter."

"Not with a man, of course." Talwyn nodded, advancing even closer to Lancelot. "But couldn't I spar with you?"

Before Lancelot could catch her breath, the girl added, "Wouldn't it be good for me to be able to fight in case I am ever in danger?"

Lancelot paled under this unexpected onslaught. "Take care what you say." Her voice trembled. She seemed ready to plunge out into the rain.

Reading the fear in her hero's face, Talwyn almost regretted her foray, but not quite. "Of course. You have always been so kind to me. I'd never let anyone know, not if they tortured me for weeks!"

Lancelot smiled faintly. "You have my leave to reveal it under the slightest hint of torture. I hope that no one ever will threaten you in any way, but if you would feel safer, perhaps a few lessons would not be amiss. Now let us brave the rain." She gave Talwyn her crimson cloak as they dashed across the flooding courtyard.

It was not long before Talwyn came to Guinevere's room, and so did Lancelot. They clashed with wooden swords while Guinevere and old Fencha watched. Lancelot was more serious about the lessons than she had been when Talwyn was younger. "Your stance is terrible," she said. "No, that angle won't do."

When they paused for a moment, Guinevere remarked, "What a strict teacher you are!"

"But a woman warrior, *mirabile dicta*," Talwyn exclaimed.

"That's *mirabile dictu*," Guinevere reproved her instantly,

Lancelot laughed. "Now who's the strict teacher?"

Talwyn tried not to giggle and pretended not to notice the look that passed between the two.

On Talwyn's birthday, Lancelot gave her a real sword and some of her old chain mail. Talwyn spent much time learning to handle the sword, which seemed astonishingly heavy.

The chain mail, which had been loose on Lancelot's chest, was snug on Talwyn.

5 TO THE CONVENT

Lancelot rode through a forest and spied a caer. She smiled, for she was hungry and had eaten nothing but salted pork, which she had now finished, and stale bread. The caer's stones looked to be in good repair, so the food might be worth eating. She could almost taste roasted fowl.

She had no reason to believe the caer was held by an enemy, so she approached it and hailed the guards. "I am Lancelot of the Lake, a warrior of King Arthur's," she said. "Pray open your gate to me."

"Lancelot!" someone called out. "Open the gate for the hero!"

Although Lancelot had received such greetings before, she always felt her cheeks flush with embarrassment.

Guards opened the gate, and a man she remembered well rushed out to her.

"Antonius!" she exclaimed with pleasure, for he had fought well in the Saxon War years before.

Antonius was still well-favored in his looks, Lancelot thought. His cheeks were still clean-shaven. She rejoiced that not all men grew beards. The spreading fashion to grow them made her more conspicuous.

It bothered her only a little that Antonius bore the name that had been hers when she was young and was first disguised as a boy. What would her life have been like if she had remained Antonius and stayed close to home at the villa in Lesser Britain instead of becoming Lancelot the warrior? Would she have become morose like her father? She shook her head. She had already become morose living with the ghosts of her parents, and that was why she had left.

Antonius welcomed her to his caer and brought her to the table even sooner than she could have hoped. The hall was clean, its floor covered with straw that was almost fresh. His men at arms were cordial and joked among themselves.

His mead was good, and so was the cold beef that was served. She devoured her portion. The aroma of baked pears let her know that more food was coming.

Antonius apologized that he had not had time to order a meal cooked for Lancelot, but she assured him that she had rather eat sooner than later.

There was no evidence of a wife. Lancelot said the dwelling seemed well managed for a place with no woman to care for it.

Antonius frowned. "There is indeed a lady who manages my household, but she is not my wife. If I introduce you to her, I trust that you will treat her with respect. She is a fine woman."

"Of course," Lancelot assured him. She wondered why he had not married the lady if she was so fine.

Antonius sent a serving man to bring his lady, and soon a lady of about thirty years entered the hall.

She was comely, tall, and dignified. A veil covered her hair.

"This is my lady, Branwen," Antonius said with a note of pride in his voice.

Lancelot rose and bowed to her. "I am honored to meet you, my lady," Lancelot said.

"Thank you, lord Lancelot. Of course I have heard of your deeds. You are very welcome here." Branwen spoke in a quiet, refined voice.

She sat with them. Branwen entered the conversation and spoke of many subjects, especially concerning theology and Roman poetry, of which she knew far more than Lancelot did. Branwen told how Rome had decided the teachings of Pelagius were heretical. Lancelot had heard the name, but knew little more.

Lancelot was more perplexed than ever that Antonius had not married Branwen.

The next day, when Lancelot had risen from a good sleep and was on her way to the hall, Branwen approached her.

"Lord Lancelot, would you be good enough to speak with me in private?"

The lady's face showed no signs of flirtation, but Lancelot was astonished and wondered about the lady's character.

"Of course, my lady," she said, as courteously as usual.

Branwen bade her come to an empty room, and Lancleot followed. The room appeared to be used to store jars of preserved food.

"Pray do not think ill of me, Lord Lancelot." Branwen blushed. "But I have heard of your noble character and wondered whether you might help me. Would you please listen to my story?"

"Of course, my lady," Lancelot said, wondering greatly.

"When I was young, I took vows as a nun." Branwen looked at the ground.

Lancelot tried to keep her face from showing her surprise.

"I was happy in the convent. It was the Convent of the Holy Mother. Have you heard of it?"

"Indeed I have," Lancelot said warmly, for she had a good friend there, a kind old nun.

"One day an injured warrior was brought there. He had taken the wound fever and was sorely ill. We cared for him. It was Antonius.

"When he recovered, he wooed me, and I came to love him." Branwen blushed. "He persuaded me to leave, and I did. I have lived with him ever since."

"He should marry you!" Lancelot's voice was sharp. Making it gentler, she said, "Of course I shall try to persuade him to do so, my lady."

Branwen shook her head. "At one time I wanted that, but no longer. It hurt me deeply that he laughed at the idea of marriage and refused to wed me because I had no living father or brother to force him. He said I had come with him willingly, and that he would look foolish if he married a woman who had openly lived as his leman. I have borne him no children, and I fear that someday he will marry a woman who can. I have been humiliated for years at being his mistress. All I want now is to return to the convent. I do not know whether the sisters will take me back, or if they do, what penance they will ask me to perform, but I was far happier there than I have been with Antonius."

Lancelot paused and considered what Branwen had to say. Lancelot could imagine feeling the same way if she were in Branwen's position, but then Lancelot had never loved a man.

"Are you sure that you no longer love him, my lady?" she asked.

"I am certain that I no longer want to live with him."

Branwen's voice was low but steady. "I have told him that I want to return to the convent, but he only laughs at me and refuses to listen. Would you help me leave? I know no one else who would take me back to the convent."

Lancelot's estimation of Antonius plummeted still further. "If you truly wish this, I will do so, but if I help you leave, it might look as if I were running away with you. I would not want to fight Antonius."

"No, of course not," Branwen said. "It is true that he might fight you if he caught me leaving with you. But I would do anything to get back to the convent. It was so peaceful there."

Branwen's firmness impressed Lancelot. "The women of that convent are so good that I believe they will take you back. How can I best escort you?"

"I have thought of a plan. You could not take me as Lancelot. But monks come to pray at the caer's chapel. I have told them what I wish to do, and they have said they would bring two monks' robes if I could find a good man to escort me back to the convent. One monk could enter the chapel and bring two robes. He could come at the time the guards change watches. We could slip in through the sacristy, and don the robes. He would remain there a long time and pray, and the new guards would not know that only one monk came while three left."

"That plan might work, my lady." Lancelot knew that her friendship with Antonius would be over, but she no longer wanted it.

The plan worked well enough. Lancelot left her horse outside the caer's walls, and the monk had left a horse for the lady outside as well.

Lancelot much admired the brave lady who rode away beside her. Branwen said little and looked only at the path ahead of her.

How strange it was that love could fail, Lancelot pondered, sure that her own never would. But how could Antonius ever have loved Branwen if he did not care if she was humiliated? It was base not to marry her because she had no male relatives to force him to do so. If Antonius was leaving himself free to marry a woman who could bear him children, Lancelot had little sympathy for that scheme.

Lancelot and Branwen rode hastily through the forest. Fortunately the convent was only two days ride away from Antonius's holding.

It was spring, but warm for the season. At night, Lancelot made a fire and spread out her horse blanket for the lady to lie on. Branwen had brought bread and cheese from the caer for them to eat.

The lady went early to rest.

Lancelot could not sleep. She worried that Antonius might follow them and challenge her to fight. The forest looked less beautiful than usual therefore. She watched the stars appear and thought of Guinevere. If only Guinevere were the one who wanted to leave the man she lived with.

The next day, Lancelot heard a noise and believed someone followed them, but it was only a herd of red deer. She sighed with relief. She had no wish to shed Antonius's blood.

Just as she and Branwen arrived at the stone wall that surrounded the convent, they heard the sound of horses' hooves and Antonius appeared behind them.

"Fools!" he shouted. "Lancelot, only you would be mad enough to take my lady back to a convent. Branwen, my patience with you is almost at an end, but come back with me and I shall try to forget your foolishness."

"I am not your lady any longer, Antonius." Branwen spoke without faltering. "Return home. I truly want to be here."

Antonius rode up to her, but Lancelot moved her horse between them. "You must listen to the lady, Antonius."

"Will they even take you back?" he jeered.

The sister porter opened the gate, and the Abbess Perpetua, a tall and formidable woman, appeared.

"Cease this clamor," the abbess demanded. "You could be heard from a mile away. If Sister Branwen wishes to return here, she may. Please enter, sister, and Lancelot also."

"Farewell, then." Antonius's face reddened. "Don't think you can ever come back to me after this. And Lancelot, don't you ever trespass on my hospitality again."

He turned his horse and rode away.

Lancelot exhaled. She thanked St. Agnes, whose relic she wore in a pouch hanging from a leather strap around her neck, that she did not have to injure Antonius in order to protect Branwen.

Branwen entered the convent gate, and Lancelot followed. They dismounted, and went through the heavy door to the convent proper.

As soon as the door was shut behind them, Branwen went down on her knees. She glanced from a statue of the Virgin to the abbess. "Please forgive me for leaving, reverend mother," she begged. "I will do any penance you designate.

The abbess put her hand on Branwen's arm and lifted her up. "Sister Branwen, you have shown that you never left. Perhaps you need some refreshment in the refectory before we go to the chapel."

At these words, tears started in Branwen's eyes. "Thank you," she choked.

"We are glad to see you," the abbess said, in a voice as calm as if she were telling the sisters to commence prayers. "Remember the parable of the prodigal son. A prodigal daughter is just the same. And we also thank Lancelot for bringing you." She smiled at Lancelot. "You cannot come into our refectory, Lancelot, but we can have some food brought to you in our room for guests. We are grateful."

Lancelot was much moved by the abbess's graciousness, and rejoiced that she had helped Branwen. Perhaps this was the kindest convent in Britain. Lancelot looked forward to telling Guinevere the story.

Then plump old Mother Ninian, smiling as ever, rushed in and hugged Branwen. The abbess shook her head over this undecorous behavior, but her face showed no disapproval.

"Branwen! It will be good to see you in black and white again," Mother Ninian said. "Those are the most becoming colors, I assure you."

Ninian breeched propriety even further by giving Lancelot a wink. "Don't you dare leave until I've had a chance to talk with you," she told Lancelot.

Lancelot nodded in happy agreement. She rejoiced at seeing this nun who had counseled her well during the Saxon War and after it.

Ninian swept Branwen away.

"There is also someone else who will want to see you, I believe," Mother Perpetua said. "Thank you again, Lancelot."

Soon after the abbess exited the room, leaving Lancelot to stare at the statue of Saint Mary holding a book (which Lancelot thought it unlikely that a poor carpenter's wife would have read), a woman in simple clothes, but not a nun's habit, entered.

Maire and Lancelot smiled at each other. Lancelot would of course never refer to the fact that she had brought Maire to the convent to help her leave off serving Arthur's army as a camp follower.

Maire handed her a cup of wine, and Lancelot accepted it gratefully and asked how she was.

After a chat with Maire and a longer conversation with Mother Ninian, Lancelot left satisfied. She wondered whether she would be forgiven for her sins as easily as Branwen was.

Lancelot rode into the forest. She wondered whether Antonius might lurk there and want to fight after all. But she saw nothing out of the ordinary.

Except that at the foot of a large oak tree lay the corpse of the girl she had killed accidentally in the Saxon War.

Lancelot almost fell off her horse. She shook her head, and looked again. Only a lichen-covered rock sat near the tree roots.

Lancelot made the sign of the cross and told herself there was nothing the matter with her.

6 THE WARRIOR OF THE HAWTHORN BUSH

Newly acquired dignity forgotten, Galahad ran down the convent stairs, almost bumping into the statue of the Virgin holding a book in her hands. Galahad dashed past the plump sister porter, flung open the heavy oak door as if it had been the flimsy door of a peasant's hut, and rushed to meet the lady approaching on a roan horse.

"Mother!" Galahad ran to the fine horse and swung down the tall and elegant lady who had ridden on it.

The Lady Morgan of Cornwalll beamed as she embraced Galahad and tousled the already tangled reddish hair that didn't quite match her own red-gold.

Galahad's breeches had a hole in the knee, but perhaps Morgan hadn't noticed that.

Morgan pulled back enough to have a good look at Galahad's face, and Galahad knew she was the only one who thought it handsome. Galahad breathed in Morgan's perfume, which smelled of lavender.

"What a ruffian you've become. Do you embrace all ladies who come here? Are the sisters safe around you?" Morgan teased.

"Oh, mother!" Galahad looked around to make sure no one had heard this comment. "Of course they are. But then, none of them are as beautiful as you."

Morgan laughed. "With a tongue like that, you'll do well at court."

Galahad cried out with excitement, "May I go to court now? Is it finally time?"

"Yes. But I must greet the sisters now," she said, smiling at the nuns who were standing at the portal. Only the youngest ones looked puzzled at the sight of a commanding lady in riding breeches. "We can talk about it later. Must you wear that thing around your neck?" She glanced disapprovingly at the silver cross that swung there. "Christians used to wear a ChiRo. This new fashion of wearing a symbol of death is much worse."

Before Galahad could reply that it was a nun's gift that could not be rejected, an infinity of nuns greeted the lady and Galahad nearly pawed the ground in impatience. Morgan must talk at length to the dignified abbess, who embraced her, and, in shorter bursts, with the others.

Then Morgan had to be offered bread and honey, which she ate in the refectory with the abbess, while Galahad stayed discreetly silent. Galahad stared at a tapestry of the miracle of the loaves and fishes. The fishes looked so real that they seemed ready to swim off the wall. Too excited to eat, Galahad cut a few pieces from an apple but didn't finish it.

After the meal had ended, Galahad, the lady Morgan, and old Mother Ninian went off to the convent garden, where roses and foxglove bloomed. The scent tantalized Galahad. Would the flowers at Camelot smell as sweet or sweeter?

"How are Galahad's lessons going, Lady Ninian?" Morgan asked, for she never used the Christian title Mother Ninian to another who used to serve the goddess at Avalon before the shrine had been abandoned.

Very well, Lady Morgan," the old woman answered, patting Galahad's arm fondly. "But this one has more of a head for the riding and swordplay."

Morgan nodded her approval. "Good. It is time that you learned more about such things than you can at a convent."

"Sister Darerca is not bad with a sword," Galahad objected, "though I always defeat her now. I'd like to learn from Lancelot of the Lightning Arm, the greatest warrior in the world." Galahad had never been allowed to meet Lancelot when the warrior came to the convent, but now at last the meeting could take place. But perhaps Lancelot would pay no heed to Galahad at Camelot. Lancelot might be too important to pay attention to those who came for training. Galahad hoped not.

Darerca, large as many warriors, was Ninian's dear friend, and Ninian smiled as always at hearing the name.

"No doubt you will learn from Lancelot." Morgan frowned. Her red-gold hair gleamed in the sun. "But keep your distance, even from Lancelot. Remember that you are a king's son."

The wrinkles on Ninian's brow grew much more pronounced than the one on Morgan's.

"You cannot tell anyone, even Lancelot, that you are not a man," Morgan commanded. "Swear, by the womb that bore you and the breasts that nursed you--mine--that you will never tell Lancelot." She extended her hand, indicating that Galahad should clasp it.

Galahad trembled at taking such an oath. Why did her mother care so much whether Lancelot knew? But Morgan did not always explain her commands. She clasped Morgan's hand.

"I swear by the womb that bore me and the breasts that nursed me that I will never tell Lancelot."

Morgan seated herself on a stone bench, and Galahad sprawled on the ground in front of her. This posture displayed the tear in the right leg of Galahad's breeches.

"What is my father like? All that you have told me are stories for children about swords and lakes, skill with horses, and fondness for dogs."

Morgan's countenance grew sterner, which made her more beautiful than ever. "Arthur is above all a king. He lives for that. He would make any sacrifice for his people, and he would expect his people to make any sacrifice for him. He sees all things in a view from the throne. Anything that does not seem fitting for a king he casts away, as he did me. Never imagine that he would not do the same to you." There was some pity in her eyes, but her mouth was bitter.

Galahad shook. "Of course I'm no likely child for a king." She bit her lip.

"Never tell him. Never in his lifetime can you say whose child you are, and perhaps never."

"Never in his lifetime." Galahad moaned slightly, and Ninian patted her trembling shoulder.

"He can be fooled, of course, and has been by Lancelot, but if he thought you were his son he would look too closely," Morgan instructed. "No father could understand."

"No, of course not." Galahad tried to keep her eyes dry but looked over the convent wall towards the forest beyond.

"Don't weep, I can't bear it," Morgan said, opening her arms and surrounding Galahad, who joined her on the bench and sought shelter in them.

A thrush sang, its sweet song accentuating life's sadness.

After a short time, Morgan pulled back a little and scrutinized Galahad. "Are you indeed strong enough to live at court? Can you truly be so restrained?"

"To become a warrior of King Arthur's? Of course I can." If Lancelot could live disguised as a man, so could she. Could she hold back from embracing her father? She would have to.

"Very good. And if you ever hear gossip at court that I have plotted against Arthur, don't believe it. It is true that I once pretended that I would marry old King Uriens of Rheged if he would try to restore the old gods..."

"Mother! You wouldn't! Not some old man!" Galahad objected, nearly falling off the bench.

Morgan shook her head. "No, dear, of course not. I meant only to prod Arthur, not to injure him." Morgan lightened her voice. "Tell me, have you fallen in love with any of the novices?"

"Oh, no, mother. Then I would have to stay here and never go out into the world. I have liked it well here." Galahad smiled at Mother Ninian. "But I want to see the world."

"So you shall. You must be very careful, of course, but surely no child of mine could live forever without loving. I suppose embracing a man at Beltane is not to be thought of?" Morgan asked, watching Galahad's face.

"Oh, no, mother!" Galahad felt her face grow hot. "Nothing like that. No stranger in the dark. But I do hope to find love," she ventured. "From a woman."

Morgan's face showed no change. "You are like Lancelot, perhaps? Well, disguised as you are, that will be easier, no doubt. But do not fear to try men either, if you wish, though it's best if you go to them in another guise, or in the dark at Beltane. I can give you a potion to prevent childbearing."

"Oh, mother, I don't need a potion," Galahad insisted. "I have no inclination for men at all."

"You have lived in a convent, which is hardly the best place to discover that," Morgan suggested with a hint of a smile. "We shall see. There is only one warning that I should give you." Her sea-green eyes narrowed. "Never lie with any of the family of Lot of Lothian. They are too closely related to us through my aunt, Morgause."

Ninian snorted. "They are all men anyway, my lady, so there surely is no great difficulty."

"I am much too shy to approach anyone, mother," Galahad said, laughing nervously. "Of course I shall do as you say."

Morgan shook her head and sighed. "This is what comes of growing up in a convent. I hope you have taught Galahad about something more than Christianity, Ninian," she said sternly.

"Even as I taught you all that you know," replied the old woman, not much more cheerfully. "Would I leave anyone to wallow in the misery of a religion that says there is only one life and whose only god is a murdered man?"

Then the abbess appeared in a doorway and Morgan rose. "I must speak with Perpetua." She left them in the garden.

Galahad rose when her mother stood.

Galahad glanced around the familiar garden, which she would now leave. It seemed smaller than it had when she was a child, but still beautiful. A robin redbreast searched for bugs near a rose bush covered with white blossoms.

Bells pealed for prayers, but Galahad was relieved to see that Ninian did not leave for the chapel.

"So now I shall go into the world, Mother Ninian. Do you have any advice for me?" Galahad's attention turned to the old nun.

It was difficult to notice anyone else when Morgan was present. Ninian plucked a white rose, which she offered to Galahad. Hopping close to Ninian, the robin caught a bug. "Where do you think you have lived all of your life? The world is here, and everywhere. Will you have advice? Have I not given it ever since you could understand my words? I must be a poor teacher if you have not learned until now."

"No, no, you are the best of teachers!" Galahad protested, for she loved Ninian dearly and did not want to offend her.

"If you wish, you shall have more of my words," the old nun said, seating herself on the bench that Morgan had vacated and patting it, indicating that Galahad should sit beside her. "You must love without possessing or being possessed. You must fight without killing or being killed. And you must conceal much without becoming deceptive or being deceived. Is that advice enough?"

"Enough, or too much." Galahad shook her head. It would be difficult enough to understand Mother Ninian's advice, much less to follow it. She twirled the rose in her fingers.

"That was interesting advice from your mother. How strange that a woman who thought nothing about lying with her brother should think it wrong for you to lie with cousins. Use your head, Galahad. What do you think would disturb her?" She scrutinized Galahad's face.

Galahad found this question perplexing. Who knew what would disturb her mother? All she could think of was her mother's great news. "Oh, Mother Ninian, I'm finally going to see the court. And my father."

"Yes, you'll see him. No doubt about that." Ninian was not given to sighs, but she let one escape. "Why must you think so much about this father you have never seen? Have we not loved you?"

Galahad was embarrassed, as if discovered in some rudeness. She looked into the old nun's kind gray eyes. "Of course. But my mother has told me about him all my life. And people say he is the best and the greatest king in the world."

Ninian clicked her tongue. "And if your father were not the greatest king in the world, but were kind to you, you would be fond of him anyway, would you not?"

"Of course. But he won't know me. Am I something awful that must be hidden?" Galahad's voice trembled again.

"No, no, you're not." Ninian put her arms around Galahad. "Think of your concealment as a game. Laugh when you fool everyone, and that should keep you in a constant state of mirth."

In a less cheerful tone, she added, "Mind you keep concealed, though, for if they learned your sex it could endanger not only you, but Lancelot as well. If you were discovered, it might be easier for them to guess her secret, for you look more like a man, with that little beard of yours." She smiled at the tuft of red hair on Galahad's chin.

A large nun, both tall and stout, came rushing up to them. "So you think those warriors are better fighters than I am, do you, ungrateful child?" Although the nun complained, her blue eyes showed no anger. "Which of them were taught by the greatest teacher of all, the woman warrior Scathach? Which of them were schooled with Cuchulain, as I was? And how many of them are from Ireland, country of the greatest fighters in the world?" Sister Darerca demanded, her robes flapping around her.

"A few of them may be Irish like you, but none of them has such a history, I should think." Used to Darerca's tall tales about long-dead heroes, Galahad grinned. Darerca, like Ninian, used humor as a form of instruction, and Galahad hoped that some of the warriors at Camelot might have a shred of like wit.

Morgan called Galahad to her, and Ninian and Darerca were left alone in the garden. Ninian picked up the white rose that Galahad had left on the stone bench and handed it to Darerca, who sniffed it.

"We'll be losing Galahad, my pagan rose. Will you grieve much?" Darerca asked.

Ninian sighed and brushed the black veil back from her face. "Save your worry for Galahad. She'll need it. Why must Morgan fill her head with dreams of being the king's child? Galahad is not the sort to claim a throne, and I have raised her to seek happiness, not power. Morgan warned her not to lie with Gawaine, but Galahad does not guess that he is her father." She felt pity for Galahad and even some for Gawaine.

Darerca shrugged and fingered the rose deftly, not pricking herself. Over the wall, the sun grew large and bright in the west as the day's end drew near.

"Have you told Morgan that you do not see Galahad on the throne? She believes in your powers of sight, pagan that she is."

Ninian closed her eyes. "What I have seen will not bear telling," she whispered.

Darerca put an arm around her and Ninian clutched at her.

"So, are you prepared for the court?" Morgan asked, brushing the red hair out of Galahad's face. She had spent some days at the convent, adding her own instructions to those of the nuns, and those instructions had been rather different.

"Yes, Mother." Galahad tried to keep from picking at her tunic with her hands. She should leave them at her side like a proper warrior. Now that the day for going to court drew near, her stomach was tense at the thought, much though she had anticipated the event. "But will they take someone as old as I am? Don't boys have to spend years studying there?"

"Many do, under the new way of doing things, but few of the old warriors went through such steps. They merely came and fought when Arthur needed men. You have learned enough of fighting to pass among lads of your age," said Ninian, who sat on a stool in Galahad's tiny convent cell with the mother and daughter, who both were seated on a pallet. A wall hanging with strange designs that was a gift from Morgan vied with a plain cross on the walls.

Wondering how the old woman came to know so much about warriors, Galahad asked, "But won't they want to know whose son I am? I can't say that I am yours, can I, Mother? What family shall I name?"

"None," Morgan said calmly.

Galahad gasped.

Morgan made her face hard at the sight of Galahad's dismay. "No one has inquired too closely into Lancelot's origins, so why should they into yours?"

"But don't they have to know that I am of noble blood?" Galahad winced at the thought of arriving at the caer's gates and simply announcing "I am Galahad."

"Who would dare to doubt that you are noble?" Rising, Morgan drew herself up, looking taller than her full height, which was considerable for a woman, and frowned at the thought of such audacity.

Ninian patted Galahad's hand. "Just wander around the wood's edge nearest to the hill on which the caer sits. You will find Merlin. Tell him that you are Galahad and that Ninian sent you, and he will know who you are. Don't worry yourself."

Galahad nevertheless was full of trepidation as she set off. Although she rode a fine white horse, Galahad felt like a beggar--an unfamiliar and unpleasant feeling.

Ninian told her the way, but said that Galahad must ride alone. The road to Camelot was not difficult to find. The woods were full of birds and squirrels, and Galahad imagined that they were clothed in gowns and tunics. In fact, they might be little people, half caught in another creature's body. That robin-- wasn't it really a little man in a red tunic? And that squirrel-- an old woman in a reddish gown? Hadn't Ninian told of such things when Galahad was a child?

Thus comforted with imaginings, Galahad slept in the forest for the first time. The hoots of owls and the flapping of bats unnerved her, but a warrior must be brave. She told herself that there was nothing dangerous in the forest except for warriors, robbers, wolves, and the occasional adder. Finally Galahad fell asleep. Toward morning, there was a faint drizzle. Galahad woke and thought the drizzle the worst part of the night.

Trying to ignore her damp clothes, Galahad rode to the wood's edge and saw the farms beyond and the gray stone caer on the hill. Now it seemed certain that this was a fairy world, for nothing built by human hands could be so large.

It took no persuasion to keep Galahad lingering near the forest. Galahad's horse, allowed to wander as it would, found a pond and drank. By the pond sat a white-bearded man in a white tunic that was the worse for wear. His glance darted hither and thither, following dragonflies that skittered over the pond's surface.

He gave Galahad only a glance, then resumed watching the dragonflies.

Galahad dismounted because it seemed discourteous to be on a horse while one so senior was seated.

"My Lord?" Galahad's voice quavered. "Are you the Lord Merlin?"

"I am." The voice was much gentler than Galahad had expected. "Who are you?"

"I am Galahad. The Lady Ninian" (Galahad had been schooled not to call her Mother Ninian to this listener, who would not like to be reminded that she was in a convent) "said I should tell you that I have come from her. I hope to become a warrior of King Arthur's." Galahad could not pronounce the king's name without a certain warmth and pride.

Merlin rose from the mossy bank. "Galahad? Why, of course you are. Why have you taken so many years to arrive?"

Galahad stared at him. "They said I wasn't old enough before."

"Not old enough." Merlin stared back. "That's what all these young people say. That's what Percival said when I asked why he had taken so long. There's one whom I hope never to see, but no doubt he'll come here, too." He shuddered. "Yes, you are young." The old man nodded and walked around the tiny pond to clasp Galahad's hand. "Let me take you to the court. Is Ninian well?" he asked, but he scarcely seemed to hear Galahad's assurances that she was.

Galahad offered to help Merlin mount his gray horse, but the old man laughed and shook his head.

Galahad hoped for some obscure, fascinating words whose meaning must be pondered, but they rode to the caer in silence.

The great gates opened to them. Why, Camelot was like a city, with many buildings! It was grand--except for a dreadful smell that proclaimed that the caer's many people had many wastes. But Galahad knew she could not hold her nose or show any other sign of dainty tastes.

They entered a courtyard full of warriors and stablehands. Galahad had never seen so many men before. Their voices were so much louder than the nuns' that Galahad thought they all must be shouting. Their clatter seemed deafening. But, beside Merlin, Galahad passed through crowds that parted like the Red Sea before Moses.

They passed a building that must have been the kitchen because an unbelievable medley of scents from roasting meats, baking bread, and honeycakes wafted from its door.

It was not long before Galahad found herself inside a building that proved to be a barracks. The smells of many men clung to it, and Galahad marveled at how different they were from the nuns' scent. No traces of incense lingered here.

A frowning warrior of middle age with thinning hair was complaining to a boy about untidiness. The boy stood still, accepting the criticism.

"Galihodin!" Merlin said, with no ceremony.

The warrior regarded him without reverence but with some semblance of respect. He nodded. "Yes, Lord Merlin?" The words held more acknowledgment of superior position than admiration.

"This is Galahad. Galahad will train here," the old man proclaimed, as if he brought in young men every day.

Galihodin raised his eyebrows. "What is your family, boy?"

Galahad felt herself flush. "I'm Galahad." The answer seemed quite foolish.

Galihodin raised his eyebrows still higher and turned his glance to Merlin. "Does he have noble blood?"

"Of course Galahad has noble blood," Merlin snapped. "Does Galahad have noble blood? What a question. The noblest."

Galahad flushed deeper, thinking that Merlin had given too much away.

But Galihodin merely frowned and barked at Galahad, "Put your things here. You'll sleep in the hall, next to Percival. While you are training, you will obey me and every other warrior. Do you understand?"

Galahad nodded, and had to hold back a sigh as Merlin disappeared without thinking to say farewell.

Galihodin shook his head. "No doubt you were made under a hawthorn bush," he said with disgust, "if you don't even know who your father was."

Galahad flushed. She supposed she would have to hear many such taunts.

A few days later, the king and the older warriors met the new recruits. Galahad stared at the king, who was graying but still handsome, with an air of authority even greater than the abbess's. Red-bearded Gawaine was even taller than the king. Lancelot she recognized. She had peered through the window when the great warrior of the lake had visited Ninian at the convent.

Galihodin barked out their names. "Percival ap Aglovale..."

Percy, a handsome, brown-haired young man with a ready smile, was already Galahad's favorite of the others in training.

"A good man, Aglovale," Gawaine interrupted, smiling at Aglovale's son.

"Welcome, Percy," said Lancelot, with a familiarity that made Galahad envy Percy.

"Lionel ap Brendan," Galihodin continued, "Galahad ap...Galahad ap?" He surveyed Galahad with impersonal derision.

She flashed a grin. "Galahad ap Hawthorn Bush."

Gawaine and Arthur laughed heartily. Gawaine clapped Galahad on the back. "Never mind, lad. Many a good man was gotten under a hawthorn bush. Let no one tax you for it," he said, looking meaningfully at Galihodin.

"It's true about the hawthorn bush. All I know of my father was that he had a prick," Galahad replied, and Gawaine and Arthur roared again.

"That's all that was needed," Arthur told Galahad. "I was born the same way myself, as everyone knows, though my father married my mother not long afterwards. If anyone insults you, he must answer to me."

"Thank you, Lord Arthur," Galahad said with a voice full of devotion.

Lancelot smiled warmly at Galahad, as if she agreed it was not so bad to be a bastard.

The king and Gawaine left the hall, but Lancelot lingered and spoke briefly with Percy, whose eyes shone as if he were seeing a holy vision.

Galahad's gaze followed the woman warrior.

Lancelot seemed to notice Galahad's extreme attention to her, and, after the youths had dispersed, followed Galahad to the courtyard.

"Come walk by the horse pasture with me, lad," she said, in a tone that was distant yet kind.

Galahad regarded her almost worshipfully. "Yes, Lord Lancelot." If only she could be like Lancelot! Galahad marveled at Lancelot's strong hands and weather-worn, hairless cheeks. What muscles Lancelot had developed!

Doves wandered about the pasture, cooing, but flew up as they drew near.

As they approached the grazing horses, which looked little like war steeds at the moment but larger and tougher than the convent horses, Lancelot spoke. "You may have heard that I have a son called Galahad. But that is only a tale. I have no son. A woman who falsely claims to have lain with me recently bore a child whom she called Galahad. I hope that you don't think I am your father."

Galahad's gaze surveyed the weeds at their feet. She choked, "No, Lord Lancelot." Her eyes suddenly looked into Lancelot's. "And I don't think you're my mother, either, Lord Lancelot."

"What did you say to me?" Lancelot's brown eyes widened with astonishment.

A dark mare whinnied, swifts swooped over the pasture, and Galahad tried to smother the beginnings of a laugh. "Pardon me, Lord Lancelot, but I can't help seeing that you're a woman. You see, my sister decided to dress as a man because she wanted to marry a woman. That's how I know. But never fear, I would never tell."

"Mary Virgin preserve me, see that you don't," Lancelot gasped. "Your sister must be an amazing woman, and she's fortunate to have a brother like you. I hope that I can meet her someday. It would be good to meet someone like myself."

"No doubt you will. She would be honored, Lord Lancelot."

Lancelot turned away, as if unable to face Galahad any longer.

Galahad choked on a laugh that threatened to turn into a sob. If only she could tell Lancelot about herself, and get both sympathy and suggestions on how best to conceal her secret. But she had sworn the oath to her mother and could never tell. She had tried to give Lancelot a hint without breaking her oath, but Lancelot had not guessed.

The young men slept on the floor of the hall. Each was wrapped only in a single cloak or blanket. Dawn seemed far away.

Galahad lay awake. She must find a way to convince their trainers to give her another place to sleep. Lying so close to a large number of young men made her too nervous to rest, and how could she undress around them? Their snores grated on her ears.

She let out a long, terrible series of moans that sounded like the spirits of the dead. The moans rang through the hall. Was this how a person having a nightmare sounded? What if her companions didn't believe that she made the sounds in her sleep? She tried not to tremble at her audacity. One might thrash during a nightmare, but not tremble. Her eyes firmly shut, she tossed and turned, and moaned again.

Percy, who slept next to Galahad on the crowded floor, shook her.

"Wake up, Galahad! This is unbearable!" he called out.

Galahad's eyes opened hazily.

"What's the matter?"

"You're wailing again! It wakes everyone but you." Percy's voice was much less friendly than usual.

"It's the same thing night after night," called out another young man angrily.

"I'll beat you if you keep this up, Galahad," cried another.

"Maybe if we give him a thrashing, he'll stop it," still another one called out.

"How good it is to be with kind, Christian companions," Galahad mumbled sweetly, hoping they would not act on their words.

"Don't hit him, that's not the answer," said Percy, turning angrily towards the ones who had suggested it. "He might wail all the louder. Let's ask if he can be transferred out of here to an alcove somewhere. He's been here only a few nights, but the rest of us are going mad."

"I'm so terribly sorry," Galahad said meekly. "I always had a room of my own. I had no idea that I made so much noise." She was greatly pleased that her moans had had the hoped-for effect.

It was after supper, and a harper was playing poignant strains. Lancelot relaxed, still tasting the honey-drenched pears she had just eaten. Their smell clung to her fingers. She took a sip of sweet wine. The harper was Irish, and perhaps they were the finest at that art.

Lancelot rose and walked down the great hall to the distant trestles where the new students sat, and stopped beside Percy and Galahad. She smiled at them, Percy because he was the son of her friend Aglovale, who had fought beside her in the Saxon War and later discovered her secret, and Galahad because he seemed to be trustworthy. The two gazed up at her as if they were more enthused at her presence than at the music. They had still been eating their honeyed pears, but they stopped when Lancelot stood by them.

She paused a moment, and when the harper had finished his tune, said, "Fine music. It brings every season of the year within the space of a few moments."

"I enjoyed it," Percy said. "My brother is learning to play and is mad about it, but I have no time. A warrior's arts are more important."

"Are they indeed?" Lancelot asked. "I'm not so sure."

The two youths appeared to drink in her every word. She was a little embarrassed at being a hero to them.

Gawaine had picked up his pipes and begun to play.

"What a wail!" Percy exclaimed. "How shall I learn to listen to the men of the North playing?"

But Galahad's blue eyes sparkled. "It's wonderful. This moves me much more than the harp. The pipes are like a creature from another world. Aren't they grand, Lord Lancelot?"

"Perhaps," Lancelot replied. "But I prefer the harp."

Gawaine stopped playing, and put the pipes aside. Arthur leaned over, no doubt to say some light words of praise. A young serving woman slipped onto Gawaine's lap, and he laughed and put an arm around her.

An older serving woman who was carrying a bowl of fruit flinched.

Lancelot walked up to her. "Put the food aside, Ragnal, and kindly go see that the fire in Lady Guinevere's room is lit. Old Fencha has not been well of late and might have fallen asleep. The nights are still cold and the queen might take a chill."

Ragnal passed the bowl to another serving woman and cast a grateful look at Lancelot. When she turned to leave the great hall, Lancelot walked with her.

In the entry way, Ragnal said, "You're a kind man, Lord Lancelot. Only you would care what a serving woman is feeling. I never know what woman Gawaine will want next. It's foolish of me to be bothered. He of course does what he pleases."

Lancelot squeezed her hand, then returned to the hall. When she resumed her place, Gawaine said, "Run along, Ewa," and the young serving woman went back to her duties.

Ragnal smiled on the way to the queen's chamber.

When Ragnal was studying everyone so she could mimic them, she had seen in what way Lancelot was different. And she later learned that Lancelot was the one person Gawaine did not like her to imitate.

Ragnal knew that Gawaine was likely to come to her bed as usual that night. She had somewhat exaggerated his wenching, because Lancelot was the only rival she feared.

As the evening drew to a close and the warriors were departing, Galahad approached Gawaine."Oh, Lord Gawaine, the pipes are splendid. I wish I could learn."

Gawaine smiled. "Of course you can, lad. I'll teach you."

Galahad felt almost as thrilled as she had when her mother had said she could go to court. "Truly? Many thanks. I know that I have much to learn about fighting, but I should like to learn music, too. The pipes spoke to my soul like nothing else I've heard."

Gawaine beamed at her. "Rare words from a southerner. You have not heard them before?"

"No, I think not."

So after jousting lessons, Galahad went to Gawaine's house to learn to play the pipes. Gawaine's walls were covered with weapons, but Galahad looked for his pipes.

Gawaine produced a set of pipes and said, "They're yours."

Galahad eyed them eagerly. "You're too kind."

"No, it's rare to find a youth who wants to play them, at least this far south it is. You can learn much from the pipes, Galahad. They're like a woman. Most men think that there is only one organ to touch them with, but they are fools." The red-bearded warrior chuckled.

Galahad felt herself flush.

Gawaine smiled. "I don't mean to embarrass you, lad, but as you have no father to tell you...not that mine ever taught me any such thing. He was more like a bull, who knew only enough to get my mother with child, and many other women as well.

One of the first women I was with told me many ways to please women. If you ask women what they want, you'll learn a great deal."

Galahad stared at the rushes on the floor. No doubt that was true. If only a woman wanted her, but that might never happen.

"Never been with a woman, have you? There are many here..."

Galahad gasped. "I don't love any of them yet."

The tall warrior's voice became gentler. "Sorry, lad, don't mind me. Do as you please. Now, about the pipes . . ." He went on to the work at hand, and Galahad set about finding the world of music through this Pan.

When Gawaine talked, he jested a great deal. But Galahad saw that when he played the pipes, he was serious.

Gawaine's sword struck Galahad's. He pushed aside the youth's sword as if it were made of stale bread. "You must do far better, or you'll be dead," Gawaine told him. "Go practice with Gareth."

Galahad sighed.

"Yes, I know he's as large and strong as I am. That's why I charge you to fight with him every day." Gawaine turned to the group of young warriors that watched his every move. "Gareth, practice every day with Galahad, and don't go easy on him."

"Willingly." Gareth smiled at Galahad.

"And start now," Gawaine added. "Don't groan, Galahad. I know you're tired. But the enemy won't let you rest in a battle."

Gawaine sauntered over to Peredur and Bedwyr, who also had been training the young men. He drank from his flask.

"They aren't too bad," Peredur said.

"Galahad is fast, at least."

"He'll need more than speed," Gawaine said.

"We must talk with you." Bedwyr looked Gawaine in the eye. "We've been discussing the kingdom. We suppose that Arthur has secretly named you as his heir, but he needs to do so publicly. You should tell him that."

Peredur nodded. "It's only right that there be a formal heir to ease people's worries and prevent speculation."

Gawaine sighed. "Of course I won't ask to be named formally. How would that look? I don't even want to be king, much less to be thought lusting for the title. If you're so anxious, you ask him."

"I have." Bedwyr compressed his mouth. "But he won't listen to me. He puts me off with tales of finding the sword and tells me that it will find a new king when the time comes. That's nonsense."

"He wants to be immortal," Peredur said. "He's a great king, but he needs to assure the succession."

"I wouldn't keep a barren wife, not to mention a barren queen." Bedwyr offered Perdur his flask.

"I would," Peredur replied stiffly, declining the drink. "Marriage is sacred. I wouldn't have abandoned Claudia if she had failed to bear a child."

Bedwyr snorted. "But we're talking about a kingdom. I suppose Arthur doesn't worry because he has you, Gawaine. You would be a fine king, though there's nobody like Arthur."

Gawaine shifted his feet. He wanted to walk away. "True, I could never be as great as Arthur. And I'll probably die first in some fight."

"And you're only a nominal Christian," Perdur said. "I wouldn't mind if Arthur picked someone else, but I can't imagine who that could be."

"What about Gareth?" Gawaine asked. "He has every virtue and is a fine fighter, and he's just as closely related to Arthur."

Bedwyr shook his head violently. "Pah! He's fitter for a monastery than a throne. Arthur would never choose him. And there are those who'd prefer a king from the south. King Mark of Dumnonia might contest any of the Orkney clan."

"I hope it doesn't come to that." Peredur sighed "Yes, it is sad that Guinevere couldn't bear a child, poor lady."

"I am tired of this subject. Gossip does no good." Gawaine strode off. He agreed that it would be best if he did not have to be king.

Young Percy was friendly with Galahad when he no longer had to sleep nearby. Galahad was just right--reverent, but not excessively pious, and always ready for a jest.

"Lancelot of the Lake likes you a great deal. You're very fortunate," said Percy when they rested after practicing fighting each other with swords. Sitting on a bench, they leaned back against the practice room's stone wall.

"I am, but he likes you, too. You were lucky enough to know him when you were a child," Galahad replied, sighing with apparent envy.

"I did," Percy affirmed, puffing out his chest. "He taught my brother and me all about the forest. We lived in the forest, you know, and wore the skins of animals. I was the only one at home who could protect my mother."

"Yes, I've heard you tell how knew nothing about warriors until Lancelot came. You tell the most fanciful tales of anyone here." Galahad grinned, poured some water from a jar to a cup, and offered it to Percy.

Embarrassed, Percy looked at his boots, which he regretted were not as new as some of the other young warriors' boots. "I admit I exaggerate the story a little. But Lancelot really did teach me to think as if I lived in the skins of animals."

"But why do you say that you lived only with your mother? I have heard that your father lives all the time at home with his family, unlike many other fathers." Galahad poured another cup of water and drank from it.

"Oh, God's truth, does everyone know that?" Percy moaned, holding his head. "How embarrassing. It sounds as if he were a poor farmer, not a warrior. He truly did fight in the Saxon War, though." It had seemed better never to refer to his father than to admit that he had not fought in many years, not since the war.

"Your story about the visiting the fisher king's caer, riding on a magical boat, and seeing a magical goblet is perhaps a little exaggerated, too," Galahad suggested, smirking.

"No, that's the truth," Percy insisted, looking away into the air beyond Galahad. "I really found him when I was with the great Lancelot. The fisher king was old and lonely, and we comforted him." He remembered an enchanted golden cup and a caer of silver and gold. Some might think they looked like a bucket and a fisherman's hut, but such people did not see with the eyes of faith. Some might believe that the fisher king's disguise as a poor fisherman was his true aspect, but Percy would never be so deluded. Would they even deny that the boat he had ridden with Lancelot moved by itself, or that it had gone on to the Holy Land after Lancelot had jumped out of it and bade him to do the same because of a foolish fear that the boat might sink? Was Galahad one of the unbelievers? Percy sighed.

"And what does Lancelot think of your telling the story?" Galahad asked.

"He smiled at me," Percy said proudly, "and told me, 'Hold onto your dreams, Percy, and you won't be just an ordinary young warrior.'"

Percy jumped up and moved about the room. Could he dare to ask Galahad the question he had been longing to put to him?

"I've heard that . . ." Percy's voice was a little less certain, but if Galahad was going to ask about his father, he might as well ask about Galahad's. "I've heard that Lancelot might be your father? Is that possible?"

Surprisingly, Galahad laughed, as if the question were foolish. "No, it isn't. I certainly don't look like him, do I? I wish I did. People say that I look like an elf."

Percy was moderately proud of his own looks, from his abundant dark brown locks to the dimple on his chin. With a slight feeling of pity, he regarded the skinny Galahad. "Yes, that sums it up. But really, you look very pleasant."

Galahad groaned. "Elfin looks are not exactly what attract women."

"Oh, I'm sure that won't matter if you become a great warrior," said Percy, trying to be kind. "Women love great men no matter what they look like."

"Thanks," said Galahad, still not sounding cheered.

"You might shave off that beard," Percy suggested. "It isn't much of one, and it only increases the elfin look."

"I'll never do that," Galahad said, patting the wispy tuft.

"You're stubborn, but likeable now that I don't have to sleep near you," Percy said. "I've never heard anything like the way you scream in your sleep. Don't sleep with a lady before you marry her, or she'll never marry you!"

"Pardon my moaning in my sleep," Galahad replied. "It was good of you to ask the lord Cai to get me an alcove of my own. They put me in a place where I can't disturb anyone."

Percival shrugged. "It was a matter of our sanity. Your noises made nights unbearable for everyone else in the hall. Just don't ever ask me to go on a mission with you, or sleep far off if you do."

"Don't worry, I shall." Galahad chuckled rather than being offended by this insulting comment, and Percy was a little embarrassed at having been so rude.

Merlin wandered away from the table long before the supper was finished, as was usual for him. He had partaken only of a little trout and some greens. The warriors slashed at roasts with their knives, but he paid them no heed. He stared at Lancelot in confusion, as he usually did, then shook his head. Something about Lancelot was strange, but he didn't remember what it was.

Supper tonight was different from other nights. A pale, dark-haired young lady rose from her bench at the other end of the great hall and drifted after him. He noticed her but pretended that he did not.

He murmured theorems from geometry under his breath and walked towards the ramparts. The girl approached him and touched his sleeve.

"Lord Merlin?" Her voice was deferential and perhaps a trifle timid, but she must be bold to follow a man in the starlit night.

Turning his head, he regarded her through weary eyes.

He saw a girl of marriageable age, whose dark hair and gray eyes like his own might mean that there was some trace of the Old Ones' blood in her. Her gown was brown and simple, but finely cut, and an amber bead hung on a chain round her neck.

"Yes, child? You had better return to the ladies and not go wandering around the caer."

The girl stayed where she was. "Please, my lord, my name is Nimue and it's you I want to speak with. My mother was schooled at Avalon."

He looked at her with greater interest. Few people now spoke to him about the once sacred island of Avalon, now deserted by the holy and desecrated by the presence of Christian monks. "Did she, now? And what was her name?"

She named a name that he vaguely recalled. The old man nodded, inviting her to proceed. He took her arm and walked on the ramparts with her, looking at the star-studded summer sky.

An owl that lived in one of the towers flew out on its nightly quest, and it reminded him of the story of Blouddewen, the woman made of flowers who was turned into an owl for her faithlessness. So many stories warned of women, and he had been cautious about them.

The girl's voice was full of the aching earnestness of the young. "My mother and my father are both dead. She told me a little about the old ways, and I want to learn more. But those who knew them are dispersed. I know the whereabouts only of the Lady Morgan of Cornwall, and you. My uncle, who is my guardian, would never send me to her caer, for everyone calls her a witch. But I was able to persuade him to send me to court because he thinks I can make a match with one of the warriors. He doesn't know that all I want is to study with you." She looked up with eyes full of hope.

Most unaccustomed to having young women regard him in such a way, or indeed to having them pay him any heed at all, Merlin spoke more gently than was usual for him. "My mind weaves back on itself now, but if I can help you, I shall. What do you want to learn? Astronomy? Geometry? Healing? Engineering?"

"I want to learn about the gods. I want to know why things are the way they are." She was all attention.

He shook his head. "That is what everyone who has thought much wants to know. Can you expect me to have the answer? I know only some of the questions. If only Ninian were here. She might be able to help you more than I can. But where did she go? I don't remember." Merlin looked about him, as if she might appear around a corner. He cleared his throat. "Oh, to be sure, she's in a convent. But I ramble. Do you still think you can learn from such a one?"

Nimue nodded.

"Well, we shall see, we shall see." For some reason the night air did not hurt his joints as it usually did.

"I am not going to spin today. Instead, I'll spin words with Master Merlin, for he will teach me," Nimue made bold to say to Lysanda, the lady who supervised the girls' spinning.

"We'll see about that," snapped sharp-faced Lysanda. "You must have the queen's permission."

Guinevere soon passed through the room where the ladies were spinning. She spent little time there, but said a few kind things about the spinning and needlework.

"Lady Guinevere!" Lysanda called out. "This girl has taken it into her head that she is going to take lessons from Master Merlin. It is improper for a girl to take lessons from a man, let alone that old pagan, isn't it? What would he teach her?" She sneered.

The queen raised her eyebrows. "Lessons with Merlin? Whatever for?"

Nimue did not quail. Perhaps the queen would not be as narrow as Lysanda. "My mother had lessons on Avalon when she was a girl, and I want to learn some of the old ways."

Guinevere nodded. "If it's old ways you want to learn, surely no one could tell you better than that ancient man. Why shouldn't a girl learn from a man?" she asked Lysanda. "I learned Latin and Greek from a priest, and that was proper. Surely Merlin is as wholesome as any priest. In all the years that I have lived at Camelot, I have never seen him show the least interest in any woman."

One morning, the golden-haired lady Gwyl came to Guinevere's room. She was Arthur's favorite mistress, and Guinevere liked her well, and was glad that some women truly wanted to be with him.

"I wanted to say farewell to you," Gwyl said. Her eyes were red. "You have been very kind to me."

Guinevere jumped up from the table where she had been reading. "You're leaving? Has Arthur sent you away? Or are you leaving him?" She knew it was unlikely that a mistress, especially one whose means were limited, would leave, but she liked to think that the woman might have a choice, too.

Gwyl laughed sharply, almost a bark. "Of course, he doesn't want me anymore. So I shall leave."

"How dare he, after the years you have been with him! I'll speak to him about it!" Guinevere exclaimed immediately, putting her arm around Gwyl.

Gwyl accepted the arm but remained rigid. There were delicate lines on her face and her waist was a trifle thicker than it had been, but she still was a beauty. "No," she said firmly. "If he doesn't want me, I don't want to stay. But I would like my son Colles to continue training as a warrior here, and my daughter Felicia to stay as one of your ladies."

"Of course, if you want, but won't you be lonely without them?" Guinevere scrutinized her face solicitously.

"I'll miss them, but I won't be entirely lonely," said Gwyl, returning Guinevere's look without embarrassment. "I have no intention of living without a man in my bed. But that's no way to raise my daughter. It's best if she stays here with you."

"You deserve better." Guinevere hugged her, but she let her leave.

When Gwyl had left, Guinevere sighed. It was unlikely that Arthur would have another mistress whom she liked so much. She smiled at the thought of all the jewels that had found their way to Gwyl's box of fancy things.

But, above all, Guinevere feared that Arthur might want her in his bed when Gwyl was gone. She would never be unfaithful to Lancelot, of course, but she didn't want a battle with her husband. Fortunately, she had always been so frozen in bed with him that he could hardly imagine she would give him much pleasure.

7 THE SAXON GIRL

One summer day, Arthur called Lancelot and Gawaine to his private chamber. The herbs and flower petals strewn among the rushes on the floor did not disguise the smell of wet dog. One of Arthur's Irish wolfhound pups, which sprawled beside his chair, had damp fur, no doubt from his morning run.

Making a slight gesture towards the hanging on the wall that depicted a battle scene, the king said, "I haven't heard much in recent years about Saxon raids, but I would like the two of you to travel along the borders of their lands, speak with the British people there, and make sure that the Saxons aren't disturbing them. Also, I need them to pay more tribute. Gawaine should go because, as my closest kinsman, he can speak for me. He is likely to succeed me--don't make gestures of dismissal, Gawaine, you know you are. And Lancelot is perhaps a little more diplomatic."

They nodded in agreement, but Lancelot felt less than enthusiastic about asking for more tribute.

"They should pay all they can," Gawaine said. "I don't trust those devil-spawn Saxons. If they're quiet it probably means they're preparing for another war. But if they have to give more tribute, they won't be able to make as many war plans."

"Certes we cannot trust that they will never make war again." Arthur nodded. "It is good for them to meet you and know that there is a strong man to replace me should anything happen."

Gawaine grunted. "Your words only make me pray more earnestly that you will live forever. I have no desire to shoulder your burdens."

The sun pouring in the window belied their words. Another war seemed impossible. The dozing wolfhound pup added to the feeling of peace.

"You will be meeting with Saxon thanes," Arthur said, glancing at Gawaine's arm. "Therefore you should put off wearing the gold you have taken from the bodies of Saxon warriors you killed."

Gawaine touched one of his Saxon armrings. "Very well. I have enough gold to wear without them."

Lancelot smiled. Indeed he did. She wore little ornament herself, and had given all of her plunder from the Saxon War to the Church and the poor.

Lancelot hoped that her journey with Gawaine would be as pleasant as earlier ones, when he hadn't known she was a woman.

In a room brightened by only one candle, Guinevere watched Lancelot step into her breeches and pull on her boots. Not for an instant did Guinevere cease her scrutiny, for it would be long before she saw the dear face again. She wanted to moan about Lancelot's departure, but refrained.

Lancelot turned to the bed, and Guinevere leapt up and flung her arms about her. They held each other for a moment, then Lancelot moved away.

"May your journey be safe."

Guinevere tried to keep anxiety out of her voice.

"It will be. This time there is no danger. I'll be back in a month or two, never fear. I shall miss you as I know you will miss me." Lancelot looked into her eyes one last time, then opened the secret door and, pulling it behind her, went quietly down the steps.

Guinevere sighed deeply, as she had not in Lancelot's presence. She might have liked to go to the stables and see Lancelot depart, but that would have seemed too great a mark of favor. It was better to part away from curious eyes.

Looking from the window, she watched Lancelot cross the courtyard to her own house to gather the few possessions she would take on the trip. Even though Lancelot was only a dark shape in a dark courtyard, Guinevere could make her out.

Then, not waiting for Fencha, Guinevere dressed herself.

Although this departure was nothing like as painful as it had been when Lancelot left to fight in the Saxon War, Guinevere felt a pang in her chest. Danger might come at any time from brigands or Saxons. Guinevere liked Saxons as little as anyone at Camelot did. They had killed some who were dear to her.

As dawn's first rays brightened the sky, Lancelot made her way from her house to the stables, and Guinevere was at the window watching her. Near the stables, Gawaine joined the handsome warrior.

Although Guinevere thought Gawaine would be an intolerable companion on a journey, she was just as glad that he was going with Lancelot. Men who would assault a lone warrior might be less likely to attack two. It was reassuring that

Gawaine fought nearly as well as Lancelot, and thus was the best one to travel with her. On an earlier journey, Lancelot had been nearly killed by robbers when she was traveling alone.

Guinevere saw the two ride away from the stable, and then they were hidden by walls.

She would be so lonely while Lancelot was gone. Guinevere looked around her room and sighed. Lancelot did not know what it was like to be always penned in one place, like the livestock. Although the dear warrior would miss her queen, she enjoyed traveling. What would it be like to be able to see mountains--though not on this journey, for Lancelot traveled east, where there were none--and rivers, forests, and marshes, to wake every day to a new scene? When Guinevere had been a girl, she had dreamed of traveling, but now she knew she never would. She had never even returned to her childhood home at Powys for a visit. Arthur did not wish it. Did she envy Lancelot's freedom? Oh yes, Guinevere acknowledged, she did.

The two warriors appeared again as they traveled down the hill and across the fields to the woods. Guinevere's gaze was fixed on Lancelot. When they entered the forest, she kept watching for a time, as if Lancelot might emerge again, although that would not happen.

Nothing mattered as much as Lancelot. Not even Guinevere's beloved books and scrolls. She would have cast them into the fire if so doing would somehow have kept Lancelot from harm.

How could she bear it if she never saw Lancelot again?

But it was wrong to harbor such morbid thoughts. Guinevere sat down at her table and tried to choose a Greek play to read, but none of them seemed likely to cheer her. Instead, she worked on her own verses about Lancelot. In her head only, of course, for they would be too scandalous if written down.

Lancelot and Gawaine set off through wheat fields and waved back to farmers who saluted them as they passed.

Who would remember the farmers who fed the people of Camelot? Lancelot wondered. She saw women washing clothes in the river and wondered who would remember them. But they probably had children to remember them, and she did not have any.

She and Gawaine rode towards the east, a direction that reminded Lancelot of war, although of course battles also had taken place in other parts of the country where the Saxons had attacked them. When they passed the scenes of earlier battles, she tried not to see rotting bodies instead of grain or grasses in the fields. They rode through woods where every tree had hidden an enemy, or so it had seemed. Some burned towns had been rebuilt, and others had faded away, with only a little rubble left.

"Saxons," grumbled Gawaine. "I'm longing to see their stupid faces and their piss yellow hair again."

Lancelot groaned. She had no great affection for Saxons, but Gawaine's antagonism to their looks seemed unnecessary. "What difference does their hair make? We know some Britons whose hair is yellow, too."

"No doubt some of their mothers were raped by Saxons," Gawaine retorted. Lancelot winced, remembering how a brigand had raped and murdered her mother, and Gawaine, who knew about that, looked sorry for his comment. She tried not to see her mother's body lying on bloody pine needles.

They passed the site of one of the Saxon towns that Arthur's army had burned. Shuddering, Lancelot remembered the sight of the fleeing women and children, the deserted huts she had searched to make sure no one was still in them, the torches of her companions who fired the huts, and the British warriors' yells of exaltation. Forgive me, forgive me, she repeated to herself. She wanted to beat her breast. How could anyone who had fought in a war ever believe again in their own goodness? she wondered.

On the first evening of their journey, they stopped by a lake and ate cold venison that Ragnal had packed for them. The horses munched on grass and a thrush sang its evening prayer.

Lancelot stared at the lake's waters, which were darkening from blue to green. She sighed. "If I were a bard, I would be able to tell how the water's blue is like but different from the blue of the sky, and how the green of the water is like but different from the green of the trees."

"We could ask the spirit of the lake," Gawaine said. "Every lake has its spirit, not just the one where Arthur received his sword."

Lancelot smiled at the tale of the arm reaching from the water. "And have you ever seen such a spirit?"

Gawaine stroked his beard. "Of course, for they are female. They have appeared to me and I have pleased them."

Lancelot rolled her eyes. Aging had not stopped Gawaine's tales about how women threw themselves at him, the more fanciful the better.

"And I know well the spirits of the sky also, for in former lives I was a hawk, as my childhood name Gwalchmai says. I rode the winds, looked over the world, and, of course, wooed female hawks. No easy task, as they are larger than the males." He drank from his wine flask.

Lancelot picked up a small pebble and threw it at him. It bounced off his shoulder.

"All of your tales end that way." Lancelot took a bite of the cold venison. "The very goddesses come to earth just so that you will lie with them."

"Of course they do." He began to munch his own dinner.

"I know. Hundreds of women could vouch for your prowess-- and even more could vouch for your constancy," Lancelot said, catching a fallen bit of venison before it could reach the ground.

Gawaine chuckled.

"Ragnal is such a witty woman," Lancelot said, changing the subject from tales of females to a real one.

Gawaine slapped his knee and took another swig from his flask. "She is indeed. It was she who chose me. One day I was walking past her in the courtyard. She carried a large basket of apples, but she paused and said, in a voice that mimicked mine exactly, 'I am Gawaine, Prince of Lothian and Orkney and cousin to King Arthur. I am far too important to notice you, little serving woman.' Of course I turned, saw her grin, and burst out laughing. I have noticed her ever since. She is one of the cleverest women at court, or anywhere. She matches me jest for jest and can imitate any voice that she has ever heard."

"I know that to my chagrin," Lancelot replied, not chagrined in the least.

"She said that you had heard her imitate you and made a jest yourself. Few others warriors would do that." He grinned broadly.

"Did you offer to carry her basket of apples?" Lancelot asked.

Gawaine lifted his eyebrows. "Yes, but why do you want to know?"

"Because it's what you'd have done if you had any regard for her."

So the journey was much like those they had shared many times before, except that Lancelot slept some ten yards away from Gawaine, whereas when Gawaine had believed that she was a man she had found the distance of ten feet sufficient. When he had first learned that she was a woman, it was winter, so she had slept on the other side of the fire from him, but now the nights were warm so there was no need to be that close.

As they proceeded in the vicinity of their former enemies, they found without discussion a route that did not go through the places where they had seen the bodies of many women who had been raped and mutilated--first a town of British women raped and killed by Saxons, and then a town of Saxon women raped and killed by the Britons--after which Lancelot had sunk into a deep misery and did not speak.

She was now quieter than usual and tense. She smiled only at little things, such as a hare running across the road. Unlike many, she did not believe that hares were linked to evil.

The ghosts of the yellow-haired Saxon women and children who had seemed to follow her in the war were returning. They said nothing, but they seemed to chide her for her happiness. She had no right to be happy, no right to forget the sight of their bodies.

"It frightens me to see you so silent again," Gawaine said.

Looking at her mare's mane, she forced herself to speak. "It's different. I am well, but I feel as if I shouldn't be, here in the country of death."

"Aren't all places lands of death?" he asked. "Surely every place has been fought over."

Lancelot shuddered. "What a terrible thought, but no doubt true."

"Damned Saxon barbarians wreck every place they go," Gawaine grumbled. "They tear down the trees and replace them with grain. The Romans cut enough of our forests. We don't need any new invaders destroying more of them."

"Who could like fields better than trees?" Lancelot agreed, looking with less than great enthusiasm at a field of meadowsweet, where goldfinches fed on thistles. A flock of fieldfares flew up. "Still, our people also cut down forests for farms because we have to eat."

"There's always roasted Saxon," Gawaine said, grinning.

Lancelot made a face at that. "We must treat them fairly," she said.

"Must you be so solemn, Lance? Of course we will. They have submitted to our treaties and pay us tribute. We should be gracious but wary."

"If Arthur intends that you succeed him, why doesn't he formally make you his heir?" Lancelot asked. "The people at court often speculate. Why not end the speculation?"

Gawaine grinned. "I hope he postpones that day as long as possible. I have no wish to be king. Perhaps some worthier man will emerge. I wonder whether my brother Gareth could grow to become kingly."

Lancelot considered the idea. "I'm not so sure he could."

"But he is more Christian than I am, and people could accept that better. Yet there are also those at court who believe that my whole clan has too much power, so none of us would please them. As long as Arthur keeps them guessing, they may hope that he will make a different choice."

Lancelot frowned. "That sounds dangerous to me. We need no factions."

Gawaine shook his head.

"Factions we will always have. It is dangerous to choose no heir publicly, but choosing one has its disadvantages also. If only Guinevere had given him one."

Lancelot was silent because that thought pleased her little.

As the day grew older, the winds whipped through a forest they traversed. Leaves still green scattered as if autumn had come early. A great tree crashed just in front of Lancelot's horse. Raven reared, and Lancelot barely clung to her. She pressed her knees to the mare's flanks in an attempt to subdue her. Gawaine's horse also pawed the air. Both riders kept to their horses and calmed them, first with force and then with soothing words. Lancelot's heart beat fast from the narrow escape. The trees she loved could be killers. Like some of the people she loved. She thought she would prefer to be killed by a tree, but not at the moment.

Gawaine's face had paled, and Lancelot suspected that hers was pale also. His gaze was fixed on her.

"If that tree had come any closer, I would have had to carry a sad message to Guinevere," he said. His voice mimicked its usual hearty tone but did not quite achieve it. "I wish you would let me ride first."

His words annoyed Lancelot. She said, "If you're so eager to be buried, just let someone kill you in your next fight." She urged Raven to go off the path, around the roots that extended from the great fallen trunk. "You don't need to protect me."

Gawaine followed her. "It's not that I want to protect you. I'd just rather not face Guinevere. If you were to come to grief, I doubt that she'd believe my account of it."

It was difficult for Lancelot to gather enough breath to chide him. She silently said a prayer of thanks that she would live and see the queen's face again. "You shouldn't exaggerate. True, Guinevere is not fond of you, but surely she doesn't distrust you so much. She's known you for twenty years."

She turned back to look at Gawaine. Some leaves had stuck in his red hair, giving him the look of a large woodland spirit.

"Guinevere trusts me, then? And have you told her that I know you are a woman?"

Lancelot frowned. "No. Why should I give her more worries? She'd fear that when you were drinking you would give away my secret." She turned away from him and felt the wind sting her face.

Her companion chuckled. "You are commendably discreet. But even were I as drunk as a berserker, I wouldn't tell."

Hoping that was true, Lancelot studied the trees ahead of her as if she could tell in advance which might fall. Dying near a friend would not be as terrible as dying alone, she thought. She might be killed in some remote place, and Guinevere would never know what happened to her, but would keep hoping that she would return. The thought nearly brought tears to Lancelot's eyes.

When they came to a meadow, Lancelot sighed with relief at being away from the trees. The two warriors dismounted and made a camp for the night. There was no need to comment about the wisdom of this plan.

The next day, the wind had died down. Fallen trees covered the earth like warriors slaughtered in a battlefield, but the danger was over.

They came upon a Saxon village that they had burned, and Lancelot silently rejoiced at seeing it sprung up again from the ashes. They rode around the collection of huts, not too close. Lancelot wondered whether any of the Saxons would recognize their faces. A dog barked at them, but no one came to look at the British warriors. Perhaps the people feared them still. Smelling the smoke of the cooking fires, Lancelot remembered that other, thicker smoke of so many years before.

As the warriors progressed, they stopped at outposts and asked if the men there had had troubles with Saxons, but there was nothing much to report. The last skirmish had been a couple of years before. One outpost said that some farmers were missing livestock and blamed the Saxons, but Lancelot thought it unlikely that Saxons were the thieves. Many British clans engaged in a little cattle stealing when they had the chance.

Of course the meals at the garrisons were enlivened with the usual stories about women. Lancelot tried as always to shield her feelings. When the beefy Plenorius, the head of one fort, told some particularly detailed stories, Gawaine put his hand up.

"Enough of such tales for tonight," Gawaine said. "Lancelot is a very pious Christian. He is very fond of holy books, particularly the Book of Judith."

Lancelot frowned and refrained from looking at him. This was the first time she had ever heard Gawaine refer to the holy book, which he had certainly never read. She was surprised that he might actually have listened to a little preaching.

After Gawaine had left for the night, Lancelot still sat at the table and argued with the commander. Plenorius tried to distract her with ale and old war stories, but to no avail. The man's beard was graying, but he seemed to have learned nothing since the Saxon Wars. There was no gleam of intelligence in his beady eyes.

"And then we encircled the Saxons..."

"I remember it well, Plenorius," she said, cutting him off. "There's no need to remind me. Gawaine's men saved the day."

"That Gawaine's worse than ever," chuckled Plenorius, stroking his beard in apparent imitation of the tall warrior.

"No doubt he is," Lancelot replied, unwilling to be distracted. "Now, about the fortifications. Why haven't you reinforced your walls, as you were ordered to do last year?"

LANCELOT AND GUINEVERE

"All in good time," he said, quaffing his ale. "We don't have enough men. There's only so much labor we can get from the local people. Now, if you could persuade Cai to send me some more goods or men . . ."

Lancelot had heard the same complaint from Plenorius several times already. Her voice was testy. "I'll see about it. You have men, you have stones. There's no excuse for not improving the walls. The Saxons could wipe you out."

Plenorius smiled without warmth. "No doubt you great warriors who spend all your time at Camelot understand these things much better than we do here in the outposts. You're certainly full of zeal in examining our buildings. Gawaine is off examining the bawdy houses. I told him what the best one was, and he actually said he wanted to know where all of them were, not just the best! Now, there's a man for you! This may be a place forsaken by the gods, but we have enough soldiers for more than one brothel."

"This fortress may not be a desirable post, but if you don't repair it, I have no doubt that you'll get a worse one," Lancelot warned, scowling. She found it disgusting that men would buy women, and was angry at her friend.

The next morning when they mounted their horses, Gawaine groaned. He had scarcely slept, and he was getting old to go without sleep. The only sight that pleased him was a spiderweb glistening on a bush. He patted his gray horse, which was aging also. "I'm tired today."

"What a pity," Lancelot said, in a tone that showed absolutely none.

"You might be a little more sympathetic," he grumbled.

"No, I might not," she snapped.

He groaned louder. It seemed that other men were always getting him in trouble with Lancelot. That old fool Plenorius had told Lancelot where he had gone, no doubt. First, Arthur had tried to make him tell a story about something he had never done. His tastes were not so exotic. But Lancelot had been repulsed, and now she believed he was buying women, which she detested. He wondered whether to tell her about his search for the daughter he had never seen, whom an old nun had told him years ago was living in a place with many women, which of course must mean a brothel. Since then, it was no pleasure to go to brothels, but rather a misery to see young girls who might have been his daughter, though he didn't see any with bright blue eyes like his, which the nun had said he should look for. He no longer wanted whores, now that he believed his daughter was one. He decided against telling Lancelot about his daughter. She would believe that he should spend every moment of his life on the search, even though it was probably futile, and be horrified that he ever did anything else. He had searched off and on for years, but less frequently, as finding his daughter seemed less likely.

The unfairness of it! He had been positively a monk. He hadn't lain with a woman in nearly two weeks, since they had started this journey, and now he had to travel with a woman who was so disgusted that she would scarcely speak to him.

"I don't suppose you'll believe this," he said querulously. "But I go to bawdy houses now because I have a quest to find and free a . . . a certain woman . . . who is in one."

Lancelot's eyes widened. She looked surprised, but not entirely skeptical. "I hope that you are telling me the truth, because I am likely to believe what you say. If this really is true, I'd go to brothels myself to look for this woman and help her."

"Gods!" he exclaimed, staring at her. "No, you won't. This is my quest, not yours, friend. It's not fitting for you."

"Surely helping a woman is always fitting for anyone," Lancelot said, but he shook his head.

Thank the gods he had not told her the whole story, or she really might have gone to such places looking for a woman with eyes like his. Lancelot was the only friend he had who would have undertaken to help him in this task, and therefore the best friend he had. But she would be miserable if she saw the conditions of whores' lives. Seeing camp followers had grieved her during the Saxon War.

He knew how Lancelot felt about injuries to women. Before he had learned Lancelot was a woman, she had told him about seeing her mother raped and murdered. He thought that Lancelot was as she was, liking women rather than men, because she had seen the attack on her mother.

That evening, when they camped for the night and ate the food they had been given at the last fort, Gawaine brought out his gwyddbwyll board. "Shall we play a game, Noble Black Warrior?"

She nodded. "Bring on the game pieces, Noble Red Warrior."

Gawaine's set, unlike most, had red pieces, not white, to contest with the black. Gawaine's stories about the game pieces, usually bawdy, were on this journey scrupulously clean.

Lancelot tended to see the pieces taken as real soldiers fallen in war, but his jests distracted her from her solemnity.

Lancelot and Gawaine came to a village of crude wooden buildings. Saxon men yelled at them, and some rushed at their horses. All her nerves tensed, Lancelot put her hand on the hilt of her sword. Gawaine had already drawn his.

A guttural voice called out a command, and the Saxons stopped in their tracks.

"Why are you seeking us? You have come at a strange time," the Saxon leader said, walking up to their horses. Although he had a strong accent, he seemed to know their language well. He wore a bearskin cloak and many golden ornaments.

Lancelot took her hand from her sword and Gawaine sheathed his.

"I am Gawaine ap Lot, cousin to King Arthur, and this is Lancelot of the Lake," Gawaine said, speaking because he was the closer to the High King. "We have come in the High King's name."

"I am Aldwulf, these people's thane," said the man, who was about their age. His face was lined, but his yellow beard showed no signs of graying. "A British warrior carried off my daughter this morning." His voice was controlled, but his fists were clenched and his eyes filled with rage. "We were about to set out to capture him. My men would have attacked you, but I told them that if you had anything to do with his crime, you would not have been stupid enough to come here."

"Do you know the brute who took her?" Lancelot felt her blood surge with anger as it did when any man tried to injure a woman.

Aldwulf's voice still maintained a deadly calm. "I don't know his name, but her thrall, who saw her carried off, said he had a long cut on his cheek, and his shield had green stripes on it."

"Sangremore! We know him." Lancelot said, her heart sinking at the thought that another of Arthur's warriors had abducted a woman. Sangremore was rough and rude, but she had not imagined he could do such a thing. "Let us pursue him and return your daughter!" she cried, ready to see Sangremore executed. "If we take him to the High King for punishment, we can avoid bloodshed between our peoples."

The thane paused a moment, as if considering her offer. "I have heard of Gawaine and Lancelot. You have slain many of our warriors and burned our villages."

Lancelot sucked in her breath.

"But," Aldwulf continued, "I also know that when Gawaine and Lancelot burned villages, they spared the women and children and checked to make sure every home was empty before they burned it." He scrutinized them as if reading the pores on their skin. "So perhaps you would rescue my daughter, Hilda. But we must be the ones to punish the man who attacked her. I don't want to start a war. If Hilda's betrothed were here, I would not be able to hold him back, but he is visiting his kin in the North. So I will let one of you go after this Sangremore, but the other must stay here as a hostage."

Lancelot gasped, and she saw that Gawaine turned pale. "We will keep our word and rescue her. No hostage is needed to ensure that," Lancelot said, trying to keep her voice calm but not succeeding.

The thane's men glared at the British warriors.

"My people would never accept letting you both go," the thane told them, his gaze cold as a winter's day. "One will stay here, and the other must return Hilda and bring back her abductor by dawn. If he fails, I will let my people do as they wish with his companion."

Lancelot froze in horror. The Saxon warriors, who now seemed to number in the hundreds though there were only dozens, looked fierce as a pack of wolves.

"We will do as you say, but remember we have come as the High King's delegates," Gawaine told Aldwulf. "May we have a moment to ourselves to decide who will go and who will stay?"

The thane nodded. "A moment. That's all." Backing off, he began speaking to his men, no doubt telling them his plan.

Most grunted in response, but some appeared to argue with him.

Lancelot knew what Gawaine would say.

"Of course I will stay and you will rescue the thane's daughter," Gawaine said, keeping all emotion out of his voice and his face. "I didn't want to tell him too quickly, or he might guess why the answer was so easy."

"We could draw straws," Lancelot said. "I hate to think of you staying here."

"No drawing straws. There's no question." Gawaine's voice still was flat.

Lancelot sighed. It was useless to protest. Gawaine would never let her stay while he went off. And she had to admit that she dreaded the prospect of being a hostage. "I'll get them back here somehow. I swear it."

"Better bring Sangremore back dead. It will be easier that way, and more merciful. The Saxons would torture him to death. Sangremore saved Agravaine's life in the war, and I'd rather not see him torn limb from limb." Gawaine seemed to have aged ten years. "But don't you come back. Just get Hilda within a mile of here and send her back with his body."

"Of course I'll come back to get you!" Lancelot exclaimed.

"I don't want you to." Gawaine shook his head.

"Sangremore has no doubt raped the girl, and even if he's dead, the Saxons still might take revenge."

"All the more reason for me to return." Lancelot felt as if her arm, not her friend, was being torn from her.

"Listen to me. They are more likely to spare me because I am Arthur's kinsman, and my death would mean war, than they would be to spare you. But we cannot trust them enough to be certain. It is best if you send Hilda home and wait for me in the forest."

Aldwulf turned to them. "One of you must go to save my daughter. Now. She doesn't know your language, so you must show that you are harmless."

"Lancelot will go and I'll stay here." His voice still toneless, Gawaine dismounted.

Aldwulf extended his hand. "Give me your sword, and your knife as well."

Gawaine relinquished his sword and the knife he kept in his belt. Then he pulled a knife out of his boot, and handed that over, too.

Lancelot felt like screaming, *don't give up your weapons.* Instead, she told the thane, "Remember, Gawaine is the High King's closest kinsman. If any harm comes to him, you'll regret it." With one final--no, it must not be final--look at Gawaine, she turned her horse away from Aldwulf's village.

Lancelot sped across fields and through forests. She had never thought she would force her mare to run so far, so fast. Sangremore had not passed them when they had ridden to the village, so she guessed what direction he must have gone, and prayed that she was right. She had never been to his holding, but she had an idea where it was. She must reach him before he got to his own land, with men to fight for him.

Lancelot found recent tracks and, hoping they were Sangremore's, followed them. She had to admit that she worried even more about Gawaine than about a girl she had never seen.

Twilight filled the woods, and Lancelot's pursuit became more frenzied. An owl called. No, it must be too early for owls. There must be more time.

Pausing a moment to let Raven rest--killing her mare would do Gawaine no good--Lancelot heard sounds ahead of her. Hooves pounded, branches were breaking.

"Just a little more, please, Raven," she whispered in her horse's ear. "For Gawaine. You like Gawaine, don't you?"

But when Lancelot caught sight of Sangremore and the girl slumped in his arms, Hilda's suffering became real to her.

"Sangremore! Where are you going? What are you doing?" Lancelot cried.

"Lancelot!" Sangremore called out, reining in his horse. "What good fortune." His voice was full of false cheer. "I thought I was followed by Saxons or robbers. I just saved this girl from brigands, but she's been through so much that she's deluded and is afraid of me. I'm taking her to my home, where she'll be cared for, poor thing."

The Saxon girl--Hilda, of course--looked to be about fifteen. Her face and arms were badly bruised and her clothes were torn and covered with blood. Both eyes were blackened, and a cut on her forehead had bloodied her face. Apparently she had struggled much, and been overpowered. Now she seemed limp, but her eyes were filled with horror. She looked at Lancelot as if this was yet another man who would rape her, too.

"Put her down, Sangremore." Lancelot spoke in the voice she had used to command a hundred men.

Sangremore flinched, but he continued his pretense.

"That would be unkind. She's so terrified that she'd run off and get lost."

"You are the one who attacked her. Put her down." Lancelot trembled with rage.

"Oh, Lancelot, you've saved so many women that you see rape everywhere. You're becoming quite mad. But I'll put her down, just to humor you." Sangremore set the girl none too gently on the ground.

Hilda staggered, then rushed off into the trees. Lancelot called out, "No, come back" and started to follow her.

Sangremore began to ride off.

"No, you're not going anywhere!" Lancelot yelled at him. If Sangremore got away, the Saxons would kill Gawaine.

Hoping she could find Hilda later, Lancelot rode in pursuit. She kept Sangremore in eyesight, but she did not gain on him.

Fearing that he would disappear among the trees, she pulled out her throwing spear and cast it. Impaled, Sangremore fell from his horse.

As a hostage rather than a prisoner--at least, not in name-- Gawaine was not bound, but he felt as if he was watched every moment. He had been taken to a one-room dwelling that had only a chair and a bed. He was alone, but he knew he could not step outside without being seen. In the evening, a man brought him food, but he could not eat. Who wanted food Saxons had prepared, though it seemed to be some kind of meat? He sat on the bed but would not lie down.

Gawaine did not wonder whether he could escape, because he knew Lancelot would return. If Gawaine had escaped, the Saxons would take out their anger on her.

But he did want to see the night sky again, perhaps for the last time. He went out to take a leak, and lingered a short distance from the house. Thinking of his mother, Gawaine watched the moon, which was waning, and tried to count the numberless stars.

Gawaine heard a whirring noise and felt a stab of pain in his leg. He fell to the ground.

A Saxon loomed over him and roughly pulled out the axe that had cut his leg. He aimed a kick at Gawaine's balls.

Resisting a lifetime of training to fight back, Gawaine curled up like a hedgehog, so his thigh took the blow. If he resisted, the Saxon would surely kill him and say Gawaine had attacked him. And if he died, the returning Lancelot would fly into a rage and get herself killed. But at least that would be a quick death, not what she could have faced as a hostage.

The Saxon struck Gawaine's head. Death was coming. The certainty that Arthur would fight a war to avenge his death did not console him. Morgause help me, Gawaine cried silently. Mother!

Other Saxons ran up to them, exclaiming in their ugly language.

Then another voice, speaking in Saxon but with a strange accent, called out loudly, and another man pushed through the group.

An arm grabbed Gawaine's shoulder, but the grip was not fierce. "What happened? Did you try to escape?" asked a man who spoke British. In the moonlight, Gawaine could see that it was a priest with dark hair and a Roman profile.

Never had he been so astonished.

"No. I went out for a leak and this man attacked me."

The Saxons yelled at the priest, but bending over Gawaine to protect him, the cleric replied in an angry, authoritative voice.

The Saxons backed off. Gawaine and the priest were alone.

"Your leg!" The priest tore off his own cloak and bound up Gawaine's leg to stop the bleeding.

"A throwing axe," Gawaine explained, groaning. Perhaps he would live--at least until the morning.

"That wound needs tending. Shall I get a healer?"

"A Saxon healer? No."

"Let me help you back to the house."

Although the priest was not a tall man, Gawaine leaned on him. The priest helped him get through the doorway and lie on the bed. Only then did Gawaine have a chance to think about the pain.

"We should thank God that you are saved. Let us pray," the priest said, looking at Gawaine's wound.

"I thank all the gods--and goddesses. Cerridwen especially." He named Cerridwen because he didn't want to admit that he had prayed to his mother.

The priest groaned. "How can you blaspheme when you have almost died, and still might? You must repent, and I will shrive you."

"I have been baptized, but I have never been shriven. And never will be. But I thank you for saving my life, Father." Gawaine did not like calling an unrelated man "father," but he thought he should use that title out of respect for the one who had rescued him.

"Saving your soul is more important!" the priest cried.

"Not to me." Gawaine tried to laugh, but he was in too much pain. "How did you come to be with the Saxons? They have sacked many monasteries and convents and killed priests."

"Some have, but there is good to be found in Saxon souls." He looked more closely at Gawaine's leg. "I go where I am most needed."

"You surely did just now," Gawaine admitted.

"I am Father Paulus. What is your name?"

"I am Gawaine ap Lot."

"That explains everything." The priest nodded sagely. "You're just as bad as your reputation."

"Thank you." Gawaine managed a smile.

"I urge you to repent," the priest said, putting a hand on his shoulder.

The priest had been so kind to him that Gawaine did not mind talking to him, though he did not feel that he was being shrived. "I am not sorry for what I have done to any man. I have treated my friends as friends and my enemies as enemies. I have killed my enemies cleanly without torture, and I hope they'll do the same to me. But I regret the pain I have caused to women."

"Does that mean if you live you will sin with women no more?" the priest asked.

"No, I will as soon as I can," Gawaine told him. "But I'll try to be kind to them, for goddesses have always saved my life, and if I live this time it will be a female spirit who saves me." A true Diana, he thought.

"There are no goddesses!" the priest exclaimed in anger.

"There are kind goddesses and cruel goddesses, and with gods it is likewise," Gawaine said.

The priest groaned.

"Please confess your sins and affirm the true God. God's blessing may help you undergo whatever might happen."

"You mean that the Saxons might not just kill me, but might serve me as they would have served Sangremore." Gawaine kept his voice quiet.

"I fear that is possible," the priest acknowledged.

"I had thought of that." Gawaine tried to numb himself. "I must ask for your help, Father. My friend Lancelot will surely return with Sangremore's body and Aldwulf's daughter. If Lancelot learns that I have been killed, he will immediately attack and kill as many Saxons as he can before they kill him."

"Do you want me to try to stop him? I have heard that he is a very good man, almost a saint."

"Lancelot is good indeed. But there is no way that you can stop Lancelot from flying into a rage and killing those who killed me. I have seen that you are brave. What I charge you to do, if you have any influence with Aldwulf, is to claim

Lancelot's body and take it intact to Camelot. Even if the Saxons mutilate my body, don't let them do harm to Lancelot's."

Father Paulus stared at Gawaine. "Despite your lack of repentance, you're a rare man, caring more about your friend's body than your own. Yes, if things go as you say, I'll preserve his body and bring it back intact to King Arthur for a Christian burial."

"Thank you. Please take Lancelot's body directly to the queen, for it should be her women who prepare it for burial." Seeing the priest frown, he said, "No, despite the rumors, Lancelot and the queen are not guilty of the sin you are thinking of."

Gawaine slumped in his chair. How little he felt able to do. But perhaps he could spare Lancelot some last indignity--and spare poor Guinevere a horror to compound her grief.

A horse shot out of the trees and ran off, away from Lancelot. Its rider gave her a terrified glance, as if she were mad.

It was Sangremore's serving man, whose name Lancelot did not know. He had seen her kill Sangremore, seen her slay a fellow warrior of the round table by throwing a spear into his back.

She did not want to kill the servant, for he was likely not to blame for his master's deeds, but she was not so pleased that he would tell the tale.

Riding up to Sangremore's body, Lancelot realized that his horse had also run away. There was no time to try to find the horse. How would she get Sangremore's body back to the Saxons, to show that she had killed him? Raven couldn't carry Lancelot, Hilda, and the corpse.

There was only one way. Lancelot dismounted and regarded the body of her former companion. He was a brute, and she did not regret his death.

Stifling her disgust at what she had to do, Lancelot drew her sword and cut Sangremore's head from his body. The task was not easy. His bones resisted, and his blood poured over her.

Finally, she severed the head and put it in her saddlebag. Then she bent over and vomited.

Now she must find Hilda. Lancelot rode back to the place where she had left the girl, which was not far. There was no sign of her.

Lancelot dismounted. "Hilda!" she called. "Come here. Don't be afraid. I'll take you to your father. Fa-der. Aldwulf sent me. Ald-wulf."

Hilda did not appear, and did not make a sound.

Frightened for the girl alone in the woods, but fearing that trying to follow her might scare Hilda even more, Lancelot cried out. "Hilda! Aldwulf sent me. And I'm a woman. Wo-mon. Femina!"

Lancelot heard a sound in the brush. She thought she saw a movement behind branches. "Wo-mon," she said in a softer voice. She pointed to herself, then made a universal gesture of the hands trying to depict a woman's body--curvaceous, as hers was not--a gesture she had often seen men make.

The girl stepped out from behind a bush. Lancelot sighed with relief, but wept when she saw how bruised and bloody Hilda was.

Lancelot extended her hands, palms up. She let the tears fall down her cheeks. "Oh Hilda, I'm so sorry that he hurt you."

Walking tentatively, Hilda approached her. Perhaps the tears had been proof that Lancelot was a woman.

"Home to your father. Let me take you home to Aldwulf."

Hilda moaned.

"Come, let's find a stream, and you can wash off," Lancelot said in her gentlest voice, the one she used with young animals. If she had been Hilda, she would have wanted to wash, so she mimicked the gestures of washing.

The Saxon girl nodded.

Lancelot rode through the night. Hilda clung to her, so exhausted that she could barely hang on, but Lancelot dared not stop. Her heart raced. The sky grayed, showing that dawn would soon appear. Never had Lancelot dreaded dawn more.

Finally, they reached the Saxon village. Tall men bearing torches ran out to them, and the women were not far behind.

Lancelot quickly dismounted and helped Hilda down. The girl tried to stand proudly.

Exclaiming women rushed to her, and yelling men rushed to Lancelot.

Aldwulf emerged from the largest building.

"My daughter." His face still impassive at the sight of the wounded girl, he put out a hand, and Hilda walked to him and clasped it. Then the girl went to the arms of an older woman, probably her mother, who took her into the house.

"What of the man who abducted her? Did you let him get away?" Aldwulf's cold stare was fixed on Lancelot.

She pulled Sangremore's head from her saddlebag.

The Saxons yelled, this time in triumph.

The thane strode up to Lancelot, took the head, and held it high. He shouted something in his language, and his people cried out in response. Then he dropped it on the ground, and the men began kicking it. The pink light of dawn emerged to light up the gory sight.

"Where's Gawaine?" Lancelot demanded, almost panicking because she did not see him.

Aldwulf gestured to some men standing outside a small house. One darted inside, and, in a moment, Gawaine emerged. He limped, and there was a cloth tied around the lower part of one of his legs. His breeches were torn and bloody.

"What have you done to him?" Lancelot cried, relieved that he was alive, worried about his leg, and angry that he had been hurt--all at the same time.

"One of my men says he tried to escape. Gawaine says he did not. He's fortunate." Aldwulf was stone-faced as ever.

"I did not try to escape. A Saxon attacked me and a priest--of all people--saved me," Gawaine said. He was clearly having difficulty standing. He regarded Lancelot with a weary--and apprehensive--gaze.

The men clamored around Aldwulf. A red sun rose over the horizon, as bloody as their faces were angry.

"My men say that Hilda was injured, and you two should pay the price," Aldwulf told the British warriors. And gold was clearly not the price under discussion.

"I saved your daughter and killed the man who attacked her! Have you no honor?" Lancelot seethed.

"Yes, you have saved her and killed Sangremore." Aldwulf put a hand on Lancelot's shoulder. "I thank you, but it is better if you go now. May I give you a gift?"

Lancelot felt the anger seep out of her. "No, I wanted to save Hilda and would have done so if there had been no other threat."

"Where's Sangremore?" Gawaine asked, looking around.

Lancelot pointed to the head, now some distance off, just as a boy was kicking it.

Gawaine shuddered and put his hand to his mouth, as if to keep himself from crying out, or vomiting.

Lancelot realized the head could have been Gawaine's. She shook with rage and fought to keep control of herself. How dare the Saxons even imagine treating Gawaine as if he were Sangremore?

Aldwulf turned to Gawaine. "One of my men injured you while you were my hostage. I must give you compensation."

"Thank you, but I need nothing," Gawaine said, nodding in acknowledgment of the offer. "However, King Arthur will require more tribute."

Lancelot felt incapable of saying gracious words, but she was relieved that Gawaine could.

Aldwulf gestured to one of his men, who brought Gawaine's sword and his knives. The thane took them and handed them to Gawaine.

The thane spoke calmly, as if this had been a normal diplomatic mission. "I know that King Arthur will want more gold as compensation for our treatment of his emissaries. Tell him I'll give all I can."

"The High King will appreciate that," Gawaine said formally, but it was clear that he could hardly stand.

Lancelot moved beside him so he could lean on her.

Then a priest, no doubt the one who had saved Gawaine, walked up to them. He led Gawaine's horse and another, which must be his own.

"The monastery where I live is not far from here," he said, addressing Gawaine. "Our healer can look at your wound." He turned to Aldwulf. "Thank you as always for your hospitality."

"May you all go in peace," the thane said, making a final command to his men and then returning to his house.

Lancelot tried to stand unobtrusively beside Gawaine so he could put his hand on her shoulder without too much embarrassment when he swung onto his horse. He doubtless did not want to appear weak in front of the Saxons, but the daylight showed his condition all too clearly.

As they rode off, the priest said, "I am Father Paulus." His voice sounded as Roman as he looked. "Saving the thane's daughter was a good act. You can both rest at the monastery. Are you Lancelot of the Lake?"

"I am indeed. Thank you, Father. We would be right glad of a place to rest," Lancelot replied. She had never before stayed in a monastery, but she was too weary to ponder much about whether it was wrong to deceive the monks. Of far greater importance was that Gawaine's leg must be tended.

"King Arthur's court must be very holy," said the priest.

"The court is Christian," said Lancelot, though she thought there was little holiness to boast of.

"I have been with the Saxons for two years now, and I have baptized a few of them," Father Paulus told them, not a little pride in his voice. "I think even the thane is ripe for conversion. Soon, all Britain will be Christian, thank God."

"How wonderful," Gawaine said. "No doubt that will end all fighting and cruelty. Sangremore was, of course, a Christian," he added in an undertone.

"I hate Saxons!" Lancelot had never said such words before, surely never with such vehemence. Indeed, she had never felt such hatred until she had heard the threat to kill Gawaine in Sangremore's place.

"You don't hate the girl you saved, do you?" the priest reproached her.

"Not the women and girls." Lancelot's voice was much calmer. "Women everywhere are the same." She paused, recalling that she would be angry if any man had said those words.

But mostly the two warriors were too tired to talk. During the ride to the monastery, Father Paulus told them how glad he was to minister to the Saxons, although he said that no place was truly civilized, except perhaps Constantinopolis, since Rome had been sacked by barbarians.

At one point, the priest rode ahead of them, and Gawaine pulled his horse close to Lancelot's. The lines in his face were more pronounced than usual, and sweat covered his forehead.

"You look the worse for wear, but you have survived," Lancelot said, though her voice showed she still worried about him.

"I knew you'd save the girl and kill Sangremore. But I did worry that they might kill me before you returned." He smiled at her. Then his smile turned to a frown. "Don't tell anyone at Camelot that you cut off Sangremore's head and gave it to the Saxons."

"Everyone will learn of it, I fear." Lancelot's stomach heaved at the thought of Sangremore's fate. "His servant saw me throw my spear into Sangremore's back, and doubtless returned to retrieve his body."

Gawaine groaned. "Gods! At least Arthur will back you up and say you were doing your duty."

"I know it was ugly, but I couldn't take a chance that he'd get away."

"Thank you." Gawaine's voice was much softer than usual.

"I hope that Hilda's betrothed will still marry her," Lancelot said, wondering what the girl's life would be like.

"That's a pretty idea," Gawaine said, shaking his head. "I doubt that any man will, unless her father orders him to and gives him a lot of land."

"Men!" Lancelot exclaimed with disgust. "If a man raped a woman you were betrothed to, wouldn't you marry her?"

"If I loved a woman, I'd marry her no matter what any man had done to her--or what she might have done with anyone," Gawaine replied.

"Would you marry a woman who has been with as many men as you have women?" Lancelot demanded.

Gawaine simply raised his eyebrows. "You know the answer."

She did. But she saw that blood was seeping through his bandage, and her indignation turned to anxiety.

8 THE MONASTERY

They came to a monastery that was little more than a collection of stone huts. A bevy of monks greeted them.

A short but strong-looking monk hurried up to them. "You shouldn't be walking on that leg," he scolded Gawaine. "I am the infirmarian. Come and let me take a look at it. Lean on me, unless you want to be carried."

Gawaine grunted, doubtless irritated at the indignity, but leaned on the shorter man.

"I'll go with you," Lancelot said, following them.

"No, you won't," Gawaine told her.

Reluctantly, she obeyed him.

The abbot, a bald old man with a smile that lit up his face, approached Lancelot. Introducing himself as Abbot Ulfin, he explained that the place was very simple, but Lancelot said they were glad for the hospitality. A monk showed Lancelot to her cell.

She fell asleep, waking only when the sky was darkening, though the stars were not yet visible. She joined the monks and priests in the stone-walled refectory, for her stomach was quite empty, but she ate the meal of bread and honey quickly.

The infirmarian had not come to the refectory, so Lancelot went in search of the infirmary. The short monk emerged from a stone hut and told her, "I believe your friend will be well."

"Will he lose his leg?" she asked anxiously, knowing how that would distress Gawaine, who would find it hard to bear being kept out of battle. "Will he get the wound sickness?"

Smiling kindly, the monk shook his head. "No, he just needs rest. He shouldn't ride off too soon. How good that he has such a devoted friend."

"I must see him." As soon as the monk nodded his permission, Lancelot entered the hut.

Gawaine was lying on a pallet. Sweat covered his face.

Lancelot sat on a stool that was the only other furniture, except for a cabinet filled with jars of herbs and the tools of medicine, and the usual cross on the wall. "How are you faring?"

"I'm enjoying myself greatly," Gawaine said, gritting his teeth. "You should go and rest."

"No, I've rested. I'll remain here a while." Her voice cracked. "Staying in that Saxon village as a hostage is bravest thing you've ever done."

"It was certainly the most difficult," he admitted in a voice that was not as strong as usual. "But your task was even harder. I'd rather fear facing death than fear that a friend might be killed."

"But you had to wait, unable to act, while I could at least act. You chose to protect me. You have sometimes before tried too hard to do so, but this time you were right." She didn't say that he had feared that if she were hostage, the Saxons could have discovered she was a woman, and raped her.

"I'm just glad I knew that you're a woman. What if I hadn't known and I had let you draw straws? You should have told me long ago," he grumbled.

"Stop complaining and rest," she said, wiping his brow with a clean cloth that hung on the wall, no doubt for such a purpose.

Lancelot sat there well into the night, even after Gawaine fell asleep. She pushed her stool against the wall, so she could lean against it. Tears escaped onto her cheeks, and she wiped them away. How near she had come to losing her best friend.

A monk tapped her on the shoulder, waking her. "You should go to your own hut," he whispered. "I'll sit with your friend. No harm will come to him tonight." Sleepily, she agreed.

"There is no need to sit with him every moment," the monk said. "He told me that he wanted a monk, not a fellow warrior, to help him with private matters."

"I understand." Indeed she did, better than the monk could.

Only a few days later, Gawaine insisted on limping to the refectory for meals. The monks had given him a large staff to lean on, but his face was drawn with pain.

"You should have stayed in bed," Lancelot chided Gawaine.

"There was too little company there," he replied.

Lancelot had sat with him every day, but she knew that wasn't the kind of company he meant. She couldn't resist laughing. It was good to hear him jest.

Lancelot was surprised to see that both fish and fowl had been prepared.

"We know that you aren't used to our food," the wrinkled old Abbot Ulfin said gently. Britain was stamped on his face as clearly as Rome was stamped on the countenance of Father Paulus.

"How kind of you," Lancelot said, smiling, and Gawaine thanked him heartily.

Father Paulus sat with them and asked them about Camelot, and they told all of the decent news they could. But he observed that they were still fatigued, and said that he hoped he could talk with them more the next day.

Lancelot rose early, having slept well. The hut where she slept was not much plainer than her house at Camelot, though it had a large crucifix and hers did not. There was little dawn birdsong because of the season, but she heard rooks calling, and walked out to greet the sun.

The monks were making their way to their chapel, and she joined them as they heard Mass.

Afterwards, Lancelot strolled around the small monastery garden, a mixture of vegetables such as turnips and medicinal plants such as foxglove.

Lancelot walked under the apple trees and pondered. Perhaps one could be happy in a place like this monastery.

She saw that Gawaine had finally awakened. Leaning on his staff, the red-bearded warrior limped across the garden.

"You seem to like the monastery well enough. Perhaps you'll stay and become a monk," Gawaine teased her.

"Of course I can't," she said, feeling her face grow hot. "But it's quiet. I do like that."

After they had broken their fast with good bannock and porridge, Abbot Ulfin came to join them.

The abbot embraced both warriors and told them, "I am glad Gawaine is feeling better. Though we preach to the Saxons now, they came here as savages, and it is thanks to King Arthur and all who fought them that we are safe. You have given your blood to save Britain as Our Lord gave his to redeem us all."

Lancelot shuddered slightly at this comparison, for she had shed much more blood than she had given. She thought particularly of the British girl she had slain by striking into a bush during the Saxon War. She felt that sin would never leave her soul, though she had been shriven. After years had passed, she had finally dared to tell Guinevere and had not lost her love. When the girl was killed, Gawaine had protected Lancelot by telling Arthur he had done the deed, and she had remained silent about it for years before finally confessing to the king and some of their brother warriors. She was ashamed of her long silence and thankful that Gawaine had remained her friend nevertheless.

After the abbot left them alone, they went out of the refectory. Lancelot turned to Gawaine. "I wish Sangremore had had a chance to be shriven and perhaps escape the fires of hell."

Gawaine grunted. "You did the kindest thing by killing him, not leaving him to the Saxons. Don't worry about his soul. He was a cruel man. If there is a hell, no doubt he would have gone there anyway."

Lancelot sighed. "I still must pray for him. God help me, I would rather pray for others instead." She looked at her hands, as if they still were bloodied.

Nodding to him, she went off and walked around the orchard.

Gawaine sat on a bench under the trees.

Some of the young monks were picking apples and laughing as they did. Not a bad occupation for young men, Lancelot thought. Better than learning to kill.

Lancelot wondered whether it was much worse to deceive these monks about her sex than it was to deceive King Arthur and the other warriors at court. She didn't return until the midday meal.

She saw Gawaine still sitting on his bench, tapping the ground restlessly with his staff, and realized that he must want to leave.

She, on the other hand, thought that she could never get enough of such rest. They sat down to a meal in the refectory and saw that everyone was served a fish stew, so she didn't feel conspicuous for eating better than the others. During the meal, one monk read to the others from St. Paul's epistles.

Then, Father Paulus began to give them a homily. "I would speak to you from the Acts of Paul and Thecla."

Lancelot looked down at her trencher of bread. She knew that Thecla had dressed as a man so she could go off and serve God. Could Father Paulus have guessed her secret?

"The monastic life is a good and holy one," the priest said, his eyes gleaming with fervor. "Although we all know what temptation is, and no one is safe from the snares of the devil, at least here we are removed from the uncleanness of women. St. Paul spoke truly when he bade them cover their heads, for their so-called beauty is that of whitened sepulchers. They take on the guise of loveliness, but there is only corruption underneath. According to the Acts of Paul and Thecla, virgins are the only women who will be resurrected. Saint Jerome wrote 'As long as a woman is for birth and children, she is different from man as body is from soul. But if she wishes to serve Christ more than the world, then she will cease to be a woman and will be called man.'"

Lancelot with difficulty held back a gasp.

The priest's voice grew louder and even fuller of passion. Stretching out his hands, he leaned towards his listeners. "The Gospel of the Egyptians says that Christ came to destroy the works of the female and to put an end to the use of the sex to bring people into the world. Truly is it said that an unclean woman--I mean when they are at their most unclean, which comes every month--is not worthy to take the sacraments. If you search for love from them, slime only will be your reward, for that is all they are..."

Gawaine got up noisily from the bench and limped out.

Lancelot, who had been shaking with anger, rose also and left. She met him outside the refectory.

"You don't have to listen to that shit," he said, hitting the ground with his stick.

"Who are you to talk?" she snapped. "When I think of all the crap I've heard you say..."

"Well, you've never heard me say that," he replied indignantly. "I never said that women are disgusting, or that they are worse than men. Nobody could be foolish enough to believe that women do more evil than men."

"Very well, you didn't say that, but I don't want to talk about it." The question of whether women were disgusting certainly was no point to be debated. "I think it's time to go, before I pollute the place--if you're well enough to travel," she added, remembering his leg.

"Of course I am."

"If the dressing on your wound needs to be changed, will you let me do it?"

He frowned. "I'd rather not."

"We can't go unless you agree. I'll not let you bleed or your wound fester."

"If your leg were wounded, would you let me change the bandage?"

"If it were necessary," she agreed, impatient at his reluctance.

"Then you can change mine--if it's necessary."

"Very well, then. Let's get our horses and go."

Just as they were saddling their horses, Father Paulus rushed up to them.

"Lancelot, you're not leaving?" he exclaimed in considerable distress. He did not address Gawaine.

"We are. Thank you for letting us rest here." Lancelot gave him only the curtest possible nod.

"Please speak with me a moment first," Father Paulus beseeched, putting a hand on her arm.

Lancelot tried to curb her anger. "For a moment, but we really must depart. It is our duty to report to the king about the Saxons."

She followed him towards the garden, but stood at its edge and would not go further. Gawaine waited with the horses, out of earshot.

Father Paulus tried a conciliatory tone. "I understand that your friend was angry when I preached against his sins, but surely you have no reason to be disturbed. I hope that you will return here."

"You preached not only against his sins, but against all women. I dislike such talk."

She hastened to her horse.

Father Paulus then approached Gawaine. "Be grateful to God for you deliverance, and sin no more," he said.

"I am grateful to you for all the good you have done for me," Gawaine told him.

The two warriors rode off.

Lancelot thought of her sins. She wanted to be in harmony with all that was good and just in the world. If she was damned, must she spend eternity with companions like Sangremore? Perhaps those who believed the old religion were right, and she might just be reborn to try to do better in her next life. She hoped so, for the Church said there was no love in hell, and she could not imagine life without love.

As the sun climbed higher in the sky, it beat down on them. They came to a stream, and stopped to drink. Lancelot took water in her hands and splashed it on her face. Then she filled Gawaine's water flask and brought it to him so he would not have to dismount and strain his leg.

"You look solemn. Are you thinking about Sangremore?" he asked, taking a drink.

Lancelot nodded.

"I regret that you had to impale him in the back to kill him. It was nobly done, but some will say it is a stain on your honor."

"I don't mind losing my honor for you," she said.

Gawaine choked with laughter, spluttering the water.

"You know I didn't mean it that way," Lancelot protested, flushing. "Can't you stop thinking of me as a woman?"

"Could you stop thinking of me as a man?" he asked.

"Of course not!"

"There's your answer." He spilled some water on his face and let it trickle down.

"Not so," Lancelot complained. "You act always like a man, but I don't act like a woman."

Gawaine grinned at her. "Indeed you do. I didn't see it before, but now that I know you're a woman, I can see that you act exactly like one."

"That's not true!" She leapt back on her horse and refused to speak with him for a while.

"I was just teasing you out of your gloom, and it worked easily," Gawaine said, with an infuriating smile.

Lancelot grimaced. "How kind of you." Her voice dripped with sarcasm. "But I want to ask a serious question. What about that saying of St. Jerome's that a woman who is always a virgin is more like a man than like a woman? Could that be true?"

Gawaine rolled his eyes. "Only a hermit like Jerome would say so."

When they returned to Camelot, Lancelot and Gawaine went to report to Arthur privately, in his room. Gawaine climbed the steps as fast as he could with his staff, but Lancelot was sure the climb pained him.

The king embraced them and exclaimed over Gawaine's leg. "Did the Saxons do that to you? Be seated, pray."

Gawaine accepted the chair, and before Lancelot could open her mouth, said, "It's not so bad a wound. They were angry because Sangremore abducted and raped a Saxon's thane's daughter, endangering your peace. He's dead now."

Arthur looked grave and shook his head. "I've heard that he was dead. What a bloody fool."

"I'm the one who killed him," Lancelot insisted.

Arthur patted Lancelot on the shoulder. "I've already heard that, Lance. Of course, I'll back you. Did you have to cut off his head, though?"

Gawaine spoke up. "Yes, he had to. The Saxons were holding me hostage and would have killed me if Lance hadn't brought back proof that Sangremore was dead."

Turning purple, Arthur pounded the table. "How dare they! I'll show them they can't threaten my kinsman."

Gawaine shook his head. "No, the thane Aldwulf was right. His men would have rebelled if he had not done as he did. And he's said he'll pay you more tribute because of how he treated us. You should like that."

Arthur's face returned to its normal color.

"They should pay the tribute. That's only right. But if they had killed you, I would have spilled their blood like wine."

Lancelot shuddered.

"Speaking of wine, I shall call for some." Arthur smiled at them. "You both should rest."

He beckoned, and Tewdar, his body servant, brought them the finest of red wines. Although he was aging, Tewdar's hair still stood up in a cowlick.

"You both behaved bravely, of course," Arthur said, "but I would have thought Lancelot might have chosen to be the hostage to preserve Gawaine, who after all is the heir to my throne."

Lancelot flushed.

"That's the reason I was the hostage, because I am kin to you," Gawaine told him. "I knew Aldwulf didn't want to start a war. Lancelot was more than brave, and I am grateful to him for saving my life." He quaffed his wine.

"So am I, of course." Arthur slapped Gawaine's shoulder. "Had the wound been a little higher, the ladies would have grieved," he said. "What a pity you have no wife to tend you."

"You should find one for him. He's too shy to find one for himself." Lancelot grinned.

"Then no doubt I'd be too shy to lie with her," Gawaine replied, swilling down the wine.

Gawaine went to his house and let Hywel remove his boots and exclaim over his leg. Agravaine and Gaheris burst in on him. "Your leg is wounded!" Gaheris cried, eyeing the large bandage that bound it.

"You let Lancelot kill Sangremore!" Ignoring the wounded leg, Agravaine yelled at his older brother.

"It was necessary," Gawaine said, not looking at him.

"Necessary! Necessary to stab him in the back, and then cut off his head! No other man has ever treated another member of the round table that way. And you defend that sanctimonious bastard!" He shook his fist in Gawaine's face. "You know that Sangremore saved my life in the Saxon War. Is my life nothing to you?"

"We all saved each other's lives in the Saxon War. I saved your life then, and I have saved it since. And Lancelot has saved it too, if you recall." Ignoring the fist, Gawaine strove to remain calm and dignified although his boots were off.

Gaheris merely stared at them, for he was ever a follower, even in family fights.

"Sangremore raped a thane's daughter. That could have started a war," Gawaine explained, though he guessed his brother would not be moved. He was pretty sure that Agravaine himself had raped at least one woman when he had served under their father. The memory weighed on Gawaine's heart.

Agravaine spat on the floor. "What do I care about those Saxon women? They're all whores."

Gawaine expected no better from Agravaine, who had said the same when British soldiers raped and murdered Saxon women and children during the war. Gawaine had lowered Agravaine's rank for that reason, a slight Agravaine had never forgotten. "The Saxons were holding me hostage. If Lancelot had not brought Sangremore--or his body--back, they would have killed me. Would you have preferred that?"

"They held you hostage! That means war!" Agravaine gasped. "Will Arthur declare war on them?"

"No, and I agree with him." Gawaine strove for patience. "They'll pay him more tribute."

"Tribute! That's not enough to compensate for holding the king's cousin! You care too much about peace. Did Lancelot give Sangremore's head to the Saxons?"

Gawaine nodded.

"What did they do with it?" Agravaine demanded, shaking with rage.

"Why ask?" Gawaine sighed. "If a Saxon had raped a British noble's daughter and you were given the Saxon's head, what would you do? At least cutting off the head left the family something to bury."

"You defend Lancelot? You care more about him than your own kin," Agravaine growled, turning away from him and leaving the room.

Gaheris looked uncertain whether to follow him, but Gawaine said, "Stay, Gaheris, and drink with me," so he stayed.

"How is your leg?" Gaheris asked.

"It'll be a while before I can run, but I can ride." He gestured to Hywel to pour his brother some ale.

Gawaine had little desire to drink ale with him at the moment, but he thought he should let Gaheris know that he had a friend other than Agravaine. Gaheris did not have many.

"I wish I had been the one to save you," Gaheris said with a sigh. "Then you might like me as well as Lancelot."

Gawaine clasped his hand. "You're my brother. Never imagine that I don't care about you." No doubt he should pay more attention to poor Gaheris.

Gawaine felt a strange ache, far worse than the still sharp pain in his leg, in the place where his love for Agravaine used to reside. Could he, as the oldest brother, have taught Agravaine to be a better man?

He could never bear to tell Lancelot that Sangremore had not been the only rapist at the round table, that his own brother was likely one. The less Lancelot and Agravaine knew about each other, the better.

All Gawaine truly wanted was to see Ragnal, and have her tend his wound. And other parts as well.

Lancelot eagerly climbed the hidden stairway to see Guinevere that night. As soon as the door was closed, Guinevere kissed her. "How was your journey? Is it true that you killed Sangremore?"

"Yes. He raped a thane's daughter." Lancelot shuddered.

Guinevere grimaced. "What a brute! I never did like him."

Apparently Guinevere had not yet heard about the beheading. Wanting to think about other things at the moment, Lancelot postponed telling her. "The journey was difficult. A Saxon injured Gawaine's leg, and we went to a monastery to recover."

"I suppose he'll be all right? I thank God that you aren't the one who was hurt." Guinevere stroked Lancelot's hair.

Frowning, Lancelot pulled away. "Believe me, it is just as hard to see a friend wounded as to be hurt oneself."

Guinevere's brow wrinkled. "I'll never understand how you can like him so much."

"Must you still dislike him?" Lancelot's voice was much sharper.

Guinevere's smile vanished. "How should I like a man who is always wenching? He consumes women in quantities, as he does mead."

Lancelot almost said that the king was not so different, but she checked herself, for she had no right to criticize Arthur on that ground. Instead, she said, "Well, they want him. I wonder what it would be like to lie with many women, as Gawaine does."

Guinevere shook her head. Her dark hair cascaded down her shoulders, and Lancelot longed to stroke it. "I would rather be with you than a hundred other women," the queen said.

Lancelot smiled. "I have thought the same."

"That you are better than a hundred women? How modest," Guinevere teased her.

"Of course not. That you are. You know that's what I meant." Lancelot grabbed her hand and they both laughed. Candlelight made Guinevere's face glow, and the scent of her almost drove Lancelot mad. "But please don't harp on your dislike for my friend." She could see no reason for Guinevere to have such an antipathy to Gawaine. Once Guinevere had believed that Gawaine had killed the girl in the Saxon War, but Lancelot had confessed that she was the one who had done that.

Guinevere, like everyone else, apparently assumed that Gawaine was the hostage only because his rank was higher than Lancelot's. Lancelot could have told her the truth, but she was not ready to explain that Gawaine knew she was a woman.

Guinevere sighed. "I'll try not to criticize him. I don't want to distress you. I'm glad enough to have you back, sweet." She kissed Lancelot's lips.

Lancelot surrendered to the queen's kisses.

Gawaine approached Ragnal in the shadows of the courtyard as she carried an empty flagon back to the kitchen. She wanted to fling herself on him, but held back.

Without speaking of it, Cai had assigned her fewer tasks than usual to allow her time to make herself ready, and she had bathed and washed her hair.

"I've heard too much of monks and virginity," Gawaine said, grimacing. The grime of the road did not cling to him, and his red hair appeared damp from washing. What other man would have washed to be clean for a serving woman?

"Why, I thought I might become a Christian so I could enter a convent." Ragnal spoke in a meek little voice unlike her own. He would always rather that she jest than greet him with sweet words. And he wouldn't want her to exclaim over his leg when he was flirting with her.

"You'll never do that." He took the flagon from her and set it on a ledge, where some other servant no doubt would find it and return it to its proper place. Cai would guess what had happened and would not scold Gawaine's mistress.

"Why not?" she continued in a voice of utter innocence.

Gawaine looked around to see whether anyone was near, then slid his tongue across his lips.

Ragnal made the same gesture back at him.

She was the luckiest woman at court, she thought. Those ladies with their fine gowns and jewels and thousand commands had such dull husbands--and she knew, from the years before Gawaine, just how dull some of them were. When Gawaine returned from a journey, he invariably turned to her, and for days or even weeks she had him to herself. He never said a harsh word to her, but kissed and petted her as if she were a noble lady who needed to be wooed, instead of a serving woman who could just be taken.

Envious serving women and ladies gossiped that she had cast a spell over him. Some claimed that she could turn into a beautiful woman at night in her room. But she knew that she held him with jests, tales, and a ready laugh. And, of course, by never making any complaint.

Life had been hard. Children had been her only other joy, but they had died early. She had learned how to hold onto this happiness with her warrior.

As they crossed the courtyard to Gawaine's house, Gawaine flourished his new walking stick, as if to say he didn't need it, but he leaned on Ragnal as never before.

Ragnal smiled to herself. She had watched Gawaine and Lancelot at supper, and seen that they seemed closer than ever, but not in the way she dreaded.

9 MISTAKEN FOR LANCELOT

Drian rode merrily through a forest. Her green tunic was good enough to wear in summer, and it was that season, so what did it matter that she had no warm clothes for winter? If cold winds blew, she could find a cloak--or borrow one from an unwary traveler. Her friend Lancelot called such acts stealing. Lancelot was lovable, but could be such a prig. She was the only other woman Drian knew who pretended to be a man.

The scent of the forest filled her as if it were a lover's breath. It was pleasanter than the scent of most great halls, and the forest would not cheat her or reject her.

Patting her harp, Drian hummed a tune that told of hidden love. She didn't know whose hall she would next play in, but she thought she had enough new songs to convince a steward that his lord would be delighted with her playing, and so would the ladies. Especially the ladies, Drian hoped.

A fox darted across her path, and Drian, thinking she was like a fox herself, nodded to it. The creature was not good to eat, or she would have taken up her bow and an arrow.

Smelling the carcass of some long-dead animal, she made her horse hurry. True, not all smells in the forest were sweet.

Drian's tunic matched the green leaves--all the better to surprise travelers if she wanted to borrow something from them, or to conceal herself if a group of warriors passed. Drian was not fond of men, for some had raped her when they learned she was a woman. And how had they learned? Drian sighed. A woman she had lain with had betrayed her. Most of the many women she had been with had been glad to keep her secret, though.

Lancelot trusted too many men. Shaking her head, Drian hoped that Lancelot was safe.

Drian heard a horse coming down the road and peered through the trees to see who was passing. A pretty brown-haired lady, not quite young, rode by. She was dressed in fine clothes. But of course any woman riding a horse would be a lady and would wear fine clothes. No man in fine clothes rode with her.

Drian emerged from the trees. Perhaps fortune smiled on her. She might get a good meal--and a good deal more.

She hailed the lady. "God grant you good day, my lady! Is it safe for such a pretty lady to ride through the forest alone?"

Stopping her horse, the lady stared at Drian. "Why, it is Lancelot of the Lake. I have always wanted to meet you," she simpered.

Astonishment made Drian unable to speak, which was unusual for her. True, she had the same build as Lancelot, and perhaps there was some vague similarity in the face, although her hair was not as dark. Would she gain favor with this lady more easily if she pretended to be Lancelot? She wasn't sure whether she should try it.

"Greetings, lovely lady," Drian said, bowing to her.

Some half dozen men in chain mail rode up behind the lady. Drian pulled back. Were they with the lady, or threatening her?

"These are my men," the lady said, not giving them another glance. "They wear my badge." Indeed, they wore peacock badges that seemed too gaudy for fighting men. "Will you honor me by coming to my caer, Lord Lancelot?"

Not being overly eager for the company of groups of men in chain mail, Drian replied, "I fear I cannot, my lady. Perhaps some other time."

The lady smiled, but her expression was not pleasant. "You will come now," she commanded.

Drian turned her horse back on the path through the trees. "Not today," she said.

The lady made a gesture to her men. "Make sure that he comes with me, but don't hurt him too much," she told them.

Armed men surrounded Drian. Drawing her knife, she tried to stab the nearest one, but blows fell on her, she dropped her knife, and the world turned black.

Waking, Drian felt her whole body ache. She vaguely remembered a fight. She had been captured, but her clothes were still on her, so likely no one had yet discovered that she had a woman's body underneath them.

"Lord Lancelot," murmured a woman who was stroking the hair back from Drian's forehead.

Drian's eyes opened wide and saw the pretty brown-haired lady, dressed in an elegant silver-gray gown. Most nobles made Drian uncomfortable, and this lady was no exception. Glancing around, she saw that she was in a bare-walled dungeon. "Who are you?" her groggy voice inquired. "Don't like Lancelot much, do you, if you'd shut him up in a dungeon?"

Brown eyes met hers. "I love you, Lancelot. I can't live without you." But the lady held onto her fine skirts so they would not brush the floor, which was not bad as dungeon floors go, but of course dirty.

"You'll have to live without Lancelot because I'm not he," Drian mumbled, putting a hand on her aching jaw. "Let me go, lady."

The lady scowled. "It ill becomes you to deny your name. Mine is Cecilia, and I have seen you in fighting contests. No one is as handsome as you are."

Drian grinned. "Sounds like Lancelot is. I'm not Lancelot. I'm no noble warrior, lady. Can't you tell from my voice?"

"Don't think you can fool me by pretending to sound common," Cecilia complained. "You shouldn't demean yourself so. I once tried to speak with you after a contest, but you didn't notice anyone but that wanton queen."

Drian sat up straight, which made every muscle in her body ache. She had met Guinevere and didn't care for her. But her friend Lancelot would not endure any insult to the queen. "The queen's not a wanton, lady. She's as pure as the snow that's never fallen. You shouldn't talk about her that way."

Cecilia chortled. "You are Lancelot. I knew that by criticizing the queen I could provoke you to disclose your identity. I love you greatly and you must love me. I won't let you go unless you do."

"Funny kind of love that is." Drian's voice showed her disgust. "Can't say that it interests me. Let me go, lady. My name's Drian and I'm a harper." Drian stood up and moved away, despite the pain in her throbbing head. She took up her small harp, which fortunately was in a corner of her cell, though one of the strings was broken.

"Many nobles have their own harps. You truly are Lancelot. Refusing to love me proves it. Everyone knows that Lancelot won't touch anyone but the queen." There was a look of triumph on Cecilia's face.

"That doesn't prove a thing," Drian objected. "And he's just the kind to have some foolish, dreamy love with no touching."

"No one could be fool enough to believe that," the lady insisted, putting a hand on Drian's arm. "I don't care whether you say you're Lancelot or not. You're handsome, and you can't leave unless you love me." Though she spoke of love, her eyes had no warmth in them.

"Care to bet on that?" Drian darted past her, raced to the cell door, and rattled it. It was locked fast, and a man, whose voice Drian recognized as one of the captors', called out, "Lady Cecilia, is that man threatening you?"

"No, be still and stay away, I am safe," Cecilia replied. "That was a foolish move, my dear Lancelot. Why must you object to making love to me? It could be very pleasant," she purred, fluttering her eyelashes.

"Love's not forced," Drian objected. The dungeon was cold and she wished she was wearing warmer clothing. "I'm not about to bare myself to someone like you. If this is how you'd treat Lancelot, I can guess how badly you'd treat me." Drian shuddered, thankful that those men who fought her hadn't torn her clothing enough to see through her disguise and learn that she was a woman, like her noble friend Lancelot. She had no faith that the lady would free her--or love her, either--if she discovered Drian's secret. Cecilia would just be angry at having been fooled.

The lady left Drian in the dungeon, provided with only barley bannock and water and a pail for her wastes. Drian was used to simple living and sleeping on the hard earth, but the dungeon's ancient stench of urine was hard to bear and she hated confinement. She shut her eyes and tried to imagine that she was in a forest.

She held back from using the pail as long as she could. That night, when she was finally forced to do so, no guards spied on her. Drian sighed with relief.

The next day the lady returned. "Will you love me now, my beloved Lancelot?"

Drian shook her head vigorously. "Lady, you don't want me. You don't want to know what I'm like, and I know too much about what you're like."

"I am displeased," Cecilia announced, stamping her foot. "If you don't make love to me, you must at least fight in a contest for me." She reminded Drian of a cat playing with a mouse.

Drian groaned. "Lady, can't you tell I'm no warrior? I don't know anything about that kind of fighting. I can use my fists as well as anybody, and I've used a sword more than once, but I've never even held a spear in my hands."

"Whether you know it or not, that's the only way you can escape this dungeon, if you don't love me," Cecilia insisted. "You must acknowledge that I am your lady, one way or another."

"I guess fighting's not so bad after all. It sounds better than the other. Maybe I have a chance. So let me give it a try," Drian said, hoping she would not die in the contest.

"You certainly are not noble to speak to me so. I am much aggrieved." Cecilia pouted. "You cannot be Lancelot, but at least people will believe that Lancelot fought for love of me."

No, they won't, Drian thought.

So, accompanied by the fair lady and several of her strong men, Drian rode to a fighting contest at a nearby dun. She tied her harp to her saddle on the chance that she might escape. Cecilia had procured some chain mail and an unmarked shield for Drian, but did not give her a sword until they had already arrived at the contest field.

Cecilia attached a red sleeve of hers to Drian's helmet.

"Fight nobly for me," she urged.

"Why don't you try fighting if you like it so much?" Drian grumbled, closing the helmet and riding off to the field.

Cecilia gasped, "How could you tell a woman to fight?"

It was a true contest, with a group of men on one side fighting a group on the other, as if it were a battle.

Drian had never been in a battle, nor wanted to be in one. Warriors charged up to test her mettle, so she hacked away with the sword as well as she could, and soon several men had injured arms.

"That warrior does not fight well, but he's a menace," one older warrior said.

"Who are you, strange warrior?" a gray-mustached fighter called out.

Hoping that they would guess that she was not a true warrior, Drian opened the visor briefly, then closed it again.

"St. Joseph's hammer, it's Lancelot, fighting other warriors of King Arthur's!" Gray Mustaches exclaimed.

"That pious bastard!" snarled another, who had sustained several cuts. He resembled Lancelot's obnoxious friend Gawaine, whom Drian had encountered before, but was not he.

"Lancelot must be doing this for some strange reason," the gray-mustached fighter suggested. "And Lancelot never wears ladies' favors. Perhaps that's a sign that he's not himself."

"He just wants to make fools of us," the snarler complained.

"Lancelot, it's Bors. What ails you? Why do you attack other warriors from Camelot so fiercely?" the gray-mustached one asked. Drian darted past him and rode straight off the field and into the forest.

"God's wounds, he's mad!" the warrior cried out, and rode after her.

But Drian found a way to slip off among the trees, for she was used to concealing herself in the forest.

Lancelot was riding through the forest when a voice called out to her, "Lance!"

She surveyed the rider in chain mail who came upon her. The rider opened her visor.

"Drian! What are you doing in chain mail?" Lancelot smiled at the sight of the only other woman she had ever known who disguised herself as a man. Though Drian was from a different class and was not unwilling to steal jewels from men who did not pay for her harping, she was a friend.

"I was fighting some of your friends from Camelot at a contest." Drian grinned. "Didn't do so badly, either. At least I didn't get killed. And your red-bearded friend wasn't there, but somebody who looked a lot like him was."

"Why did you fight in a contest? Are you unhurt?" Lancelot asked. She was just as glad that Gawaine had not been present, though on remembering that Drian was her friend he surely would not have fought her. No doubt the one who had fought had been his brother Agravaine.

"Some lady named Cecilia held me in her dungeon and kept insisting that I was you. She said I'd have to either make love to her or fight, and I trusted her too little to embrace her." Drian grimaced. "I kept your reputation for loving Guinevere alone, and I claimed that it was all pure." She rolled her eyes. "Aren't you pleased with me?"

Shaking her head, Lancelot threw her arms around Drian. "Yes, especially that you are safe. Foolish lady to treat you so ungently. Had she only known it, she had a far more experienced lover than I am close by. No doubt you make love better than I do."

Drian winked. "Perhaps I'd better learn how Lancelot makes love, then, if I'm to impersonate you."

Lancelot just laughed. "Sorry, you know I am true to Guinevere, as you said." But she found it so pleasant to have her arms around Drian that she pulled away with some haste.

"Too attractive, am I?" Drian asked.

"Don't seek flattery from me," Lancelot told her.

"Why not? I'd be happy to flatter you. I'd sing your praises, but I have to get new harp strings first. One of the brutes who cast me into the dungeon broke some of them." Drian patted the harp as if it were an injured child.

"At least you got out of the dungeon. I'll never forget how you helped me escape from one." Lancelot smiled at her, for Drian had saved her after King Uriens had imprisoned her because she wouldn't acquiesce to his taking Arthur's purloined sword. And she had once saved Drian, when an angry husband attacked the harper.

"We're both much too handsome to rot in dungeons, aren't we?" Drian replied.

They chatted for some time, then Lancelot went on her way. She could not invite Drian to Camelot since Drian had just fought some of Arthur's warriors. Not that Guinevere would have been pleased to see Drian, who all too openly flirted with Lancelot, under any circumstances.

And both Guinevere and Gawaine had told Lancelot that when she was standing side by side with Drian, the sight of the two of them together made it more obvious that they were women.

When Lancelot returned to Camelot she found that the other warriors believed that she was the one who had fought them. They complained about their injuries, for Lancelot had always before been so courteous that she rarely wounded them in contests.

When she entered a room, she sometimes heard muttering against her. Not infrequently she heard the words "Sangremore" and "brutal treatment," and she knew they meant her brutality, not his.

Guinevere, sitting at the small table in her own room, sipped red wine imported from Gaul. The light from her beeswax candles made the silver goblets shimmer. A bit of gold embroidery on her blue sleeve also glimmered in the light. But, Lancelot thought, Guinevere's face was far fairer than shining silver or gold.

The queen sighed. "It's a good thing that your mission led the Saxons to give Arthur more tribute. He wants more, always more, so he can have more men and more weapons. It's all that Merlin, Cai, and I can do to restrain him. I don't like to think how hard it will be when Merlin is no longer with us."

"But we need the men and weapons to defend Britain," Lancelot objected. "The Saxons will always be a threat. I hate Saxons, I hate them!" she cried, surprising herself.

Guinevere stared at her. "You needn't shout. I've never heard you say you hated anyone, not even after the war."

"Perhaps I need to shout sometimes, as most men do." Lancelot found herself thinking "how can a woman understand that," but chided herself for the thought.

"But what would men do if a woman shouted?" Guinevere asked. "At least Arthur doesn't yell much." She looked into her winecup as if reading the future in it. "But I would do some things differently from him, if I could ever rule."

Lancelot did not want to hear what Guinevere would do. The very subject, premised on Arthur's death, made her want to walk away. Instead, she gulped down her wine.

"I would set up a council to help me govern, and there would be women on it as well as men."

Lancelot gasped at the strange idea. "But what women could you ask to take on such a weighty task?"

"An abbess or two. Certainly the abbess of the Convent of the Holy Mother is wise, is she not?" Guinevere calmly sipped her wine.

"Indeed," Lancelot admitted.

"And, as I would have to ask the advice of the lesser kings, I would consult Queen Morgause of Lothian and Orkney. She has ruled for many years." Guinevere fingered the end of one of her black braids. She had never looked more beautiful--or less appealing.

"But why all of these plans?" Lancelot stirred restlessly in her seat. "Surely Arthur will rule for many more years, and he is the best of kings." She refilled her goblet sooner than she usually did, almost spilling the wine from its silver flagon.

"Arthur won't last forever," Guinevere said impatiently, pursing her lips. "You cannot depend on just one man."

"I can hope that the generations after him will remember his justice and keep his laws," Lancelot insisted.

Guinevere made a disparaging sound. "Men speak of imitating the Christ, but they don't, so why should they keep on following Arthur after he is gone?"

Lancelot shifted in her carved chair. "I have to hope that there is some chance for the world to be better."

"Only if men do not rule alone," Guinevere retorted, setting down her goblet for emphasis. "And I think the Athenian way of electing leaders was better, although women should have voted, too."

"I doubt that it makes much difference how leaders are chosen," Lancelot said, looking out of the window at the waning moon. "I think that a man like Arthur would become the leader in any land. Good kings past must have been like Arthur, and future ones will be, too."

"Past, present, and future, the best we have to hope for is Arthur?" Guinevere asked, sighing.

Lancelot felt her heart race with anger. "Likely he is the best. But you should not count on ruling after he dies." She raised her voice, in spite of Guinevere's disdain for loudness, or perhaps because of it. "Don't you realize that most people think Gawaine will inherit the throne?"

Guinevere pulled back as if slapped. "I suspect that he may," she said with some disgust. "He is a fighter, and that seems to be all men care about."

Lancelot frowned. "Those who have fought have no great desire to follow a ruler who has not."

Guinevere's eyes narrowed. "And you agree with them that a woman should not be a ruler. I cannot imagine Gawaine as the High King. What kind of ruler would he be?"

"Probably not a bad one, not least because he does not want such power." Lancelot rose from the table.

"You would rather see him rule than me?" Guinevere's eyes blazed, but her lip trembled.

"I have no wish to be a ruler's lover," Lancelot said, turning from her. "Still less do I want to continue this conversation. I hope that Arthur's life is long."

So agitated was she that she bumped into a chair on her way to the hidden doorway.

"Please stay," Guinevere begged her, but she did not.

Lancelot retired to her own house. Much as she loved Guinevere, sometimes she wondered what it would be like to be with a gentler woman who did not seek power and did not criticize her friends. A wife of her own. Because no woman she knew fit that description--certainly Drian did not--Lancelot did not believe the thought was too disloyal to Guinevere.

10 THE YOUNG WARRIORS

Morgan sat alone in her room, but her every muscle tensed with anticipation. The winter night was cold, but she wore her finest gown, which was not overly warm. She did not sit near the brazier with burning coals.

This was the night of nights, the time she waited for all year. This was the time of the visitor, the only man who mattered.

She wished that he would let her live near him, so she could see him often, instead of just once a year, but he never would. When people guessed at their love, he had repudiated and punished her. But, despite her anger, she could never say no to him. She was sure she was the only woman he had ever loved, as he was the only man she had ever loved.

There was a gust of wind, and he was in the room with her. Brought by the sword that Merlin had enchanted, her lover was almost a specter. But he was real enough to lie with her.

Arthur took her in his arms.

It was late and the warriors had dispersed for the evening. Lancelot was away, and Talwyn had gone to bed in tears because she had seen her mad father, who had raved more than usual.

Guinevere's eyes were tired from reading. Restless, she decided to make an unusual nighttime visit to the stable to see that a sore on her horse's back was healing. She wrapped her fur-lined cloak around her and descended the stairs. Carrying a torch, she crossed the courtyard.

Guinevere was not fond of the dark, but what could happen to her at Camelot? She was, after all, the queen. She took care on the cobbles in case some water on them had frozen.

She might wake some sleeping stablehands or disturb their dice games, but that prospect did not worry her.

But when Guinevere reached the stable, she saw two stablehands outside, shifting nervously on their feet. Although they did not appear to be doing anything illicit, they almost jumped when they saw her.

"Why aren't you inside guarding the horses?" Guinevere asked, moving towards the stable door.

"A warrior ordered us to stay outside, your highness," one young man said in a strained voice. "We can't disobey him."

"Best not go inside, highness." The other stablehand trembled with apprehension.

"I shall go wherever I please," Guinevere told them. "You may not disobey a warrior, but I don't have to obey him."

She pushed open the door and heard sounds of a struggle.

"Get away from me!" cried a woman.

"You hit me, you bitch! You'll pay for that."

"Halt!" Guinevere commanded. She shone her rushlight in the direction of the voices and saw a serving girl break away from a man who had been holding her down. The man raised his head, and Guinevere saw that it was Agravaine.

The girl, whose skirt was torn, threw herself against the wall near Guinevere. She grabbed a pitchfork.

"That won't be necessary now," Guinevere told the girl. "Be calm. Agravaine, explain yourself."

"There's nothing to explain, Lady Guinevere." Panting, he struggled to his feet. "We had an assignation, but the girl demanded more money."

"I did not!" the girl exclaimed. "I don't want you. I didn't come here to meet him, highness. He followed me here and grabbed me."

"She's a whore!" Agravaine spat out the words. "Why would a serving girl go to the stable at night, except to meet a man?"

"Evidently she did not plan to meet you," Guinevere said in a voice of ice. "Your own words suggest that."

"What difference does that make? She's just a kitchen wench." He was shaking with anger.

"You may leave us, Agravaine, and never disturb this girl again, unless you want me to tell the king that you tried to rape a serving woman." Guinevere spoke as if from a throne.

"Yes, Lady Guinevere. I realize you're the guardian of purity." Agravaine's tone was insolent, but he strode out of the stable.

"Were you meeting a sweetheart?" Guinevere asked the girl, who looked about the same age as Talwyn. "As you can see, this isn't a safe place."

"No!" the girl cried, only now dropping the pitchfork. "I went here to get away from one of the cooks, who's been after me."

"The chapel might be safer," Guinevere said.

"Hah! A man grabbed me there once."

The girl shivered.

"No place is safe. I want to leave here and find some dun where all the men are too old to care, if there is any such."

"I doubt that there is." Guinevere wanted to embrace her, but she held back. "What is your name?"

"Creirwy, highness. I work in the kitchen."

"Doesn't Cai protect the kitchen workers?"

"As much as he can, highness. He's a good master. But he isn't there all the time."

Guinevere was relieved to hear that Cai tried his best to look after the serving women. She would tell him about the cook. But her heart still raced with anger.

"Come with me," Guinevere told the serving girl. She wanted to accuse Agravaine of attempting rape, but she thought no one, not even Arthur, would want to believe Creirwy's account over Agravaine's.

When they left the stable, Guinevere turned to the stablehands, who were shaking as if Agravaine had just cursed them, which he undoubtedly had.

"If any warriors try such a thing again, you must go to someone in authority, like Bors or Lancelot, who will put a stop to it," Guinevere ordered them. "Or wake Cuall, and he'll summon them." She was sure the old stablemaster would never countenance any misbehavior, much less crimes, in his jurisdiction. "And if any man bribes you, you'll be judged as guilty as he is. Now watch over the horses, as is your duty."

"Yes, highness," they said in unison.

Silently, the girl followed Guinevere across through the shadowy courtyard back to her room.

Guinevere told her to enter and bade her light some beeswax candles. In the flickering light, she saw the young face, tousled brown hair, strong arms, and rough hands.

"You're a fighter, are you, Creirwy?" Guinevere smiled, showing that she did not disapprove.

Creirwy nodded. "I don't want to be had again."

"Indeed not," Guinevere agreed. "My chief serving woman is old now. You could work for me and be one of my serving women."

"I never worked with ladies' gowns, highness." Creirwy looked less than excited at the prospect.

"Never mind, you can learn. And you will be working at a little more distance from the men. And perhaps you might learn a bit more about fighting, so that you might guard me, just in case the guards need guarding. Will you do that?" Guinevere scrutinized her face.

"Yes, Lady Guinevere." The words were innocuous enough, but the voice was not submissive, and Guinevere liked that.

Lancelot stood with Creirwy in the queen's room, where old Fencha had left them after assuring the girl that Guinevere had asked the warrior to speak with her.

"Queen Guinevere says that you would like to learn how to fight. Is that so?" She was not overly enthused about this scheme of Guinevere's, but the queen had spent half a night persuading her.

Creirwy eyed Lancelot coolly. The serving girl's hands were on her hips. "You never bothered me and I never heard of you botherin' anyone else, Lord Lancelot, but I don't want to be off alone with you much more than with any other man. And I don't want the lessons enough to give you anything for 'em."

"No," Lancelot agreed in a calm voice. She should not be offended, for the girl undoubtedly had good reason to be so wary.

"That would be a poor bargain, wouldn't it, letting one man help you fight the others if he extracted a price for it. You are right that people help each other for reasons. Mine is that it would please the queen."

"Why learn to fight? If I cut any of the warriors, they'd hang me." She shook her head defiantly, and her braids swayed.

Lancelot felt her face flush. This girl was no fool. "Perhaps. But not all men who might attack you are warriors."

"I know that well enough." Creirwy grimaced.

"I don't want to teach you if you don't want to learn. You must tell me whether you do." Lancelot stood there quietly, waiting for her to think about the matter.

After a pause, the girl said "I do."

"Very good." Lancelot nodded, as if she had struck a bargain. She saw that Creirwy had muscles that would help her fight and work-reddened hands that had calluses enough so the girl likely wouldn't fear getting more from handling a sword.

"Want a new cloak?" Creirwy asked. "Get me some wool and I'll make one for you. Then I won't owe you nothin'."

"I teach one of the young ladies, and she gives me nothing, so why should you?"

"Talwyn? The queen told me." There was a note of scorn in her voice. "That's because you think of her like a daughter, the queen says. That's not how you'd see me."

"Why not? The queen herself had a sister who was a serving girl," Lancelot began to explain.

Creirwy hooted. "So do all the ladies, if they'd own it. Much good that it does us."

"Perhaps you're right." Lancelot felt herself blush again. Yes, bastards were common enough, and generally not acknowledged. "I could use a new cloak. I'll get some wool and bring it to you. And if you make a tunic as well, I'll give you some of my old chain mail and a sword."

"Two tunics."

"Two tunics. Agreed."

The chain mail would not be as tight on the wiry Creirwy as it was on Talwyn, Lancelot reflected.

Lancelot stood with Talwyn in Guinevere's room and told her that Creirwy would join in her lessons.

"Let a serving girl strike at me?" Talwyn flinched at this horrible idea. Why would Lancelot want her to undergo such humiliation? "Can you truly mean that? Won't it turn her bad?"

Lancelot frowned. Her voice was grave. "She wants to escape whoring for the men. Is that bad?"

The bluntness of this speech made Talwyn stare at the floor. "No."

"If she struck you when not at practice with me, you could no doubt have her hand cut off. And if you struck her, she could not say or do anything. So why is it that you fear her?" Lancelot examined her face.

"I'd never strike a serving woman," Talwyn protested. She had never even thought of doing such a thing.

"Some ladies do, Guinevere tells me. See that you don't." Lancelot patted her shoulder.

Talwyn sighed. If the queen and Lancelot wanted her to cross wooden swords with a serving girl, she would have to do it as a price for the lessons. Talwyn vowed that she would be kind to the poor serving girl. But when Creirwy came to the queen's room there was a hint of scorn in the serving girl's gray eyes.

When they fought, with Lancelot watching every move, listening to every word, it was clear that Creirwy was the stronger.

The two girls circled around each other, trying to take each other's measure.

Talwyn had thought she cared nothing about clothes, but as she looked at Creirwy's rough, undyed gown, she knew that she did. Talwyn also had imagined that she worked hard, spinning and sewing every day, though it was less than most ladies did because the queen took her off for lessons. When she looked closely at Creirwy's raw, red hands, she realized that she had scarcely worked at all by comparison.

Then Creirwy's wooden sword hit her shoulder and Talwyn could barely keep from staggering. She bit her lip to keep from anger at being hit by a servant. Creirwy was stronger than she was, but then, so would men be. She lunged at Creirwy, and missed.

"Don't just thrash around, Talwyn. Keep your stance," Lancelot urged her. "Don't just stab, Creirwy. That may work against Talwyn, but it wouldn't against a trained man."

Creirwy looked up boldly at their teacher. "How likely am I to be wearin' a sword when a man grabs at me? Better teach us how to fight with our fists, too."

Talwyn sucked in her breath. Fighting with a sword was somehow splendid, but fighting with fists seemed low.

Nonetheless, Lancelot nodded. "I suspect you know some of that already. You can show Talwyn the rudiments. And as for grabbing, come from behind and grab me around the neck, and watch how I break free."

Creirwy grabbed Lancelot, but Lancelot stepped back and threw her off balance.

"It is good to know more than one way of fighting. Like foxes, you must have many strategies for escaping," Lancelot said.

"And a good kick in the groin is one of the best," the handsome warrior told them. "You can try it on me. I have padded myself so much that you can't hurt me."

Creirwy eyed Lancelot with amazement, and Talwyn thought she must guess that a man would never teach her this form of attack. Lancelot did not look like a padded man; in fact, just the opposite.

Gareth seemed to brood more than any of the other young fighters. Gawaine noticed how much time Gareth spent alone, or praying in the chapel, and so one evening when they were in their house, he said, "Surely you must want a woman, Gareth. Don't be shy. Let me tell you how you can please one," and put an arm on his shoulder.

But Gareth pulled away, exclaiming vehemently, "Stay away from me. Everything you say is evil and I can't bear for you to touch me."

Stung, Gawaine retreated. What misfortune that he had one brother who barely suppressed his violence, another who was a foolish lout, and the third was the world's worst prig, and hated him as well.

"I did passing well, did I not?" Mordred laughed triumphantly over Gereint, one of King Arthur's warriors, whose shoulder he had just nicked in fighting practice. Gereint was of no account, being nearly forty years old and having no imagination.

"Passing well," Gereint agreed, his hand on his shoulder.

"No one could guess that you learned sword fighting only this year."

They stood in the cool cellar of the brothel that Mordred owned. Casks of wine and ale surrounded them and lent the air a pungent smell.

Mordred wiped his sword--a fine one, with lapis on the hilt--and sat down on a wine barrel. He had done well to kill the panderers who raised him and take the brothel for his own, he reflected with glee.

"My language is also polished enough for the High King's court, is it not?" Mordred asked, keeping the anxiety he felt out of his voice. Never could he show anyone a hint of uncertainty. Only fools did that.

"Usually, but at times you slip," Gereint said, also seating himself on a wine barrel. He had stanched the blood that had dripped through his doublet.

Mordred frowned. How dare this fool criticize him, when he was paying the man so much to teach him sword fighting and noble speech. "My father will be proud of me, won't he?"

"You do resemble the High King, but you must never speak of that," Gereint warned, running his fingers through his brown hair, which showed a touch of gray.

Mordred turned away from the warrior. How dare Gereint suggest that he might not be King Arthur's son. His whore of a mother had died before he was old enough to remember her, and that was just as well. Why couldn't he have had a lady, or even a queen, for a mother? His red-gold hair, his gray eyes, and the features of his face showed whose son he was. The panderers had taunted him with that knowledge, but soon no one would ever taunt him again.

"My father will not welcome me." Mordred stated these words, but they were really a question.

"The king will no doubt show mercy to you. It was commendable that you sought to learn how to behave properly before you met him, but he would not be pleased to learn that you own this place." Gereint looked around the brothel's cellar with distaste, as if he could see what was taking place in the rooms above it.

"I've told you that you can have any of the girls."

"And I have told you that I am true to my wife." Gereint brushed his sleeve as if wiping off a spot of grease.

"How noble." Mordred had learned to modify his sneer so it sounded genteel rather than coarse. "But your nobility doesn't prevent you from taking my money. Or would you prefer not to be paid anymore?"

"I have told you that I need it, for my caer is in a state of disrepair and my cattle sickened and died last winter. I have done much for you. You would do well to show me respect." Gereint spoke not just in the tones of teacher to student but also in the tones of a superior to a social inferior.

"I do respect you. Have you kept your promise and told no one, not even your so beloved wife, that you are teaching me?" Mordred ran his finger along the blade of his sword.

"I have done as you asked. It is better that your whereabouts be secret until you present yourself to the king." Gereint wiped his brow.

"I am in your debt. Do go up to the tavern and at least drink some of my best wine. As you know, I have said that you should be given only the finest." Mordred made a mock bow.

"Thank you. I am a trifle thirsty." Gereint began to climb the cellar steps.

As Gereint reached the third step, Mordred moved up behind him and stabbed him in the back.

Gereint cried out and collapsed.

The fool had believed that Mordred would let him live, so he could tell how low Mordred's origins were. Mordred laughed scornfully. These warriors of the king's were simple-minded. It would be child's play to deceive them.

Mordred took Gereint's purse, not because he wanted the money, but so it would look as if robbers had attacked the warrior. He would have his men take Gereint and his horse far away, and leave them in the road, with signs of a scuffle nearby.

No one at Camelot could ever know that he had been raised in a brothel, for they would despise him if they did.

Stepping over the corpse, Mordred walked upstairs. Might as well have a woman now, as a reward for his clever deed.

Soon he would see his father. Was there a chance that Arthur, who was believed to be childless, would welcome a son and acknowledge him? Mordred's heart beat a little faster at the thought. He pictured the king embracing him. But it was unlikely that the king would embrace a bastard. Mordred chided himself for his sentimentality.

Arthur saw a tall young man with red-gold hair stride into the great hall as if he belonged there. He wore an elegant tunic and cloak of a blue that was almost royal in color, and not worn by lesser nobles. Gold and bronze armrings gleamed on his arms. His face was familiar--indeed, it was much like Arthur's own. The king felt as if he might fall off this throne, but he tried to remain expressionless.

Arthur was hearing petitioners, and the young man came up before him.

Arthur drew back and asked, "What is your petition?" He wasn't sure that he wanted to hear it.

The young man bowed, but not as deeply as some petitioners. His voice was bold. He stated, rather than requesting, "I want to be one of your warriors."

"Who are you?" Arthur asked, not wanting to know.

"My name is Mordred."

"Mordred ap?" the king queried.

"Mordred son of Morgan," he replied, and when there were faint gasps in the hall, he added, "There are men as well as women named Morgan."

Arthur tried not to flinch. Was this young man claiming to be his sister's son, and his own son by his sister? But he had never heard that she had borne a child, and surely she would have taxed him with it if she had.

"My warriors shall test your mettle, and if you show promise you can become a warrior here," Arthur said.

Heads shook as if everyone in the hall marveled at the speed with which he granted the presumptuous request. Everyone stared at the newcomer, as if trying to calculate whether he was Arthur's son.

Arthur was eager for the young man to leave, so he could think about the matter.

That very day, Mordred proved himself in fighting on the practice field. Arthur came to watch, though he knew that in doing so he fed the speculation. This Mordred managed to slightly cut the shoulder of Gareth, the best of the young warriors, and suffered no blows himself.

At least Mordred could fight. Arthur gave him a friendlier smile than he had before.

Striding up to the young man, who was barely sweating, Arthur said, "You fight well. You may become one of my men."

"Thank you, sire," Mordred said, provoking muffled gasps from the warriors who surrounded them.

Arthur did not deign to notice the double meaning of the word, but only said, "Do your best."

He remembered that years ago he had dreamed of a boy baby biting him in the throat and trying to kill him. He had feared having a son of his body so much that he had asked Guinevere to lie with Lancelot. But that match had produced nothing.

It had been foolish to imagine that a son might kill him. Arthur often regretted that he did not have one. But Guinevere's lack of issue with Lancelot proved that she was barren.

When Arthur thought of Mordred, he was uncertain whether he should rejoice.

That night he dreamed again of the infant attacking his throat, then his chest.

In the next few days, warrior after warrior came to Arthur and told him that Mordred claimed to be his son. Arthur demanded that Mordred be sent to his room for a private audience.

When Mordred arrived, he said nothing but a greeting. There was only a trace of a smile on his young face. He surveyed the room, eyeing the carved furniture with lions' and dragons' heads and tapestries with scenes of war and hunting.

Arthur tried to be formal but not entirely unfriendly. Perhaps, after all, this strong young man was his own flesh and blood. Perhaps he could name a woman who plausibly might have been his mother. If not, perhaps Mordred was the son of some bastard of Arthur's father, King Uther, and thus kin of a sort.

Arthur sat, and gestured for Mordred to be seated also. "You must know why I have asked you here. Of course I have heard that you claim to be my son. Why do you tell others this tale? Will you make this claim to me?"

Mordred's smile widened. His red-gold hair shone in the light of Arthur's oil lamp, which was shaped like a dragon. "See for yourself, sire. Don't you believe that I am your sister's son?"

Arthur frowned. "Perhaps I don't believe that my sister bore a child."

Mordred shrugged. His face still wore the insolent smile. "Believe what you want. You can see that I'm your son, plainly enough, if you'll but look. If she wasn't the mother, perhaps it was someone else. Perhaps an even more powerful woman, such as Queen Morgause of Lothian."

Arthur felt the blood surge in his veins. As if he had ever touched his aunt! What a rotten lie! Now he was free to totally disbelieve Mordred. He raged and shook his fist. "My aunt! At the time you must have been born, I'd never even met her. This is incredible. And you'd better not let Gawaine hear you speak such filth about his mother. He adores her."

"That would make a pretty tale." Mordred was smirking as if unmoved by Arthur's anger.

"By the Cross, what a filthy mind you have! And you're not very clever to talk so about such a great fighter." Arthur wiped his hands on his gold-trimmed white tunic, as if washing himself of Mordred.

"No doubt you would rather have him inherit the throne than see your son inherit it." Mordred's voice was expressionless.

"I have no son," Arthur said.

There was a bitter smile on Mordred's face. "It's wise of you to deny that you do."

Arthur's heart hardened. "I have allowed you to become one of my men. That should be enough for you."

Mordred bowed. "Indeed it is, my lord Arthur. I am grateful."

"I shall watch your progress." Arthur thought that was a grand concession.

"I am honored." Mordred bowed.

"You may go now."

When Mordred left, Arthur breathed a sigh of relief. Of course this was not his son.

Mordred stalked off and went for a ride. He did not see the forest around him, except to note whether there were any dangers, which he could sense easily. He rode only for the motion, to carry the rage he could not speak. Audacious as his speech with the king had been, it showed only the slightest part of his anger. He had been a fool ever to imagine that his father might care for him. His dreams of taking vengeance against the king had been far wiser than hoping for his father's love.

His heart was full of bitterness. He hated all of them, these men who had always lived in caers and had servants at their command. His father he hated the most, of course, but he did not spare the others, who prated about childish ideas such as duty, honor, justice, and love. No one cared about anyone else; they only pretended that they did.

The only one who intrigued him even a little was Gawaine, who had come to the brothel when Mordred was there as a boy. He had often wondered what would have happened if Gawaine had seen him. No doubt Gawaine would have recognized him as the king's son, and perhaps saved him. But why should Gawaine have done that, when he was the most likely heir to the throne himself? Why rescue a rival heir? No, it was foolish to imagine that anyone would have helped him. Why should he like Gawaine? He was just another obstacle to gaining the throne. That would be after King Arthur died, a time to be anticipated with pleasure.

Mordred sat in the great hall. He acted as if he was used to such huge rooms, though it was much larger than his whole brothel. It irked him that he sat with the young warriors, far from the king.

He saw who sat nearest to Arthur. Gawaine, the king's cousin. Mordred couldn't quarrel much with that, but he observed that Gawaine's brothers sat nowhere near the king. They might be discontented with their seats. The queen sat on the king's other side. Perhaps Arthur could watch her better there. Women would get away with whatever they could. Merlin sat beside the queen, but he was too old to matter. He seemed to stare into space, and no doubt was doddering. Lancelot sat next to Gawaine. This Lancelot was a famous warrior and a handsome one, but Mordred saw nothing special about him.

Lancelot said something and Arthur gave him the kind of smile that he should have given to Mordred. Mordred winced inwardly. Why did the king favor Lancelot?

"The king seems to like Lancelot," he said to a handsome young warrior who sat next to him. The young man, who was named Percy, looked too gentle for a warrior. So did Lancelot, come to that.

"Everyone loves Lancelot of the Lake," Percy said, smiling foolishly. "He is close to the king. They even go riding together at times."

Mordred felt a surge of jealousy such as he had never experienced over a woman. He wanted to fight this Lancelot, but perhaps Lancelot would defeat him, which would be unbearable.

Mordred tried to concentrate on his mutton, which was nicely flavored with mint, no doubt because of that seneschal Cai. Why did Arthur have a seneschal who was perfumed? Cai must bugger men. But Cai didn't look strong enough to rape anyone, like the panderers who had forced Mordred.

The queen was not bad-looking, though it was a mystery why the king had not put her away when she bore no children. She was making a strange move with her knife that had nothing to do with cutting meat. Lancelot also made an odd move. They were signaling each other! How could his father countenance such carrying on? What was the good of being High King if your wife flirted with--and no doubt laid with-- other men? Mordred's arms ached to strike Lancelot.

"Which of the girls do you think is the prettiest?" Percy whispered to Galahad when they were waiting outside the great hall watching the young ladies go in for the evening meal.

"I like Talwyn the best," Galahad said, smiling to herself. Talwyn had glanced at Galahad, then quickly looked away.

"Talwyn? But she's not the prettiest." Percy's eyes widened.

"She's very pretty, indeed, and her looks suit me well." Galahad frowned.

Percy flushed. "Sorry. I didn't mean to offend you. I think Gralla is the most beautiful, but she won't look at me. I tried speaking with her, and she said, 'Percy, you're handsome, but you're poor, so please don't try to court me.' What do you think of that?"

Galahad whistled, amazed that anyone as handsome as Percy could have trouble with girls. "I think you're fortunate that she was so honest."

Percy nodded. "Don't tell anyone about what she said to me."

"Of course I won't." Galahad patted his arm.

The young warriors had just finished their practice, and Lancelot was striding away from the practice field. Seeing that Galahad was trying to catch up with her, she slowed her pace.

The skinny youth hastened to her side.

"Could I ask a boon, Lord Lancelot?" Galahad asked breathlessly.

"You may ask. You did well against Percy today, but watch your left side as well as your right." What boon could the lad want, more lessons?

"I shall. Could I go riding with you in the forest at times?" Galahad's voice had only a hint of pleading.

Jealous of her solitude, Lancelot tried to find a gentle way to put off Galahad. "I have little time for quests, now that I am teaching so much. And of course you know that I generally go alone."

"It doesn't have to be a quest. I'd just like to learn more about the forest, and you know more than anyone else," Galahad begged. Doves pecking at spilled crumbs on the cobblestones cooed, as if to say that the world outside the caer's walls beckoned them. Lancelot wondered whether the doves would be served for dinner.

Lancelot smiled. It was good that this young man cared about the forest. "Very well, perhaps I have time for that."

Some mornings and evenings they rode out, pausing by each new thing they saw. Lancelot was surprised to find that Galahad knew a great deal already and could identify as many bird songs as she could.

They found red fawns hidden in tall grasses, and stayed late in the evening to watch badgers come out of their dens. Galahad could be quiet at such times.

One day they found a fox's den, with four cubs playing outside of it. They silently agreed to sit at a distance and watch the cubs leap in the grass, catching insects.

"See how they move," Lancelot whispered. "They look like dogs, but they jump and pounce just like cats. What are they, then? It interests me, perhaps because I am not entirely sure what I am."

Occasionally the vixen came, bringing a rabbit or a mouse, but she was not disturbed by the two warriors sitting at a respectful distance.

The fragrance of meadowsweet scented the air and larks filled it with song. Blue cornflowers contrasted with the foxes' red fur.

The two denizens of Camelot finally left, Lancelot almost surprised that they had hands and feet instead of paws.

They rode along in silence as the afternoon light faded. Birds bade their last farewell to the day, and animals that had slept began to stir.

As twilight obscured their features, Galahad asked, "Lord Lancelot, how did you woo Queen Guinevere?"

Lancelot felt so comfortable with Galahad that she answered the question instead of denying that she and the queen loved each other. Galahad had not told about her sex, and so could also be trusted with this secret. "What a question! I wouldn't tell this to anyone else, but I didn't woo her at all. She wooed me, and I fled from her. I was afraid that she wanted me because she believed I was a man, but she knew all the time that I wasn't. I am ashamed to say that I even kissed her when I thought that she believed I was a man."

Galahad's eyebrows shot up. "Was that so wrong, to kiss a woman who believed you were a man?"

"Of course it was." Lancelot insisted. "I can see that you wouldn't understand, as it's a question just for me and no one else. But it's deceitful, not perhaps as bad as pretending you were unmarried if you were married, but almost."

"I see." Galahad regarded his horse's mane. "And Queen Guinevere always knew that you were a woman?"

Lancelot nodded. "Yes, she said that she would not have loved me otherwise. I suppose it's clear whether one loves women or men. It always has been for me. Thank the Blessed Virgin I did not fall in love with a lady who longed for a man."

"Yes, I can see that could have been very unpleasant." Galahad's tone was warmly sympathetic.

Lancelot silently chided herself for talking too much about her own situation, which couldn't help this lad. "But you should ask some other warrior, who is a more likely example for you, about courting. You might ask Bors how he courted his wife. Of course the marriage was arranged, but he met her first."

"I suppose I could," said Galahad, sighing a little.

An owl hooted, and they rode on.

When they returned to the stable, Lancelot saw Percy moping among the horses. As soon as Galahad had departed, Percy came up to her.

"When I was a young boy, you would kindly go out in the forest with me. Would you perhaps grant me that favor again someday?" Percy asked, his foot tracing a circle in the dirt of the stableyard.

"Of course. That would be a pleasure." Smiling at him, Lancelot put her hand on his shoulder. He was a boy still.

The next day, they rode far, passing an old villa with crumbling walls.

Percy gasped as if the sight astonished him. "Could we go inside?"

"Of course, but let's be careful. The walls might collapse." Lancelot never knew what strange thing would interest Percy.

They dismounted and entered the villa. Percy stared about in the dark as if he had never seen old walls before. A few chunks of plaster still clung to them, but most had disintegrated long before. Ants and spiders made the villa their home. A bat disturbed by their intrusion flew out of the villa. The villa smelled of mold. Lancelot almost gagged, but Percy didn't seem to notice.

Lancelot suggested that they should leave. When they returned to the sunlight, they saw an old peasant woman who was stooped from her many years of work. She hailed them, and they returned her greeting.

"Blessings on you, my lords," she said.

"Thank you, my lady. God grant you a good day," Lancelot said, inclining her head.

Percy bowed deeply to her. "I shall cherish your blessing forever," he intoned solemnly.

"Will you now?" The old woman grinned, displaying her lack of teeth.

Lancelot and Percy rode away. Percy was silent for a long time. Then he said, "What a wonderful day! No doubt she was a fair maiden under an enchantment who guards that enchanted caer."

"No doubt," Lancelot agreed. Yes, Percy was the same as ever.

Returning from a silversmith's shop where she had surreptitiously purchased a gift to send her mother--for she was supposed to be a poor bastard with no family--Galahad saw Talwyn enter the walled garden.

Galahad shivered. Here was a chance to speak with the girl she liked, so she should take it, come what may. For good luck, she touched her chest in the place where an amulet her mother had given her hung under her tunic. The silver cross from the nuns she wore in plain sight.

Galahad sauntered into the garden as if she believed no one else was there.

Talwyn was in a fighting stance, thrusting an imaginary sword at an unseen foe.

Galahad stared, but she recovered enough to say, "Well done! You struck him down."

Talwyn whirled around. "What are you doing here? I thought I was alone."

"I just happened by and wanted to look at the roses." Now that she was pretending to be a young man, Galahad was becoming accustomed to telling lies. "I didn't know you could fight."

Talwyn put her hands behind her back. "I can't. I was just pretending."

"No, your fighting stance was too good for that. You must be learning, and I can guess who is teaching you--and why he would." Galahad grinned.

Talwyn flushed. "I don't know what you're talking about."

"Don't worry. I know his secret, but would never tell. And now I know yours."

Galahad was tempted to say, "Give me a kiss and I won't tell," but she knew that would be wrong.

"You men don't want girls to be able to fight so we could fend you off," Talwyn complained, frowning. She was prickly as the pink roses, and just as pretty. How sweetly Talwyn's curly hair hung down her back.

"You don't need any defenses against me, Lady Talwyn. I'm so smitten with your beauty that I'm helpless around you." Galahad moved near a stone bench as if waiting for Talwyn to sit on it, but Talwyn remained standing.

"Don't talk such nonsense." Talwyn shook her head. "I don't want to flirt with men."

"Good, that's understood." Galahad smiled. She had an inspiration. "In fact, I'll help you learn to fight, if you'd like extra tutoring." She executed several swift fighting moves, though like Talwyn she was weaponless.

For the first time, Talwyn smiled. "Perhaps you can help. I'm learning how to fight in rooms only. I want to know how to fight on horseback, but my teacher won't let me. Would you?"

"Go out riding in the woods alone with you? Yes, indeed. Of course I'll show you how to fight on horseback." Galahad wanted to shout with delight. Things with Talwyn were going to be even better than Galahad had hoped.

"That's the only reason I'm going to ride with you. Don't flatter yourself." Talwyn rapped Galahad's knuckles lightly. "I know you have more training than I have. Just don't lord it over me. I can't bear that," Talwyn warned.

"I won't. I'm not a lord, so no lording." Galahad tried to hold Talwyn's hand.

"You sound as if you're used to having secret meetings with girls. Perhaps I shouldn't go with you." Talwyn stepped back.

"No, I'm not. I swear, no secret meetings ever before." Galahad assumed an air of innocence that was, unfortunately, real.

"Queen Guinevere allows me a little time to myself, which few other girls have. I think I can get away tomorrow morning at breakfast time. No one else but Lancelot goes riding that early. I'll tell the stablehands I'm taking my horse to the pasture, but not that we're going beyond the gates." Talwyn walked to the garden's gate. "I'll meet you just outside the outer wall."

"Nothing would keep me away." Galahad went off whistling. Strange, no one had whistled at the convent, but she always had. Some of the guards at Camelot whistled, but none of the warriors did except Gawaine, who could whistle entire tunes.

The next morning they set off. Galahad's heart beat fast. Talwyn had pulled back her generally unruly hair and concealed something, obviously a sword, under her cloak.

Thrushes sang, but Talwyn's voice, telling about a book she had read, sounded sweeter. "Why didn't the Trojans heed what Cassandra was saying? Men don't pay enough attention to women's words."

"Indeed they don't," Galahad readily agreed.

"Do you really believe that?" Talwyn scrutinized Galahad's face.

Galahad crossed her heart. "More than you can imagine."

"But do you honestly believe that girls should learn to fight, too?"

Galahad smiled. "I have a sister who passes for a man, and I approve wholeheartedly."

"Oh, how splendid!" Talwyn's eyes lit up. "I'd love to meet her!"

"I hope you will someday." Everything was perfect. The sunlight streamed through the trees. Galahad thought she had never been so happy. The light made traces of gold in Talwyn's brown hair. "What pretty hair you have."

Talwyn frowned. "Please don't flirt with me. I stay away from flirting because I don't want to marry and have babies. I saw my mother die in childbed." She shuddered.

Galahad bowed her head. "How sad. I don't want children, either."

Wide-eyed, Talwyn pulled back. "You can't be telling the truth! I never heard of a man who thought such a thing, except for a monk."

"It's true, I care nothing about having children. I have nothing for them to inherit, anyway," Galahad insisted, wondering how much she dared to tell. "I promise you, I'll never make you with child." She was telling only the truth.

"You certainly won't, because I'll never let you." Talwyn tossed her head. "You shouldn't even say such a thing to me."

They came to a clearing, where only bracken grew. It would be a perfect place to dismount, and to do a great many other things.

"I need to learn how to rescue maidens." Talwyn took off the cloak that covered her sword. "So you can pretend to be a maiden, and I'll rescue you."

"What!" Galahad gasped. "I can't pretend to be a girl."

"Oh, indeed!" Talwyn tossed her head. "So that's what you really think about women. You believe you're so much better than we are that you won't even pretend to be one for a morning."

"No, no, that's not what I mean." Galahad felt more trapped than she had when another aspiring warrior had backed her up against the wall in fighting practice.

"If you won't pretend to be a maiden in distress, I'll go back to Camelot right now." Talwyn began to turn her horse.

"But Talwyn, if I am the maiden, who would you fight?" Galahad pleaded.

"I want to learn how to sweep a maiden off her horse and onto mine. All you have to do is let your horse run as if you couldn't control it," Talwyn explained, though her voice still showed exasperation.

Galahad thought fast. "As you wish. That I can do." Lancelot had taught her how to swing to the side of her horse and to leap from her horse onto another. She dug her heels into her horse's flanks, making it run so suddenly that it was startled.

Talwyn rode behind her.

"Help! Help! I'm falling!" Galahad cried, and let herself slip from her saddle, just a bit, until Talwyn could catch up with her.

Talwyn rode beside her. "I'll save you!"

Appearing to let herself fall, Galahad actually leapt onto Talwyn's horse, landing in Talwyn's arms. She then kissed Talwyn on the lips.

"How dare you!" Talwyn exclaimed--after returning the kiss.

"But that's how maidens thank fighters who rescue them. All the tales say so." Galahad held onto to Talwyn as if she might fall off otherwise.

"Not if Lancelot rescues them!" Talwyn protested, but she didn't pull away.

"I'm pretending you're someone else, not Lancelot," Galahad said.

Suddenly, as if summoned, Lancelot rode into the clearing, and she called out, "Galahad! Talwyn! What are you doing?"

Galahad had never been less eager to see the woman warrior.

"I was teaching Talwyn how to fight on horseback, and she wanted to learn how to rescue a maiden who was falling off her horse," Galahad explained, thinking the excuse sounded feeble.

Talwyn stopped her horse, and Galahad slipped off it.

"Talwyn, I've told you that you can't practice outdoors because someone might see you!" Lancelot's voice was stern. "And you both know that it's improper for you to be alone together, much less to hold each other. I'm very disappointed in you."

"Please, Lord Lancelot, I just wanted to learn how to fight." Talwyn used a wheedling tone.

"To fight, or to kiss?" Lancelot demanded, frowning at them.

"The kiss was entirely my fault. Talwyn is blameless," Galahad asserted, whistling for her own horse.

"You could destroy Talwyn's reputation. You know better than that," Lancelot chided her. "You must never meet like this again. The lessons Talwyn has with me should be adequate."

Oh, have mercy, Galahad thought but did not say. She sighed.

Lancelot looked from one of them to the other. "Talwyn, I hope you understand that you must maintain some distance from any young man. You must be a little shy with each other," she admonished in her most teacherly voice.

"Oh, please, I'm shy enough," exclaimed Galahad.

"So am I. I am excessively shy and modest," Talwyn asserted. "I am a maiden's maiden."

"Would that you were," Galahad muttered, then added in a louder voice, "Of course you are."

"This was my first kiss." Talwyn blushed prettily.

"Mine, too," Galahad said.

"Truly?" Talwyn and Lancelot asked in unison, and they both raised their eyebrows.

Galahad nodded. Of course it was unusual for a male of her age to never have kissed a girl. Wouldn't this revelation help Lancelot guess the truth? Why couldn't she see it? "It would be proper for us to meet at times if you accompanied us, wouldn't it? Would that be asking too much?"

"I'm not at all sure that I should encourage you." Lancelot's voice still was stern. "And of course Queen Guinevere would have to give her permission for you to spend time with Talwyn."

"It's no use to ask her, she never would," Talwyn whined. She pouted at her teacher. "Galahad says that he likes me. Is there any proper way that he can show that?"

Lancelot's frown took in both of them. "Has he made bold to say such a thing?"

Galahad flinched, but Talwyn quickly spoke up. "I have thought of a way that he could show he is fond of me without doing anything improper."

"What is it?" Galahad was a little apprehensive, but surely the plan could not be too bold if Talwyn would speak of it before Lancelot. "Do you want me to fight someone for you?"

"You could make me a gown. That would be a great test. I have never heard of a man doing that for a woman." Talwyn smiled as if proud of her idea.

Galahad groaned with dismay. "Make you a gown! I have no idea how to sew."

"You couldn't be worse at it than I am," Talwyn insisted, making a gesture with her sword. "I have sewn for years, but I can't make a seam straight and my stitches always fall out in no time at all."

Galahad's heart sank. What if someone saw her sewing and guessed that she was a woman? "But must sweethearts sew for each other? Lord Lancelot and Queen Guinevere don't make or repair each other's clothing, do you, Lord Lancelot?"

"No, neither of us ever thought of such a thing," Lancelot said, her mouth twitching as if she suppressed a laugh.

"I want to know that you don't think you're better than I am because you are a man." Talwyn sheathed her sword. "Don't you think it's a fair test, Lord Lancelot?"

"It's certainly a difficult test," Lancelot replied, shaking her head. "I can't think of any man who would be willing to take it."

Galahad sighed. In this way at least, she could vie for Talwyn's affections in a way that no man might match. "What material do you want the gown made of, Talwyn? Will you show me how to do it?"

"Of course I'll show you, but that only means that you'll learn from the worst seamstress at Camelot," Talwyn chortled, triumphant.

Then Galahad began to grin. "At least I can look forward to the fittings."

"Galahad!" Lancelot scowled.

"You certainly cannot," Talwyn snapped, moving her horse away. "One of the serving women can do those."

"No unseemly jests, Galahad," Lancelot warned. "I'll ride back with you, but I'll go ahead of you and allow you to speak with each other."

As soon as Lancelot had ridden off ahead, Galahad asked, "Could you be attracted to Lancelot?"

Talwyn stared at Galahad. "Why would you ask me such a question? I never thought about it. He of course would never flirt with a student, and worships the queen, I believe."

"But could you be attracted to Lancelot, if Lancelot were free?" Could Talwyn want a woman?

Talwyn looked like a bristling cat. "Why would you want me to be attracted to Lancelot? I've never thought of wanting Lancelot. I think I might like someone who is more manly, jests more, and is perhaps a little wicked--rather like Gawaine, only younger."

"Like Gawaine!" Galahad groaned loudly. Must Talwyn choose the most manly warrior at court?

Talwyn frowned. "Don't upset yourself. I said younger. You are more like Gawaine than like Lancelot."

"I don't think so," said Galahad quietly, despairing of winning Talwyn's love. She could barely meet Talwyn's gaze.

"Don't be silly, you aren't at all like a saint, as the lord Lancelot is," Talwyn insisted.

Talwyn brought some linen and showed Galahad how to sew, which Galahad did as surreptitiously as possible, not wanting any of the young men to know.

"I'm so proud to have a gown made by a man," Talwyn said. "I don't even mind that your seams are just as crooked as my own."

"Come with me and let's learn what Camelot's brothels are like. I've heard there's a good one near the wine shop," Mordred said to several young warriors after jousting practice. It was well to win over as many men as possible, and what better way could there be? He was careful to make this suggestion when Gareth, Percy, and Galahad were absent, for those fools would have gasped.

But several young men grinned as they put away their practice swords.

"Grand idea," said Clegis, a handsome and strong young warrior.

Bleoberis wrinkled his plain face with a frown. "I would, but I have no money."

Mordred smiled. "Don't let that worry you. I'll pay for everyone. Why not help my friends?" He flourished his bulging purse.

"That's decent of you," Bleoberis replied, grinning.

"Generous, very generous." Colles chuckled with pleasure in anticipation of the night's revelry.

"Why shouldn't we young men have some fun? The older ones always boast about what they did in their day, fighting and whoring," said Camlach.

"It's our turn now," said his younger brother Cildydd.

"Our father pays little heed to us, but you'd think he'd at least have taken us to a brothel," Camlach complained.

Those two were reputed to be Gawaine's bastards, but looked nothing like him. Mordred thought Camlach resembled Bedwyr.

Mordred laughed inwardly. How easy it was to draw men to him! He could succeed without magic swords, round tables, or elderly sages.

"Would you rather ride into the fires of hell, or ascend to the clouds and join the heavenly host?" Gareth admonished Galahad, Percy, and few of the other young warriors who were known to pray. They had just left the chapel and were standing outside it, in the misty morning dew.

"I want to go to heaven, of course, but not just yet." Percy shifted his weight from one leg to the other. He was not fond of Gareth's admonishing tone.

"Those of us who are pure should pray in the chapel all night, as counter to the wickedness that others do in the dark," Gareth said.

"A good idea," Galahad replied. "Perhaps we might try it once a year. But my own body is more likely to resist temptation if I get a good night's sleep."

"I had hoped for better." Sighing, Gareth walked off. Some of the others followed him.

Percy and Galahad lagged behind.

Percy was greatly relieved by Galahad's words. "I am not quite in accord with Gareth," Percy said, "but it does seem that we might be able to be still nobler than many of the older warriors. I had thought that King Arthur's men might be like angels, yet they are not." Percy looked up at the clouds that soared above them. "Few of them speak of much but their fighting prowess and their horses. I had hoped for a more glorious life, in God's service and the king's."

"So had I." Galahad looked to the clouds, as if hoping that Percy had seen a vision there, one that might be shared. "We can try to be nobler, certainly."

11 THE HIGH QUEEN

Tewdar, Arthur's body servant, helped him on with his good leather boots. Arthur stretched, contented. It was a fine winter's day, with no snow on the ground. He and his men had hunted for deer the day before, and there had been venison on the table. Today he must attend to reports from the outposts, but he could do so at a leisurely pace. He strode over to his table and drank a little more of the ale that Tewdar had poured to break his fast.

Tewdar left the room, but immediately returned.

"Sire, the Lady Enid begs to have an audience with you."

A lady wanted to have an audience in his room? That was most unusual. Was she throwing herself at him? He thought Enid was too recently a widow for such wanton behavior. Her husband had died only a few months before. She had, however, been Arthur's mistress before she married--secretly his mistress, of course, or Gereint never would have wedded her--and the memory was pleasant, though vague. There had been so many women.

"Let her enter." And take yourself off, he might have said, but Tewdar would understand that without his speaking.

The lady entered. She was plumper than he remembered--plumper than Guinevere, who was not slim--and of course Enid wore black, which did not become her. She still was fair, nonetheless, with thick brown braids and a sensuous mouth that now trembled as if she would weep. He hoped that she would not.

"Lady Enid. I shall miss Gereint, as I have told you. He was a fine man, a fine warrior. Is there anything I can do for you and your children that I have not yet done?" Arthur did not remember whether she had three children or four. He made a gesture indicating that she should be seated, and sat down himself. Did she want him to find another husband for her? No doubt he could.

Enid did not sit. "Lord Arthur, you have been too kind, allowing me to keep Gereint's land." She sniffled. "I could ask for nothing more. Indeed, I deserve much less. I fear that Gereint's death is my fault." She looked at him piteously.

"What!" She could not mean that. "Gereint was killed by robbers, was he not? Surely that was not your fault."

The lady threw herself on her knees before him. "I fear that my sins killed him. I did not deserve to be so happy, and God has punished me. The priest told me that I should confess to you, and would not give me absolution unless I did."

Arthur pulled back. "Confess your sins to me? Why should he tell you to do that? I am no priest, I don't want to hear them." How distasteful! What a fool priest. "Mayhap you should seek another confessor."

"Please let me speak, Lord Arthur," she begged, wringing her hands. "You are the one I have wronged. When I was your mistress, you got me with child, but I knew that I would lose Gereint's love if I bore it. So I went to an old woman, who destroyed it."

"You did what!" He felt as if he had been attacked by an assassin--and he had. "But it cannot be. I have never gotten any woman with child. Another man must have been the father." He tried to calm himself. What the woman had done was disgusting, but it could not have concerned him.

She gasped. "Lord Arthur! No man but you had ever touched me, until I married Gereint, and then only he did. It was your child. I went to Queen Guinevere, and she told her old serving woman to help me."

"Guinevere!" he shouted. Suddenly believing Enid, Arthur shook with rage. Clenching his fists, he felt as if his veins would burst and his heart would break through his chest. "She destroyed my child!"

Cowering before him, Enid stammered, "She did not know. I did not tell her the child was yours until after it was done."

"She must have known." He still shook. Enid's face was now hideous to him. If he had to look at it any longer, he would vomit--or strike her. "Leave me now, and never let me see your face again. Go to your home and stay there. You're right, it's a far better fate than you deserve."

Trembling, she rose from her knees. "Yes, majesty. I know that you can never forgive me, but I greatly regret what I have done."

"Go!" He flung the word at her, and shook his fist.

Enid fled.

He looked out of the window. The winter fields now seemed as barren as his life. He could have had a child, no doubt a son to rule after him. He had gotten a son on a woman, but evil women had killed it. His own wife, whom he had cosseted all these years, had seen to it that the child was killed. What a fool he had been ever to trust a woman. Great racking sobs tore through his body.

When he was too weak to weep any longer, he stared at the walls of his hill fortress, and the fields and forests that lay beyond them. There would be no son to rule this land after him. And Gawaine might die before he did. Britain would fall apart. And all because Guinevere, who could not bear a child for him herself, was jealous that another woman could.

If he could father one child, perhaps he could father another, if he put Guinevere aside and married a young woman. Guinevere deserved a far worse punishment.

But if Guinevere left, Lancelot would doubtless leave also, and take her to Lesser Britain, where Lancelot still had land.

Arthur would lose one of his best men. Worse, he would be disgraced as a cuckold. And he would have to take an army to Lesser Britain on a mission to destroy Lancelot. Arthur groaned. He did not want to kill Lancelot, who had served him well.

If he could not put Guinevere aside, how could he punish her?

Guinevere was explaining a fine point of Latin grammar to Talwyn when a knock came on the door. A young guard of the king's burst in before Fencha could open it.

"The king is ill, Lady Guinevere! He asks you to come and see him." His voice was breathless, as if he had run to her room.

She jumped up immediately. "Of course. Go off and read by yourself," she told the girl. Arthur had almost never been willing to acknowledge sickness.

Stunned, Guinevere walked quickly back with the guard.

"What ails him?" she asked, feeling almost as concerned as any other wife might be. He was the king, after all, and the land depended on his good health. She sometimes dreamed of succeeding him when he died, but she knew well that some strong man might seize the throne instead. Or Gawaine might be king.

"I don't know, Lady Guinevere."

"Has he seen the physician?"

He stammered. "I don't know, Lady Guinevere. I just came on duty."

She opened the door to the king's room. Arthur was alone, slumping in a chair and staring out of the window.

He never slumped, but always sat erect and kingly.

"What is the matter?" she asked.

Arthur turned and looked at her. Every wrinkle in his face looked deeper than it had before, and his gray eyes were like storm clouds.

"You killed my child." His voice was low, but shaking with rage.

Guinevere gasped. "What do you mean, my lord?" Had he somehow discovered that she had used a potion to prevent childbearing when he had wanted her to bear his child, before he had his mad dreams about a murderous baby boy and had tried to prevent conception? But he couldn't know that she had taken a potion. Only Fencha knew, and she would never have told anyone. "Do you have a fever?"

"Enid told me that the vile old witch who serves you, acting on your orders, destroyed her child. My child, the hope of all Britain." His eyes were like knives carving her.

Guinevere felt as if she had been run over by a horse. For a moment, she had no breath to speak. "My lord," she gasped. "I did not know the child she was carrying was yours."

"I don't believe you." Standing, he towered over her. His breath smelled rank, as if the bitterness rising within him had tainted it. "You are barren yourself, and you could not endure seeing another woman be the mother of my heir. If Britain falls apart when I am gone, you are to blame. You have betrayed not only me, but all of Britain."

He grabbed her wrists and held them tightly, so that they ached.

Sure that appearing weak would only incite his rage, Guinevere tried to keep as calm as possible. She took a deep breath. "My Lord Arthur, you are hurting me," she said in a voice that was not begging.

Arthur laughed bitterly. "Not as much as you deserve. What should I do with you? How should I punish you?"

"I did not try to injure you, so you should not injure me. I only tried to help the girl because she was with child, and no man of her station would ever marry her. You should release me." She looked him in the eye, not flinching at his furious expression.

"Release you? I shall." He flung her away from him, so she fell on the floor.

Guinevere's arm and one of her ankles hurt, but she made no outcry. Instead, she rose as quickly as she could and sat in a chair. "You have sworn never to strike a woman," she said.

An ugly laugh answered her. "I have not struck you, have I? Indeed, I should never strike a woman, not even the murderer of my child. What should I do to that murdering old witch?"

Guinevere shuddered inwardly, she hoped not outwardly. "Fencha is ancient. You surely would not injure her. There is no honor in hurting an old woman."

"Shall I hurt you instead?" His voice was a mockery of pleasantness.

"Instead of Fencha? Of course." She sat up straight, trying to radiate defiance.

"Send the old witch away. Today. Immediately. I can't answer for what I would do if I saw her face." His voice was calmer now.

Guinevere sucked in her breath. Send away Fencha, who was almost like a mother to her? Perhaps never see her again? Guinevere realized that she had no choice. "If you insist."

"But that does not answer what I should do to you." Moving closer, he stood over her. "Shall I hurt you?" he asked again.

Guinevere gripped the arms of the chair so hard that they cut into her hands. "If you did, you would lose Lancelot forever." She could guess what her best protection would be.

Arthur clenched his fists. "Hide behind Lancelot, will you? I doubt that he knows what you have done."

"Of course he does not." Lancelot might not approve of helping a woman rid herself of a pregnancy, but even if that were true, Guinevere was sure that Lancelot would not be angry at her.

"Should I put you aside?"

"If you wish to do so, then you will." She could sense that she was winning this battle. "Lancelot could take me to Lesser Britain."

"You bitch!" Arthur glared at her, but he unclenched his fists. "You know I won't stand for the disgrace of having my wife run away with another man. You will not find it pleasant to live with me after what you have done. How will you try to placate me? Will you return to my bed?"

Guinevere gasped. "My lord, I cannot. I will not lie with anyone but Lancelot." The thought of being touched by the raging man nauseated her. "Surely you cannot want me when you are so angry at me."

"Why not? Why should I be gentle? I have spoiled you. But you are my wife, and should obey me." His voice and face were grim.

"I cannot lie with anyone but Lancelot," she insisted.

"I have let you be with Lancelot. I have been the kindest husband in the world, and the most badly treated." His voice now held sorrow as well as anger.

She realized that he believed his words.

"Forgive me if I have hurt you, Lord Arthur. I have not been all that a wife could be, but I have been a friend to you..."

"A friend!" he yelled, shaking with anger again. "A friend who killed my child? I wish I had never heard your name. Go off to your books. I can find ways to cause you pain without touching you. In public, I shall still pretend that you are my wife, but I know you for what you truly are--my enemy."

She rose from the chair as quickly as she could. "I do not wish to be your enemy. I shall still do my best to be a good queen."

His response was a hollow laugh. "Remember, there are always accidents. Lancelot would commiserate with me if something happened to my wife."

Guinevere put her hand to her chest as if she had been attacked--and, indeed, she knew she had been.

"Are you threatening me? What if I told Lancelot?"

"You won't," he said with great certainty, "For then Lancelot would attack me and be killed in punishment if he succeeded."

Guinevere stifled a gasp. Of course that was true. "I can't tell him now, but I could leave a letter for him to read if I died." She turned and left the room.

Guinevere could not stop shaking. She returned to her room, and bade Fencha to close the door.

Guinevere fought back tears. "Oh Fencha, Enid told Arthur what we did for her years ago. He is in a rage, and says that you must leave Camelot forever. Immediately, before he sees your face. I had to agree."

Fencha cried out like a woman whose child had been torn from her. "Leave you? Oh, my lady!"

Guinevere extended her arms, and the old woman fell into them.

"I'm so sorry, Fencha. There's nothing I can do. Is there a place for you to go?"

"My youngest son has a farm about ten miles from here. He has a kind wife. I'm sure they'll take me in." Fencha choked on the words.

Guinevere's cat, which had been sleeping on a cushion, came up to them and rubbed against Fencha's ankles. The old woman bent over with difficulty and patted the cat.

"Good-bye, puss," she said.

"Fencha!" Guinevere could no longer hold back her tears at the sight of her serving woman's damp cheeks. "I shall miss you sorely."

"I'll miss you like I miss my daughter who died, if it isn't bad luck to say so," Fencha said, rubbing her eyes. "Oh, my lady, I fear that the king will be cruel to you."

Guinevere could not deny that, and did not try. "Whatever he does, I can endure it." She bit her lips. "Luned must be my chief serving woman now."

"I'll always love you, my lady," Fencha choked.

"And I shall always love you, Fencha," Guinevere said, putting into words what she had never said before.

Sobbing, the old woman left the room.

Guinevere collapsed in her chair.

She thought she could not tell Lancelot any of this. She would have to tell Lancelot that Fencha had gone because she wanted to be with her grandchildren and great-grandchildren.

Guinevere knew that she was the one woman whom Lancelot could not rescue without bringing the world crashing down around them. How could Lancelot bear to hear about the way Arthur had grabbed her wrists, much less how he had threatened her? Lancelot would . . . Lancelot would be dead.

Guinevere felt there was no way to protect herself, except that she would allow only Cuall the stablemaster to saddle her horse. He would never put it on in such a way that it would fall off.

Guinevere would have run away, but she could not. All she had to hold onto was Lancelot. Their love was all she had to live for. Oh, Talwyn too. But chiefly Lancelot. Talwyn would find her own life.

Guinevere entered Cai's office. Holding her body stiff and proud, she said, "Will you please order a locksmith you trust to change the lock on my door? And give me the only key. It must be done today, and in secret."

Cai's face froze. "It will be done," he said, asking no questions.

Later, he gave her the key, again without making any remark.

Fencha had had the only key but Guinevere's, yet Guinevere feared that Arthur had found a way to make a copy.

How could she face her husband at supper? Guinevere wondered. She went to the great hall as usual, of course, and prepared to sit with the women.

But Arthur called out, "No, my dear, sit near me. I don't see enough of you," flung his arms around her, and kissed her on the lips. He pulled her into the chair beside his and draped his arm over her. She could feel his hatred pouring into her, but she had to keep her face as calm as usual and try to eat her trout. So this was his revenge. At least Lancelot wasn't there.

A chill crept up the back of her neck as she realized that Arthur would likely act the same when Lancelot was present.

In the middle of the night, Guinevere's door rattled, as if someone was trying the lock but failed to open it. The attempt ended.

She shuddered, but she wagered with herself that Arthur would be too proud to speak about the changed lock.

Her luck, such as it was, held. He never mentioned it.

Arthur watched Guinevere enter his great hall. Truly, her beauty had faded. Why hadn't he noticed before? Even in the torchlight he could see that tiny lines had begun to form in her face, and a few gray hairs showed among the black. She was too short for a queen. Oh, she had bearing, all too much, in that straight back, that head held high. Those blue eyes hadn't looked so steady when he had uncovered her secret. He had seen fear in them; he would see it again.

Yes, she must sit by him because he gestured that she should. He would kiss her cheek, less fondly than the cheek of any whore.

She was his queen, his. Happen the only wife he would ever have, more's the pity. He could dash her down, he could trample over her, but he would not. Let her live with the knowledge that he could.

She was no idle flirt, no weak woman overcome by passion. No, her adultery was of the mind as well as the body. She did not love Lancelot: Oh no, such as she could not love. She loved her pride. She would be queen with one subject--her husband's friend.

He bade her sit on one side and Lancelot on the other. He gave Lancelot his warmest look. Poor fool drawn in by a woman's smile, poor trusting fool! Lancelot was too innocent, could not see that the woman lusted only for power.

Let Lancelot learn not to trust the woman.

Arthur pressed his arm around Guinevere, and left it there.

She could not object, she must eat her supper in this posture.

He smiled and jested with Lancelot, who shifted uneasily on the bench.

Lancelot lay awake in the middle of the night. Something was different in Guinevere. Guinevere was holding something back. No, it was just Lancelot's own foolish imagination. The woman who slept beside her loved her as much as ever. She must stop imagining things. At supper she had imagined that Arthur touched Guinevere more than usual. It was nothing but Lancelot's own absurd jealousy.

Guinevere stirred and Lancelot realized that she was awake also. Lancelot pressed her cheek to Guinevere's shoulder. "Is anything the matter, sweet?" she asked gently.

"No, nothing. Go to sleep," Guinevere mumbled.

Lancelot woke again and shifted from her stomach to her side.

Guinevere asked, "Are you awake?"

"Mmm," she mumbled.

Guinevere touched her arm. "I want you to teach me how to fight in case anyone ever attacks me."

Startled into full wakefulness, Lancelot sat up. "Surely no one would ever dare to try to harm you." She stared at Guinevere's dim shape.

"How do you know? Perhaps someday a man might. I need to know how to stop a man from hurting me without killing him. And also how to kill him if I have to."

Lancelot felt her blood run faster at the mere thought of Guinevere being hurt. "If any man hurt you, I would kill him, or Arthur would," she averred.

Guinevere turned away from her. "It seems that you want me to be weak so I must depend on you to protect me. Are you so much like a man?"

Lancelot apologized and agreed to teach her. Lancelot sighed audibly.

Lancelot had no great desire to try giving lessons to a pupil who seemed so unlikely to learn the skill well and was never going to need it. She didn't want to have to correct Guinevere when the queen made mistakes.

Seeing that swords were too heavy for the small Guinevere, Lancelot taught her how to use a dagger, and bought her a small one that she could keep concealed on her person if she chose.

"A small blade can be just as effective as a large one," she told Guinevere, who laughed sharply.

Lancelot also taught her how to kick, and where to place such kicks. And how to press at the temples in a way that might kill a man who could not be deterred otherwise.

At the end of a long meal, fruits and sweets sat on the round table. Guinevere took a bite of her honeycake. It was sweet enough, but not too sweet.

Gawaine reached for an apple.

Bors eyed the apples reproachfully, as if they could leap off the plate and induce him to sin. "Eve's weakness led us to misery and death," he said.

"What Eve wanted was power," Arthur said in a harsher tone than usual. "She deceived Adam."

"No, it must have been Adam who tempted Eve," Gawaine said, taking a bite. "She was a maiden and innocent."

"Adam was innocent, too," Bors insisted.

"Are men ever innocent?" Gawaine asked, letting the juice drip down his chin. Laughing, Lancelot reached past the apples and took a honeycake.

Guinevere thought that it must have been Eve who took the first bite, because she wanted knowledge and men think they already know everything. Only a few months ago, she might have spoken those words, but now she didn't dare.

"Adam was foolish to trust Eve," Arthur said. "Who can trust a woman who deceives her husband?"

Lancelot shifted in her seat.

Clearly Arthur was trying to sow the seeds of distrust.

Guinevere wanted to strike at him like a cornered animal. Never having had such a violent impulse before, she felt sick to her stomach.

Talwyn visited her father in his cell of a room, and walked with him to the ramparts so that he might have some air. His room was not so different from others in the caer, except that he was kept in it, which made it seem more dismal. His serving man, Huw, was always half a step away from them, lest Gryffyd's madness show itself. Gryffyd believed that all men were Saxons, save only Huw. Warriors and guards were warned in advance of his coming, so they might not cross his path.

Guinevere joined them, for Gryffyd admired her exceedingly and was fond of her because Talwyn's mother, who had died in childbed, also had been named Guinevere.

"Still a captive of the Saxons, my lady queen?" he asked sadly.

"Still a captive," she answered with a brave smile, and Talwyn suppressed a giggle at the improbable idea of the golden-torqued queen being a prisoner.

Talwyn spoke with her father about things that would not disturb him. It took some ingenuity to devise such mild subjects for conversation.

"The queen has given me a new mare, Da. She's a fine chestnut."

He scrutinized her and said, "Aren't you of an age to marry, daughter?"

Most of the girls her age were married or betrothed, but she said, "Not yet, Da." At least his madness prevented him from betrothing her. It was better to stay with Queen Guinevere.

Gryffd groaned. "I fear that you are. What can be done about it? You're living among Saxons. Be wary, child. Don't forget that all of the men around you are killers."

"Yes, Da." It occurred to her that, excluding the young warriors who had not yet fought anyone, the priests, and the serving men, he was right.

Gawaine lolled over his wine at the king's private table, the small one in his room. Arthur cleared his throat, preparing to speak, perhaps about some new mistress or Saxon War memories.

"You are, of course, my heir and successor."

Had the king truly spoken those words? Slightly dazed, Gawaine gawked at him. Arthur seldom mentioned the subject of his own death.

"We needn't tell the whole world, but you know that I once wrote it on vellum. I shall write it again with the date and seal it with my great seal." Arthur tapped the finger that bore that ring with his seal.

Truly, he had drunk too much, and perhaps Arthur had, too. There seemed to be no possible response to this statement. No thanks found their way to Gawaine's lips because he felt none. He tried not to belch.

"What about my brother Gareth? He might be a good choice."

"Nonsense. Gareth is all very well as a warrior, but he will never have the strength of mind needed for kingship."

Gawaine sighed. "That may be true. I wish there was someone other than me. I hope you live long."

"You will keep that woman from ever being on the throne, do you hear?" Arthur seemed to be talking to himself, and Gawaine was to play the audience.

"What woman?" he muttered stupidly, wondering whether Arthur imagined that his mother, Queen Morgause, would sweep down from Lothian with a horde of northerners and seize the whole of Britain.

"My wife, of course!"

Arthur's voice held a note of contempt for Gawaine's greater state of drunkenness.

Gawaine flinched just slightly. True, he was too old to get drunk, if he wanted to keep in fighting shape. "Oh, her. Well, no doubt she'd like to rule. Why not?"

"Never," Arthur proclaimed decidedly. "It must be you."

"If you say so. But I'll likely die before you, don't you know?"

Arthur sighed. "What a pity that I cannot be king forever. That would be best for the people."

Gawaine nearly fell out of his chair. King forever? He was not too drunk to know that such an ambition bordered on madness. All he could do was leave. "Gods, it's late," he said. "Time to be abed. Hope I can wake Ragnal." Lately Ragnal had been so tired and slept so deeply that he had not had the heart to wake her.

"You may take your leave," Arthur consented.

Gawaine almost stumbled out of the room.

Bedwyr saw Talwyn carrying a large book with sewn leather binding to the queen's room, and called her aside.

"Such a weighty tome for a maid. I hope that the queen's teaching is not worrying you with thoughts too solemn," he said in a kindly voice. She would make a fine daughter-in-law. Pity about her father.

Talwyn smiled. "Oh, no, my lord Bedwyr. She does not tax me with any thoughts that are too solemn for me."

He smiled to show his benevolence. "Very good. I have a far more pleasant message for you. The king and I have discussed the possibility of your marrying my son. What say you?"

He was rewarded with a broader smile. Talwyn's face softened and she breathed, "Marry, marry, baby, happy."

Bedwyr stiffened. "What did you say, child?"

Talwyn began to chant. "Marry, marry, baby, happy." Her face was sweeter than honey. "Marry, marry, baby, happy," she sang again and again, nodding her head. She went on and on with the refrain.

The warrior froze. "Stop this, child. Stop it," he commanded. "Nothing is settled," he told her and hurried away.

The poor girl was addled like her father. Thank Mithras he had found out in time.

Bors pulled Talwyn aside outside the chapel after a Mass. A proper time for such a solemn occasion.

"I have thought of marrying you to my eldest son, dear child," he said. "I suppose that you would be a good Christian wife?"

Talwyn beamed. "Surely, my lord Bors. I pray to the three Christs."

He jerked back as if struck. "No, child, there is only one Christ," he admonished.

She still smiled and nodded. "Three Christs, three crosses."

"No, no, Christ was hung between two thieves. It is the Trinity that is triune. Of course that mystery is too difficult for a girl to understand." Why must the queen daze the poor girl with so much reading? It boded ill.

"Three gods," she nodded.

Despite this stunning lapse in theology, she might be a good girl, he told himself.

"Just listen to your elders and repeat exactly what they say," he cautioned her. "Exactly. For Eve was tempted to believe that she could eat the fruit of the tree of knowledge, and she was rebuked. Pray to the Holy Virgin Mary."

"Eve is Mary, Mary is Eve," said Talwyn in the most innocent of tones. His gasps did not stop her from repeating it.

Bors made the sign of the cross. She was mad like her father after all.

Mordred unhorsed the other young warriors with such force that they could hardly fight when he came to batter them on the ground. Seeing that the king was watching the practice, he fought harder than ever. He could tell that Arthur's gaze lingered on him.

"Well done, Mordred, you'll be a fine warrior." The king condescended to walk over and give him this encouragement after the practice. "The Saxons don't ride to war, of course. They fight on foot."

"Perhaps you might want the treaty Saxons to be tied closer to you, sire." Mordred used this word whenever possible. "They'll be better allies against invaders that way. They have no wish to yield their hard-won land to others newly come. I speak passable Saxon. Perhaps I could be of use to you in dealing with them."

Arthur regarded him with more interest. "Saxon? Can you really? Say something."

Mordred began to discourse on the art of war in the Saxon speech.

Arthur nodded, apparently understanding at least enough to realize that Mordred knew the language. "Very good. How did you learn to speak it?"

"I have done some trading with them, sire." He neglected to say that what he had traded was women. The Saxons seemed to find the black-haired British women as exotic as some Britons found the yellow-haired Saxon women.

The king hemmed and hawed. "I will send you to spend six months of every year with them. You will report to me everything you learn about them." He patted Mordred's shoulder.

Some bird sang. Mordred didn't know or care what it was.

Mordred smiled faintly, saying, "Never fear, I'll tell you everything. Thank you for entrusting me with this mission, sire."

Arthur sighed. "Their language is ugly and difficult. They have no beautiful music like ours and their culture will never be so fine. But we must try to civilize them, for we shall have to live with them in this land."

Mordred continued to smile. He cared nothing about this culture of which his father was so proud, the culture that assigned him to humiliation every day of his life. The Saxons would mark how much he resembled the king, and they would treat him well, no doubt. And Arthur would be glad to have him out of sight.

Mordred couldn't quite admit that he hoped to make his father proud of him.

And of course practice at dealing with the Saxons would help him when he became High King.

"I have just one other request, sire." Mordred felt his heart beat faster than it ever had. "Would you cut my hair publicly?"

The king sucked in his breath. "How could you ask such a thing of me? That is never done. You are a brave young man. Be content with what I have already given you." He turned away.

Even though Mordred had expected this blow, it shook him. Of course Arthur would never cut his hair, because that would mean acknowledging him as a son. He had been a fool to ask. He must never be so soft-hearted again. He must never let himself be rejected again.

Guinevere noticed that a serving woman who passed her in the courtyard looked ill. Her face had become thin and haggard. "Ragnal," she said to the gray-haired woman, "you must see a physician."

"Yes, my lady," said Ragnal, flinching.

"Today," Guinevere told her, and sent for Cassius, the king's physician, though it was not usual for him to see servants.

Guinevere demanded that he report to her afterwards, so he came to her room.

"What is the matter with Ragnal?" Guinevere asked in a commanding voice.

"She's dying," the short but dignified physician said simply. "Some wasting sickness."

"Is there nothing that you can do?" she demanded. Death had always seemed an enemy to Guinevere. Tales of heaven had never moved her. They might if they had come from someone who had actually been there.

He shook his balding head.

"Does she know that she is going to die?" Sunlight poured in the window as if death were impossible.

"I think she does, Lady Guinevere."

"You think?" Her voice rose. "You didn't tell her?"

"Not in so many words, my lady."

"I shall tell her, then. Thank you," said Guinevere, dismissing him with a gesture. What cowards men were. Only women could bear the truth.

She sighed because Fencha was no longer with her. Fencha had been such a fine healer. The old woman had tried to teach some of her skill to Luned.

Guinevere asked Luned whether she knew of any way to save the woman, and Luned said that she did not, but could abate the pain. Guinevere asked her to bring Ragnal to her.

Guinevere did not know Ragnal well, for she seldom served the queen. However, she thought Ragnal seemed rather pleasant, with a nice although not extremely pretty face and a perhaps excessively loud laugh.

The woman came into Guinevere's room and curtseyed to her.

"Never mind that," Guinevere said. Queen or serving woman, they all faced the same fate eventually, if not in life. "You are seriously ill and should not have to worry about pleasing anyone. You are relieved of all your duties." She had no idea what Ragnal's duties were, but Cai would have to do what the queen decreed.

"I am dying, then," Ragnal said in a voice that strove for resignation. Moved by her dignity, Guinevere tried to make her voice gentle. "Yes, I am so sorry to tell you, it seems that you are. Luned says that she can do nothing but ease the pain. I wish she could do more. Do you want to go visit your family?"

Ragnal drew back. "Oh no, I want to stay here."

Guinevere was a little surprised at this rejection of her magnanimity. Perhaps Ragnal had nowhere else to go. "Of course you can if that is what you want. Do you want to stay in a room near mine, so I can see how you are doing?"

"No thank you, Lady Guinevere."

Ragnal's reluctance seemed strange to her, so Guinevere spoke with Luned. "Don't you think we should put her in a little room near mine, so you could look after her better? Surely she is too ill for me to worry about her gossiping about my locked door."

Luned shook her head.

"No, my dear lady. A great warrior visits Ragnal regularly, and she doesn't want to do anything to disturb that. She lives in a small house that he gave her."

Guinevere raised her eyebrows. "A warrior visits a gray-haired serving woman? I never heard of such a thing. I thought they were interested only in the young ones." She had never bothered to notice which warrior liked which serving woman, except to rescue girls like Creirwy who did not want to be touched.

Luned shrugged. "Lady Guinevere, Ragnal has loved the same warrior for many years. All she wants is to see him while she can."

"But will he still see her when she is sick?" Guinevere asked, shaking her head as if that were unbelievable.

"She wants to be left alone so that he will at least have the chance to do so," Luned insisted.

"I shall do as Ragnal wishes," Guinevere said.

"Lady Guinevere?" Luned almost whispered.

"Yes?"

"I, too, am fond of a man. Cathbad, one of the stablehands."

"Yes, I know who he is. Is he kind to you?" Guinevere searched her face.

Luned blushed. "He is."

"Do you want to marry him?"

"I think so. I am not yet certain." A smile strayed across Luned's face. "If I do, can I stay in your service and spend fewer nights by your room?"

"Of course you may. I am glad if he is kind to you." Guinevere smiled at her.

When Luned left the room, Guinevere pondered how many years it had been since Luned had served her. Luned's father had treated her shamefully, and she had fled to Guinevere. Luned had shown no interest in men. If there was finally a man who was gentle to Luned, that might be a good thing. Guinevere hoped for Luned's happiness. Creirwy could be near her when Luned could not, and Creirwy showed no signs of wanting to be with a man instead.

Guinevere did as Ragnal wanted. Luned showed her where Ragnal's small mud-daub house was in the town, and Guinevere visited her there once or twice.

One morning she decided to start her day by visiting Ragnal. When she went to Ragnal's house, she saw Gawaine leaving, his face pale and his eyes red.

Never having seen him sorrowful, Guinevere was jolted. She stopped and looked at him.

"I think she has only a few days more," he said in a broken voice.

"Yes, I'm afraid that's true," Guinevere replied, patting him on the shoulder.

She could scarcely have been more astonished. Ragnal was perhaps a few years older than Gawaine, or at least she looked older, which was not so unusual in a serving woman.

Back in her room, she demanded of Luned, "Is Gawaine so fond of Ragnal?"

"Can't you see it, my lady?" Luned asked.

"Yes," she said reluctantly.

She thought that Lancelot might believe it to be a touching romance, but Guinevere herself could imagine not so pretty reasons why a man might want a mistress whose rank was so much lower than his. However, she could not deny the grief on his face, so she was gentle with him when she saw him over the next few days. On the night that Ragnal died, Guinevere saw Gawaine weeping, so she patted his shoulder again and said that death was always very hard.

"Other men did not think Ragnal beautiful, but she was beautiful to me," he choked.

Guinevere held back the retort that he certainly ought to think so after the woman had given him years of devotion.

Lancelot had been away on a mission for the king. She had ridden for many hours, and was resting in Guinevere's room. Luned brought her pears and watered wine, and Guinevere fondly watched her eat the fruit.

"Has anything happened while I was gone?" Lancelot asked Luned. She would ask Guinevere a little later, more privately. "How are you?"

"I am well, thank you, my lord," Luned said, as always. She was not one to complain. "Not much has changed in the world of the serving people, except that Ragnal has died."

Lancelot dropped her pear. "That's terrible! Poor Ragnal! Poor Gawaine!" she exclaimed.

"You knew about that? I suppose he talks about everything with you," said Guinevere with little pleasure.

Luned slipped away.

"It's hard to keep such things secret in a place like Camelot-- unfortunately, I have often thought," Lancelot said, sighing. "I think he was embarrassed to care about her."

"How dare he be ashamed of her birth! What kind of life did she have?" Guinevere demanded, frowning. "How terrible to be a mistress, loving but unacknowledged, visited only after dark."

Lancelot looked out of the window at the night and could keep silent no longer. She spoke sharply. "Yes, it is. Will you come away with me?"

Guinevere gasped and her face reddened with anger.

"How dare you compare me to that man. He could have married any woman . . ."

"King's sons do not marry serving women, except in tales," Lancelot objected.

"But he can do almost anything he wants, whereas I . . ."

"Could run away," Lancelot said gravely. For the first time she dared to say the words that she had scarcely allowed herself to dream.

"How can you speak to me so harshly? Don't you love me?" Guinevere demanded.

"That's why I speak so. And I'm tired of hearing you criticize a man who has so often faced danger. You have no idea what that's like. You've never known anything but safety and comfort." Lancelot turned away and looked out at the dark again. A few torches gleamed in the courtyard. She had never before thought that Guinevere would leave with her, but she was not pleased to have her fears confirmed. Did Guinevere truly love her as much as she loved Guinevere? She fought back tears.

"But why talk about going now? I can't leave Talwyn until she is married to a good husband."

Guinevere's voice was pitched high.

"There will always be a reason not to go. Then someday, one of us will die, and the other will sigh because it's too late." Lancelot stared at the night sky where only a sliver of a moon was visible. It had been too much to hope that Guinevere would leave with her.

Guinevere put an arm on her shoulder. "It won't be like that. Arthur will die before either of us does."

"Is that my hope?" Lancelot exclaimed, flung off her arm, and ran out of the secret passage and down the stairs. She did not say that she faced many times the dangers Arthur did, or that if she saw him threatened she was sworn and honor bound to give her life to protect his.

But when she had gone to her own small house, she wondered whether she was being too hard on Guinevere. Perhaps Guinevere realized that Lancelot was the one who was likely to die first, and how would it be for her alone in an unfamiliar country like Lesser Britain? Perhaps Guinevere would be better off staying with Arthur, Lancelot told herself. But did Guinevere care more about being a queen than about being with her? She buried her head in her pillow.

Guinevere put her arms on the table and let her head lie on them. Lancelot did not understand, could not understand. It was impossible to leave Arthur. He would not simply let them go. The king's men would pursue them--far too many men for Lancelot to fight.

How Guinevere now hated the sight of her husband's face! But she could never tell Lancelot the reason why. The wife dreaded the husband because the husband hated the wife.

Lancelot did not understand what it was not to be free.

Guinevere looked with loathing at the gold ring on her finger. And Lancelot believed that there were no dangers in a queen's life. Guinevere prayed that Lancelot would never know the truth.

The next morning on her way through the mist to the stables, Lancelot saw a figure, bent over but clearly tall, sitting on the fence by the pasture.

"Gawaine," she said. The face that turned to her looked older than it had a month or so before, so she added, "I'm sorry."

He began to weep, not putting up a hand to cover the tears. Never having seen him do such a thing before, she was astonished.

"I didn't treat her well enough." His voice sounded hollow. "I was afraid that men would think I was foolish to love a serving woman. But I was the fool to care what they thought."

It was undeniable that Gawaine had not treated Ragnal well enough for one he loved, though no other man she knew would have treated a serving woman better. Lancelot patted him on the back and said, in her most manly voice, "There, there, old man. At least she knew that she was the one you always returned to. And she died while you were at Camelot, so you could say farewell. That's little enough, but some don't even have that."

Gawaine sighed deeply.

Lancelot gestured towards the stable. "Why don't you go for a ride in the forest? That always helps me."

He shook his head. "I have to teach the boys some riding maneuvers this morning."

"I'll take your class. I may need to ask you to take my classes for some days soon. Tristram is running away with King Mark's wife, Iseult, and I'm helping them."

"You're the patron saint of adulterers, aren't you?" Gawaine shook his head. "Thanks for taking my class. Of course I'll teach yours anytime." He paused. "As you know, both my wives died in childbed when I was young. I often thought, what was the good of loving women, only to see them die in childbed? Perhaps I liked it that Ragnal was beyond the age for that. But death has claimed her nonetheless." He sighed, and lumbered off to get his horse.

Lancelot vowed again to find a way to persuade Guinevere to leave. If Iseult could run away, why couldn't Guinevere? Life was too short not to be together. If by some strange chance Guinevere died first, it would be unbearable, knowing that they hadn't made every effort to have some years alone together.

When Lancelot was changing her clothes--her serving man was blind, so he could be present--Catwal said to her, "Ragnal gave me a message for you."

"A message for me?" Lancelot was surprised, for she hadn't known Ragnal well.

"Yes." Catwal handed Lancelot her green tunic. How good he was at recognizing clothes by their feel. "She wanted me to tell you that she had exaggerated Gawaine's faults, that he was good to her."

"Why would she want to tell me that?" Lancelot paused before putting on the new tunic.

Catwal shrugged.

That was how people were when they were dying, Lancelot thought. No doubt they felt guilty about even the slightest things. Surely if Lancelot were dying, she would regret any critical thoughts she ever had about Guinevere, though she never expressed them to anyone else. And if Guinevere died first . . . no, that couldn't happen. It was too horrible to contemplate.

Rubbing her face with a towel, Lancelot looked up and saw a man--scarcely more than a boy, about sixteen years of age--she had killed in the war. Blood still poured from his side.

Lancelot groaned and looked away. When she turned back, the specter was no longer there.

Was she mad? How dare she urge Guinevere to go away with her? Tears streamed down Lancelot's cheeks, but she dried them. She must pretend that nothing was wrong, and perhaps the strange visions would go away.

12 TRISTAM AND ISEULT

Guinevere finished her breakfast of wheaten bread and marched off to the stables. It was the first sunny day after a week of rain and she was determined to go riding, although Lancelot had said that she could not accompany her. Lancelot might have to leave at any moment to help Tristram, who was fleeing with Iseult, wife of King Mark of Dumnonia. Tristram had sent word that they would be passing through the forest near Camelot and would need Lancelot's aid.

Arthur required Guinevere to have an escort, so she asked Bors, who had always admired her and imagined that she was more pious than she truly was. Bors had led the escort that had brought her from her father's land to Camelot, and had been impressed that she wanted to spend a night on the journey at a convent. He of course did not know that during that night Guinevere had made love with her childhood friend, Valeria, who had been fostered at her father Leodegran's caer before an uncle sent her off to the convent of the Holy Mother. That night had been a hidden treasure that Guinevere had mulled over until she met and loved Lancelot.

When Guinevere arrived at the stables, half a dozen warriors, including Agravaine, the one she liked least, were mounted and prepared to ride with her.

"The king said that he wanted you to have a proper escort in case of danger," Agravaine explained, gloating as if he knew that he was intruding and it pleased him.

Her husband would let her ride, but he would make it as unpleasant as possible for her. Well, she would not turn back to her room.

Riding through the forest, Guinevere tried to listen to it as Lancelot did, hearing every woodpecker's tap and thrush's song. The bluebells were just beginning to open their blossoms, but they were not as fair as they would have been if Lancelot had been with her. She ignored the warriors' noisy talk.

A man hailed the queen's party.

Tristram, his tall frame thin and grimy, was riding with a woman veiled in green.

The men hailed Tristram, whom they had not seen in many a day. Guinevere merely nodded, for she was not overly fond of him.

Making none of the customary salutations to the queen, Tristram called out, "Brother warriors of King Arthur, I am in dire straits. Tell no one that you have seen me."

Most of them readily agreed that they would not, but Bors challenged him. "Who is this lady, then? Are you wronging her, or her family?" Like everyone else, Bors must have heard the tales that Tristram had a sinful love for King Mark's wife. Guinevere was grateful that Bors seemed to believe that Lancelot's obvious love for her was pure and hopeless.

Tristram glowered.

"Let me speak with the lady," Guinevere said, moving her horse towards theirs. "Are you well, my dear?" She guessed who wore the once fine gown now stained and torn so one could scarcely tell what its original color had been. "I am Guinevere."

The lady rode to her at once and lifted the green veil. "Do you understand, then?" she asked in a thin, reedy voice that only Guinevere could hear. "I am Iseult. I could bear it no longer. I felt as if Mark raped me. Can a husband rape his wife, or am I mad?"

Guinevere softened her voice. "You are not mad."

Iseult sighed. "I knew what it was to be touched with love by Tristram, and Mark was nothing like that. I thought you were the only woman who might understand me. We have hidden in forests and in caves, but still they follow us. But it's worth it, it's worth it."

Guinevere was much moved, although she guessed that their journey would end in grief. She asked, "Where are you going?"

"Don't you know? We go to meet Lancelot of the Lake, who is helping us. We are going to a caer in Lothian because we have heard that Queen Morgause would let us live there unmolested."

"It is just what he would do." Guinevere smiled. "I can do no less. Here, change veils with me. That might delay your pursuers." She removed her own white veil trimmed with a scarlet ribbon, showing the still black braids underneath.

"How kind you are!" Iseult exclaimed, doffing her own veil and receiving Guinevere's.

"What are you doing, sweeting? We must make haste," Tristram fretted, speaking in a tone gentler than he had used at Camelot.

Contrary to gossip, Iseult was not a beautiful woman, but had ordinary brown hair and a face covered with freckles. Her green eyes were those of a small, frightened creature. Guinevere thought the better of Tristram therefore. Most men would not have risked their lives for a woman like Iseult, but Tristram looked at her as if she were the most beautiful woman in the world.

"A thousand thanks. You know what it is to be a lover," Iseult said, and Guinevere pressed her hand.

"I do," she whispered. "Take care, and my prayers go with you."

When they rode off, the warriors wished Tristram Godspeed, but Bors did not join in.

"Lady Guinevere, you should not have taken that sinful woman's veil," he exclaimed.

"It becomes her well," Agravaine said in a voice that was just audible.

As the afternoon light began to dim, they heard a great clamor. Suddenly, a number of warriors with shields and helmets in the style of Dumnonia crashed through the trees.

They saw Guinevere in Iseult's green veil, and attacked.

"There's King Mark's wife! Seize her!"

Of course the warriors from Camelot fought back to defend Guinevere.

"Cease this, fools!" Guinevere yelled, but her voice was lost in the din.

Almost before she knew it, there were injuries on both sides. As she saw a Dumnonian sword cut through Bors's shoulder, Guinevere drove her horse towards the Dumnonian warriors.

"End this foolery! I am Guinevere!" she cried out, pulling the veil from her head. The warriors from Camelot put up their swords and moved their horses protectively around her. The men from Dumnonia saw that she was not Iseult, and the skirmish ended.

"Have you seen our Queen Iseult with Tristram?" demanded a Dumnonian warrior.

"Indeed, we saw them on their way to the coast, where they said they would board a ship for Lesser Britain," Guinevere told him.

None of the men from Camelot contradicted her, and the Dumnonian warriors turned west with much grumbling.

All of the small party of warriors from Camelot bled, although only Bors had a serious wound. Grimacing, he seemed barely able to sit on his horse.

"Forgive me for endangering you," Guinevere said to the grumbling men, and indeed she was sorry about their wounds. "Let us stay in the first shelter we come to, so you can rest. I fear that Bors is not sound enough to travel back to Camelot by nightfall."

They had passed by an abandoned holding not long before, so they returned and quartered there for the night. Guinevere thanked each man and surveyed the state of their injuries.

Lancelot waited at a certain clearing in the forest, as she had at the appointed time every day for several days. The surrounding oaks and beeches were so thick that little sunlight permitted flowers to sprout up among them, but new bluebells grew in the clearing. She was about to leave when she heard horses, and the riders came into view. It was Tristram with a lady wearing Guinevere's scarlet-trimmed veil.

"What are you doing with Lady Guinevere's veil?" Lancelot called out, startled.

"What way is that to greet my lady?" exclaimed Tristram, quick to anger as usual.

Iseult parted the veil. "Are you Lancelot of the Lake? I am Iseult. The kind queen exchanged veils with me, but I fear that it may endanger her. Mark's men still pursue us."

Lancelot was moved by Iseult's sweet, frightened face, but even more by the thought of Guinevere in danger. She had imagined that Tristram would be able to evade Mark's men much sooner.

"Bah, his men are nothing. Mark does not even bother to come himself," snorted Tristram with contempt. "But if they find us on the way north, you and I can easily fight them off, Lancelot."

"How can I travel with you if Queen Guinevere might be in danger? I must go and make sure that she is safe." It had taken no time at all for Lancelot to decide to look for Guinevere instead of traveling with them. "I shall tell all the world that I have given you my protection, and claim that the caer in Lothian where you will stay belongs to me. That is all I can do. You will also be under the protection of Queen Morgause, who is no friend to cruel husbands. Her son Gawaine assures me that she will never let Mark's men fight in Lothian."

Tristram howled like a wounded animal. "You told me that you'd travel with us. False friend! Don't pretend that you care about Guinevere, when you let her stay with her husband. What kind of a man are you? If you loved her at all, you'd run away as we have."

Shaking with anger, Lancelot tried to control her rage. She could not fight this man, who was all that Iseult had. Nor could she tell Tristram that Arthur did not lie with Guinevere, for that, like all else about their love, was secret.

"Tristram!" cried Iseult in a pained voice. "Why must you attack all those who help us? First you insulted Dinadan, now

Lancelot and Guinevere. Forgive him, Lord Lancelot. He just worries about me."

Tristram put his hand on his sword, as if he might draw it to keep Lancelot from leaving them. "And well I should. Do you have any idea what it is to have to hide the woman you love in clammy caves and feed her on what game you can snare? You know nothing of love, Lancelot. And as for that filthy Dinadan! You must not think of that sodomite, sweeting."

"It is those who know what it is to hide love who help you," Lancelot told him. "Forget this foolish quarrel, and go north with the lady. I wish you Godspeed, but I must find Guinevere."

"Pray, do. I wish you Godspeed as well, and many thanks," said Iseult, inclining her head.

Lancelot rode off, realizing that Tristram was one of those men who fought the whole world and let himself be close to only one woman, and that was why he so prized Iseult.

Lancelot worried herself into a frenzy, and by evening, when she found an abandoned building with horses from Camelot, including Guinevere's, tethered outside it, she thought that Guinevere and some of her brother warriors must be held prisoner within.

"Who holds Queen Guinevere in this place? Release her, or forfeit your life!" she yelled in fierce challenge.

Guinevere walked through the door frame, which lacked a door. "Be calm, Lancelot, I am free and well, but some of our men been injured by Dumnonian warriors. Bors's shoulder is sorely hurt. I thought it better that they rest here until morning."

"This is no fit shelter for you," Lancelot grumbled, but she tethered her horse near the others and went in to hear the tale and inspect the men's wounds.

She agreed that they had to stay the night, although she gasped at the state of the second floor room where Guinevere intended to sleep on an ancient bed. Lancelot shook out the rotten coverings, only to see them fall apart in her hands as dead insects and mouse droppings fell out of them.

"You must take my cloak as a covering, Lady Guinevere," she demanded, whipping off her crimson cloak and spreading it on the rotting boards.

"If you insist, Lancelot. But I shall manage quite well," Guinevere said publicly and formally.

The only problem was that Lancelot and Guinevere could not easily be together because the wounded warriors were lying in the hall outside the door of Guinevere's room.

Lancelot was determined to be with Guinevere and hold her, so when it was dark, she climbed up the outside wall, digging her hands and feet into the crevices between the stones. She pulled herself in through the window, and Guinevere embraced her. They made love as quietly as possible.

Before dawn, Lancelot climbed down again, which was more difficult than climbing up. When she went to relieve herself, she discovered that, perhaps because of her worry about Guinevere, her blood had flowed sooner than usual. She got a rag from her saddlebag.

Early in the morning, Guinevere left the room where she had stayed and greeted the warriors, who moved slowly and stiffly. She saw that they all stared at her with strange expressions on their faces.

Young Clegis spoke up. "The queen's face is covered with blood."

Agravaine said, "One of the wounded men must have been with her last night."

"How dare you say so?" Guinevere's voice was indignant and majestic, though her hands had darted to her cheeks. She could guess what must have happened.

"That's a terrible insult to the queen, and impossible as well," Bors exclaimed, clenching his fists as if he might strike Agravaine. "I was so uncomfortable that I laid awake all night, and I saw that no one went in the door." He advanced on Agravaine, but his steps were unsteady and he clutched his wounded shoulder.

"She must have let in one of the wounded men, and you dozed off and didn't see it," said Clegis, who often was seen in Mordred's company.

Guinevere glared at Agravaine and Clegis.

Lancelot entered the hall. Her face turned pale at the sight of Guinevere's.

"It must have been Lancelot," Agravaine charged, turning his gaze from Guinevere to Lancelot. "He must have climbed in through the window to see the queen and cut himself on the way."

"How dare you insult the queen!" Lancelot raged, putting her hand on the hilt of her sword. "I have no cuts, as anyone can see."

"There must be a cut on one of your hands. Show them to us," Agravaine demanded.

"There is no such cut," Lancelot insisted, displaying her hands. "You must not insult the queen any more, or you will have to fight me."

"These insults to the queen are vile," Bors complained, giving Agravaine a look of contempt. "There must be some other explanation. Perhaps something supernatural that we cannot grasp has taken place."

"You are all very cruel," Guinevere chided them, making her voice sound pathetic and covering her eyes with her hands. "This is not men's blood, but women's blood. I was overcome by it last night, and in such pain that I wept. I must have put my hands to my face, not realizing that they were covered with it."

She uncovered her eyes and saw that most of the warriors were red-faced with embarrassment.

"It is a great shame that we have treated the queen so. Forgive us, your highness," exclaimed Bors in a horrified voice. "We must not tell the king about this terrible insult."

Lancelot brought Guinevere a flask of water and a cloth to use as a towel.

"Leave the queen in peace," she told the warriors, and they did.

That night, when they were together back at Camelot, Lancelot apologized profusely, but Guinevere only laughed.

Guinevere left the chapel after a Sunday Mass. Her husband's arm was properly linked with hers. They smiled and nodded at those they passed. Bells pealed, but all Guinevere could think of was the unwelcome arm that imprisoned hers.

"You've heard of course that Tristram and Iseult are living at a caer that belongs to Lancelot," Arthur said in an ordinary conversational tone.

Guinevere made no reply.

"It's well that Mark has no large warband. I've heard about the position of that caer and it would be easy to besiege," he told her, "although not so easy as the old villa that belongs to Lance in Lesser Britain. Ah, Bors, that was an admirable service, wasn't it?" he called out.

Guinevere managed not to flinch at his boast that he could easily take any caer or villa of Lancelot's. She knew well enough that she could not run without risking Lancelot's life. Indeed, there was no chance that they could escape from the High King's huge warband.

13 THE DARKENING CLOUDS

Merlin rarely came to supper at the round table. He walked by the kitchen and demanded food at odd hours, or forgot it altogether. If he sat at the table, he rose and wandered off when the conversation bored him, as it generally did. What did he care about which warrior had bested the other? At this late point in his life, he wanted only to think about the gods and the world that they had made.

One evening at the table when the warriors were discussing which horses were the best mounts in jousting, Merlin rose and grabbed Arthur by the arm. "I'm getting old," he said.

Arthur did not look alarmed. He merely smiled. "Never too old. You have many years yet, I am sure."

"When I am gone, Ninian is the only one who can foresee the future for you," Merlin warned, loud enough for those who sat near the king to hear. Sighing, Merlin looked around the table. "I can no longer bear to be with all of you. I see too much. I grieve too much for you." He put his hand briefly on Lancelot's shoulder, and Lancelot shuddered.

Merlin left the hall. Later, he recalled that Arthur had not asked who Ninian was, and he had failed to tell him.

Nimue still studied with Merlin every day, sometimes walking or riding in the forest with him, for he said that it was better to learn of sacred things in the world that is sacred, which is to say, not man-made.

One spring day when they were sitting by a pond, watching a dabchick run across the surface of the water chasing another dabchick, no doubt in some nuptial dance, Nimue sighed.

"Am I boring you?" Merlin asked, suddenly retreating in the belief that that must be so.

"No, never. I could spend my whole life with you," Nimue averred.

"You'll go off and marry," he told her. Merlin had not realized that he was lonely until he had met her, and he knew that he would be twice as lonely when she went away. Her face, with its small, upturned nose and little mouth, often appeared in his dreams.

Tears formed in her gray eyes and she stared down at the mossy bank. "No, I won't. Don't you see that I love you?"

Merlin stared at her as if seeing her for the first time. She looked fairer than ever. How could a young girl imagine herself in love with him? "Nonsense, I am far too old to think of such things. You'll marry some young man."

"Some fool who spends all his time fighting other men or practicing fighting? No, I won't." Nimue shook her head defiantly. "I don't care whether you are old."

"I tell you, I am much too old to think of things of love." His voice cracked. Apparently she was too innocent to understand what he meant, but he could not bear to explain any further.

She looked into his eyes. "I don't care. We can just be together as we are now."

Merlin merely sighed. If only he could match this love.

"You don't say whether you love me, too. I think that means you do," Nimue said, apparently trying to coax an admission out of him.

"It's not right for me to promise what I can't give," he told her. His heart felt heavier than it had since he had learned that the people of the old faith had left Avalon.

A blackbird sang, but its notes sounded melancholy to him.

If only he could fade away, and return as a young man to love Nimue properly. He had served the gods all his life. Would they give him this last, greatest gift? Merlin closed his eyes in prayer.

Merlin took Nimue on a ride farther into the forest than she had ever been and showed her a hollow oak tree. "See, this tree was split by lightning, but yet it still lives."

Nimue looked at it with considerable interest. Green woodpeckers had made a few holes in its surface, but not many. An owl's nest sat high in its branches and small pellets cast by the owls were lying on the ground surrounding it. "Is it a particularly sacred tree?" She knew, of course, that oak groves were sacred places.

He took her hand gently. "This one is important to me. Here I shall rest, and I shall never waken. Merlin will never see you again, because it is time for me to go."

"No! Not yet!" she cried, throwing her arms around his neck. "You could live for years."

Merlin pulled away from her. "No, it is my time. Do not try to stop me. Just return to the caer and tell the king that I have done all I could for him. Now I need to rest."

She wept, but he would not change his mind.

Finally, after many protests, Nimue agreed to leave.

When she returned to Camelot and told her tale, the king stared at her in dismay. He sent his warriors out to search for the old man, but, look as they might, they could not find him, or even his body.

Nimue heard people whisper that she had killed Merlin. She shrank from them.

However, she did hear Guinevere tell her ladies, "Nonsense, why should Nimue kill old Merlin? Men have no great reason to fear women, so they devise strange tales about us. People claim that she killed him to steal his magic, but he had no magic, save that people believed in him. People believe that a man who is said to have magic is good, but a woman who might is evil."

Nimue returned to the oak in the hope that she might find Merlin's body. But the ground by the tree was empty, and she thought that he had decided to go off and die somewhere else after all.

Tears dripped down her cheeks, and they built up to a noisy wail. As she was keening, she heard movements in the bushes, and started up, alarmed.

A young man parted the bushes and appeared beside her. He was short, as short as Merlin had been, with darkish skin, black hair, and gray eyes, and she thought he might be one of the Old Ones. He wore a plain homespun tunic and breeches.

"Don't weep," he said in a gentle, somewhat faltering voice. "Why are you weeping?"

"My teacher is dead," Nimue sobbed.

"That is sad," he agreed, "but be glad that you had a teacher. Not everyone does."

"Who are you?" she asked, her tears slowing.

He paused. "My name is Taliesin," he said, turning the word in his mouth as if it were a question rather than an answer. "And yours?"

"I'm Nimue."

"Ah." He nodded and looked as though he was trying to remember something. He reached out as if to touch her.

Nimue quickly drew out a knife that she kept in her kirtle and pointed it at him. "Stay back."

Taliesin shrieked. "Don't hurt me," he cried, shaking.

Nimue put the knife back in her kirtle. "Are you one of the Old Ones?" she asked. "I have heard that they fear iron."

Taliesin dried his tears and tried to regain his composure. When he finally spoke, his voice was sad. "Old, young? I don't know. I don't remember anything. I know only my name. All I have are questions. If you had a teacher, can you teach me?"

"I can try," Nimue told him. She was no longer afraid, and neither did he seem to be. Nimue stayed in a hut in the forest with him.

One evening when Gawaine sat in the king's room, sharing wine, Arthur ventured, "Surely you must think about having sons."

Gawaine almost jumped in his chair. This was not a subject that men generally spoke of with Arthur, who had always grieved about having no son. He mumbled a slight acknowledgment and drank some more. "Excellent wine." He stared at the fire in the brazier as if he could see sons sprouting from the flames. His own fires had blazed, but had left him all too short of progeny.

"Why don't you marry? You're getting on in years."

This comment about his aging gave Gawaine an excuse to grumble. "Kind of you to say so. I'm still able to bed women, thank you."

"At forty? I don't doubt that." The king chuckled and his voice became conspiratorial. "Nor do I doubt that you have bastards. But you should have some children born in wedlock as well. After all, they might be kings. What do you think of my fosterling, Talwyn? A pretty girl with a pleasant laugh, isn't she?"

Gawaine choked on his wine. "What, little Talwyn? Yes, she has a pleasant laugh . . ." His voice trailed off.

"You've always liked women who laugh a great deal."

"I do, but I had no thought of marrying her." Gawaine squirmed in his chair. The wine did not taste as fine as it had a moment before. He had learned to be wary of fathers with eligible daughters, but he had never thought that Arthur would raise this subject.

"Then think of it. It would please me well to know that the poor girl had such a kind-hearted husband. You surely aren't one of those who believe that Gryffyd's madness could be inherited?" The first comment was made warmly, but there was a hint of displeasure in the final sentence.

Gawaine thumped down his winecup. "No, I know well that it is from the war. She's a fine girl, no doubt, but I have no thought of marrying a girl of--what is she, sixteen?" When he thought of Talwyn, he thought of the little girl who used to run about carrying scrolls for the queen. Yes, she was older now, but still had an almost childish look of mischief.

"Almost eighteen. What, is she too old?" Arthur demanded, frowning. "True, most girls are married younger, but Guinevere was determined that she not be married at the usual age. I'm sure that she's a maiden nevertheless."

"I don't doubt that. I'm not casting aspersions on her character," Gawaine retorted. "I'm forty, Arthur. If I wed, it won't be to some young girl."

Arthur's eyes widened and his tone suggested disbelief. "Who ever heard of a man saying that a girl was too young for him? She's the usual age, and more. I think you must doubt her sanity or her virginity. If you've heard tales about her, out with them. I won't stand having a fosterling of mine disgrace herself. If she's a loose girl, I'll marry her off, and not worry so much about the husband." He pounded his silver goblet on the table.

"By all the gods," Gawaine exclaimed, "I'm not saying a word against the girl. She's not a bit of a flirt. No doubt she's a maiden. Don't excite yourself. But if I marry, it will be to someone closer to my age." Seeing the king's incredulous stare, he added, "There are many pretty widows."

"Why should you want used goods if you can have fresh? You want someone young enough to bear you sons, after all," Arthur argued.

"Leave me be." Gawaine rose from his chair. "Why not find the girl a younger husband?" It occurred to him that Guinevere might have her own reasons for keeping the girl around her. If she had seduced Lancelot, why not others as well? Perhaps that was why Lancelot had seemed less happy lately. Well, what happened to Talwyn was no concern of his. At worst, Guinevere wouldn't take her maidenhead and make her unmarriageable. But no, Guinevere couldn't have touched her. Talwyn had such a pleasant, open manner, neither shy nor flirtatious, the manner of a girl who'd never been made love to.

"Too many think that Talwyn might have inherited her father's sad state, though I've never seen a touch of madness in her myself," Arthur confessed.

"So I wasn't exactly the first choice." Gawaine chuckled at this admission. "No doubt someone will ask you for her. Be patient."

Staring at the flaming brazier, Gawaine remembered his first wife, whom he had wed when he was only eighteen. She had brought him nothing but joy, but she had soon died in childbed. He had been fool enough to marry a girl who resembled her not long afterwards, and had been miserable when he realized that she was not at all the same. That one had died in childbed also, and he had vowed never to marry again unless he was sure that he would never weary of the woman.

As it happened, there was not even a mistress he was especially fond of. More than a few women had tried to replace Ragnal, but none had.

If he did choose to marry a girl, Talwyn would not be such a bad choice, not bad at all. She did have a merry laugh.

He wondered in passing why Arthur would seek him as a husband for Talwyn, although Guinevere surely would not want him for her fosterling.

Looking into the fire, Gawaine realized there was a woman he wanted to marry. When he thought of who she was, he groaned.

Arthur played gwyddbwyll with Lancelot, defeating her easily as usual. If she had cared more about the game, she would have been bothered, but she was resigned to losing in this field of play. The king had urged her to come to his room for some wine, and she felt she could not refuse. She wondered how soon she could leave and go to Guinevere.

"Just a little," she said, honored that he poured the wine for her.

He laughed genially. "Of course, you will drink little, as you always do. I know you well."

And as usual she felt a twinge of guilt because he didn't know that she was a woman, but she thought it was probably better so.

The bronze oil lamps carved in the shape of dragons cast their dancing lights about the room, making it seem almost magical.

She looked at the familiar wall hangings depicting scenes of hunting and war. As always, she wondered how anyone who had seen war could want to be reminded of it. The warriors falling from their horses seemed almost real to her, and far from beautiful. She had to look away.

"Those were the days, weren't they, Lance?" Arthur said, seeing her glance at the hanging. "I know it was difficult and painful, but we were great against those Saxons, weren't we?"

Lancelot sighed and stared down at the game board. "We fought to keep them from taking our lands and enslaving our people, and they did not."

"Thoughts too gloomy for you? Never mind. At least we knew who the enemy was then." Arthur sighed even more deeply than Lancelot.

"Well, of course." She looked up at him and tried to read his thoughts. Did he think there were more mysterious enemies now? Did he distrust some of the subject kings?

"A sword is a man's weapon, Lance. Women are more devious. Poison is their weapon." Arthur spoke in a low voice, as if he were confiding in Lancelot. "I hope the queen doesn't want to rid herself of me that much."

Lancelot almost fell out of her chair. "How can you think such a thing?"

Arthur shrugged and downed his wine. "Of course I'd never suspect you."

Lancelot felt her cheeks flush with anger. She stood and moved away from the table. "And you should not suspect anyone else who is close to you, Arthur. I am sure you have no reason for such morbid thoughts."

He shrugged again and poured more wine. He offered some to Lancelot, but she shook her head.

"Perhaps not. But much more goes on between husbands and wives than you could ever guess." The king smiled kindly. "Sure you won't have some more wine?"

"No thank you, I am weary," she said, and she told the truth.

Lancelot left and went to her own plain house, not Guinevere's room. She could say the next day that she had had a headache. She sank down on the bed and buried her head in her one pillow. It was a mean thought, a horrible thought. She was betraying Guinevere by thinking for a moment that there was a chance that Guinevere could kill anyone.

But hadn't she herself killed many men? Hadn't she even killed a girl during the war? What did it matter that it was by accident? The girl was just as dead as if it had not been. It had taken her years to tell Guinevere what she had done, so how could she know whether Guinevere had terrible secrets of her own? Why did she talk about Arthur's death as if it were something to look forward to?

And what did he mean by saying that there was more between husbands and wives than Lancelot knew? Was it possible that Guinevere wasn't faithful to her after all?

Lancelot tried not to think of that idea. Jealousy grabbed her and she fought it, as if it were a powerful warrior riding against her.

Lancelot felt that Guinevere was hiding something.

But the next night she smiled at Guinevere, touched her, and pretended that nothing was wrong.

Guinevere's body was tense, and never seemed to relax. For the first time, Lancelot suspected that Guinevere did not desire her as much as previously. Guinevere had not truly relaxed for several months, but Lancelot only now admitted that there might be more of a problem than she had recognized.

"Are my touches really as good as ever for you?" Lancelot ventured, afraid to hear the answer.

"Of course, dearest," Guinevere said, kissing Lancelot's neck.

But Lancelot was not reassured. She remained awake, not daring to ask any more questions, even though she knew that Guinevere was still awake also.

Lancelot and Gawaine taught the young warriors how to ride in battle, showing such maneuvers as slipping to the side of the horse and riding so that one was not a target, and could scarcely be seen.

In so doing, Lancelot could reach nearly to the ground, but none of the young men could. A few of them could reach the ground with their spears, but none could do so with their hands. She smiled as she watched them. She was not so old after all. The day was fair and the sun shone on the warriors' chain mail.

"Now it is time to fight with your spears," she told them.

A forest of spears was lifted to the skies, and the young men all covered their left sides with their shields.

"And how would you fight on horseback if you lost your shield?" Gawaine challenged them. "Take up your spears and try yourselves against me." His leg had healed from the previous year's wound.

The young warriors put aside their shields. Bearing spears, they charged Gawaine, and he fought them off. Feeling no anxiety for her friend's safety or his dignity, Lancelot watched Clegis attack Gawaine. Gawaine's spear held him off. Gawaine raised his spear like a barrier, and Clegis pressed against it, as if they were fighting with swords. They seemed to wrestle, trying to push each other off their horses. Gawaine was heavier, but Clegis was also heavy and strong. Their pressure on the wooden spears was so great that both broke.

Clegis yelled with pleasure.

Gawaine merely smiled and let the young man gloat. "Ah, my fighting strength wanes as the day does," he said. "I fight my best in the morning."

Lancelot smiled to herself. She knew he could fight almost beyond match at any time.

She then showed the young men the trick of leaping from one's horse to the enemy's. This technique Lancelot demonstrated with Dinadan playing the enemy. After several demonstrations, Dinadan begged to take his leave.

Gawaine then said that he would willingly take Dinadan's place in this arduous task, but Lancelot said that she had demonstrated the move enough, and the young warriors could practice this trick with Gawaine. Whereupon Gawaine said it would be much better if they practiced it with each other.

After an afternoon of practice, some of the young warriors made moan that they were tired and aching because they had fallen any number of times.

The older warriors just smiled and said it couldn't be so bad, but when the younger ones had dispersed and gone off to rest, and Lancelot and Gawaine had taken their own horses back to the pasture, they relaxed a little.

Gawaine's gray gelding and Lancelot's dark mare both eagerly sank their teeth into the grass.

Although it was late in the day, a few larks sang.

A red kite flew overhead, and Lancelot winced because she remembered seeing them eat the dead on battlefields.

"You didn't take up your sword to fight Clegis after the spears were broken, as you would have done in a real battle," Lancelot observed, wiping sweat from her brow. "You haven't shown them how to fight with swords on horseback."

Gawaine grinned. "Time enough for that later. I enjoy knowing a few things they don't know. There's no war on the horizon, and this way I may have an advantage over them in fighting contests when I grow old. I notice you showed them how to leap behind an opponent on horseback, but not how to throw someone off if he leapt up behind them."

"Perhaps I also want to keep some tricks of my own," Lancelot admitted. "You know how to do that, and I do, and we can show the younger warriors how if war comes. That was quite a tale about your being unable to fight as well in the afternoon as you do in the morning." She returned his smile.

"They may decide to wait until the afternoon to challenge me in fighting contests, and then get a surprise." Gawaine chuckled.

Lancelot rubbed her back. "To tell the truth, I'm a little old to leap from horse to horse," she said. "Next year, I'll be forty. My back is killing me." She ached much more than she should from a mere practice.

"I am forty, but I have fought enough for forty men, or at least that's what all of my bones tell me," Gawaine moaned, rubbing his right shoulder. "I'm not sure which of them protests the most. That pasture has begun to look more appealing. I almost want to join those horses."

He gestured not to the horses they had just released, but to the older horses, including a bay that had been his, that spent the whole day in the pasture.

"I never will go to pasture, of course," he added, with some haste.

"You? You'll go to the horse pasture only if they decide to bury you there," Lancelot replied, grinning and rubbing one of her legs, which was almost as sore as her back.

"True. But there are some things that I wish I had done and have not." Gawaine sighed.

She refused to be serious. "You've lived your life exactly as you wanted to. No one more so."

"Yes, I have lived a life of sacrifice, but indeed I chose it." He rolled his eyes heavenwards. "But really, I wish that I had children."

"But you have sons, and pay them little enough heed," Lancelot objected, completely unsympathetic. One of the stallions in the pasture was approaching a mare, and Lancelot turned and started walking away. "Everyone knows that Brendan of the Isles' sister Ysaive's boys are yours. You should have married her."

"Well, in fact Camlach and Cildydd are not mine, or probably not," he said, following her. "True, I laid with Ysaive, but so did almost everyone else. When she found she was with child, she came and asked me whether I would say that it was mine, because no one else would, so I agreed, and settled some money on Camlach, too. But the boy bears no resemblance to me, and I was never fond of him. Frankly, I think he looks like Bedwyr.

"And, as for the second one," Gawaine continued, "I didn't even lie with her in a month that could have made me his father, although I did many other times. I was not so happy when she asked me to say again that he was mine, but what else could I do? She was in a bad place, and it would have been hard for the boy. So I said that Cildydd was mine, too, and settled some money on him also. They're not such bad boys, although I think they've joined Mordred's group."

"Which will make them bad in the end. If you went so far as to say that they were yours, you might have taken a little more trouble with them," Lancelot admonished, frowning at a thrush that sang in a bush near them.

"I can't do anything right, apparently. I've been very courteous to Ysaive and her boys, almost like a saint to them, and still you reproach me," Gawaine complained, rubbing his red beard.

"Your idea of sainthood is a little different from mine," she replied, stepping around a pile of horseshit and glancing at it pointedly. "I suppose you want sons."

"A son, perhaps, or a daughter. I wouldn't want to wear my wife out with overmuch childbearing." He looked at Lancelot. "But what about you?" he inquired. "Do you ever wish you had children?"

She choked. "Good Lord, no, I never give it a thought."

"True, children may not be so important after all," Gawaine said agreeably. "But are there things that you have never done that you wish you had?"

"Everyone has such things, I suppose," Lancelot replied, looking at the caer and particularly at a certain window. "Of course if I could change my life in any way, I would marry Guinevere and go off to live with her, far away from any man's claims."

"Indeed?" Gawaine raised his eyebrows. "Well, at any rate, I can't marry. I'm afraid you'd steal my wife if I did."

Lancelot started to say, "Don't wor . . ." then paused. "But I shouldn't make any promises to you. I should wait and meet her first."

Gawaine groaned and they both laughed.

"I would have to marry the one woman who won't fall in love with you," Gawaine said.

"Only one? And who is she?" Lancelot asked.

But Gawaine only laughed more uproariously.

"Did you hear that Tristram died?" Bors told Guinevere on the way to the great hall for supper. "He was finally killed by King Mark's men."

Guinevere winced. "Poor Iseult," she said almost involuntarily.

Bors frowned. "Her husband has forgiven her sin and taken her back. We can only hope that Tristram repented at the end and saved his soul. There will be a Mass for him tomorrow morning."

Guinevere shuddered at the thought of Iseult having to live again with her husband. She remembered that Iseult had said that lying with him was like being raped.

As Arthur accompanied Guinevere to the Mass for Tristram, he said, "Of course Iseult will never escape again."

Guinevere had never liked Tristram, but she battled to refrain from weeping at the Mass, and, as usual, she succeeded.

Wearing her chain mail away from fighting lessons, although Lancelot had forbidden her to do so, Talwyn rode through the woods. She came to a pond, shimmering in the late spring air. Swallows swept over it, apparently in random madness, like warriors on a quest, looking for something, they knew not what.

People said they were the devil's birds who visited hell, but Talwyn doubted that.

Talwyn dismounted and went to drink. On the other side of the pond, she saw a slim woman bathing.

She had never really looked at another naked woman before. She noticed the slender legs and arms, the small breasts. Talwyn had never been able to see well in the distance, so she couldn't make out the woman's face. It was all very sweet, a peaceful scene on a peaceful day.

The woman saw her and fled to the shore.

"Don't worry," Talwyn hastened to call out. "I'm really another woman. You're safe."

Still the woman ran crashing through the bushes.

Worried about her, Talwyn hurried around the pond, through the willows and alders, to reassure her. She called out a number of times, saying that she was a woman, but there was no reply.

Not finding the woman, she abandoned her attempt and went back to her horse. She hated to think that she had frightened another woman.

After she had ridden a short distance, another horse trotted up to hers. The rider was Galahad.

"How are you today, Talwyn?" Galahad asked, with a proper bow of the head.

"I'm a little disturbed," Talwyn admitted. "A while ago I saw a woman bathing in a pond, but she ran away from me. It's awful to think that I could have frightened her because I'm wearing mail." A thought crossed her mind. "You didn't see her, too, did you?"

"No, I didn't see any women bathing," Galahad assured her, but there was an annoying grin on Galahad's face.

"I certainly hope you wouldn't spy on her, but you probably would have," Talwyn chided the young warrior.

"Of course I wouldn't watch a woman bathing--unless it was you." Before Talwyn could snap back, Galahad said, "Why shouldn't I look if you did?"

Talwyn scowled. "It's entirely different. I was just looking because it made a pretty picture. It was innocent."

"But she ran away from you," Galahad reminded her.

"It's a good thing she didn't run into you, or you would have taken advantage of her," she retorted. Staring at Galahad, she gasped. "I think you did! Your hair is damp."

Galahad's red hair lay flatter than usual, unmistakably moist.

Galahad sighed. "What can I say? It's true. She was so afraid of you that she threw her arms around me for protection, and nuzzled her head against mine."

"I knew that you were untrue to me. Good day, I don't want to ride with you." Talwyn made her horse go ahead of Galahad's.

"I should have admitted it immediately, because I can never fool you," Galahad tried to cajole her, but Talwyn tossed her head and rode away.

14 KINDRED

Lancelot strode across the courtyard. Every stone she trod on was familiar, beloved, different from stones that were condemned to lie far from Camelot. Surely being at Camelot was enough to make even the stones feel important.

Lancelot wondered whether she would win the next day's fighting contest. A blazing sunset streaked across the western sky, and she paused to look at its red and purple clouds. Pentecost was a time of light, and she should pray rather than thinking of the contest, she chided herself. Even though she was probably damned, she should give glory where glory was due. She prayed less often than she used to, and felt ashamed therefore. Sunset bathed Arthur's dragon banner in red light, and Lancelot hoped that no other red stain would ever touch it.

She was not eager to enter the great hall and consume what was no doubt a fine supper. It was better not to eat too much so she was not weighed down for tomorrow's contest--and certainly not to drink much wine.

"Lancelot!" A voice more imperious than those usually heard at Camelot demanded her attention.

She turned to see Queen Morgause of Lothian and Orkney, a guest who had come for Arthur's Pentecost celebration. The queen was fine-looking for a woman aged between fifty and sixty years. Her hair, wonderful to relate, was still red, and she was tall enough to tower over most other women--about the same height as Lancelot.

Lancelot bowed her head. "Yes, my lady?"

Morgause did not smile. "You have set yourself up as being a greater warrior than my son Gawaine. That is impossible. I have little use for idle boasts. Tomorrow's contest will prove who is the better man."

"Indeed, I agree with you, Lady Morgause." Lancelot had heard that the queen worshiped her eldest son even more than he did her. Despite the queen's insulting tone, her maternal devotion moved Lancelot. "Gawaine certainly is the best man at Camelot. No man can match him as a warrior. I have never boasted that I was better than he is."

"At least you will not make your shameful boasts before me. See that you do not make them over your cups either." Queen Morgause swept past her into the great hall.

Lancelot smiled to herself. The queen would see her son victorious. Surely Gawaine would not insist that Lancelot win this time.

It was Pentecost, time for Galahad's first serious fighting contest. Mail polished spotless, she rode out onto the jousting field. The view was different than it was for a watcher. Galahad could scarcely look at the stands to see the viewers. She glanced towards the royal stand with the dragon banner, but could not see any faces, nor was it possible to look at the warriors who earlier had offered encouragement. The onlookers were all melded into one overwhelming pair of eyes.

Galahad's opponent was Lionel, a young warrior just a bit older and not a great deal larger than Galahad. There was a real chance of winning. Galahad had trained with Lionel many times, and found him generally unobjectionable, except that he sometimes liked to claim, apparently because he was from Lesser Britain and had black hair, that he was a cousin of Lancelot's. Lancelot heard the claim and was too courteous to dispute it publicly, but privately said that it was not true. But then, almost any noble in Britain who had black hair (and some who did not) seemed eager to claim a relationship to the perfect warrior.

Galahad's horse was ready, and so was Lionel's. They charged at each other, and their spears clashed on each other's shields. Neither was unhorsed. They turned, and charged again.

Galahad was in a trance. This was far different from practice. True, it was not real fighting, but it was a real spectacle, and Galahad was enveloped in her part.

This time, Galahad knocked Lionel from his horse, and dismounted to the sound of cheers. Sword drawn, keeping in mind Lionel's strong and weak points, she advanced on him. Lionel stood and drew his sword.

Galahad began slashing, trying to confuse Lionel, moving in so many ways at once that Lionel could hardly keep track of his opponent's movements, much less have a chance to strike. Always a little slow, Lionel fumbled.

Remembering years of lessons, Galahad pressed the advantage, driving against Lionel, keeping him on the defensive, and then dealing a blow to his shield that knocked Lionel on the ground.

"Will you yield?" Galahad asked.

Lionel pulled up his visor, displaying a gray face. He tried to open his mouth and speak, but he could not. He shook as if something had seized him, and passed out.

Galahad stood frozen, staring at Lionel.

Shouts resounded from the viewers. Warriors ran onto the contest field.

Lancelot arrived first and knelt by Lionel.

She choked. "He's dead."

Galahad shook like the pennants that rippled from the stands. She had killed a man. She had killed Lionel, whom she had liked.

Other warriors crowded around, then parted to make way for Cassius the physician, who confirmed that Lionel was dead. Cassius closed Lionel's eyes.

Gawaine shook his head. "What pity. Such a young man. The only other time I ever saw this happen at a contest, the man was much older."

Lancelot rose and put an arm around Galahad, who could barely stand. "Don't blame yourself. You did just as you were taught. No one knew that Lionel had a weak heart."

Other warriors came over and said similar things. Percy tried to say some words of consolation. Gareth said it must have been God's will. Even the king hurried to them, sighed over Lionel, then turned to Galahad. "Don't blame yourself, you fought well and courteously."

Galahad began to sob, and Lancelot walked her off the field. She took Galahad to her small, spartan house, which Galahad had never visited before.

"He's dead," choked Galahad, slumping onto Lancelot's bed. "I killed a man. I killed a friend." Lionel had not been a good friend, but they had always been cordial to each other. "I don't want to face the others. I don't want to kill. I don't want to be a warrior."

Lancelot clasped Galahad's shoulder. "You didn't kill him. His own weakness did. Nothing you did was unfair or brutal."

"It was for nothing. No life was saved, no battles won. I'll never fight in a contest again." Galahad's heart felt unbearably heavy. She had never known that hearts really felt that way.

Lancelot patted Galahad's back. "It was terrible. Of course you must think and pray about it. But really, it wasn't your fault. I must go back to the contest. Rest here as long as you wish."

But Galahad thought Lionel's death was indeed her fault. Why had she slashed again and again at Lionel, why had she so wanted to win? For what purpose?

Gawaine chatted with his mother. Queen Morgause had come for the Pentecost celebration--not to pray, of course, but to see how things were at Camelot. And to see him.

They sat in Camelot's finest guest house, made much finer than usual with elegant wall hangings that Cai must have procured from every room but the king's and queen's.

Morgause still was not an old woman, Gawaine thought. She was just fifteen years older than he was, and her red hair had no gray. The lines in her face showed only strength, he believed, not diminishing beauty. She wore a fine gown of the darkest green and heavy chains of gold.

She had dismissed all of her serving women--and Lamorak, her war leader, on perpetual loan from Arthur and not so secretly her lover--so she could be alone with her favorite son.

Although Gawaine had won the chief prize in the fighting contests the day before and had feasted well into the night, he had slept only a trifle late because he wanted to spend time with his mother.

Morgause pressed his hand and gave him her warmest smile, which indeed she seldom withheld from him. "Your fighting outshines all the others. You are golden, and they are but silver, or lesser still."

He returned her smile. "Lancelot is a fine fighter also." This time he had won, as he had known Lancelot would let him do in front of his mother. Indeed he had fought well, but he could tell that Lancelot had held something back, and this time he was not displeased. He might have won even if Lancelot had not done so, but it would have been a pity to have his mother see him defeated.

"Hmpf." Morgause made a low sound that was almost a growl. "Lancelot is nothing compared with you. I wonder why people make so much of him. No doubt it is because he is handsome, in a weak sort of way. He seems almost womanish to me."

"Mother! You mustn't say such things!" Gawaine gasped. Her eyes were too sharp.

"It wouldn't surprise me if he went looking for men," Morgause continued, fingering a golden goblet that was fine enough to be used as a chalice at Mass.

"Lancelot would never do that," Gawaine insisted, moving to stir up the coals in the brazier and escape his mother's scrutiny. "He has been my friend for many years, and has saved my life more than once. Aren't you grateful for that?"

"Of course, my son." Her voice softened. "But no doubt you have saved his also."

"No doubt."

"Still, he seems as bloodless as Guinevere. Little drinking, no flirting. Perhaps that's why they are so fond of each other. Oh so serious, both of them, and who could possibly accuse them of wrongdoing?" She laughed, not pleasantly, and drank from the chalice-like goblet that Cai had provided in her honor.

Gawaine put his hands on her shoulders. "You must not speak of that with anyone but me."

"Never fear, I shan't." Morgause shrugged. "Why should I care if Guinevere wants both Arthur and Lancelot? Many women would think her fortunate, but she scorns the finest man at Camelot. I shall never like a woman who looks with disfavor on you. She never smiles at you." Her mouth twisted in a grimace.

Gawaine laughed and took his hands from her shoulders. "What, do you want me to be a rival to Arthur and Lancelot in the queen's affections? I like her no better than she likes me, so we are agreed about each other."

"You might be excused for not liking her, but I don't excuse her for disliking you," Morgause insisted. "Everyone at Camelot should be grateful that you deign to live here instead of ruling in Lothian and Orkney. Oh, Gawaine," she said in a softer, sadder tone, "I know that you are happy here, but at times it is so lonely in the North without you. I watch the seabirds return in the spring and I wish that my own son returned more often." She sighed--a great, tremulous sigh. "Lothian's lochs are lonely without you, and the heather does not bloom as brightly when you are gone. And Orkney is more deserted than every without you."

As she spoke, he could almost smell the sea salt of Orkney and hear the cries of shorebirds, the demented-cow bellows of the puffins.

He tried to jest. "The gulls are moaning for me, no doubt."

Morgause gave him a brave little smile. "And they would be laughing if you were there. No one jests as well as you do."

Gawaine winced. He sat beside her and took her hands in his. "Ah, Mother, I should hate for you to be lonely. How goes it with Lamorak?"

"He is devoted to me, and I am devoted to him," Morgause said impatiently, pulling her hands away. "But I am a mother, and a mother does not forget her children."

"Your other sons might also want to visit Lothian and Orkney," he teased her, knowing well that she had little eagerness to see Agravaine and Gaheris, though she was fond of Gareth.

"Indeed I do not want them." Morgause twisted her gold chain in her hands. "When Gareth was there, he urged me ten times a day to get baptized. It was tiresome. As for Agravaine and Gaheris, let them stay in the South. Keep Agravaine far from me, Gawaine. He eyes my crown with rage and lust."

"How dare he!" Gawaine made an angry gesture with his fist. "I was only jesting, Mother. Of course I'll keep him from bothering you in Lothian."

"If Agravaine were to try to unseat me, he might face the same fate as his father." Morgause ran her finger around the edge of her golden cup, as if testing it.

Gawaine gulped. His mother had poisoned his father after he had told her that Lot was a rapist--and after Lot, angry that Gawaine had gone to Arthur's warband, had ordered her never to see her eldest son again.

"If you wore the crown, Agravaine would accept it," Morgause told him. "Someday I won't be here any longer, and you'll have to go to rule in Lothian. You'll rule when that time comes, won't you?" Her eyes were pleading, as they rarely did.

He leaned forwarded and pressed her hands again. "Yes, yes, if I must."

"Arthur should name you formally as his heir. I take it very ill that he has not. Your becoming king of Lothian should be no obstacle to that."

"As far as I know, I am his heir, but there's no need for it to be public. But the day of kingship should be far away, Mother. You will live long, I pray, and so will Arthur."

Morgause returned the pressure on his hands. "None of us live forever, Gawaine. Even you won't. You must marry and have sons."

He dropped her hands. "Must you mention marriage every time you see me? I will marry someday, no doubt." He picked up a silver goblet lined in gold--even Cai could not find two goblets like the one Morgause drank from--and gulped down a quantity of wine.

"But if you do not marry, one of Agravaine's sons might rule, and they are little better than he is." Morgause showed her contempt in her face. "Agravaine's poor wife wouldn't make the journey with me because she feels safer away from him in Lothian."

Gawaine sighed. "You have a good point, Mother. But there is no woman whom I wish to marry."

"Perhaps you would like the girls in Lothian better than those here," Morgause countered.

"But you came from Cornwall, so the ladies there must be the best. Having you here is like a breath of heather. How can I be pleased with any of these ladies when none are as fair as you are?" He gave her what he believed was his most winning smile.

His mother laughed. "Oh, Gawaine, you always turn me away with flattery."

His laughter joined with hers. It was grand to have her at Camelot, and he would be sad to see her go, but he would also feel relieved. He certainly couldn't tell her that he fancied the only woman in the world who would be horrified at the idea of being a queen.

That night a less welcome visitor came to Gawaine's house. It was late, but Gawaine's servant had left the lamps burning. Gareth was off praying in the chapel, though Gawaine wished his younger brother were wenching instead. Gawaine scratched the ears of an old hound and told the dog that he looked foolish with his tongue hanging out. The hound licked Gawaine's face.

A knock sounded at the door, but Agravaine entered almost before Gawaine could bid him to do so.

"You should lock your door." Agravaine's tone was unpleasant, which was no uncommon occurrence.

Gawaine relaxed in his chair and indicated a chair for Agravaine. "Who would dare to try to attack me in my own home? Anyone who did would not live long."

"Your dog didn't even bark." Agravaine regarded the hound with some disgust.

"He knows you, of course. What is your business that cannot wait until the morrow?" Although Agravaine was eyeing a jar of mead, Gawaine refrained from offering him anything to drink.

Scowling, Agravaine leaned forward. "Will our mother never step down from her throne? Why don't you ask her? It shames us that an old woman rules in our stead."

Gawaine straightened his back. "In my stead, you mean. I shall thank you not to refer to Queen Morgause as an old woman. She is cleverer than any ruler in the land, save Arthur. No one could rule Lothian and Orkney better."

Agravaine snorted. "I say she shames us. As if she didn't shame us enough by having a lover always hanging about her.

I've said many times, we should force her to dismiss him--or we should take action ourselves."

Gawaine leapt up from his chair. "If you dare to make any move against her, or against Lamorak, I'll see that you regret it. Don't try anything." He brandished his fist.

"Ever the good son, Gawaine, but not such a good brother." Agravaine rose and stared at the fist as if daring Gawaine to strike.

"Better than you deserve. Stop this quarreling and be off." Gawaine indicated the door.

"Whatever you say, Elder Brother." Agravaine's voice mocked him, but he went out into the night.

Gawaine groaned and poured himself some mead. He knew that his warning would keep Agravaine at Camelot. Why weren't his brothers more of a comfort to him? Then he remembered that for years he had thought of Lancelot as a brother, and he laughed.

Galahad stayed away from everyone else as much as possible, speaking only when sought out.

She avoided even Talwyn's sympathetic glances, for she feared to weep in front of Talwyn.

Gawaine taught Galahad a tune on the pipes that was even sadder than any Galahad had heard before. It was almost like weeping, but more calming. Galahad played it again and again, but knew that the whole of life could not be spent with the pipes.

Galahad thought it necessary to speak with the king. Almost creeping to Arthur's rooms, Galahad asked meekly for a moment's talk.

"Of course, Galahad." The king smiled at her kindly.

"I want to tell you how sorry I am. I killed another of your warriors, who wanted only to serve well. I failed you. Please forgive me." Galahad knelt down and sobbed.

Arthur motioned for her to rise. "Nonsense, no one knew that this could happen. You didn't fail. Of course you're sorry, but don't grieve so over it. You have to be a warrior, after all." He seemed a little displeased at Galahad's strong emotion.

Talwyn took a slice of bread and another of cold meat from one of the tables that had been set out with food for the people of Camelot to break their fast. In the morning, eating was hurried as people went about their tasks. Before Talwyn left the great hall, King Arthur walked in her direction. After curtseying, she tried to scurry out of his path, but he stopped to speak with her. He never had before, so Talwyn stared at him.

"You should make yourself attractive to Gawaine," the king said in an undertone. "There's a chance that he might marry you, and there's no need to tell you that's the best marriage you could make."

Talwyn was unable to speak. She realized that her mouth was hanging open with astonishment.

The king gave her an impatient look, so she nodded and said, "Yes, my lord," as she was expected to do.

"Good girl." Then the king was off, to do whatever kings did.

Talwyn staggered out to the courtyard. What should she do? By good fortune--or, perhaps, not so good--she saw Gawaine walking to the great hall, no doubt for a morning meal.

She rushed over to him. "Noble lord, I must speak with you," she said in a breathless voice.

Gawaine's eyes widened. "What's the matter? Has someone been injured? Is your father unwell?"

"No, no, I just need to speak with you, pray." Talwyn blushed.

Gawaine frowned. "What in the name of Cerridwen? Lady Talwyn, you should go to the lady Lionors. I will come soon and speak with you at her house. Bors will no doubt be at Mass at this hour."

Mirabile dictu! What strange instructions! But Talwyn followed them.

She entered the house and, walking past an uncountable number of children with toys, bade good-day to the Lady Lionors, who was settling a dispute about some marbles.

"God grant you good day, Talwyn." Lionors looked only mildly surprised to see her. "Would you help me by getting that kitten down?"

Looking up, Talwyn saw a black kitten climbing to the top of a wall hanging that depicted several apostles. Jumping up on a stool, she plucked the protesting kitten off the hanging. The kitten scratched her, but she put it down gently nevertheless.

A little girl grabbed up the kitten and scolded it.

"Thank you, Talwyn. You'll see what it's like when you have children of your own," Lionors said.

Talwyn vowed that day would never come.

A servant showed Gawaine into the room.

"Good-day, Lady Lionors." He bowed his head first to her, and then to Talwyn.

"Gawaine!" Lionors exclaimed with pleasure, running her fingers through her hair, although it was braided like a proper married lady's. "How good to see you. I'm afraid that Bors left long ago. You might find him at the chapel, or by now at the practice field."

"I have come to see you, my lady." He inclined his head again. "It's always good to see your delightful family. Your children are looking well." A little boy ran up to Gawaine, who picked him up and swung him around, then set him down again. "My errand concerns the Lady Talwyn. Could the three of us go to another room?"

Looking as astonished as Talwyn felt, Lionors bade a serving woman watch for the younger children, then showed the way to another room, where Bors's armor and weapons, rather than toys, predominated.

"What is this all about?" Lionors asked, shutting the door behind them.

"The Lady Talwyn approached me in the courtyard and said she needed to speak with me urgently." Gawaine nodded to Talwyn. "But I fear that my reputation is such that even having a conversation with me, especially in agitated manner, might hurt her good name. Therefore I thought it best if we speak in your presence." He turned to Talwyn. "Pardon me for my presumption, but I was only thinking of you."

"Of course it's proper that you should speak in front of me," Lionors said, "although it would have been even more so in front of the Lady Guinevere..."

Gawaine cleared his throat.

"Well, perhaps not," Lionors admitted. Guinevere's dislike for Gawaine was well known. "Talwyn, why on earth do you have to speak with Gawaine?"

Talwyn felt herself blush, though she had done nothing to blush about.

"Could we perhaps go to the other side of the room?" she asked.

"I suppose so." Lionors sat down in her chair and picked up a garment that needed mending.

Talwyn walked to the other side of the small room, and Gawaine followed her.

"Pardon me for causing all this trouble, Lord Gawaine," she said, forcing herself to speak. "But the king told me I should try to make myself agreeable to you in the hope that you might ask to marry me."

"Indeed?" Gawaine raised his eyebrows.

"I couldn't tell him, but I care about someone else."

Gawaine smiled.

"Other people have approached me about marriage--I don't want the Lady Lionors to hear me because one of the offers concerned her own son--but I have pretended to be mad so I could avoid the matches." She told him the details of her pretenses.

Gawaine appeared to be holding back laughter, but he shook his head. "Pretending to be mad could be a perilous game, Talwyn. Take care when and how you do it."

"I know." She nodded. "But I like you too much to lie to you. I wanted to tell you the truth."

Gawaine's face held the warmest look she had ever seen on it. "Thank you. I am honored. May I ask you which young man--I assume he is young--is fortunate enough to win your affections?"

Talwyn's face felt hot with blushing. "Galahad. I've never told anyone before."

"Galahad. A fine young man. I hope that he returns your affections and you will marry." Gawaine beamed at her. "I know that young girls aren't likely to find old men attractive."

"Oh, I didn't mean that," Talwyn said hastily. "I've always thought you were. If it weren't for Galahad..." She clapped her hand over her mouth.

"Ah." Gawaine smiled with his eyes. "I'd be your second choice, then? In a way, that's more flattering than being the first choice. Far too many women flirt with me because they want to marry a king's son. But second choice, and honest about it, means that you truly like me."

Talwyn's face couldn't be any hotter. She wanted to cover it with her hands. "I was so rude."

"Not at all," he replied graciously. "Your candor is very pleasing."

"Lady Lionors," Gawaine said, striding back across the room. "Talwyn had good reason to have words with me. The king had suggested that I might be a suitable husband for her, but we have discussed the matter and decided that such a match was not appropriate."

Lionors dropped the garment she had been working on. "The king! I can't believe he said such a thing. The queen would..." She left the thought unfinished.

"Exactly." Gawaine nodded. "It might be best not to tell her, as nothing came from it anyway. Talwyn is a fine girl, and perhaps I'm a little sorry that the king was mistaken."

Bowing to both of them, he departed.

"Talwyn, Talwyn, what have you done?" Lionors shook her head.

"Nothing," Talwyn said, blushing.

"I have never seen Gawaine show so much liking for a girl. You mustn't discourage an offer of marriage!"

"Because he's so high-placed?" Talwyn shrugged.

"He is indeed, but I meant because he's kind. Kindness is the best a girl can hope for in a husband, Talwyn. Don't imagine that anything else is more important. Never mind what the queen says about Gawaine. He's always treated me with great respect. I think he just needs a good wife, and then he'll settle down." Lionors patted Talwyn's shoulder. "Oh, dear child, let me go to him and tell him not to take your protests too seriously. And don't worry about Queen Guinevere's objections. I'll persuade her not to oppose the match."

Talwyn wondered for a moment whether she had said the right thing. Then she thought of Galahad and was sure that she had, even though Galahad had paid little attention to her since the Pentecost contest. "No, no, please don't speak with either of them. It's very good of you, Lady Lionors, but I know what I want."

"Nonsense." Lionors frowned. "Think on this matter. I can't go to the queen if you'll tell her you don't want him."

Talwyn didn't at all agree with Queen Guinevere's view of Gawaine, but at the moment she was just as glad that the queen was not fond of him.

Gawaine whistled as he walked to the kitchens. Most food would already have been cleared away from the table in the great hall, but the serving people would give him whatever breakfast he wanted.

Talwyn was a delightful girl. If she had liked a youth who was rich, handsome, and cocky, Gawaine might have enjoyed contesting the young man for her affections. But Galahad was none of those things. He was a fine youth who deserved Talwyn and should have her.

But Gawaine couldn't help plotting what he would have done if he had tried to get Talwyn for a wife. There was one way to overcome Guinevere's objections. He could have claimed that he had dishonored Talwyn--though of course he wouldn't have touched her until he married her--and Guinevere would be forced to give her consent to the marriage. Then he realized that Lancelot would never forgive him for saying such a thing about Talwyn. Even if he married Talwyn without subterfuge, Lancelot would be angry because she would think he was not good enough for the girl. And he would not anger Lancelot in that way.

Well, if nothing else, it was pleasant to know that such a fresh, honest girl existed.

On a hot summer day, Lancelot rode through some marshes to the East. They were not too far from Saxon territory, so she was a bit unnerved, and not just because of stinging marsh insects. Although the Saxons had sworn allegiance to King Arthur and were paying him tribute, she still didn't trust them.

She let her horse drink from the water. The croaking of the frogs reassured her that nothing terrible was about. She watched a marsh hawk swooping low, hunting with a grace that belied its deadly mission. The marsh smell both appealed to her and disgusted her. She wiped her forehead. Then the frogs stopped croaking, and a pretty, finely dressed British lady rode breathlessly up to Lancelot. The lady's dark hair flew about in a tangle and her face seemed drained of all its blood.

"Please help me, noble lord," she gasped, choking out the words with difficulty. "My husband believes that I have committed adultery, and he means to kill me."

"Of course I'll help you," Lancelot assured her. The lady's pitiful appearance roused her sympathy.

Then a large, well-dressed man on an elegant steed galloped into the marsh. The lady screamed.

"Hold up," called out Lancelot. "I am Lancelot, King Arthur's warrior, and I won't let you hurt this lady."

The man pulled up his horse just a slight distance from them. His face was red as some flowers that bloomed in the marsh, but not as attractive. "You don't understand, Lord

Lancelot. This woman is my wife, and she has committed adultery. I have every right to punish her."

"I have not, I swear it," the lady insisted, trembling like the marsh grasses.

"You lie," the husband yelled at her. His eyes glowed fiercer than the marsh hawk's.

"It doesn't matter whether she is telling the truth or not, you have no right to harm her. I shall take her to a safe place. You should go home and forget her," Lancelot told him, putting her horse between the lady's and the man's.

The husband stared at Lancelot. "Not have the right to punish my wife for adultery? I can't believe that any man would say such a thing."

"Well, I have said it, and you should go." Lancelot used her military officer's voice.

The husband changed his tone. "How can I go and leave my wife? Perhaps I was too hasty. Won't you talk with me?" he coaxed the lady.

"No, I'm afraid of you now," she replied, shrinking from him.

"We should depart," Lancelot told the lady. "And you should let her go," she said to the man.

Lancelot and the lady started to ride, but the man followed, at only a slight distance behind them.

Suddenly, he cried out, "Oh, God's mercy, it's Saxons coming, and they look as if they mean to attack!"

Lancelot turned to look, and the man sped forward and slashed his sword into his wife's neck, almost cutting off her head, before Lancelot could stop him.

"How could you?" Lancelot cried in anger, doing the same to him.

She buried the lady's body, but left the man's unburied by the road.

She returned to Camelot with a heavy heart, regretting that she had been fooled by the man.

Lancelot told Arthur what had happened, and he shook his head and said, "You were too hard on the man. No one would have executed him for killing a wife who committed adultery. You're too ready to take the woman's part."

Lancelot shuddered, but could not bear to think further. This was the first she had heard of the king being harsh toward women who committed adultery.

When the leaves had fallen from the trees, Mordred returned from living with the Saxons. When the young warrior strode into the great hall, Arthur did not know whether to feel glad. It was difficult to look at anyone but this Mordred, who looked so much like Arthur's younger self. Arthur couldn't help wondering whether this might be his son after all. No, that was a foolish fantasy.

Mordred bowed. "I have learned much about the Saxons, my lord."

"Very good. Come to my room and give me a full report," Arthur said, trying to sound just the way he did when he spoke to any other competent man in his service. He rose and led the way to his private chamber.

Mordred gave a full report on the Saxons' armaments and their disposition.

Arthur nodded. "You have learned a great deal." He had the strange feeling that it might have been just as well if Mordred had not returned.

Mordred smiled, but there was something insinuating about his smile. "Sire, I have a gift for you. Come with me to a small house in the forest near here, and I will show you."

Now this was passing strange, for young warriors did not presume to give gifts to the king, but Arthur went. He was curious to see what manner of gift Mordred had brought him. He rode out alone with the young man.

When they came through the forest to a small thatch-roofed house that was whitewashed with lime, Mordred said, "Come inside and see my gift."

Arthur followed him inside, and saw a woman in a dove gray gown who looked just like Guinevere, save that her face was haggard, and her eyes, which were gray rather than blue, had a look that was colder and harsher than any he had seen in the queen's. And there was on her neck the mark of a Saxon iron thrall-collar.

He stood there, too surprised to speak.

"Here, sire, is a woman who says that she's the queen's bastard sister, and I think that's the truth. She was taken as a Saxon thrall when she was a girl, and later they sold her to a British brothel. I thought you might find her amusing." Mordred gave an exaggeratedly deep bow, and left them.

Arthur smiled at the woman. Here was a way to get revenge on Guinevere without striking her.

Mordred rode away, thinking he had been a fool to want to gain his father's esteem. Arthur was just an ordinary man, with the same low tastes--not that he admitted them, but that was ordinary, too.

Guinevere was different. How dare a woman be so proud? It would be interesting to lie with a woman like that. Lying with her sister had been a poor substitute.

We are an incestuous family, Mordred thought, chuckling to himself. But when he thought of the queen looking at him with contempt if she learned he had been raised in a brothel, he cringed.

Arthur and Gawaine rode through the bare woods on a gray day in late autumn. Gawaine scanned the branches for the birds that had not left for the year. He wondered whether he was withering like the bracken on the forest floor.

Arthur said, "I have something to show you."

He stopped at a small house and dismounted, and Gawaine did the same.

Arthur knocked three times, and a serving woman opened the door. They entered, and a woman who looked like Guinevere came up and threw her arms around the king. Gawaine stared at her. Gods, the likeness was amazing. The nose, the mouth, the chin, the hair--everything but the eyes was the same.

Arthur laughed and kissed her mouth. "Good to see you, sweeting. And here is my good cousin, Gawaine. Go fetch some refreshments for us."

The woman curtseyed to Gawaine and smiled. "Good day, Lord Gawaine. Yes, Lord Arthur. I'll just be a moment."

Gawaine nodded to her politely, then, when she had gone, asked, "Gods, who is that?"

"Gywnhwyfach, Guinevere's bastard sister, who was captured by the Saxons, then sold to a bawdy house. Mordred brought her to me."

"And not to Guinevere?" Gawaine had a sick feeling in his stomach.

"She has no love for Guinevere. I have a better use for her." Arthur laughed unpleasantly. "You turned down your chance for the queen many years ago when I asked whether you would get her with child, but I think this one would not refuse you. Would that amuse you?"

"No," said Gawaine sharply, thinking of the daughter he had long sought. If men recognized her as his, is this how they would treat her? And how could Arthur not think about how men might treat his own possible missing daughter? Above all, why would he make his wife's sister his mistress? Gawaine could hardly look at his royal cousin.

Someone knocked at Guinevere's door. Luned, who had been mending a torn hem, went to the door.

Wide-eyed, she turned to Guinevere. "My lady, it's the lord Gawaine. Should I let him in?"

Guinevere stopped reading Talwyn's Latin exercises. She put down the tablet and rose from her chair.

"Let him in." Her voice was full of frost. "What brings you here?" she asked, with cold courtesy. Gawaine had never knocked on her door before, except once years ago when she had summoned him, and she could see no reason why he would now.

The tall warrior hemmed and hawed. He lowered his head. "I have seen today a woman who could be your sister. She says she is, and she much resembles you."

"My sister!" Guinevere let herself hope, even though it seemed impossible. "I did have a sister, who looked just like me. I thought she was killed by Saxons when she was a child. Could this be Gwynhwyfach?"

He nodded. "That's the name she gives. It must be. This woman bears the mark of a Saxon thrall collar."

"Where is she?" Guinevere felt as if she had sprouted wings and was ready to fly. Gwynhwyfach had been her serving girl, and she had not known that her father had also fathered Gwynhwyfach until after the Saxon raid. Now she could make everything up to Gwynhwyfach and treat her like a real sister.

Gawaine colored. "She lives in a small house in the forest. She is Arthur's mistress."

Guinevere caught her breath. Her joy disappeared, replaced with icy rage. "I see," she managed to say. "Thank you for this news, Gawaine. You may go now."

He bowed and departed.

She almost ran to Arthur's door and demanded to be let in.

Arthur wore a fine white tunic, one of his favorite garments. His serving man, Tewdar, was folding the king's leather riding tunic.

"Can't you wait until supper to see me, Lady Guinevere?" Arthur asked cheerfully. His handsome face had never looked so ugly to her.

"Leave us," Guinevere said to Tewdar, and the man departed.

"Such eagerness to see me is most uncommon." Arthur smiled at her as if she meant what he must know she did not.

"How dare you keep my sister from me?" She choked out the words as if she were strangling. She longed to fly at him, to scratch his eyes. She had never before had such an impulse about anyone.

"So Gawaine told you. I thought he might. I thought the message might please you, coming from him, because you are so fond of him." Arthur smiled, not sweetly. "If you had been a real wife to me, I would not have gone to your sister. Do you believe that she wants to see you? I assure you, she does not. She blames her whole hard life, from Saxon thralldom to British brothel, on you."

This was the first that Guinevere had heard of the brothel. Her voice almost choked her. "She is my sister. You will at least have the decency to bring her here to live at court, not hidden away. She must be treated like any lady here, as Gwyl was treated, and as your mistresses usually are."

She took him by surprise. His eyes widened. "Not the ones who come from brothels. You can't want her here, Gwen. She looks just like you. People would make sport of the resemblance."

"She is my sister, and I shall acknowledge her as such." She spoke with all the dignity she could summon.

Arthur looked appalled. "You can't, she's just a . . ."

"Sister!" Guinevere snapped. "You will bring her here. I demand it. I'll go and fetch her myself if you won't. I must see her."

The king shook his head. "I didn't mean that you should have to see her. It won't be pleasant for you."

She took advantage of his retreat and seized the offensive. "Arthur, you will send someone to bring her here immediately, this very evening, or I shall send Lancelot and Gawaine to do it."

"Lancelot? Oh, for God's sake, leave him out of this," Arthur muttered, frowning. "I'll send Gawaine. But you will have no joy of her. After you've met her, you'll see how unsuitable it is for her to live here."

Guinevere could not eat a bite of supper. She sat for the shortest possible time at the great table, then retired to pace her room, and occasionally sob. At least she could tell Luned what visitor she expected.

Luned said Lancelot's serving man Catwal had told her that the king had sent Lancelot off on an errand for a few days, and Guinevere suspected that it was a punishment for her because she had demanded to see her sister.

She remembered the imperious little girl she had been, giving orders to Gwynhwyfach. Guinevere had noticed the resemblance, but never guessed that Gwynhwyfach was her sister. Then, when Guinevere was about ten years old and her parents had told her she was the most beautiful girl in Britain, she had objected that Gwynhwyfach looked just like her. After that, her mother had demanded that her father send Gwynhwyfach away to an old farm of his. The Saxon raid had come not long after and burned down the farm. Then Guinevere's old nurse, Macha, had told her that Gwynhwyfach had been her sister.

Guinevere had been haunted all her life by the belief that she was responsible for Gwynhwyfach's death. She had tried to make up for it, as much as she could, by befriending serving women.

Finally, the much-awaited knock came, and a hooded figure slipped into her room. Luned let her in and departed. The figure threw off her hood and cloak. It was Gwynhwyfach, wearing a fine crimson gown and a lapis brooch.

"Gwynhwyfach!" Guinevere had been telling herself that she must be reserved because Arthur had said her sister had no fondness for her, but she could not hold back. She opened her arms. "Thank God you're alive. I have so longed for you these many years."

Gwynhwyfach spat on the floor. "Longed for me, have you? Haven't you had enough servants to fetch your things? I haven't longed for you." Her eyes blazed with hatred.

Guinevere tried to hide her own pain, because Gwynhwyfach's had been so much greater. "You'll never be a servant again, dear. Forgive me for treating you as one. I had no idea that you were my sister. All that has changed now."

"You bet it has. Your king loves me now. That's why he sent for me. Don't pretend it's not." She sneered.

Of course she could not tell Gwynhwyfach the truth, that Arthur had not wanted her at Camelot. "You must live at court now, Gwynhwyfach. A room has been prepared for you. I can understand that you have suffered too much to like me now, but I hope that after a time . . ."

Gwynhwyfach laughed bitterly, showing the lines in her face. She had a few more lines than Guinevere, not surprisingly, but her hair still was coal black. "You bet there's a room here for me, but I know that he's the one who wants me, not you. You're just pretending to make the best of it. Look at these jewels he's given me. This is how much your husband likes me." She indicated the brooch, and an amber ring on her finger.

Guinevere nodded. "I don't care about that. I am only glad to see you and to know that you're alive after all."

"Alive? I wasn't so thankful for that when the Saxons took me, after they killed my mother because she was too old to suit them. I had to wear a weight of iron around my neck for years." A veil had covered her neck, and she pulled it loose, showing the scar.

Guinevere moaned. "Oh, my poor dear." She extended her hand, but her sister pulled away from it.

"None of that, don't pretend that you care. They raped me for years, then sold me to a brothel, where the British men had their way with me, too. Everything's been done to me, but now I can live." There was a note of triumph in her voice.

"Do you want to live here? I hope you will, but if you prefer, you can go anywhere you want. I'll give some jewels so you can lead an independent life." It occurred to her that Gwynhwyfach might not really be so fond of Arthur.

Her sister threw her head back and laughed. "Sure you will. You want to buy me off. Well, you can't. I'm here to stay. Make the best of it."

"No, you don't understand. I want you to stay." Guinevere tried to explain, even though it seemed hopeless. "Pray be seated, and have some wine." She indicated her finest chair, the one she usually sat in herself.

Gwynhwyfach ignored the chair. "Sure you want me. Well, you soon won't. I'm not calling myself Gwynhwyfach. I know that's no court lady's name. I'm calling myself Guinevere now." She was like a warrior who had conquered a foe.

Guinevere made her voice gentle. "Don't, dear. It will be harder for you if you do. People will always compare us then. What about Guinlian? That sound more patrician."

"You mean you'd prefer it. I'm Guinevere now, and I'll take everything that's yours." She gestured around the room, as if to say that it would be her room soon. "I've heard about your Lancelot, and I'll take him, too. He'll like me better, just as the king does. I know how to please men. They're all the same," she gloated.

Guinevere shook her head. "Please, dear, let me help you find your place at court. The way that you have chosen will only lead you to grief."

Gwynhwyfach tossed her head so violently that her braids jumped. "You'll be the one who's grieving, and I'll be glad. Let me go, Sister Dear. I'm dead tired. There's no point in this talk. You have to take me as I am."

"I shall. You will be shown to your room," Guinevere said, her voice weary. She could see that Gwynhwyfach had suffered so much that she had walls that might have no gates.

When her sister was gone, Guinevere slumped in a chair and fought back tears. It was too late to love her sister. If only Guinevere had known the truth when they were children.

So Gwynhwyfach called herself Guinevere, and everyone started calling her False Guinevere, although Guinevere demanded that they not do so.

After Lancelot had been away for a few days on a mission to inspect a watchtower, she returned late at night and slipped off to her own house because Guinevere would not be expecting her.

But to her surprise, an old lady named Brisane who was new to Camelot followed her and whispered, "Lord Lancelot, have some of this wine. The queen sent it for you and bade you to come later to her room. I'm to knock on your door when the time is come."

This message was odd, but Lancelot felt too tired to wonder. She had not heard that Guinevere had taken Brisane into her confidence, but the woman was surely too old to dissemble. Lancelot drank the wine and went off to rest before she saw Guinevere.

She was sleeping soundly when a knock on her door woke her. Lancelot staggered up and followed the old woman down passageways. She wondered why Guinevere would want her to come through her door rather than the secret stairway Lancelot always used, but she was so tired that she accepted it. The passage seemed unfamiliar.

She entered a darkened room. Strange, Guinevere usually had candles burning. Lancelot pulled off her boots and climbed into the bed, where Guinevere sat in her shift.

"Love," Lancelot mumbled incoherently, put her arms around her and gave her a sleepy kiss. "I'm too tired to undress." Strangely, Guinevere did not answer, so Lancelot sprawled face down in her usual sleeping posture and almost instantly fell asleep. When she woke, the gray light made it seem that dawn was on its way.

"I had best go, Love. I'll see you tonight." Planting a kiss on Guinevere's cheek, she pulled on her boots. She was so groggy that she could not find the tapestry that hung in front of the secret passage. Praying for good fortune, she stumbled out of the door through which she had entered. There were no guards in the passageway.

Guinevere was breaking her fast in her room when Luned announced, "Your sister, Lady Guinevere."

The queen rose as if she were greeting someone of equal station. "Well come. Will you join me, sister? I have wheaten bread and dried fruit."

Gwynhwyfach smirked. "No, I'm much too happy to eat. Your handsome warrior joined me in my bed last night. He thought I was you. He's a fine swiver, Gwen. I told you I'd have him."

Guinevere found the lie pathetic. "He is indeed a fine lover. Too fine to betray me. Don't try to deceive me."

"He's the one who'll try to deceive you. No doubt he'll say he did nothing, but you're a fool if you believe him." Gwynhwyfach tossed her head, laughed, and left.

Guinevere sent Luned to summon Lancelot.

Lancelot appeared a little later, looking tired and heavy-lidded. "What does this mean?" she complained. "I must be off training the young men. I cannot come hither at your beck and call during the day. Surely you know that."

"I do. I merely thought you should know that I was not the one you slept with last night." Guinevere was not pleased that Lancelot had been deceived, though it was obvious that her beloved had done no wrong.

Lancelot flushed with anger.

"It surely was you. What game is this? I have no time for such foolery. Are you angry that I slept and barely spoke to you? I have been strangely weary."

"In fact, it was not me. My sister is alive, come to the caer, and hates me. This was a shabby little game indeed, but not mine." She spoke softly and extended her hand.

Lancelot gasped. "Not you! By the Virgin, what did I do? I kissed her cheek only. You must believe me."

She looked so distraught that Guinevere quickly took her hand and kissed her mouth. "I know you did nothing, dearest. Gwynhwyfach still thinks you are a man."

"But how could she hate you? Why?"

So Guinevere explained.

Gwynhwyfach still cast soft glances at Lancelot, followed her down passageways, and said, "Lord Lancelot, wouldn't you like to try my bed again?"

Lancelot sighed and said, "Of course not, my lady. Your sister loves you. Can't you see it? She has told me many times about the Saxons killing you, as she thought they had, and she has wept bitterly. Can't you forgive her for being your father's lawful child? She had no more choice about her birth than you did about yours."

But Gwynhwyfach rolled her eyes and said, "Her tears didn't do me any good, did they?"

Lancelot dared not say anything to the king about Gwynhwyfach, but went about puzzled.

Arthur called Lancelot aside and took her by the arm. "Embarrassing about this False Guinevere, isn't it? At first I thought she was the true Guinevere. I was deceived."

Lancelot knew that was a lie, but said nothing.

Gwynhwyfach stroked the elegant saffron gown that she wore. She sat back in a chair that graced her room. Never had she felt so comfortable. Good food, fine clothes, nice furniture. Only one man she had to lie with, though she wouldn't mind trying Lancelot too. If she felt tired, she could rest. Servants did her bidding. She tried not to remember all the Saxon men and women who had struck her if she didn't obey them quickly enough. She wished that Arthur would kill them all.

Brisane knocked on the door and brought an old woman to her.

"I have a new silver mirror that the queen sent for, and I must put it in her hands," the old woman said. Her clothes were poor and she was bent with age, but her voice was proud.

"I brought her straight to you, highness," Brisane said.

"Thank you, good woman," Gwynhwyfach said, inclining her head. No one else believed that she was the queen, but she was pleased to fool even this poor old woman.

The old woman pulled a sealed vellum from her bosom, and gave her that as well as the mirror.

Gwynhwyfach could not read, but she thought the message must be from Lancelot. Or perhaps Guinevere had another lover, for why take the risk of sending a message when Lancelot could see her at any time?

That night, Gwynhwyfach delivered the packet to her visitor. "Dear Arthur, someone is sending messages to your wife. Very improper. You should know about it."

Arthur broke the seal and scanned the vellum. He exclaimed in anger.

"Poor Arthur. Yet another lover?"

He frowned. "No. It is from my sister, Morgan, who is my enemy. Its words show that it is not the first. So Guinevere betrays me by exchanging messages with the one I sent away. Say nothing of this to her, or anyone. Ever." There was no affection in his voice, but Gwynhwyfach smiled with satisfaction nevertheless.

Luned bowed to the king and of course had to let him into Guinevere's room, but she stayed, as she had been instructed to do if he ever came there.

"Tell your woman to leave us," Arthur said, frowning at her. "I have come to talk about your sister." He spoke the last word contemptuously, almost spitting.

"You may leave us, Luned." Not glad to see her depart, Guinevere waited for his words.

Snow fell past her window, but Arthur's face was colder than the day.

"She's an embarrassment. I won't have here any longer. I'm sending her away." His voice issued a challenge, as if he expected Guinevere to protest.

"You must tell her yourself. I shall send for her," Guinevere said. She did not argue, but her heart felt heavy. Gywnhwyfach had brought her no joy, yet it would be sad not to see her anymore.

Arthur sent a servant to bring Gwynhwyfach.

While he was thus occupied, Guinevere slipped jewels into a packet for Gwynhwyfach.

"You're not giving her all those!" Arthur protested, turning and seeing her.

"I am."

She did not look at him, but continued wrapping the packet in white linen.

"Giving presents to a woman who hates you is foolish. I didn't think you were a fool, at least."

Guinevere did not deign to reply.

When Gwynhwyfach came, her eyes widened at the sight of the king standing beside Guinevere.

"Arthur, sweet," she said, moving towards him and opening her arms.

He pulled back. "No more of that. All things must end. You must leave here today."

She stopped in her tracks, then turned on Guinevere, screaming, "You tried to turn him against me! Don't believe her, Arthur. I care more about you than she does. I'm a better queen to you than she is."

"Nonsense, I won't have a whore for a queen, or even as a mistress living in my caer. I would never have brought you here except that Guinevere insisted on it." He looked at Gwynhwyfach with disgust. "Guinevere is a lady, and has a brain, while your best features lie elsewhere."

Gwynhwyfach shrieked, "You sister-fucking bastard! Everybody knows that the sister you like best is your own!"

"How dare you!" His arm trembled. Apparently ready to forget his vow never to strike a woman, he made a move towards her.

Guinevere placed herself between them, her voice commanding as if he were a serving man. "She is my sister, and you will treat her with respect. Leave us."

Arthur relaxed his arm and nodded. "I shall leave, but make sure that I never see this creature again."

Gwynhwyfach still screamed at him. "If you send me away, I just might start a house of my own, and call it the Queen's Arms."

Arthur's glared as if she were a captive Saxon. "If you dare to do anything more to embarrass me, you'll wish that you still wore the Saxon thrall collar." He stalked out.

Gwynhwyfach paled, but she gave a barking laugh. "I should have known better than to believe a man."

"Yes, dear, you should have," Guinevere said gently. "I have a packet of jewels for you, and you shall have the best villa in Londinium to live in. That's far enough from Camelot so that Arthur will never have to see you and be reminded. But you had better live a quiet life, or he'll be angry."

"I see that. I'm not a fool, or I'd never have survived." She grabbed the packet from Guinevere and examined its contents. She gasped at their obvious value.

"Of course you're not a fool. I'm glad that you survived. I wish that we could have known each other in a different way," Guinevere said to her, making one last try.

"So do I, Gwen, but it's too late," Gwynhwyfach replied, in a softer voice than Guinevere had heard from her before.

Guinevere put an arm out to touch her, but Gwynhwyfach cried out, "I can't feel anything, Gwen, don't try to make me feel," turned, and fled.

15 THE GRAIL

The priest came to shrive Arthur in his own room, as befitted a king. Arthur smiled at how mild the penance was. Father Donatus, who had been at Camelot for years, did not dare give a penance that would be too difficult, Arthur reckoned. It would be easy to give more money to the poor and attend more masses.

Arthur spoke in a confidential tone.

"Good Father, I see that my foolish mistake may have hurt the conscience of my court. How can I turn their minds to things of the spirit?" And away from the scandal of the False Guinevere.

Seldom honored by a request to advise the king, the aging and gentle Father Donatus seemed too overwhelmed to worry about whether there was true repentance. He bowed his balding head.

"It is well that they should ponder things of the spirit, and whatever turns their minds to that is good," the priest ventured.

Arthur smiled. This priest would give him no trouble. When he was young, he had listened too much to priests, even sending away his sister and making all his men get baptized.

Now religion would serve him, for a change. He would produce a miracle. Let no one say that his reign was sinful. He would prove that his court was the holiest in the world.

"Father, what if the cup that was used at the Last Supper were found? Would that be a great thing?"

The priest gasped with amazement. "Indeed it would. Have you heard of such a vessel?"

"That may be. And it may come to Camelot." Arthur made his voice reverent.

"And may I see this wonder?" The priest's face was all aglow.

"Indeed, we should all see it." Arthur smiled at the priest's guilelessness. The world had praised him for being a good king, but those praises had become routine. He wanted more honor; it was scarcely possible to have enough. He wanted to know that his name would live forever, that he was more than just another king, however good. He was the one favored by God to rule.

He had asked a goldsmith to fashion a cup that was like no other, and to let no one know from whence it came.

But it should not appear at Mass like an ordinary chalice. Its appearance must seem miraculous. It should be borne by a woman, a woman who could seem mysterious. Nimue came to mind, so he sent for her to be brought secretly from the forest.

On the day of the Christ Mass, when the court was gathered for feasting, a sudden stillness came over the great hall. Fewer torches than usual blazed from the walls, so the hall was filled with mysterious lights and shadows. Music of an almost unearthly quality, played by an unseen harper, wafted around the court. Arthur was pleased with the effect. He wore his finest purple cloak, trimmed with ermine, over a snow white tunic.

A woman with the austere look of a nun, bearing a chalice that gleamed in the dark, like marsh lights, swept through the hall, and was gone. Bors was not the only one who gasped. No one seemed to see that it was Nimue, much thinner than she had been. The evening was proceeding just as Arthur had hoped.

Arthur stood solemnly and held up his sword in a patch of light, so that its shadow appeared to be a cross on the wall behind him. Many gasped again. After a long pause, he sheathed his sword and was seated again.

"Could that cup have been the holy grail, the vessel Christ used at the Last Supper? Legend says that Joseph of Arimethea brought it to Britain, but that it was lost," Arthur asked Bors, who had been honored with a seat beside him. Arthur's voice was deep enough to be heard throughout the quiet hall. Of course he had just made up the legend himself.

But Bors seemed too moved to speak.

"How can it be that my humble court would be favored with a vision?" Arthur asked, again in the deep voice, shaking his head. "Let us all keep in mind that we are a Christian court doing the work of the Lord."

"If that is the grail, we must go forth and seek it!" Bors exclaimed, and several other warriors cried out the same.

Surprised, Arthur told them, "Who among us can hope to see it more than once in his lifetime?" He did not want them to leave his side on a fruitless journey.

But he had triumphed. Now they would think of the court as a holy place, and stop talking about his sin with Gwynhwyfach. And the tale of miracles at his court would spread far and wide.

Lancelot had seen that the woman bearing the cup was Nimue, and she thought the sight was no vision. She sat silent while Bors marveled at the glowing cup.

Lancelot saw the way the light reflected from Excalibur. She had seen the sword covered with the blood of Saxons. How could it be holy?

She looked around the hall, and saw other faces lit up with joy.

She knew that they wanted something wonderful, perfect, and beautiful. She saw ecstasy on Percy's face, and Galahad's. Gareth had left his seat and knelt on the floor. She had no wish to destroy their dreams.

But she saw the hall filled with blood, with the bodies of Saxons, with the bodies of Britons, with the bodies of Arthur's warriors.

Would all these warriors who sat around her be cut down? Would the young hearts stop beating? Would their bodies be trampled? Would they live, but be haunted by those they had killed, as she was haunted by those she had killed?

What was she doing, training boys to be killers?

What was Arthur doing, leading men to be warriors?

Was his talk of a grail an attempt to repent, to create something beautiful?

She did not feel that she saw repentance in his face, but how could she know?

Guinevere's face was stiff, her muscles straining to smile. Her eyes held no warmth. She must be thinking of her sister. The grail, or whatever it was, must hold no beauty for her. Lancelot could see that Guinevere's rage was barely suppressed.

Arthur put his arm around Guinevere and kissed her cheek. Lancelot could bear it no more. She wanted to leap from her seat and strike him. Holy Grail, indeed!

Not many days before, Arthur had been touching and kissing Guinevere's sister. Lancelot felt her chest constrict. Her hand went to the place where her sword would be, though she was not wearing it for the feast day supper.

She wanted to kill. She was nothing but a killer, and never would be more. Never could she create anything good or beautiful. Her soul must be dead indeed.

This wasn't Arthur. This couldn't be Arthur, the man she had sworn to follow.

Camelot just another hill fort, a bigger one. She and her friends were nothing but killers. This wasn't the Camelot she had thought she knew. She reeled.

She almost ran out of the hall, barely managing to conceal her panic.

Galahad and Percy did not linger late at the table.

Percy did not eat. He sat so still that Galahad wondered if he might be ill, but his eyes shone and he gazed up at the roof, which held only a smoke hole.

Galahad managed to eat some venison and sweet cakes, and noticed that the wine was the finest ever served, at least to the young warriors.

"Percy." Putting a hand on his arm, Galahad tried to wake him from his daze.

"Yes?" Percy blinked as if surprised that any human voice would speak to him.

"Shall we leave?" Galahad saw that many other warriors were beginning to drink as much as they usually did at such a feast, and wanted to spare Percy from being rudely pulled from his bliss.

Percy nodded. They went to the courtyard.

The winter stars lit the heavens. The air was cold, but Galahad knew that Percy would be impervious to mere temperatures.

"Was that the grail?" Percy asked in a wondering tone. "It seemed somehow too splendid. I would have expected it to have a simpler earthly aspect."

"Indeed," Galahad said, cautious lest she offend. "I would not think the Christ used elegant vessels. His supper was only at a simple inn, after all."

Percy shook his head. "A king's caer has too much earthly grandeur for such a rare treasure. I think this vessel must just be a sign that we should seek the true grail. It may well be in a caer of gold and silver, but I think the outward appearance would be very different." He turned his eyes from the stars to Galahad. "Will you seek for the grail?"

"I don't know. Perhaps I'm afraid that I might find it." Galahad shivered. Was it from the cold, or the idea of some terrible spiritual duty? She wondered.

Snow began to fall, and Percy stared at it as if it were a miracle. "Is this a sign from heaven?" he asked.

"It doesn't seem like an auspicious sign for a quest." Galahad pulled her cloak tighter. It was black, made from the same material as nuns' habits.

Lancelot burst into Guinevere's room. Snow covered Lancelot's shoulders, but she didn't bother to brush it off. "You can't stay with a man who'd lie with your own sister!" she said in a voice that was much louder than usual. "It's repulsive. And to pretend that he's a great friend of the Christ's, and the court is full of visions--it's vile, too vile to believe. I'm surprised that Nimue would lend herself to such a deception. A chalice that glows in the dark! How blasphemous! It's time for us to leave."

Guinevere grabbed the arms of her chair. "Leave? We cannot."

"Of course we can, and must." Lancelot paced about the room like a wild creature penned. Its familiar candlelight did not soothe her. "How can you bear to be kissed by a man who lay with your sister? Won't you leave?" she pleaded.

Guinevere's mouth was set in a tight, grim line. "I find it hard to bear the way he treated my sister, but my situation is not so different from what it was before."

"Not different for you? How not? I can see that you are angry at him." Lancelot searched her face.

"I am no more able to leave now than I was before." Guinevere sighed.

"What is it that you like so much here, though you complain? Perhaps you stay because he can make you a queen, and I cannot." Shaking with anger, Lancelot said the words that she had scarcely let herself think before.

Guinevere shook also and grasped the gold torque around her neck, almost tearing it off. "True, gold and thrones mean much more to me than you do. If you believe that, you're a fool. I won't be free until Arthur dies, can't you understand that?"

With a strangled scream, Lancelot rushed out of the queen's room and plunged down the secret staircase. Did Guinevere want her to kill Arthur? The thought was intolerable.

The next morning, Galahad saw Talwyn in the cobbled courtyard, leaving her footprints in the fine covering of snow. Galahad not seen much of Talwyn in the months since Pentecost. What could Talwyn know about how it felt to kill?

Now Galahad approached her. "Please walk into the garden with me."

She stepped carefully around patches of ice on the cobbles. She offered Talwyn her arm, but Talwyn did not put her arm in Galahad's.

"There are no flowers at this time of year," Talwyn replied, but she followed Galahad into the walled garden nevertheless. The rosebushes sparkled with droplets of ice. Talwyn shivered, perhaps with anticipation as well as cold, or so Galahad hoped.

"I have decided to go away on a quest, perhaps for the Holy Grail," Galahad told her. Galahad tried to give her a winning smile, doubting that it would be successful.

Talwyn frowned. "You're going away."

Galahad's heart beat faster. "Do you care?"

Talwyn's face became blank. "Not at all."

Galahad's heart sank to her boots. She looked at the icicles on the garden's bench. "I'll miss you. Could I have a kiss?"

"Of course not." Talwyn took a step away from Galahad. "You think I'm a loose girl, but I'm not. I don't think you're pure enough to find the grail."

"Unfortunately, I am. Thank you for keeping me pure, Talwyn."

"Go off with the other men, and have your adventures. I shall be just fine here with Lady Guinevere." She turned away from Galahad and pulled her green wool cloak tight around her.

Galahad tried to take Talwyn's hand, but she wouldn't permit it. She began to stride to the garden gate, but Galahad pursued her.

"Wait, there's something I have to tell you." Galahad's voice became urgent.

"I don't want to hear it! Nothing you could say would make any difference in how I feel about you." She darted through the gate.

"I hope that's true," Galahad called after her, backing off. Perhaps it was not a good time to tell Talwyn that she was a woman.

Lancelot went to Arthur's room, but turned down a glass of wine proffered by the king's own hand.

"I am fasting," she said for an excuse. "I am going off to try to find the grail."

The king raised his eyebrows. "There is no grail, but what people want to see," Arthur said. "I thought you knew that. It is only an outward sign of the Lord's majesty, sent to help us look for grace."

"I need to go away." Lancelot stood adamant, barely controlling her anger at him. "Or else my soul may be wounded beyond repair."

Arthur's frowned. "Nonsense. You must not desert me. I need you here."

"I must go away to save my soul." She tried to remember that he was the protector of Britain, not simply the man who angered her. She must control her temper. Her arms still ached to strike him.

"But must you go in the middle of winter? That's no time for journeys." The king shook his head. "Why not wait until Easter?"

"No, I must go now," Lancelot insisted, feeling that she could not control herself any longer.

"If you insist, you may go." Arthur sighed. "But return soon."

Not too soon, she thought, turning away so he would not see her face.

"Lancelot is going off to find the Holy Grail, isn't that splendid?" Bors said to Gawaine after they had demonstrated some fighting techniques to the young warriors in a practice room. They were rubbing their faces with towels. "I will go too."

"Oh, Daghdha's cauldron that has no bottom, but provides food for all those who come to it," Gawaine replied, not wanting to speak about Lancelot's going away. "I always liked that story."

Bors crossed himself. "You know well that I don't mean any such pagan tale. It is Christ's cup from the Last Supper."

"You think that is easier to find?" Gawaine couldn't refrain from smiling, although he didn't want to insult Bors. "I think this grail is like young Percy's caer of the fisher king--a fine story, but nothing to be found in this world."

"I saw the grail with my own eyes, and so did you!" Bors exclaimed indignantly.

"If I saw it, then I didn't recognize it," Gawaine replied with as much courtesy as possible.

Surely Lancelot was not pious enough to go on such a fool errand. She might have done so when she was young, but now a different reason was more likely, Gawaine thought, sighing inwardly. Doubtless she was sad. There had been dark shadows under her eyes lately. Had that cold Guinevere driven Lancelot to leave?

Not daring to look out of the window, Morgan waited in her room. As always on these most important of nights, the room was cold. That was just as well, because fevers consumed her. Perhaps this year the flush came from her aging as well as her desire.

She thought only of Arthur. His body, still as strong as ever, even though he came to her as almost a specter. His face--no other man was as handsome. She remembered his touch, though she had not felt it for a year.

Surely it was later than usual. He should have arrived by now. Her heart raced, but she chided herself. One should not expect enchantments to be prompt, like a servant summoned.

Although she did not look towards the window, Morgan could see rosy streaks streaming across the floor. She shuddered.

He had not come. He would not come. How could he bear to stay away? He had said he never would, that he would always come just this one night a year.

Arthur must be angry at her, angrier than ever. He would never come to her again.

Morgan howled.

16 GUINEVERE'S TEST

After Lancelot had told the young warriors who studied with her that she would be going off on a quest and advised each of them about what he should practice, Gawaine joined her on the walk back from the practice field. The sky was bleak and they could see their breath in the cold air. Two hounds raced play-fighting about the field.

Gawaine paused as if reluctant to go to the warm hall, rather than hurrying on for some hot mead as he was wont to do. He turned to Lancelot.

"I'd like to accompany you on your quest for the grail," he said.

She stared at him. Gawaine wasn't even truly Christian, and he surely couldn't have believed that the vessel they had seen had been what Arthur claimed. Perhaps he was jesting, so she decided to respond in kind. "Don't tell me that you want to look for the grail, you old sinner."

"How do you know I don't?" he asked quietly. The expression on his face was unusually thoughtful. "I wouldn't look for it by myself, but I would like to go with you. And you aren't really going on a pilgrimage. I think you're going off because you're unhappy here."

Lancelot tensed. His manner was too quiet and serious and his eyes were looking into hers in an unfamiliar way. "Even if that were true, I have to go alone."

"I'm not such a bad companion, surely." Gawaine sounded as if he made an effort to speak lightly. "I laugh more than Guinevere does."

"Gawaine, you have more reason to laugh than she does." Lancelot frowned. "How can a woman whose husband lies with her sister be expected to jest?"

"No doubt you're right." He accepted the reproach. "But it is madness to travel alone in winter if there is no need," he protested, putting out his hand as if to keep her at Camelot.

She moved away. "There is a need."

"If you say so," Gawaine said, his face becoming as blank as the shield of a warrior who was keeping his identity unknown.

Walking to her house to change to a clean tunic for supper, Lancelot marveled at the strange expression that had been in his eyes for a moment. No, she was not imagining things. He was wondering whether she would ever . . . How could he? Surely he could not imagine that they could be more than good friends.

She remembered Gawaine's jest of some months ago that he would have to marry the only woman who wouldn't fall in love with her. Belatedly, she guessed that he had meant Lancelot herself. It was a jest, but perhaps not only a jest.

How could she ever feel about Gawaine the way she felt about Guinevere? She shook her head. She felt neither attraction nor repulsion, only amazement and grave misgivings.

Pulling off her stained and sweat-smelling leather tunic, she could think only about Guinevere. To be away from Guinevere's kisses would be a terrible penance. She did not want anyone else's.

Shortly after Lancelot donned her scarlet tunic, Catwal entered, carrying wood that he began to feed into the fire. "How can you undertake a spiritual journey when your heart is so unquiet?" he asked in a somber voice.

Lancelot gasped. Even a blind man could tell that she was in turmoil--perhaps because she paced around the room. "That is why I must go," she told him.

"You might let me go with you to look after you," Catwal said. He addressed her without title because she did not like him to call her "lord" or "master." "My horse has good eyesight and can find his way although I cannot guide him."

"Thank you for your concern, but I must go alone," she said, holding herself back from pacing any further. "All will be well."

"I hope so." Catwal leaned away from the fire as it flared up.

That evening, when Gawaine, Lancelot, Bedwyr, Bors, and Peredur sat in Arthur's room after supper, Lancelot said, "I'd like to tell a story."

Gawaine raised his eyebrows and watched her carefully. Lancelot never told stories. What meaning did she want to convey, and to whom?

Tewdar the serving man poured another round of wine.

"I suspect this won't be much like Gawaine's bawdy tales," Bedwyr sighed, signaling to have his cup refilled. "No doubt it will have a moral."

"Perhaps it will," Lancelot admitted. "Once there was a lady who was betrothed to a lord whom she did not want to marry, so she decided to run away." Avoiding her friends' faces, Lancelot looked out of the window into the night. "She asked a warrior who was her friend to help her. It was dangerous to oppose this lord, but the warrior agreed."

"Of course he did, if she was beautiful. You didn't say whether she was," Arthur commented, quaffing his wine.

Lancelot shrugged. "People said that she was handsome. Very well, I suppose she was beautiful."

"You don't know how to tell a story," Bedwyr complained.

Gawaine could barely refrain from ordering him to be silent and listen.

"The lord sent many warriors in pursuit of them," Lancelot said, "They had to go to distant forests, and had many adventures, which they faced together with good cheer. They liked each other."

"This sounds like the tale of Grania and Diarmuid. Of course she ran away only to seduce him." Bedwyr snickered.

Gawaine listened attentively, for he did not think it was Grania's tale. The expression on Lancelot's face was hard to read.

"This is a different story. Then, one day," Lancelot continued, still looking out of the window, "the warrior suggested that they should be more to each other, and the lady was distressed. 'You don't understand,' she said. 'I didn't just want to avoid the lord I fled from. I don't want any man.'"

"Coy, was she?" Arthur asked.

"No," Lancelot insisted, shaking her head. "She meant what she said. But the warrior said that she didn't understand these things because she was a maiden, and that she would be very happy with him. She doubted that, but after a time she let him persuade her."

"Obviously," Bedwyr said.

"But she found that she had been right. She was not happy. And because he was clever, and she was not able to hide her feelings, he soon saw that she was not. And everything was dust and ashes for him because she was unhappy. It was hard to say which of them was the more miserable. Finally, one day she said, 'Please go off and find another woman, who could love you in the way you want,' but he said, 'I can't leave you.' She insisted that he should. Then, after some time, he did leave, and one day he returned, bringing another lady, and he introduced his old friend as his sister. She was happy, and said, 'I am glad that my brother has found someone,'" Lancelot concluded, and took a drink of wine.

Gawaine took a large drink himself and almost choked.

"That's the most ridiculous story I have ever heard," Arthur scoffed, setting his silver goblet firmly on the table. "She was a foolish woman, but she got what she deserved. I certainly don't believe she would be glad that he'd found another woman. Even if she didn't want him, she wouldn't want anyone else to have him."

"No one could be that selfish," Lancelot said, sounding appalled. She now looked at the king instead of the dark outside of the window.

"Don't judge by yourself," the king answered, patting a dog that was curled at his feet. "No woman is as noble-hearted as you are, Lance."

"You didn't say whether they were married," Bors reproached Lancelot. "Of course the lady was unhappy and ashamed if they were not."

"It doesn't matter whether they were married," Lancelot replied, sighing.

"Of course it does," Peredur said, turning the goblet in his hand with annoyance. "Honorable men can't just go off and leave women. He would have gotten her with child, and they would have had to wed whether they were joyful or not. Marriage isn't just about kisses, it's about raising a family."

"A child!" Lancelot exclaimed. "How horrible to have to marry because of that." She gulped down some wine.

"If the man liked her so much, he would have been glad to marry her," Gawaine said.

Lancelot gasped and shook her head.

"I suppose the man must have been ugly for her to spurn him so," Arthur said, playing with the ears of his dog, which had put its head in his lap.

"Or he was a terrible lover," Bedwyr contributed.

"No." Lancelot's voice was emphatic. "He wasn't ugly or a bad lover. That's not the point. Love is not just a matter of this act or that act, but of the whole person."

"Well, he was a soft and sentimental man to pay so much attention to a woman's whims," Arthur said, gesturing for his serving man to pour yet another round. "That running off in the forest sounds like Tristram and Iseult. Mark was a brute to kill Tristram. He was a great warrior."

"Why don't you tell one of your stories, Gawaine? Yours are much better," Bedwyr asked.

"Not at the moment," Gawaine said quietly. It would take him a while to recover from this one.

"Well, I must get some rest before I set forth tomorrow." Lancelot nodded to them all and departed after accepting their good wishes.

As soon as Lancelot left, Bedwyr said, "Lancelot must have been the man in the story. Only he would be so foolish as to listen so much to a woman who was impossible to please. And did you see how annoyed he was at the idea that the man was ugly or a bad lover?"

"How clever of you to guess that Lancelot was the man in the story," Gawaine told him. No one else would ever guess that Lancelot was the woman in the tale.

Guinevere heard the secret door open and the tapestry rustle. Lancelot entered the room. At least Lancelot would say farewell to her.

Lancelot's face was pale and unsmiling. She looked as if she might weep, but she held herself erect.

"Are you leaving tomorrow, dearest?" Guinevere asked, striving to keep her voice calm.

"Yes. A long parting would be too difficult." Lancelot's voice was just as strained as her face.

Guinevere sucked in her breath. Lancelot did not mean to stay the night. Biting her lip, Guinevere said, "Do what you must. I hope you will return soon."

"I am not certain how soon. God keep you well, my lady." Lancelot turned and pulled back the tapestry.

"I pray that you will be safe," Guinevere replied.

Then Lancelot was gone.

Guinevere sat down in a chair. She could not keep standing.

Determined not to show her grief at Lancelot's departure on what promised to be a long journey, Guinevere put on a smile and went to Cai's office. Although the day was dark, he had several oil lamps burning brightly. How little he seemed to age, she thought. He had no gray in his hair, and his skin was much less wrinkled than that of Arthur's other men. Of course he spent far less time out in the elements than they did.

"I want to hold a special feast to cheer the court in the January gloom," she said.

Cai's eyebrows shot up, but he said, "Will the guests be sustained by spiritual nourishment from the grail, or should we plan fine foods?"

Guinevere gave him a look that said she believed as little in the grail as he did. "Fine foods, of course. What everyone likes best to eat. Be sure that there is roast pork for the king, and partridges in wine for Peredur, the freshest fish for Bors, and plenty of apples for Gawaine. Surely you must have some apples that are not too dried up."

"Apples in January. Of course we have some in the cellars, but I can't make them taste as if they just came from Eden. But I doubt that you want to tempt the guests." Cai grinned at her, as if he knew just how little she wanted to tempt anyone, least of all Gawaine.

She rolled her eyes. "No, just to feed them well. Put some sort of wine sauce on the fruit, if you must, to improve the taste. The warriors will like it well enough if it tastes of wine."

The feast started off well. Several whole roasted pigs brought appreciative smiles from many warriors. The fires burned bright, warming them all, and Cai had brought out some of the best wines. Harpers played and sang of the sorrows of winter and the tantalizing joys of spring.

Just as they began to eat, a slender young warrior, Patricius, picked up an apple dripping with wine sauce. "You can't have all the apples, Gawaine, although you always find women ready to offer them to you. I shall sin now, and perhaps redeem myself later by looking for the grail," he said.

Many warriors laughed. Bors and Gareth frowned. Patricius took a bite, and, a moment later, collapsed, crying out in pain. Then he was still, his face horribly contorted.

Everyone began yelling and jumping up, upsetting the dishes. Men spat food from their mouths. Servers screamed and dropped their trenchers. Warriors who were kin to Patricius hung over him so that Arthur had to order them back to allow Cassius to reach the warrior and pronounce him dead.

Guinevere sat frozen with horror. He must have been poisoned. How could such a thing happen at Camelot?

"This poison was meant for Gawaine! Everyone knows he usually takes the first apple!" Gaheris wailed, leaping to Gawaine's side to defend him.

"It was meant for Gawaine!" Agravaine waved his fist as if menacing the whole company.

"Someone has tried to murder Gawaine!" Gareth leapt to Gawaine's other side.

Remaining seated, Gawaine put one hand on Gaheris's arm, the other on Gareth's, as if to restrain them. His face had paled.

Mador, a lean, well-muscled warrior who was cousin to Patricius, began to yell, "The queen poisoned him. It was her feast. She poisoned the apples. She must have meant to poison Gawaine. Everyone knows that she dislikes him. She must die! My Lord Arthur, I demand justice!" he shrieked, eyes fixed on the king.

Arthur stood, firm and dignified as a Caesar. "Be calm, Mador. This contemptible murder has unnerved you. Of course there will be justice for the murderer, but it could not have been the queen. Why would she do such a thing?"

"I have never poisoned anyone. I would never poison anyone," Guinevere said quietly, trying not to shudder at the accusation. She could hardly believe that anyone would imagine she could commit murder. Nor was she pleased at having to rely on her husband for justice. His first words were not bad, but would he be guided by his hatred?

"I accuse her! You must try her, my lord," Mador insisted, pointing his finger at her.

Some other warriors nodded. None spoke up to challenge the accusation.

Feeling as if she would faint, Guinevere clutched the table edge and tried to maintain her dignity.

"There will be justice," Arthur said, majestic as ever. "If you make this challenge, a defender can fight you and prove her innocence."

"I do make this challenge," Mador cried.

"And who will fight for our queen?" Arthur asked, as calmly as if he were asking the outcome of a contest, though serving men were carrying the wretched corpse away not far from him.

No one spoke.

Guinevere tried not to look around the table and see the faces of the men who refused to defend her.

Arthur raised his eyebrows and surveyed his men. "Who will fight for the queen?" His voice had grown sterner.

So, little though Arthur cared about her now, at least he wanted her to be championed, Guinevere thought. He was far too intelligent to believe that she would poison a warrior. But wouldn't this charge give him an excuse to rid himself of her?

Gray-mustached Bors bowed to the king, and then to Guinevere. "I would be honored to fight in defense of the queen's innocence, if no warrior who is greater than I will do so, but if a greater one wishes to fight in my stead, he can."

Arthur and Guinevere both nodded to him in acknowledgment. She was not surprised that Bors was willing to fight for her, but she knew that he was not one of Arthur's best fighters.

"Let the contest be held a week from today," Arthur proclaimed. "Now let us leave this distressing scene. I offer our condolences to the family of the noble Patricius. We shall bury him with the greatest honor. Meanwhile, if anyone can tell me who the guilty party is, let him come to me, and I shall reward him if his charges prove to be true."

Arthur called Gawaine to his room.

"Why did you allow Bors to say he would fight for Guinevere?" Arthur demanded, letting his annoyance show in his voice. He had never before felt so irritated at Gawaine. Arthur sat at his table, but he leaned forward towards his cousin. "He doesn't fight as well as Mador. I can't fight for her, because I can't be both judge and defender. Why didn't you offer to fight for her? She's your kin as well as your queen."

Gawaine remained standing. His face was like a mask. "Wouldn't that seem a bit odd when most people think I'm the one she tried to poison? My brothers would be displeased."

Arthur frowned. He did not ask Gawaine to be seated. He himself had not many months before suggested to Lancelot that Guinevere might be a poisoner, but of course he hadn't believed it and wouldn't have kept her around him if he had. She was his queen and it was infuriating that some mere warrior had sought to bring her to judgment. "That's completely mad. Guinevere has absolutely no reason to poison you. She was angry some fourteen or fifteen years ago when I suggested that she should lie with you to produce an heir, but nothing came of it. You didn't even try asking her. She could hardly hold a grudge that bitterly for so long. What possible reason would she have for killing you?"

"None." Gawaine's voice was expressionless.

"Then why won't you fight for her? You have sworn to defend all women, and that includes Guinevere."

"I will if I have to," Gawaine said with apparent reluctance, "although it would look very strange. But you set the contest for a week from now, so Lancelot will likely hear about it and come to fight and prove her innocence."

Arthur relaxed slightly. Yes, he could rely on Lancelot. It would be good to have Lancelot return, even for such a terrible reason. "Of course that's why I put it off. That, and the hope that someone will name the real poisoner. And of course, I won't put Guinevere to death. If worst comes to worst and her champion loses, I'll just send her to a convent for a few months, until this little storm blows over." But there was no need to tell Guinevere that decision too soon. Let her worry a little.

Guinevere retreated to her room and stayed there as much as possible, but acted calm, both there and when she went about the court, when others were around her. Talwyn had come sobbing to her, and Guinevere had comforted the dear girl and told her, and all the other ladies and serving women, not to worry. When Guinevere was alone, she sat in stunned silence.

It does no good to weep because I might die, Guinevere thought, shivering. She put on an extra shawl and invited her cat to sit in her lap.

Why hadn't Gawaine leapt up at once and said that the idea of her trying to poison him was nonsense? Surely he must know that. His silence was inexplicable.

She should not rely on men's swords to save her. Instead, she must use her mind and try to figure out who the murderer was. She looked at the courtyard, where warriors strolled. Somewhere out there was the killer, laughing inwardly because she had been accused. If she was executed, the murderer would watch her die. She shuddered. Perhaps the murderer wanted her dead? Could the plot really be against her? No, that idea was too far-fetched.

Sunlight sparkled on snow in the courtyard. She did not want to die.

Was Gawaine truly the intended victim? Why would anyone imagine that she wanted to kill him? If everyone killed the people they disliked, none of us would be left standing, she thought. There were other men--Agravaine, for instance--whom she disliked more than Gawaine.

If someone had tried to kill Gawaine, no doubt it was due to his wenching. Perhaps it was some woman he had cast aside? But how could any of the ladies have had a chance to poison the apples? The men were served first, and the bowl had been nowhere near where the ladies sat.

More likely the poisoner was the father, brother, husband, or sweetheart of some woman Gawaine had seduced, Guinevere thought, patting her cat absently. Men usually settled such grievances with swords, but this man must have known that he was unlikely to kill Gawaine in a fair fight, indeed far more likely to be killed himself if he insisted on fighting to the death.

Perhaps the murderer might even be a serving man whose woman Gawaine had taken. Poison would be the only weapon that a serving man could use against Gawaine. The serving men had more chances to poison the apples than the nobles did.

But how could she discover who the murderer was? She had little idea of which women Gawaine had lain with, and how could she find out? She rubbed the cat's cheek, and it purred loudly.

She could not go about asking who had lain with Gawaine. Was there anyone who could ask such questions for her? Lionors was the lady she liked best, and she surely would believe that Guinevere was innocent, but Lionors did not gossip and would be horrified at the idea of asking anything of kind.

Talwyn would be only too eager to try to find out who the murderer was, but Guinevere had no intention of letting her do so. Talwyn was little more than a child, and would quickly get herself in trouble.

If only Fencha were still at Camelot! She always knew who was lying with whom. Luned was much shyer.

Creirwy knew little of what was happening among the ladies, but she might ask questions of the serving people. Guinevere summoned her.

"I did not poison the apples," she told the serving girl.

"Of course not, Lady Guinevere." Creirwy nodded vigorously.

"Can you find out whether any of the serving people hated Gawaine?"

Creirwy frowned. "It would be easier to find out which ones loved him. He's very popular with the serving people, Lady Guinevere. Many of the women throw themselves at him, but the men like him, too. I don't think you'll find the killer among them, but I'll ask." Her voice became harsher. "They won't be too pleased at the idea of someone trying to put the blame on them for a murder committed by a noble."

Guinevere looked at the girl's troubled face and her red, raw hands, much like those of the other serving people who toiled to maintain the court in comfort. "I would never try to put the blame on any of them if they didn't do it."

"I know, Lady Guinevere, but they won't all know that. They'll suspect the worst. But I'll ask." Her tone was resigned, too resigned. Creirwy generally did not sound as resigned to her lot as the other serving people, and Guinevere liked that well.

"Perhaps it is better if you don't ask. Never mind, it's probably a noble, as you said." Guinevere dismissed her. If the murderer really was a serving man, he might be frightened and injure Creirwy. Guinevere did not want to risk that.

When she was alone again, Guinevere looked out of the window. Mador was speaking with another warrior in the courtyard below. He gestured so fiercely that he was probably talking about the murder.

What if Gawaine had not been the intended victim? Why had Mador been so quick to accuse Guinevere? What if he had murdered his kinsman because he expected to inherit property?

But she was in no position to ask about that. If only there was someone who could make inquiries for her, but she was alone. There was no one to ask. If she had still been on good terms with Arthur, of course she could have gone to him, and he would have asked someone to pursue the inquiries. If he had come to see her, she would have told him what her thoughts were, but he did not, and she did not feel that she could go to him. She sighed, but she wanted to beat her fists against the wall in a protest at her helplessness.

On the day when the test was set, the whole court assembled on the contest field. There was a light covering of snow on the ground, making the footing worse for a fight. No fighting contest would ever be held in the snow, but the trial by combat was not postponed.

The crowd's mood was somber, and people muttered. Guinevere did not sit beside the king as usual, but off some distance with her ladies. It was mild for a January day, but her marten-fur robe did not warm her. The sky was as gray as her mood. She might die. Surely she would not die. Sitting calmly was an effort, but she was determined not to tremble. If Bors lost, she must not weep. Would Arthur really execute her? He did not believe she was a murderer.

What madness this trial by combat was. All men cared about was their own skills, not justice. If only she could defend herself. But she could barely lift a sword, and her words did not matter. If she could rule, she would not let trials be decided by such means.

Gawaine stood near Arthur, who was looking at him with great impatience. The red-bearded warrior wore his chain mail. Perhaps he would defend her after all. Though they disliked each other, she thought it was odd that he had not risen to her defense because he was the best fighter when Lancelot was gone and, as Arthur's cousin, was kin to her. Surely he could not believe that she would try to poison him?

Bors came out on the field, shaking a little, and made the sign of the cross. Walking over to Guinevere, he bowed before her. "God grant me the strength to prove your innocence, my lady. I am sure that He will, because that is the only way that justice can be done. Have faith."

"I shall," she said, with grave courtesy. "Thank you for your kindness. Do not be distressed if you are not as successful as you hope. Tell yourself that God intended it that way." She pitied Bors having to fight for her life and wanted him not to be stricken with guilt if he failed.

"His ways are mysterious, but surely not that much so," Bors said, trembling a little more.

They saw a midnight black horse gallop up, and a smile spread over the pious warrior's face. "My prayers are answered. Here is your true champion, Lancelot. He'll make short work of Mador and his insane accusation."

Guinevere sighed with relief. Her jaws, which had been tightly clenched, relaxed. She wished she could leap from the stands and throw her arms around her beloved warrior. Of course Lancelot would save her.

Lancelot rode to the stands, bowed to Guinevere, and then to the king. Both bowed gravely in return.

It was as Bors said. Lancelot quickly bested Mador, knocking his sword out of his hand after giving him some cuts.

Mador went down on his knees. "I yield. Have mercy, Lancelot."

Lancelot held her sword to Mador's throat. Her voice was harsher than a hailstorm. "Only if you say that the queen had nothing to do with poison and promise that you will never again repeat this slander against her."

"I swear it," Mador said, and Lancelot let him scramble to his feet.

Guinevere held back tears and pulled the fur cloak tighter around her. All she wanted was to see Lancelot alone and be in her arms.

There was a contented sigh among the crowd, and people murmured that justice had been done and the process had once again proved to be the best possible.

Arthur said a few words to that effect, thanked Lancelot, praised justice, and asked for God's blessing. Guinevere nodded, and discreetly let her husband give her thanks for her.

Later, as night came, she retired to her room, and finally Lancelot came from the hidden passage.

"Thank you," Guinevere said simply, opening her arms just a little in anticipation of a possible reconciliation, but not so wide that she would look like a fool if Lancelot did not enter them.

"Of course I came to save your life," Lancelot responded, not moving close. There was no tenderness in her gaze. "But tell me, did you try to poison Gawaine?"

Guinevere recoiled as if Lancelot had struck her. "Why ever should I poison Gawaine? I have no reason to poison him." A terrible thought came into her mind. "Do I?"

"No!" Lancelot yelled. "Don't you trust me?"

"Don't you trust me?" Guinevere echoed her.

"Do you really think I'd murder anyone?" They glared at each other. "And he doesn't even know that you're a woman."

"Yes, he does," Lancelot replied defiantly.

Guinevere's stomach heaved. "You told him?"

"No, he just found out. It doesn't matter how. He's my friend, anyway."

"No doubt he wants to be more," Guinevere countered in a bitter tone. Of course Gawaine wanted more with nearly every woman.

"You don't trust me." Lancelot trembled with anger. "After all these years, you don't trust me."

Guinevere felt as if her world was collapsing. Instead of comforting her, Lancelot was harsh with her. Had Lancelot been more concerned about the possibility that someone might have tried to poison Gawaine than about the danger to Guinevere's life if her champion had lost? Her voice became more frenzied. "You're the one who doesn't trust me. You think I'd commit murder out of jealousy and spite. You think like a man."

"I suppose that's the worst possible insult, coming from you." Lancelot's eyes still held no warmth.

"You think they aren't so bad?" Guinevere felt angry blood rushing through her heart. "I hope you aren't so foolish as to trust that friend of yours."

Lancelot glowered. "Of course I trust him. He cares as much about the friendship as I do."

More thoughts flooded Guinevere's brain. "And does he know that you haven't told me that he's aware you're a woman?"

"Yes." Lancelot's voice was impatient, as if the matter was insignificant.

Guinevere trembled. "Then he must have jested about my ignorance, and you've let him laugh about it?"

"What of it?" Lancelot's face and voice showed no sign of apology.

"I call that infidelity."

Lancelot glared at her as if she were an enemy. How unnerving to see her gentle brown eyes glare! "Infidelity indeed! No one could or would be more faithful to you than I have been. Does my friendship with him bother you so? Oh, how terrible that you should have to feel for a few moments what I've had to feel for the last ten years. I hate it that you're married. I hate it!" Her face was red, and not with blushing.

Guinevere was strangely relieved to hear those words, but she just snapped back. "Oh, that old refrain again. You know I don't lie with Arthur."

"You kiss him!"

"Only in public! It's nothing. It's less than nothing." She was unwilling to remain on the defensive. "But you like Gawaine."

"Well, that's not nothing," Lancelot asserted, frowning. "It's friendship. I'm as fond of him as if he were my brother. Must you harp on this nonsense about Gawaine? I even told him a story that made it sound as if I could never possibly be attracted to a man, which might be an exaggeration. I just don't want one. Some friendships are better with a little distance."

Guinevere was stung by the absence of an avowal of love. "Oh, by all means, don't do anything to spoil your friendship. It's not as if you had some other love. If you told him a story that's not true, he probably knows it isn't."

"He is clever enough to know that we all make stories of our lives, and to see the significance of my choosing the one that is the most discouraging." Still she stormed at Guinevere. "How can you complain about me, when you act like a wife to someone else? How do I know that you are faithful to me?"

Guinevere shook with anger. As if she could do anything but pretend to be a good wife to Arthur! "How dare you accuse me! If you think I'm unfaithful, you're a fool. You understand nothing of what it is to be a woman. No one has ever touched you without love. You know nothing of what I have endured, nothing! Go back to the company of noble men. This humble lady thanks you for taking the time from your quest to save her. I'm saved now; you can go again, if you like." Her hands formed fists.

"I must, at least for a time. Will you come with me?" Lancelot did not beg, but her longing was visible in her eyes. Her face finally showed something other than anger.

"And do what? Try to live on roots and nuts in the woods in winter? With Arthur chasing after us to redeem his honor by taking me back?" Guinevere said scornfully. Even if she had been willing to go to Lesser Britain, they could not have gone at that time of year. No ships would sail until spring.

"It would be better than this misery," Lancelot said, and turned to the door.

"So you think I should show my love for you by running off and getting you killed like Tristram? I've told you I won't be free until Arthur dies."

Lancelot bolted out of the door.

Guinevere called after her, but Lancelot thudded down the stairs of the secret passage. Guinevere threw herself on the bed and sobbed.

How long would it be before she saw Lancelot again? Why didn't Lancelot understand that she couldn't leave with her? Lancelot knew only freedom; she didn't understand what it was not to be free. Guinevere stifled her sobs in the pillow. She couldn't bear to see Lancelot cut down by Arthur. Better to be captive, better even to be misjudged by the one she loved.

Gawaine was free to spend more time with Lancelot than she could, curse him, Guinevere thought bitterly. He could go out riding with Lancelot at any time; he could speak with her all day. Not while Lancelot was away, of course, but he had had such freedom for years. He could go on journeys with Lancelot; he could save Lancelot's life.

Although she could not fight, Guinevere had saved Lancelot's life more than once, but those incidents happened years ago. She could not go off and fight at Lancelot's side, which was apparently what Lancelot valued. Killing together-- how sweet. Guinevere shook with anger as well as sorrow. Lancelot had once admitted that she trusted Gawaine more than Guinevere. It appeared that she still did.

After ten years of love, Lancelot still did not trust her! Guinevere moaned. How many people would trust her? Lancelot could fight better than Mador, but that did not really prove that Guinevere was not a poisoner. Probably no one would ever know who poisoned Patricius, and no one would bother to try to discover the truth. She would always have to live under suspicion. Guinevere clutched the pillow so hard that she tore it, and feathers came tumbling out.

The next morning, Guinevere approached Gawaine in the stableyard. She could barely force herself to speak to him, now that she realized he knew Lancelot was a woman. Lancelot had told him that she and Guinevere loved each other. Did Gawaine find the idea of two women loving each other amusing, curse him?

Guinevere kept her face and her voice as expressionless as possible.

"You had better look elsewhere for your poisoner, if you think you were the intended victim. I don't stoop to such things. No one will ever die because of me."

"Thank you for the warning, your highness," he said, just as formally, his face just as impassive.

Gawaine ought to realize that some unknown person who had tried to kill him was likely to try again, and that he should attempt to find out who it was--but he probably wasn't clever enough to believe her and do that, Guinevere thought as she stalked to her horse.

17 Lancelot's Quest

Galahad rode off across snow-whitened land that was still except for the occasional call of a carrion crow. The land seemed empty, though tracks of hares, foxes, and red deer were threaded across it. She had just visited her mother's caer, Tintagel by the sea. Following directions that her mother had given her, she came to a moorland bog near a wood. Some waterfowl flew up from a pond that was only partly covered with ice, and a young woman rose up out of the reeds. Galahad rode to her.

The lady had reddish hair, tangled from the wind, and a wild, shy look. She did not hold her plaid wool cloak tight around her, but let it flap in the breeze.

"Are you the Lady Elaine?" Galahad asked, sure that she was.

She stared at Galahad. Her pale face filled with wonder.

"I am. I had the strangest feeling when I saw you ride up. The thought came to me that you are my brother, not the man who I always thought was. I don't know how that can be."

"It's true," Galahad said, smiling in what she hoped was a brotherly way. "I recently was told that you are my sister. That's why I came here to see you, although just briefly."

They looked at each other, not knowing what else to say. Galahad wanted to embrace Elaine, but hesitated for fear the girl would resent such sudden intimacy. Her mother had told her that this Elaine was her sister, but warned her not to reveal anything about their parentage.

Finally, Elaine said, "I know where owls nest. Would you like to see that?"

"Yes, that would be grand."

Galahad dismounted and followed her to a wood where a great gray owl sat high in an oak.

"There's the mate, on the next tree," Elaine said, gesturing.

"I don't see it." Galahad stared at the pine, but its thick needles hid any birds from view.

"You have to look where the branches are thickest, near the trunk, some distance from the top," Elaine replied.

Galahad peered among the branches and found the owl.

"And there's the nest," Elaine added, gesturing toward a wobbly looking nest of sticks.

"Did you see them build it?"

"Owls don't build their own nests, but take old ones made by other birds. Didn't you know that?"

"No." Galahad looked down at the snow. They had not been children together, but perhaps they could recapture a little of that lost childhood. "Did you play with snowballs when you were young?"

"Not much." Elaine picked up a handful of snow and let it fall. "I was mostly alone or with my mother. My brother is much older and was always sullen."

"Did he ever hurt you?" Galahad's stomach tightened.

"No, he mostly ignored me."

"Good." Galahad nodded. What she knew of her own parentage made her leery of how men treated their sisters. "Would you like to know how to make a good snowball?"

"Yes." Elaine smiled shyly and brushed her hair from her face.

Galahad showed her how to pack the snow into a ball. They tossed the snowballs at trees and watched them shatter on the bark.

"Would you like to have a snowball fight?"

Elaine giggled. "Yes."

They threw snowballs at each other for a while, Galahad deliberately aiming to miss. Elaine laughed like one who had been starved for laughter. She hit Galahad several times, and a few times Galahad's softly packed snowballs struck Elaine's shoulder.

The winter afternoon light grew dim, and Elaine asked, "Will you come to my father's hall for supper?"

"I fear I cannot. I have to go on a journey. But I'll be back someday." Galahad looked at her regretfully, reluctant to leave.

Elaine sighed. "I'm glad I met you anyway."

"It's better if you don't tell anyone." The suggestion of something hidden embarrassed Galahad, but she believed that she must obey her mother.

"I thought that might be true. I don't understand, but I won't tell." Elaine kissed Galahad lightly on the cheek.

Galahad hugged her and went off, wondering how meeting a grown sister could be different from this awkward tenderness, as it apparently had been for King Arthur and Galahad's mother.

But her mother had told her to use discretion, so she was glad that Elaine hadn't asked her name.

Lancelot had gone off angry for many reasons. Truly, fighting with her lover was more painful than combat with men.

Perhaps she had been wrong to imagine that Guinevere might have plotted to murder Gawaine, but Guinevere might want her to kill Arthur. That was horrible to contemplate. And worse, Lancelot sometimes wanted to do it.

In many places mud, not snow, covered the land. Everything seemed desolate, barren of beauty.

She passed a frozen pond and stared at the leaves and logs trapped beneath its dark surface. No waterfowl lingered near it. She wondered whether she, too, could freeze, if she stayed forever caught in this half-hidden love, lived out in the husband's shadow. A winter light showed bare trees reflected pale on one corner of the pond, like a ghostly world in which only saints could dwell. Such a world would have drawn her once, but it no longer did. Trying to be a celibate saint was not enough for one who had known love.

Feeling weary, Lancelot camped early for the night. She attempted to eat some of the food that Catwal had packed for her, but she could barely swallow. Nothing tasted as it should, and indeed she did not want food at all.

She wanted to sleep and escape from her troubles, but she could not. Her body was rigid. She couldn't remember long it had been since she had slept much. Not since the Christ Mass, but perhaps longer.

The next day her eyes were bleary, and all she wanted was to lie down again. But when night came, again she was so filled with fear that she had lost Guinevere that she could not sleep.

It did not seem that she ever slept, but she opened her eyes long after dawn had come. A man stood beside her. She reached for her sword, then saw he was Bellangere. She sighed with relief.

"Bellangere, good day. Why do you stand so strangely quiet before me?" Rising, she extended her hand to him.

He did not accept it. "I am calling you out to fight," he said, regarding her as if she wore scales instead of chain mail.

Stunned, Lancelot stared at him. "Fight another warrior of King Arthur's? For what cause? If you want a contest, can't we settle this next Pentecost?"

Bellangere shook his fist and exclaimed in anger, "Contests be damned! I'm fighting to avenge my cousin Sangremore, because you killed him for trifling with a Saxon wench. You gave him no chance to fight, but killed him like a dog."

All of her muscles tensed. Her heart beat faster. "It's true that I killed him, though I would have fought him if he had not fled from me. He did not trifle, as you said, but raped her."

His face almost purple, Bellangere shook with rage. "And you cut off his head and gave it to the Saxons! That's no way to treat a brother warrior."

"I did that," she admitted, trying to face him as calmly as possible. "But the Saxons would have killed Gawaine if I didn't have proof that Sangremore was dead. I don't want to fight with you. Sangremore's not worth avenging."

"You holy fanatic whoreson, he was my cousin!" Bellangere shouted. "Will you agree to fight, or must I just attack you?"

"I'll fight if you demand it, but I have no wish to shed your blood. We are both sworn to King Arthur," Lancelot replied sadly, nevertheless readying her mind for battle. She already had to pray for Sangremore's soul, and she did not want to have to pray for Bellangere's as well.

Bellangere smiled unpleasantly. "Sangremore was sworn to Arthur, but you murdered him. I'm the one who tried to poison

Gawaine, because he stood up for you, and I thought your lady"--he pronounced this word with great sarcasm--"would die for it."

Lancelot gasped. "What a cowardly act!" Her hand clutched the hilt of her sword. But she could scarcely believe his words. "Can you really be Bellangere and have done such things?" she asked.

The man smiled craftily. "I am Bellangere, but you are not Lancelot. You only imagine that you are. You aren't a great warrior at all. You aren't a true member of King Arthur's round table. You are deluded into believing that a queen loves you, but she does not. When you aren't at Camelot, she hangs on the king's arm. I see you for what you are. You're just a madman who goes about killing people."

Lancelot froze. She must be an imposter. This man had seen through her. And he could see that Guinevere didn't love her.

Panic seized Lancelot. She tried to pull her sword from its scabbard, but her hand would not move. The forest swam before her eyes. Dimly, she saw Bellangere hit her horse on the rump and drive the mare off. Then his fists moved towards her, but her body was unable to move, even when she felt his blows.

Drian rode in the forest far to the south and west of the areas she usually frequented. A commotion drew her to explore on foot and peer through the trees.

Drian's heart plunged into her boots. A large warrior, not as big as the hairy brute whom Lancelot called a friend, but big enough, considerably larger than Drian, was beating Lancelot, who was lying helpless on the ground. How could Drian stop him? If she had her bow and arrows with her it would be simple, but she had left them on her horse, which was some distance away.

Drian climbed one of the bare oak trees. She edged her way out along the largest limb, then sprang down on the man, knocking him over, away from Lancelot. Hitting and kicking, she hoped she could subdue him. He slumped like a sack of grain. She hardly dared to stop pummeling him. What if he were pretending to be unconscious, and would spring at her if she let up? Finally, she left off and got up. She saw that his neck was broken, no doubt from the impact when she jumped on him.

Lancelot had risen and was shaking not far away. Then she ran off. Drian rushed after her. Although her legs were stiff and sore from the jump, Drian could run faster than anyone she knew, and she soon caught hold of Lancelot's arm.

"Lance, it's Drian." Lancelot stared vacantly at her, but did not seem afraid. She led Lancelot to the stream, broke the ice, and washed Lancelot's face and hands, which had been hurt by the man. Then she gathered Lancelot in her arms and sat down by the bank.

Drian muttered soothing sounds and held Lancelot, who did not resist but seemed not to know who Drian was. Drian sang old songs that she had learned from her grandmother.

That night, Lancelot slept, and sometimes Drian drifted off too.

In the morning, she woke up to the sound of Lancelot's voice. "Drian! How did you get here? I dreamed of you."

Drian rubbed her eyes and hugged Lancelot. "Lance! I'm glad to hear your voice," she exclaimed heartily. She had wondered whether Lancelot ever would recover, and how she would care for Lancelot if she did not.

Lancelot flushed. "I lose myself sometimes. I hope I didn't distress you. Why, I'm covered with bruises!"

"Some man attacked you."

"And you saved me!" Lancelot hugged her tightly.

"I jumped on him from a tree."

"You might have been killed." Lancelot embraced her again and Drian felt so warm that it might have been summer. "Is his body near? Of course, he couldn't have been anyone I know, but I want to see."

"Of course he couldn't." Drian's voice was sarcastic. Lancelot's faith in the other warriors of the round table struck her as mad. She led the way to the man's body.

"It's Bellangere, another warrior of the round table!" Lancelot exclaimed. "No, it's the man who saw through me." She fell silent. Trembling, she closed her eyes.

When Lancelot opened them, she again looked at Drian as if she did not recognize her. Drian guided her away from the body, but Lancelot still did not speak. She sank to the ground as if exhausted, and Drian sat beside her.

Drian sang again, but Lancelot seemed not to notice. As the morning waned into afternoon, Lancelot still sat staring vacantly. Another cold night passed, and Drian hoped that Lancelot would again be better in the morning, but when the warrior's eyes opened, she did not know Drian.

Drian managed to coax the shaking warrior to walk off with her. She had looked for Lancelot's horse, but it was nowhere to be seen, so she helped Lancelot onto her own brown mare and walked beside her, only riding with her when she became exhausted, because it was hard for a horse to carry two riders.

For several days, Drian traveled, she knew not where, with Lancelot. She fed the warrior, and when they had used up all of her food, Drian snared some squirrels. When they came to a small village, she asked if there was a wise woman who was a healer. She was directed to a crone's hut.

The mud-daub hut was poor but cheerful, with many cats by the fire and herbs hanging from the thatched roof.

Drian led the trembling warrior into the smoky hut. A much-wrinkled little crone regarded them kindly.

"He's been attacked by another warrior who he thought was a friend, and since then he doesn't seem to know who he is or who I am," Drian said. Her voice shook.

"Don't be afraid," the old woman said soothingly, trying to hold Lancelot's hand in her gnarled one, but Lancelot put her hands over her face and sobbed.

A cat rubbed against Lancelot's ankle and she stopped weeping. She looked at the cat sadly, but she petted it.

"I can't help him," the crone said, "But a young lady who lives in a nearby dun is the daughter of a famous healer, and they say that she's a healer, too. Go down the road and turn when you come to a bog. Then take this warrior to the dun, and say that you're seekin' the help of the Lady Elaine."

"I'll do that. Thanks," Drian said, although her stomach sank at the thought of asking nobles for help. She helped Lancelot back to the horse.

They went along, and when they came to the bog, a red-headed lady in a plaid cloak appeared by a pond.

Tears were dripping down Lancelot's cheeks.

"What ails this warrior?" the lady asked, for after all it was not common to see a warrior ride by weeping.

"He's sorely troubled, and can't speak or care for himself," Drian said. "I'm looking for the Lady Elaine, who's supposed to be a healer."

"I am Elaine," she said, reaching up to pat Lancelot's hand. Her gray eyes seemed to reflect back Lancelot's sorrow. "But I don't know whether I can care for him. I have never tended a man, except for my father and brother when they had slight fevers. I usually tend women."

Drian spoke reluctantly. "Well, my friend's really not a man, but don't tell anyone. It could be dangerous."

"Not a man!" Elaine exclaimed. Her eyes widened.

"Will you promise not to tell anyone?" Drian asked. Should she trust this lady? But there was no choice.

Lancelot looked down through her tears at Elaine. She did not stop crying, but she did not seem afraid of her.

"Please do help, if you can," Drian begged her.

They took Lancelot to the dun, an old fortress with great stone buildings that had fallen into disrepair.

"I can give you some money for caring for the lord," Elaine said uncertainly.

Drian gave her an enraged look and snapped, "No. You're speaking of my friend."

"I am sorry if I offended you. Perhaps you should leave now. I don't think my father would accept you as a guest," Elaine said, looking at Drian's patched clothing, "and he cannot pay a harper," she added, noticing the harp tied to Drian's horse.

Drian rode off, but stayed only a few miles away. She did not rob, as she often had, but foraged in the forest, not an easy task at that time of year. She managed to kill a thin red deer, which fed her for a while. Her heart was still heavy with concern for Lancelot.

Elaine told her father, "Here is a poor warrior who is sorely troubled. By his clothing, you can see that he must be wealthy, and he seems gentle. Do give him a room, Father, and let me take care of him."

Her father, Bagdemagus, looked closely at the warrior, who shook terribly and backed off from him. Eyeing the warrior's fine crimson wool cloak and tunic, he assented to Elaine's request without much enthusiasm.

Elaine told her father and her brother--that is, Lanval, the man she had thought was her brother, a dull man who was nothing like her newly found true brother--that they must keep out of the sickroom, which of course they did not mind. She put her poor warrior to bed in a small house in the dun, and gave her strong teas to cure her madness, though they might at first make it seem worse.

Lancelot lay in a bed in a dark room. She could hardly bring herself to speak. Her world was gone.

Was there anything she knew for certain? She could see that her body was female. Was she indeed Lancelot, or was she some raving woman who had never held a sword but wished she could? How did she know she was Lancelot? She was locked in a room. Would Lancelot be locked in a room for who knew how many days? Surely Lancelot would have found a way to get out. But she did not want to get out until she knew where else she should go.

She had no memory of being anyone else but Lancelot, except when she was a girl named Anna and a boy named Antonius. She thought she had never been anyone else since she had grown. But perhaps if she claimed to be Lancelot, people would laugh at her.

She had no sword, so she had no way of showing that she could use one. Her sword might have been taken away. She seemed to have a great many ideas about how a sword could be moved, but perhaps they were just imaginings.

No, she had too many memories of being Lancelot. They could not all be imagined. She knew too many fine phrases to be a serving woman, but her hands were far too calloused to be a lady's, and her muscles were too firm.

She had killed. She was sure she had killed many men. She could see their blood and remember the feel of her sword piercing their bodies. Perhaps the room was a prison, and she was being punished?

She had made love with a woman whom she believed was Queen Guinevere. Again, there were too many memories for that to be a dream. Oh, let that be true! Even if Guinevere no longer loved her, Guinevere had loved her once.

She felt the bag on a strip of leather that hung around her neck. The red-haired fairie witch who fed her had tried to take it off, saying she might strangle herself, but Lancelot had held onto it fiercely.

Trembling, Lancelot looked into the bag, and counted her treasures once again. A relic, two raven feathers, a ring that was too small for her hand--surely that was Lancelot's mother's ring--and a pearl. That must be the pearl that Guinevere had given Lancelot long ago, before they had been lovers. These were Lancelot's treasures. Therefore, she must be Lancelot.

But why was Lancelot locked in a room? She began to cry, though she had wept so much that she had few tears left.

The man who had attacked her could not truly have been the Bellangere who had fought beside her in the Saxon War. Sangremore had not been the warrior she had known, either. And they were not the only ones who had been changed.

The good king she had known would never have lain with his wife's sister. And as for the queen, there was indeed a False Guinevere, far more cunningly mimicked than the one with a crude accent. The True Guinevere had loved her and might have run off with Lancelot as Iseult had with Tristram.

Some evil enchanter must have created a false king and queen, while the true king and queen were God knows where, perhaps imprisoned, perhaps sleeping some terrible sleep. Perhaps even dead.

People said that Merlin had been seduced away and put under a spell. Merlin was not the only one who was gone.

Perhaps many of the warriors had been replaced with false warriors. Perhaps this supposed grail quest had somehow been suggested to her by someone else, so subtly that she did not realize it, and she would be lost forever, and so would any other warrior who went.

Perhaps someday a false Lancelot would supplant her, and the False Guinevere would not mind. The True Guinevere would have cared.

It might be that these false people looked nothing like the true ones, and only some weird glamour they cast about them made them seem to have the same faces and voices.

She might never see the true ones again. Lancelot begged whatever god or goddess there might be to let her see the True Guinevere again, but she did not believe that her prayer was heard. She would never again see anyone she knew.

The woman who had saved her from Bellangere resembled Drian, but she probably was just some kind faerie. And she had left Lancelot with this strange red-haired lady, who seemed gentle, but who might be a witch disguised with enchantments.

Lancelot slept in a fever that pulled her further into the realm of horror than she had been since the days after her mother's death, further even than when she had seen the bodies of women raped in the Saxon War. Warriors of all colors, green warriors, blue warriors, ceaselessly attacked her. When they had vanquished her in battle, they would strip off her chain mail, discover that she was a woman, and rape her. Their faces changed constantly. They were the man who raped her mother, but then they could become other men. Some of them were men she had fought. Some had the faces of warriors at Arthur's court. She saw Mordred's face, and the faces of some of the other young warriors. While they held her helpless, they raped Guinevere and her mother. Sometimes her mother was alive again and other times they dug her corpse from the grave to rape it. Lancelot prayed for death.

But a gentle woman's voice kept saying, "I am with you. You are safe. Hold my hand." Who was this strange, red-haired lady? Was she a friend? Could Lancelot trust her, or anyone?

18 LANCELOT FOUND

Talwyn tried to read the scroll the queen had given her. But nothing interested her, certainly not mere words. Perhaps she was not meant to be a scholar after all. Life had lost its flavor since Galahad had gone. She struggled against thinking about Galahad, but the more she struggled, the more the skinny youth's face appeared to her. She tried to dismiss the memory of Galahad's lop-sided grin, but she could not. The sun shone from the window into the queen's room, illuminating the scroll, but that did not make the words come alive.

"Is everything well with you?" Guinevere asked when Talwyn kept losing her place in her lessons.

How could anyone so old understand her? Talwyn replied in a sharp voice. "I'm not. I am fond of Galahad. He has gone away on that quest and I miss him. I wonder whether he will come back, and whether he will want to marry me."

Guinevere sighed. "This the first time you have spoken of love. I suppose he is a good young man. I hope so. Be careful with your heart. Do you think he cares about you?"

"I believe he does. I think he is good. But how can I be certain?" Talwyn exhaled with relief at being able to talk about her feelings.

Guinevere patted her hand. "If you want to find out whether a man is good, it would be better to ask a serving woman. If there's a bad side, they are more likely to see it than we are."

Pulling away from her, Talwyn exclaimed indignantly, "I can't believe that Galahad would try to seduce a serving woman. I trust him too much even to ask."

"Very well, then. You trust him." Guinevere shrugged. "If you want to marry Galahad, I can ask Lancelot to speak on your behalf to Arthur. When Lancelot returns, that is." The queen turned away, looking out of the window as if she could see where her handsome warrior had gone.

How odd that Guinevere did not offer to speak with the king herself.

When Talwyn was walking down a passageway that afternoon, she saw Creirwy carrying a large earthenware jar and began to walk beside her.

"Please speak with me a moment."

The serving woman did not look into Talwyn's eyes. "I have no time to speak with you. Can't you see I'm busy?"

"When do you have time?"

"Never," she said, stepping along briskly. "I'm always working from morning to night, except when we practiced with the lord Lancelot."

Talwyn thought the serving woman had little liking for her, but she felt desperate enough to beg. "Please, Creirwy."

Finally, Creirwy gave in to Talwyn's persistence. "You can't walk along beside me like that. Come onto this stairway."

They turned into a small stairway that led to the queen's bed chamber.

The serving woman set her jar down on a stair. Her brow was damp and she smelled of sweat.

"What do you want?" Creirwy's voice was neither friendly nor unfriendly, but not in the least deferential.

Talwyn was almost too embarrassed to speak, but she knew that Creirwy could not pause for long. She forced herself to say, "The queen said that this was a question I should ask a serving woman. Is Galahad a good man?"

Creirwy grinned and tossed her head. "Galahad a good man? No."

"No?" Talwyn exclaimed in horror. She slumped against the wall. Tears began to form in her eyes. "No? He isn't? Can that be true? I must confess I'm terribly disappointed."

Creirwy met her gaze. "I thought you knew because of the way you two look at each other. Galahad uses too many rags to be a good man. I hope you aren't disappointed."

Almost losing her balance on the stairs, Talwyn stared at her. "Could you be saying what I think you are? I can't believe it's possible."

Creirwy chuckled. "Why not? All I've seen is Galahad scrounging up old clothing and tearing it up, but I think that's why."

Talwyn shook her head. It couldn't be. She was nothing like Queen Guinevere or Lancelot. She admired many young men's looks; she just preferred Galahad, even though others were handsomer.

"That's not enough to be sure. Why, I don't know whether I'm in love with a man or a woman."

"You've got at least half a chance of being lucky, then. I have to get back to work." Giving her a hint of a smile, Creirwy lifted her jar and turned back to the passageway.

Talwyn went off to ponder.

"What happened to the harper who brought me here?" Lancelot asked the red-haired woman, who gave her name as Elaine.

"I sent the harper away. Never mind about him," Elaine told her, putting a hand on Lancelot's arm.

Lancelot groaned. If the harper had gone away, it couldn't have been Drian. The true Drian wouldn't have left her. Tears dripped down her cheeks. She would never see any of her friends again.

Drian approached the dun. Lancelot was, as always, on her mind.

Seeing a serving man unloading a cart, she asked him, "Is a sick warrior still staying here?"

The man scratched his head. "Uh-huh. He's a strange one. He stays all the time in the room where my lady put him. Sometimes people hear him groan or weep." He made a sign of protection from evil. "Me, I don't like men who are possessed. I don't know why the lady keeps tending him."

"Might I see him?"

"Why'd you want to?" The man's eyes narrowed. "She don't let nobody see him anyhow."

There was no recourse but to trust Elaine.

It was nearly evening, and Gawaine was looking for a good place to camp on a moor. He came to a stream that had flooded its banks, carrying trees and bushes with it. A man waited on the other side, apparently trying to determine the best place to cross. The man was unknown to him, but was riding a familiar black horse. His packhorse was an older, far less fine chestnut.

Gawaine quickly found the most likely place to cross and rode his horse across the gushing stream. His gray gelding, Sword, also recognizing Lancelot's mare, was likewise eager to cross and plunged through the swirling waters. Gawaine's legs were soaked.

"Where in Annwyn did you get that mare? She belongs to a friend of mine. Did you kill him, or steal her?" Gawaine yelled.

The man was small, with a pinched face. "What do you mean?" he cried indignantly. "This horse is mine. I bought her last week."

It was difficult to believe that this man could have fought Lancelot. The story was probably true.

"You didn't buy it from a breeder. You must have bought it from a thief. Where did you buy it?" Gawaine shook his fist.

Cringing and querulous of voice, the man replied, "It was south of here, on the way to Cornwall. I bought it from a group of men who sold only that horse, no others."

"No doubt. You must have guessed that it was stolen. Give it to me," he demanded.

The man drew back. "Why, you're a thief yourself! I won't give you my horse. You'll have to buy her."

"Buy her!" Gawaine shouted. "I'll do that the day the seas dry up! She was stolen, and you must give her back."

"I certainly won't let you have her out here, where I'd be left stranded." The man clung tightly to the reins.

"Use your packhorse!" Gawaine yelled.

Telling himself that the man probably hadn't been the one to injure Lancelot, if someone had, Gawaine decided not to beat him. Instead, he called the black mare, which was looking eagerly at Sword. "Raven!" Then Gawaine turned and made his horse go back across the stream.

Throwing her rider, Raven followed Gawaine and his horse. Gawaine didn't even pause to see how the rider fared, but moved south with the two horses. He stopped at every town or dun he passed, looking for Lancelot.

He wished that Raven were magical, like the horses in tales, who could find their rider or at least the place where the rider had last been seen. However, when he let Raven loose to go where she wanted, she just stayed nearby and hunted unsuccessfully for a patch of grass that was not brown. He fed her some of the oats he had brought for his horse.

He came to the shabby hill fort that he knew belonged to a man named Badgemagus. Gawaine noted with disapproval that only the main building's roof was well-thatched. The outbuildings' roofs looked as if they might not survive the winter.

Bagdemagus, whom Gawaine had met on a previous journey to the area years before, had aged. His beard and thick eyebrows were gray and his steps were slow. He had gained a great deal of weight.

"Gawaine! Well met!" he cried, as if they were old friends.

"Greetings, Bagdemagus." Gawaine was barely polite because Bagdemagus had never been a great supporter of King Arthur and had to be pressed to pay his taxes.

"I am a loyal subject of the High King, one of his most loyal subjects," Bagdemagus muttered, his face twitching as if something was the matter with his right eye.

Gawaine cut him short. "Has anyone here seen a strange warrior who is black-haired and handsome? I'm looking for a friend of mine."

Bagdemagus nodded. "Indeed, my daughter found such a strange warrior near the marsh. We took him in and she cares for him. He weeps and seems quite mad. Perhaps he is your friend."

Gawaine sucked in his breath. He hardly knew whether to hope that this warrior was Lancelot.

Bagdemagus sent a serving woman to bring his daughter to what passed for his great hall. The hangings had long since faded and the benches were the worse for wear, but clean rushes lay on the floor.

The reddish-haired young woman was pretty enough, despite her plain brown gown, but she scarcely glanced at Gawaine.

"This is my daughter, Elaine. Daughter," Bagdemagus said in a tone common to proud fathers, "this is Gawaine of the Matchless Strength, Prince of Lothian and Orkney and cousin to King Arthur. See that a good supper is prepared for him, and then you might stop with us a while. It would do you good to hear about the court."

"I'll see to the supper, but then I must return to my poor patient." Her tone was only slightly deferential.

"The Lord Gawaine believes that our poor patient may be a friend of his who is lost. Why don't you take him to the building where your patient is and let him see?" her father coaxed.

The young woman frowned, her face locked like a door. "He is much too agitated to see anyone."

Gawaine spoke as gently as he could. "The warrior I am seeking is my good friend. I'll not disturb him, kind healer. If he is my friend, he might recognize me."

"I doubt it." Sighing, she added, "You may come as far as the door and look in for a moment, but that is all."

"Pardon her, Lord Gawaine. She has worn herself out caring for this stranger," Bagdemagus told him. He frowned at his daughter.

Gawaine followed Elaine out of the door and across the courtyard. He refrained from making the comments he would have made to another lady in similar circumstances.

"Is your patient missing two fingers on his left hand?" Gawaine asked.

Elaine nodded.

Gawaine groaned.

They came to a small building with a roof that, like others in the dun, was ill-repaired. Elaine opened the door halfway, barring Gawaine from entrance.

Gawaine peered into the small, dark room.

"We dare not keep a lamp or candles here," Elaine whispered. "We fear he might hurt himself in the fire."

There was no fire in the firepit, and the hut was cold. Lancelot was sitting in a chair. She looked at Gawaine, but there was no recognition in her look.

He was stung by the thought that Lancelot could actually forget his face. "It's old Gawaine, Lance," he said, as softly as his loud voice could speak. "Don't you know me?"

Lancelot glared at him. "You're not Gawaine. You're not even like him. Cease this deception."

"Lance! I am Gawaine!" he moaned, feeling as if he had been knocked from his horse.

She leapt up and pushed her way past Elaine. "Where is Gawaine? Have you injured him?"

Stunned, he tried to reassure her. He grasped her hands. "No, Lance, I'm Gawaine. I'm safe. You're among friends here."

Pulling away her hands, Lancelot yelled in his face, "Where's Gawaine? What have you done with Gawaine?"

He tried to speak calmly, but his voice cracked. "I am Gawaine," he said again. "Who else could I be?"

"You could be anyone, seeming to be him. Go away!" Lancelot demanded. "Lady?" Lancelot called to Elaine, "Are you safe?"

"I'm here," Elaine said soothingly, as if none of this had been frightening. She stepped into the room and gestured for Lancelot to follow her back into it. "I'm safe. Never fear."

Lancelot hurried to her and clasped her hand.

Elaine patted Lancelot's shoulder and stroked her hair. "All is well. Now I must leave for just a moment. Don't worry yourself, I'll be back."

Then she left the room and joined Gawaine in the courtyard.

Gawaine shook as if he had spent the night in a cold rain. His heart ached. "It is my friend Lancelot of the Lake."

"Truly?" Elaine gasped. But she frowned. "He doesn't want to see you. He has never made any violent moves before. Leave him to my care. I'm trying every remedy I know. My mother was a fine healer and I learned from her. I believe that the great Lancelot will recover. Now I must return to him."

"Of course, of course. May the gods grant you the power to help him," Gawaine said as fervently as he could. "All of his friends would be grateful. But must you keep him shut up in that hut?"

"He is afraid to leave it," Elaine told him. "His heart is so heavy that he can scarcely walk, and he sleeps a great deal."

Gawaine groaned. Elaine slipped through the door and closed it behind her.

He slumped across the courtyard. The only good thing in all this horror was that Lancelot was in the care of a healer who did not reveal that she was a woman.

"A fine girl, is she not?" Bagdemagus asked, bidding a serving man to offer Gawaine some mead. "A pity that there are so few travelers who pass here. It is lonely for her. But she has managed this dun well since her mother died. I should insist that she join us for supper."

Gawaine gulped down the proffered mead, which was not particularly good. "Pray do not. I am well pleased that she is such a diligent healer, for the warrior she is tending is my friend, the great Lancelot of the Lake."

"Lancelot?" A smile broke out on Bagdemagus's face. "The angels be praised that we took him in. I hope he recovers, but no doubt he will with her care."

Lancelot put her head in hands and wept. How cruel that man was, pretending to be Gawaine! He did look like Gawaine, but Gawaine never had such a sad, worried expression on his face. Gawaine laughed and jested.

How long had the false Gawaine been substituted for the true one? Perhaps the one who had looked so strangely into her eyes when he asked to accompany her had been the false Gawaine. The true Gawaine had never done that.

If only she could see the real Gawaine! But she would probably never see any of her friends again.

The gentle lady stroked her hair, but Lancelot did not lift her head.

As she cared for her warrior, Elaine was sorry that she was tending the famous Lancelot, for Lancelot was reputed to love the queen. Elaine tightened her grasp on Lancelot's arm. Lancelot must be hers, not anyone else's.

The next morning, Lancelot saw the man who pretended to be Gawaine enter the room again.

"How are you today, Lance?" he asked.

"You mock me!" she cried, not moving from her chair. She tried to hold back tears. "You call me Lance as if you were Gawaine, and even try to make your voice sound like his. But your mimicry is flawed. I can tell that the voice is not the same."

"Can you?" he asked. This time his voice shook, quite unlike Gawaine's.

But perhaps this man was not an enemy, even if he belonged to the enchanted world. His voice sounded kind, if not familiar. She would risk entreating him. "Do you know where Gawaine is? Do you ever see him?"

The man choked. "Yes, I must say that I do."

"I don't know how many years have gone by since I have been under this spell," Lancelot said. "Please ask him not to forget me, even if I never see him again."

The red-bearded man--at least, he seemed to be red-bearded--sucked in his breath. "Gawaine could never forget Lancelot," he said, making the words sound like a promise. "Gawaine cares more about Lancelot than about anyone else in the world."

"False!" Lancelot cried at this unconvincing double. "Gawaine cares more about his mother than about anyone else. You don't even know him."

The man smiled slightly, not unlike Gawaine, though Gawaine's smile was wider. "Why, when a man says he cares more about someone than about anyone else in the world, his mother is generally excepted. That's understood."

"You are too much like Gawaine, yet not enough." She groaned, trying not to look at him and be fooled.

"Why, what do you think of Gawaine?" the stranger asked.

"He is the best of friends--as you must know if you've been sent to perplex me," Lancelot said, unable to keep from looking at the seemingly well-known face. The eyes were not merry like Gawaine's. "But it disgusts me that he has used and hurt so many women."

"Gods!" the man exclaimed, just as if he were Gawaine himself.

"Stop imitating him! I can bear it no longer!" Lancelot exclaimed, turning away.

"Lance, you know I'm Gawaine. You'd never say such a thing about Gawaine to anyone else."

She covered her face with her hands. "I never criticize Gawaine to other people. But I don't know whether you're Gawaine. You're like him, and yet not. And I can't bear the uncertainty. Please, go away."

"If you wish. I pray that the spell cast on you will end." He turned to leave.

"Wait." She looked up. "There are two King Arthurs, one who is a great and generous leader and another who conjures up false grails. There are two Guineveres, one who loves me and one who is married to Arthur and who is above all the queen. And there are two Gawaines, the man he is with me and the man he is with most women. Which is true?"

His face, generally unwrinkled, furrowed with added years of age. "The true Gawaine is the man he is with you. With many women, he has often been foolish and arrogant."

That seemed a good answer, but not enough to convince her. "Am I truly Lancelot?" she asked him.

The seemingly red-bearded man choked. "Yes, you are Lancelot. Never doubt that."

She didn't think he would lie about that. "Yes, I am Lancelot," she said. "But how can I be Lancelot if I am locked in a room?"

"Do you want me to take you out of the room? I will, gladly."

Lancelot looked at the door and wondered what was on the other side. "No, I am under a spell. I cannot leave this room."

"As you wish," he said, but he sighed.

"If I am Lancelot, then I have killed many men." She groaned.

"That's true," he admitted. "But in war, or fair fights, or to protect those who were in danger."

"Lancelot is called great," she said, pronouncing the word "great" in no laudatory tone. "Which person is called great, the one who kills or the one who is crucified? Am I great because I have suffered, or because I have caused suffering? Is Arthur great because of his wars, or because of his peace?"

The man looked at her. "You may be under a spell, but your mind is keen. These are great questions. I try not to ask too many of them."

"Could this spell be a punishment from God for my sins?" Lancelot asked.

He shook his head. "Your god does not punish people by putting spells on them."

"That sounds right." She nodded. Because the man seemed kindly, she asked, "Tell me, will I ever see my friends again?"

"You'll see them." He tried to touch her, but withdrew when she moved back. "I know you are in pain, but you must not think of killing yourself. Please."

Lancelot gasped. How did he guess she had thought of that? The True Gawaine knew that she had tried to get herself killed in the Saxon War. She stared at the man. No, looking at him was too painful. Tears began to drip down her cheeks. She covered her face again to hide them. "Please leave me."

"If you wish. But if you want to see me again, just say the word and I'll soon be here."

She heard him walk away and close the door.

Gawaine left Raven at the dun, in case Lancelot recovered enough to ride her.

He rode some distance to the nearest outpost of the king's messengers, on one of the Roman roads. He asked for a wax tablet and stylus and bent over the tablet for some time, sealed it in a packet, then gave it to a messenger.

Should Lancelot go to Camelot, he wondered, where the many who loved the warrior might restore her senses? Or would she slip in this condition and reveal her sex? Better if Guinevere could come to see her. Guinevere would come if she truly cared about Lancelot as much as Lancelot cared about her.

Arthur hid his concern when a messenger handed him a packet from Gawaine, for Gawaine rarely sent messages. Could there be some rebellion brewing?

But the words were far different from any he could have anticipated:

Lancelot is ill, indeed mad, and staying at the hall of Bagdemagus. He did not know me. The daughter is a healer and is caring for him, but I think only Guinevere could help him. Please send her here. You could say that she has gone to Powys to settle some trouble in the land that used to be her father's.

She could be guarded by men who won't talk, like Bors and Gareth. Or, if that cannot be, shall I bring Lancelot home to Camelot?

Arthur wiped the tablet clean, sent his serving man away, and sank into his chair.

Surely Lancelot could not be mad. It must be a fever, and it would pass.

He prayed to the Christ, and other gods as well, for he had never been certain that there was only one.

But as for sending Guinevere off to see her lover--it was impossible, he would look like a fool. And perhaps be one, for they might never return. It was hard to imagine Lancelot having enough guile for such a plan, but he had seemed strained when he left. And wasn't it suspicious that the message was sent by Gawaine, who was the man most likely to play the go-between in arranging a tryst? But surely not for his cousin's wife?

No, Guinevere would never be released to run off with her lover.

Arthur also pondered Gawaine's other suggestion, that Lancelot might be brought to Camelot.

He shook his head. No, Lance should not be seen in some sad state, like Gryffyd. How would it look if his finest warrior seemed mad? What if the Saxons heard of it? Bad enough if the more restless subject kings did.

The king wrote a message on the wax tablet that Lancelot should remain where he was, but that Gawaine should keep watch to see if Lancelot needed anything that it was in his power to do.

Then he told Gareth how badly Lancelot fared, but not of Gawaine's request that Guinevere be sent.

Guinevere flinched ever so slightly when Arthur entered her room. She put down her stylus and wiped Talwyn's writing, which had been about Amazons, off a wax tablet.

"You may stay," the king said to Luned, who had not moved to leave.

"I have sad tidings," he continued, giving Guinevere a more sympathetic look and tone than he had in many months. "Gawaine sends word that Lancelot is ill."

Guinevere drew a sharp breath and rose from her chair. She could hardly refrain from crying out.

"Never fear." Arthur's voice was soothing. "By good chance, Lance is being cared for by a woman who is a healer, the daughter of a lord named Bagdemagus. No doubt he'll be back with us soon."

"How ill? What illness?" Guinevere made no attempt to hide her fear. A pain stabbed her heart.

"Some fever, I suppose. He raves. I am concerned, too. We must pray for him."

"Pray let me go to see him." She had to ask, though it was unlikely that he would grant her request.

Arthur shook the royal head. "That cannot be." His tone was harsher than it had been. "You are a queen, and your place is here. Moreover, you are no great healer." Then he turned and left.

It was no wonder that he would not let her travel to Lancelot, but Guinevere felt that she was imprisoned. She hurled her gold-tasseled, embroidered pillows against the wall. Then she sunk on her knees in prayer.

All that day and through the night she agonized over what to do. Just after dawn, she determined that she would ask Gareth to take her to see Lancelot even without Arthur's permission. The young warrior was fond of Lancelot and so might be willing to help her. The worst that her husband could do was set her aside, and what did that matter, if Lancelot was suffering and Guinevere could help her? Could Arthur try to kill Lancelot because Guinevere went to heal her? Surely not if they returned to Camelot, though Guinevere would much prefer not to do so.

She could not go alone, for she did not know the roads and feared that the king's men would find her and force her to return.

She went to the house that Gareth shared with Gawaine, and the young warrior answered her knock. His eyes widened at the sight of her.

Guinevere's voice showed her frenzy. "Have you heard that Lancelot is ill?" she asked.

"Yes, Lady Guinevere, gravely ill." He sounded weary and there were circles under his young eyes. "I have been on my knees all night praying for his recovery. Poor Lord Lancelot is suffering greatly."

Guinevere shut her eyes briefly. "Would you take me to Bagdemagus's dun, Gareth?" she pleaded.

The tall young warrior pulled back. "You must ask his majesty about that, your highness. Surely there is nothing you could do for the lord Lancelot. He is so out of his senses that he did not recognize Gawaine."

Guinevere staggered back. "Poor Lancelot! I must go to him."

Gareth stared at her as if she were as mad as Lancelot. "You must go back to your rooms and rest. Prayer is the only thing that will help the lord Lancelot. I shall pray for him, and fast for his sake, and you might, also." He shut the door.

Guinevere walked unseeingly back to her room. If only she had agreed to run off with Lancelot. Whatever dangers they might have faced, they would have been together.

Oh, my love, she thought, I would wander in the forest with you and sleep under the hawthorns. I would hunt for nuts and dig up roots, I would even eat bark with you. If you were mad, still I would gather any food I could for you and feed you.

Guinevere felt as if she were wandering through a desert. Her fine room was only a bleak and barren wasteland. The woods and streams she saw in the room when Lancelot was there had dried up.

Talwyn entered and picked up her wax tablet from the table.

The girl asked, "Lady Guinevere, are you ill?"

"No," she muttered.

"I had to ask you three times," Talwyn exclaimed.

"Read your Virgil," Guinevere answered the girl. It was impossible to imagine that anything but Lancelot mattered.

19 THE MAID ELAINE

The red-haired lady's voice always sounded sweet, and her touch always felt gentle. Whatever sort of being she might be, she did not mean harm, Lancelot believed.

The lady brought her water to drink, and Lancelot drank it gratefully. She feared that her food and drink might be poisoned, but she believed the kind lady would prevent that if she could.

"How are you today?" The lady put her hand on Lancelot's forehead. "Your fever is gone."

Lancelot thought she would never be well again, in this world of exile from all that she had known, but she said, "I am well. Thank you for troubling about me. Pardon me for not asking your name. What is it, my lady?"

Elaine."

"I have always liked that name." Little though she felt like smiling, Lancelot returned Elaine's smile. If she had a friend in the realm of enchantment, she should show her appreciation.

Elaine blushed. "You sound happier. I hope that you will be happy here."

Lancelot made an effort not to sigh. Happiness was gone forever, if Guinevere was gone. But at least there was some kindness. It would be wrong to kill herself, for that was a great sin. She must live for the moments that were tolerable. "Your presence makes this world brighter, my lady."

"Truly?" Elaine's face lit up with a smile. "Your presence also makes this world brighter for me, noble lord." Her cheeks were almost as red as her hair. She brushed some locks back from her forehead.

Lancelot shook her head. "I am no lord in this world. You should call me by another name." She paused and wondered whether she should give her name, or make up one for this enchanted world.

"Lancelot," Elaine said shyly.

"You know who I am." Lancelot was only a little surprised. Of course whoever had put everyone under a spell knew her name, and must have told this lady. Could Morgan, in her anger at being in exile from Camelot, have spun a spell that destroyed it? Lancelot closed her eyes for a moment.

"Yes. Why do you close your eyes? Does your head ache? May I get you a damp cloth?" Elaine stroked Lancelot's forehead. "I think you are well enough to have candles in your room now. I'll get some."

Lancelot opened her eyes. She must not be rude to this lady who tried to help her. "How kind you are. I had not thought to find any kindness in this world."

"Has no one been kind to you?" Elaine's eyes widened. "Never fear. I shall always be as good to you as I can. Just tell me what you want, and I will do it."

Tears started in Lancelot's eyes and began to drip down her cheeks. She reached up her hand to dry them, but Elaine's hand was there first, wiping them away.

"Don't weep, Lancelot. I shall always be with you. You will never be alone." Elaine put her arm around Lancelot.

Lancelot rested her head on Elaine's shoulder. The pretty lady--for she was pretty--brought a welcome smell of the forest to the musty room. But if only Lancelot could smell Guinevere's familiar scent! Was Guinevere gone forever?

Elaine could think of nothing but Lancelot. Never had she seen anyone so handsome, so gentle. It mattered not whether Lancelot was a woman or a man, only that she was so appealing. Lancelot was so sad. Perhaps the queen had been cruel to her. It must be strange to love a married woman. Wouldn't it be better for Lancelot to love a woman who was unmarried?

Elaine sat with Lancelot and told stories that took her away from her misery for a few moments. Lancelot listened avidly.

Looking into Lancelot's eyes, Elaine said, "The first people were trees, who spoke and felt something like we do, but they could touch each other only when the wind blew their branches in just the right way. They longed to touch, and begged for the power to do so, and so one day their wish was granted, and some of them had flesh, and legs, and could reach each other, but they had to accept a much shorter life, and much wandering, in return."

Elaine touched her hand, and Lancelot trembled. She longed to kiss Elaine's hand, and her gentle mouth. She had never imagined that she would embrace anyone but Guinevere, and the knowledge that she could made her ashamed.

But she would likely never see the true Guinevere again, so perhaps it would not be so wrong to embrace Elaine. Must she pine for what could never be?

"I should try to walk," Lancelot said, raising herself from her bed. After weeks of sitting and lying in bed, walking was difficult. Her legs felt stiff as spears. Elaine took hold of her arm, and Lancelot shook for many reasons. She slumped into an old wooden chair and looked at Elaine.

"Perhaps you aren't ready to walk yet. You need not force yourself," said Elaine, though surely she guessed that was not the reason why Lancelot had moved away from her.

Elaine was gentleness, nothing but gentleness, and Lancelot ached to immerse herself in Elaine as if she were a bed of ferns. What would it be like to meet nothing sharp or angry in one you loved?

Lancelot spoke softly. "I don't mean to offend you, but I must find a way to do these things for myself. When you touch me, I fear that I shall return your touch in ways that I should not."

Elaine looked longingly into her eyes. "I wish that you would touch me. You are very dear to me."

Lancelot sighed. She saw that she had been wrong to say anything. Of course saying the words would lead to more. Admitting any feeling betrayed Guinevere. If the true Guinevere were under an enchantment somewhere, Lancelot should be true to her.

"I have no right. My heart is pledged to one I love dearly."

"Pardon my boldness. I have heard that your life is entwined with the queen's, but I beg you to spare some love for me." Elaine held out her hand.

Lancelot took the hand.

She drew Elaine beside her and Elaine kissed her fervently. Lancelot felt a surge of warmth. She could enjoy kissing a woman other than Guinevere.

Elaine pulled her to the bed and Lancelot reclined willingly.

Elaine took off her clothes. Her body was pink and sweet. She looked so vulnerable that Lancelot took off her clothes also. Anything else would seem like an insult. Elaine pressed herself against her.

Lancelot was shy about touching a virgin, but Elaine was so eager to be touched and to return the touches that Lancelot stopped holding back. Elaine seemed so completely sweet and affectionate that Lancelot kissed her everywhere, and found that Elaine learned such kisses very quickly.

When they were lying on the bed afterwards, Elaine said, "I fear that you will leave someday, but I love you nevertheless."

Lancelot then felt nearly as guilty toward Elaine as she did toward Guinevere. She was more divided than ever. How did she dare to claim the love of two women, even if one of them was under a spell?

Lancelot gained strength, and she and Elaine walked together in the woods near the dun. Spring was coming, and they spent hours watching the first birds return.

Drian was riding in the forest when she saw Lancelot and Elaine in the distance. She was ready to shout with joy because Lancelot could walk in the forest again. Then she saw that they were holding hands, and Elaine kissed Lancelot.

Drian turned her horse away. Of course the nobles would go to each other. Was Lancelot recovered enough for love? Well, these noble ladies had no decency. Imagine throwing yourself at one so recently mad. Drian rode off towards the north. She forced back tears.

Lancelot and Elaine went to the bog pond and watched herons stalking fish. Snipe and curlews flew up as the two walked through the reeds. Lancelot had not been able to share such things with Guinevere as often as she had wished.

"My mother and I walked here often," Elaine told her. "She knew which birds would arrive each week of the spring, and when they would leave at the end of the summer. She could find remedies from leaves, roots, or bark for every illness, and she taught me all of these things. She had learned much from the Lady Morgan, who was her cousin and came here to visit us. I think of my mother every day. I thought of little else until you came here."

There were tears in her eyes, and in Lancelot's as well. She thought she should not be surprised to hear that Elaine was related to Morgan. The spell was doubtless Morgan's after all, but Elaine must be innocent of all wrongdoing.

"I walked in the woods with my mother, too," Lancelot said, "but she died when I was very young. I have always missed her so much. It is good to meet someone else who loved her mother as much as I loved mine." Somehow she could not bring herself to tell Elaine what she had told Guinevere, the story of her mother's rape and murder. It seemed indecent to weep about the same thing with Elaine.

They seemed close on their walks, but when they made love, Lancelot called out Guinevere's name. And when she woke in the middle of the night, she wished that Guinevere was beside her.

"Come and watch the moon with me," Elaine said when the moon was full, and took Lancelot by her hand. Together, they slipped into the woods and stood beneath the ghostly trees.

"Women have drawn comfort from the moon and the stars since time began," Elaine told her. "This is good, this is holy. The night is a time to listen to heaven and earth."

"There are many kinds of nights," said Lancelot, staring into the darkened woods. Once she had loved the woods at night, but now they seemed strange to her. Bats flew by, and they seemed like beings from the world of enchantment. "There are nights in the woods when you feel that thieves may attack at any moment. There are nights before battle, when you know that many men will die in the morning. I pray then, but find no comfort."

Elaine exclaimed with distaste, "How could you be comforted when you are going out to kill? That would be inhuman."

"Yes, I do not really want comfort then. Just courage--and a sense that I may be doing right." She paused. "Elaine, would you kill for the things you believe? Do you know whether Morgan would? Do women have the same thoughts of killing that men do?"

Elaine gasped. "Look at the moon. Look at the stars. Do they kill?"

"No, but the owls do." An owl had just swooped down on an unlucky mouse and was carrying the squealing thing away. "Rivers, the sea, blizzards can kill."

"For food. Or in accidents. The sea is not moved by malice." Elaine's voice sounded like a teacher's. "But if an evil warrior had burst into the chamber where you lay sick and tried to kill you, I would have grabbed your sword and struck him."

Lancelot stared off among the trees where the owl had gone.

"You care about me. If you do, please tell me the truth." She turned to Elaine and looked into her eyes. "Is this an enchanted world or the real one? I long to know whether the Guinevere at Camelot is the true Guinevere."

"What other Guinevere could there be but the queen?" Elaine trembled. "Of course this is the real world. Are you still ill? I had thought otherwise."

"No other Guinevere?" Lancelot shook. If that were true, then she had betrayed Guinevere terribly. "But she has been so strange that I hardly knew her. Can I trust Guinevere, though she speaks of ruling after her husband's death? She sounds as if she looks forward to the day Arthur dies."

Elaine sighed with exasperation. "Can't you just look at the moon with me? What can I say? Perhaps King Arthur might die before Queen Guinevere and she could hold the throne, with your help. If you go back to her." The last words came in a sad little voice.

Lancelot groaned. Again, talk of Arthur's death. What would Guinevere want her to do, fight any of her brother warriors who did not want a woman ruler? "She might hope for that. She doesn't like him, much less love him, but she won't leave him. It must be because she thinks she can rule some day. I don't know which is worse, her letting him kiss her or her wanting him to die. The combination drives me mad." She shuddered. "I think her hopes are vain, in any case," Lancelot continued, though she sensed her listener was not pleased with the subject. "I don't think the warriors would serve a woman ruler."

Elaine looked at the ground. "They wouldn't have to have 'only' a woman. You could marry her, and then they'd think they had a man, too."

Lancelot shivered, though the night was not cold.

Could she and Guinevere possibly go through with such a spectacle without discovery of her sex?

And how could Elaine bear to speak of it?

"Would anyone hasten Arthur's death? I would rather die than be part of such a scheme." Lancelot flung herself on the ground. The night seemed to enter her very being. Perhaps it would have been better if she had died of her illness. But she could stay here, with Elaine, and never have to face the court again, even if the true court was still at Camelot. Would it be better never to see Guinevere again than to chance learning that she plotted against Arthur?

Elaine sat down beside her. "Why do you ask me, not Guinevere?"

"I have trouble believing her. I am afraid that she wants me to kill Arthur." The words made her voice shake. "I don't think I could touch her again if she said such a thing. I can't bear to hear people talking about Arthur's death. Why should Guinevere mention it? Why should anyone? He is strong. He is only a little beyond forty. Forgive me for telling all of this to you."

Elaine's face shone pale in the moonlight.

"You expect me to be wise beyond my learning. I have never lived at court, but I do know that people always talk about who will succeed kings, whether they have one year to live or twenty. You may be doing the Lady Guinevere wrong to doubt her." Elaine's voice sounded forced. She twisted her hands. "I think you may have these thoughts because you are angry at the king yourself."

Lancelot closed her eyes briefly. "Could that be true? I should not blame her, when I am the one who has wronged her," she said, angry at herself--then even angrier when she realized how Elaine must feel about what she had just said.

"Wronged her, with me?" Elaine's voice shook. "I am sorry that I have grieved you. Of course it must be so. I have injured a great queen who has done no harm to me."

"Forgive me. You're so sweet. I didn't mean to hurt you." Lancelot took hold of Elaine's hands, which were cold.

"I know you don't want to hurt me, but I can see that you are constantly thinking of Queen Guinevere." Elaine choked on the words.

She turned her head away from Lancelot. "Let's look at the moon and be comforted. There is more in the world than our passing sorrows."

Lancelot put an arm around her. She knew that she was selfish in her love for Guinevere, but she felt tenderness toward this young woman. "I would like to comfort you, too, Elaine. You are always comforting me."

"Just being near you comforts me." Elaine smiled but her voice hinted at forced-back tears. "Please, let's just look at the moon."

Lancelot kissed her cheek and sang a song about a beautiful woman who lived in the woods, going to sleep in the winter and waking in the spring.

Elaine clasped Lancelot's hands tightly. "Sometimes people wish they could be trees again, and feel cool sap running through their veins instead of blood, and have skin of bark that does not tremble at a touch, and grow beside each other without joining. But they forget that trees can also be cut, and trees can also burn. And sometimes a tree that began as one is split by lightning, while others that grew at first apart become entwined."

She led Lancelot to a pond sparkling with moonlight. "You love the water so. Do you think that what we see there in daylight are our own faces reflected? No, they are ourselves leading other lives. Your likeness and mine have entered this water together, and you will live there with me."

Lancelot could marry Elaine. There would be much joy in being with this gentle woman, and so much less fear of discovery than there was in the adultery--she would always think of it that way--with Guinevere. Elaine loved wild things as much as Lancelot did, and they could be together freely.

Then Lancelot thought of her years with Guinevere, of Guinevere's voice, and scent, and sorrows, her courage, her passionate touches, and her no less passionate beliefs. Everything from her eyebrows to her toes seemed particularly delightful, more interesting than anyone else's. As for Guinevere's anger, how could she not be angry, after having to pretend for so many years that there was love where there was none?

Guinevere's love for her was part of the world she lived in, as large as a great forest. Elaine's love was like a more tranquil lake, and might be as deep, but it was not so deeply a part of her. To leave Guinevere would be like burning the forest in which Lancelot had so often ridden. If the true Guinevere lived at Camelot, Lancelot must return to her. And if Guinevere was hidden elsewhere under a spell, Lancelot must find her.

Dawn came, and Lancelot returned from her walk with Elaine. The man who looked like Gawaine was handing over his horse to one of Bagdemagus's stablehands.

He resembled Gawaine so strongly, and he wore a many-colored plaid cloak just like Gawaine's. Moreover, his horse looked just like Gawaine's horse. Could he possibly be the true Gawaine? She stared at him. The red beard was the same, and so were the blue eyes, the nose that was larger than Arthur's, the height and weight.

The man looked at her. "How are you doing, Lance?"

His voice was a little too soft, but he was otherwise so much like Gawaine.

"Will you walk with me in the garden?" he asked.

She nodded. She had to find out the truth.

"Pardon me, lady," she said to Elaine.

Elaine nodded, but her forehead wrinkled.

Lancelot joined the man, but didn't get as far as the garden. When they had walked a few steps from the stables, she asked, "Are you Gawaine?"

The man paused. "Of course I am, Lance."

He sounded sad. But perhaps the true Gawaine would be sad, indeed dumbfounded, if she didn't recognize him. She must question him further, ask him things that only Gawaine would know.

"I must be sure. When you were held by the Saxons, and attacked with a throwing axe, who saved you?"

"It was a priest, who later took us to his monastery," he replied promptly.

Lancelot trembled slightly with hope. "Why did we leave the monastery?"

"Because Father Paulus preached that women are filthy. I am Gawaine," he said, extending his hand. "Look at the scars on my hand, on my cheeks. Could another man have the same scars?"

"They are similar to Gawaine's." She nodded. "What is my secret?"

He grinned at her. "I am not supposed to speak of it, but you are a better fighter than any man."

The grin was Gawaine's! "No, we are about equal," Lancelot said. "You truly are Gawaine!" Her heart swelled with happiness. A weight had been lifted from her shoulders.

"Who else could have this ugly face?" His grin widened.

"I had thought that you were gone, gone forever." Her voice quavered. "And so was everyone else I knew." She paused, hardly daring to hope. "Does this mean that all the others are the same? Are the king and queen real, not hidden away under some enchantment?"

A sad look replaced his grin. "I assure you, they are the same as ever. Only you have been under a spell."

Relief flooded her. Tears started in her eyes. "I am the only one who has been under a spell? The world is the same as ever? My friends are still there? This news is so good, so good." She choked on the words.

"Your spell has ended." His grin returned. He reached out his hands, and she clasped them tightly.

She would have thrown her arms about him, but she remembered the look he had given her when she went away-- which was not so different from the way he was looking at her now--and decided that it was better not to do so. If he had still believed she was a man, she would have.

She shook her head. "Such a powerful spell. Who could have enchanted me so?"

"You were perhaps ill. It's good to have you back again." He beamed at her. "Or perhaps you were just pretending to be ill, greatest warrior in the world." His eyes were full of merriment.

Gawaine was jesting. The world was right again. She laughed with delight. "Indeed, I pretended so well that I convinced myself."

Gawaine dined at Bagdemagus's hall that night, and Lancelot was eager to jest with him. "Gawaine is the greatest liar in the world," she told the company.

"You must believe Lancelot. He's the greatest saint in the world, as well as the greatest warrior," Gawaine added.

Bagdemagus looked befuddled by the jests, as did his blank-faced son. Elaine, although her fey look made her seem not to fit into the family, also seemed little pleased with the new guest. She frowned, looking away from Gawaine.

"And I have become Saint Gawaine, the holy hermit, so treat me with more respect, Lance," Gawaine said, pretending to growl.

"You have taken vows to embrace a life of purity and self-abnegation. How wonderful!" Lancelot folded her hands as if in prayer.

After supper, Gawaine urged Lancelot to walk with him again in Elaine's herb garden. As soon as they were out under the moon, looking at the untended rows that Lancelot knew Elaine had neglected planting this spring in her absorption in healing, he asked, "So, you have found yourself a wife?"

She stopped dead in her tracks. "A what?"

"Surely you're going to marry the poor girl, after carrying on with her in front of her father?" He sounded almost as indignant as if he were the girl's father.

Lancelot glanced back at the hall, where Elaine was. "Surely I'm not." Not unless Guinevere no longer loved her. If the true Guinevere was indeed at Camelot, she must go to her.

Treading on a few stray plants that were starting to spring up, Gawaine professed surprise. "Why, then, you have treated Elaine very ill. What a way to treat a sweet girl who healed you!"

"Sweet Elaine may be, but I love Guinevere. There's no need for you to meddle in this, Saint Gawaine," she snapped, defending herself as if on the field of battle.

He caught hold of her arm. "Don't be a fool. Take this chance to be happy. You won't find a better wife. Guinevere's already someone else's."

She shook him off. "No matter, I am hers."

"You could still bed Guinevere, of course," Gawaine said with some exasperation. "You can have more than one love. Guinevere is not the only one who loves you." He emphasized this last sentence.

"I want only Guinevere. I won't marry Elaine." She bristled at the unwelcome advice.

Gawaine shrugged and sighed. "Then we had best leave in some haste, before her father tries to stop you."

Surprised, she looked at him. "Why should he?"

"Fool, don't you see he'll think you've gotten her with child?"

Lancelot gasped. "That I have not." She hoped the night would hide the blush that she was sure was on her cheeks.

Gawaine rolled his eyes. "Not even Saint Lancelot's miraculous powers can manage that? Well, love her or leave her. That's your only choice now," he advised.

"I'll leave," she replied decidedly.

"Are you well enough to travel?" he asked, for the first time sounding uncertain.

She nodded. "Surely I am."

"Then better leave sooner than later, to avoid a fight with the father or the brother. You could hurt them badly. And they would be right. If I were her kinsman, I'd be vexed with you." He frowned.

Lancelot bit her lip. "Don't be too vexed. I scarcely knew whether she was a mortal woman or a witch or faerie when I first laid with her. I thought I might never see the true Guinevere again."

"Gods!" Gawaine's eyes widened. "I shouldn't chide you. If Elaine had been a man, I would say he was a brute to take advantage of you when you were mad."

Lancelot sighed. "She was an innocent girl, so it is very different."

"No doubt." But there was doubt in Gawaine's voice. He shook his head.

Lancelot found Elaine that evening and walked with her to the garden. Clouds had obscured the moon.

There was no way to sweeten the message. "I'll be leaving tomorrow," Lancelot said, somewhat embarrassed.

"I knew you would." Elaine's voice strove for calm, then failed utterly. She clutched at Lancelot's arm. "I know that you love the queen, but can't you keep on with me, too? I won't be any trouble. I'll follow you, I'll hide away somewhere, and you can see me only when you choose. I'll be so grateful to see you, I'll never reproach you. Just let me love you."

Horrified, Lancelot stared at her. She clasped Elaine's hands. "That's dreadful. What kind of life would that be for you? I couldn't treat a woman like that."

"I wouldn't mind," Elaine begged. "I'll be your mistress, I'll be your servant. I'll make clothes for you--surely the queen doesn't do that. Just let me worship you."

Lancelot wanted to let go of her hands, but that seemed too cold. "I don't want to be worshiped. I don't want a servant. I am used to loving the proudest woman in Britain."

But Elaine plunged on, clutching Lancelot's hands still tighter. "I cannot be proud with you. I have no pride. I have nothing but you. I want only to be yours. I am no queen, I am your devoted servant."

Lancelot shuddered. "I could never think of you as a servant. I have thought of you as a woodland dream, a bed of ferns."

Elaine grasped eagerly at the words. "Then let me be your woodland dream forever. I shall be the bed of ferns, and you may crush them."

"No." Lancelot finally pulled away. "I am very fond of you, you know I am. But I love Guinevere and I want only to be with her. Please forgive me for hurting you."

"I knew all along that you would leave and never return. It's not your fault," said Elaine, but she began to weep.

Lancelot felt that she had to put her arms around her and comfort her, but she saw that she had been wrong ever to imagine that she wanted a woman who was not as strong as Guinevere. Her mind was full of Guinevere, and how the queen was both proud and tender.

Lancelot wondered what, if anything, she could do for this woman who wanted only love. "I cannot keep you as a mistress, I cannot be your lover, but if I can be your friend, I would be glad to be."

"A friend? What is that? I have never had one." Elaine spoke as if the offer were nothing.

These sad words gave Lancelot an idea. "Then let me take you to a convent where you surely will find friends. That's the only place I can take you."

Elaine jerked away from Lancelot. "Never will I go to a place where I would be shut in forever with a lot of old women. Is that where you send all of your castoff mistresses? I won't go!"

Lancelot flinched at the insult. "You know well that there aren't any others. I have been only with you and Guinevere. The convent I mean is a good place."

"I shall never leave my home except to be yours. But even though I never stir from this place, I shall follow you always, on the hills and through the woods, as a hunter follows a deer," Elaine sobbèd.

Lancelot hid her anger. Guinevere was the one who followed her to the remotest mountains, Guinevere was the one whose absence she felt more keenly than most people's presence.

She was worried that Guinevere might never want to touch her again after she heard what had happened. For of course she would confess it all to Guinevere.

Elaine fled, and Lancelot retired to the old building where she stayed. It was not long before she heard pounding on the door.

She opened it to find Bagdemagus's beefy face, twitching more than ever, staring into hers. "I saw Elaine weeping. What does this mean?" he demanded. "Are you going to ask for her hand at last, or not?"

Lancelot simply stood there, as if she were still too weak to talk.

"You had better decide before morning, or I'll apply to the king to make him force you to marry her," Bagdemagus threatened and slammed the door.

Lancelot shook her head. Bagdemagus was deluded. He was certainly much less important to the king than Lancelot was, and Arthur would never do such a thing to Lancelot unless the girl had a father who mattered a great deal, such as King Maelgon of Gwynedd or King Uriens of Rheged.

Lancelot wandered off to the stables, as if on a nighttime stroll. A bat flew over her head, but having no fear of the creatures, she barely noticed it. The bat was only a bat, not enchanted.

One sleepy boy generally guarded Bagdemagus's stables, but he was nowhere to be seen that night. Lancelot pushed open the creaking stable door, and found Gawaine, with both of their horses saddled.

"Ready to flee, Saint Lancelot?" he whispered in a tone that was almost as loud as his voice usually was.

She didn't look at him, but swung onto her horse.

The day had dawned and they were still riding, now slowly across a moor. Their eyes scanned the ground for possible treacherous bogs.

They rode through the gorse, and an occasional violet showed itself. Here and there a pipit sang, or a hare broke its fast, watching to be sure that all foxes had retired to their dens. A male grouse drummed, and females watched from not far away.

Gawaine broke the silence. "It's all very well to say that you love Guinevere." His voice was gruff. "But you deserve to be loved by someone who cares more about you than about anyone else--as this Elaine does. And others might also." He glanced at her, then looked away.

"You think that Guinevere does not?" She closed her eyes briefly and prayed that the fear that Guinevere did not love her was just another illusion from her time of madness.

"She does have a husband, after all, so she cannot put you first. Others might." Gawaine paid scrupulous attention to his horse, as if it might stumble if he did not. "Of course you love Guinevere, but perhaps you could love someone else also."

Lancelot shook her head. "I don't want to be divided. I don't want to be torn."

Gawaine nodded. "It is like you to do whatever you do with your whole heart. But anyone can see that you have been unhappy. Perhaps that is what led you to madness."

Lancelot gasped. "Are you saying you think Guinevere drove me mad?"

"In a sense, yes." Gawaine eyed her warily, as if he expected her to be angry.

"You have no idea of all that Guinevere has done for me." Lancelot abandoned all discretion, for what was the good of it now? She spoke as much to convince herself as her friend. At least Guinevere had loved her, whether she still did or not. "When Arthur sent me back to Camelot after the battle of Badon, mad Gryffyd imagined that I was a Saxon, and rushed at me with his sword, but Guinevere put herself between us."

Gawaine's eyebrows shot up. "Guinevere did that? Little Guinevere?" Gawaine exclaimed. "Truly, she loves you."

Lancelot sighed. "If only I could take her far away from Arthur."

"You want to leave us all?" Gawaine's voice was not as hearty as usual.

"Of course not." How selfish she was, thinking only of her love for Guinevere. "But I do wish I could be with Guinevere openly, with no husband nearby." She sighed. That was impossible, because Guinevere was unwilling to go away. But she so longed to see Guinevere and felt so guilty that she could forgive even that.

The sun was high in the sky and fewer birds were singing. Lancelot's stomach rumbled, but she had not thought to bring any food, and probably Gawaine hadn't either.

Gawaine said, "I brought some oat cakes and cheese with me."

Lancelot grinned at these welcome words, which cheered her more than the sunlight. "What a good friend you are. Let's break our fast. What are we waiting for?"

So they rested their horses by a little pond and munched on the oat cakes and cheese. Raven shat copiously, so the warriors moved their repast a little further away.

Lancelot sighed. "I hope that Guinevere will forgive me for betraying her with Elaine."

Gawaine shrugged and cut himself a slice of cheese.

"Almost no one would be foolish enough to break with you over that, and no one ever said that Guinevere was foolish. If you're so worried about it, don't tell her."

"Of course I have to tell. I could never keep such a thing secret." She felt herself blush, and Gawaine rolled his eyes.

"It seems that you keep a good many secrets, though your love for Guinevere is completely unconcealed. What was your given name?" he teased. "Judith, perhaps? Or Scathach?" he asked, naming the woman fighter who had taught the legendary Irish heroes. "Or perhaps Diana the huntress?" He bit into an oatcake.

"Well, it was a good deal pleasanter than Gwalchmai," she replied, mentioning his childhood name. "I suppose I can't convince you that I was baptized Black Warrior, so I must admit that it was Anna. Lance, to you."

Recalling that Gawaine had not asked what had happened to her, Lancelot explained what she could remember about Bellangere and Drian.

Gawaine swore a great deal, calling Bellangere every name that ever was and inventing several. When he had exhausted all possible curses, he admitted, "I'm right glad that Drian the harper saved you. If I ever see her again, I'll thank her. And even try to be polite." Then he added, "Of course I never believed that it was Guinevere who tried to poison me."

"I should hope not," Lancelot chided him. "It never entered my mind that she could have." She suspected that he was lying as much as she was. She certainly wasn't going to admit to Gawaine that she had at first suspected Guinevere, and had even feared that Guinevere would plot to kill Arthur.

"So you love Guinevere. But you might think a little more about Elaine. Her father will try to marry her off now, as he no doubt fears she is carrying your child. It's strange that he didn't get her a husband when she was younger," Gawaine mused, brushing crumbs off his chest.

"Marry her off? By the Virgin, I never thought of that," Lancelot groaned, dropping her oatcake and retrieving it just before it hit the ground. She supposed that she would have to visit Elaine again, a thought she did not much relish, to be sure that she was not married off to a man she did not want. Perhaps Elaine might find the convent more appealing if her father pressed her to marry.

"Couldn't you be happy with Elaine--or someone else--if it weren't for Guinevere?" he persisted.

"I'm tired of being asked who I'd love if I didn't love Guinevere," Lancelot complained. "How can I possibly know?" She sighed. Trembling, she asked, "Do you think Guinevere could still love me even though I have been mad? For I know this spell was truly madness."

"Anyone who loved you before you were ill will love you still," Gawaine said, using the quiet, serious voice that disturbed her.

"Perhaps." Feeling that tears were beginning, she looked away.

"Are you sure you're well enough to travel?" There was anxiety in his voice. "Shall we rest a little longer?"

She rose and strode over to Raven. "Nonsense, I am quite well."

As their journey progressed, they entered the forest, which Lancelot loved above all things. Bluebells filled the woods like bits of sky fallen to earth. Despite her nagging guilt about Guinevere and Elaine, Lancelot was newly moved by the spring's beauty, which seemed greater because she had been sick and was now healed.

Joy sprang to her heart like the flowers that sprang from the earth. Guinevere was alive, Guinevere was safe. Arthur was still on his throne. No changelings had replaced them. The world was as it had been. It had not been perfect, but perhaps the faults were all in herself. She had been granted another life, and a chance to do better.

The true Gawaine was riding beside her, smiling as if she had done something remarkable, rather than just being healed of madness.

That night Gawaine actually asked whether she was well enough to sleep under the stars and she hooted, reminding him how many times she had.

When they had made their camp, he took out his game board. "Would you like to play gwyddbwyll, Black Warrior?"

Lancelot shook her head. "Are you trying to see whether I have wits enough about me for that, Red Warrior?"

"No, I can see that you do."

She looked up at the stars, which were real enough. She did not imagine them. "How I fear going mad again." Lancelot shivered.

"You mustn't live in fear of that." His voice was kind. "Now that you know what madness is like, thinking people are not who they seem to be and such, perhaps you can reject it."

She couldn't see Gawaine well in the dark, but his presence reassured her. She would have liked to have a friendly arm around her as well, but she knew that would be unwise. What a pity that he wasn't her brother. But then Agravaine might be also. "If I do go mad again, please take me to Mother Ninian at the Convent of the Holy Mother. I think she could help me--and she wouldn't expect me to devote the rest of my life to her in repayment."

"Of course I'd take you there. But it won't be necessary."

The thought of madness was too much for her. "I'm tired, and want only to sleep." She rolled up in her cloak and, praying that there would be no evil dreams, fell asleep.

The next day they found a simple mud-daub chapel in the woods, and a great light poured from its doors. Beautiful music spilled out into the air, joining with birdsong. The birds, in turn, seemed inspired to pour out their songs.

Lancelot looked at the chapel and wished that she were innocent enough to pray there without shame.

"If you're still feeling so guilty about Elaine, why not go in and be shriven?" Gawaine suggested.

Lancelot turned her horse away from the chapel. "I have not been shriven since Guinevere and I became lovers. A priest would say that my sin was in loving Guinevere, not being unfaithful to her. I cannot be at peace until I have made my peace with Guinevere."

"Well, then, let us make haste to Camelot," Gawaine said, encouraging his horse to go faster, and Lancelot's did also.

Lancelot groaned. "What if she does not forgive me? What if she does not want me anymore? I'll go away again, as far as I can."

Gawaine put his horse in front of hers, as if she were trying to flee. "Don't go away alone so soon after your madness. If you go, let me go with you. We could travel to Lothian. You would much enjoy its mountains and lochs."

Lancelot sighed. "Perhaps. I suppose I shouldn't travel alone for a while." She paused. "I might want to go to Lothian if Guinevere didn't forgive me. But I wouldn't want to go back to Camelot."

"Then neither would I," Gawaine said quietly.

"But you love to be with Arthur." Lancelot could hardly speak the words. "You would leave his service for my sake?"

"Of course," Gawaine said, as if that went without saying.

He would do what Guinevere would not. Lancelot felt close to tears. But, she reminded herself, Gawaine could be a king in Lothian, while Guinevere had no such fine prospects if she left Camelot.

"I think I would look for Drian instead." Lancelot felt she had to tell Gawaine that.

He gulped. "I would help you to find Drian, or to visit the old nun, or to go anywhere you wanted."

Too moved to look at him, she choked. "You are indeed a friend."

"Of course I am. But talk no more of being rejected. I think Guinevere won't give you up so easily."

"I hope not."

Lancelot looked off in the direction of Camelot.

20 THE REUNION

Guinevere almost started to weep when she heard guards shouting that Lancelot had returned. It was fortunate that she was seated in her chair near to Arthur's throne, for she might have collapsed if she had been standing.

Lancelot entered the great hall. Gawaine accompanied her. She wore her crimson tunic, much faded. Her step was more hesitant than Gawaine's wide paces.

Guinevere could hardly restrain the way she looked at her beloved. Gray had spread through Lancelot's dark hair. Her pale face told that something had befallen her.

A harper ceased playing a tune about a maiden and struck up a song that he had composed years before in honor of Lancelot.

"Lancelot! Well met!" Arthur called out, standing up as if he were meeting kindred or royalty. "Are you well?" His arms enfolded Lancelot in a great embrace.

"I was mad for a time, and am recovered, thank the Lord and the Holy Mother."

A gasp went through the hall and many eyes stared at Lancelot.

Arthur frowned, though he should not have been surprised that Lancelot was honest as usual. "There is no need to speak of fevers."

"A little madness seems to have done Lance no harm," Gawaine said, grinning at Lancelot and poking her arm.

"You might try going mad yourself to see what it's like," Lancelot replied, poking his arm in return.

Guinevere was impatient for the men to finish speaking. She merely said, "Well come, Lancelot," but she felt desperate to be alone with her.

Guinevere's own black hair now had strands of gray. Would Lancelot mind?

Lancelot said only, "God grant you good day, Lady Guinevere," formal as always.

Guinevere picked at her gown with nervousness and drank more wine than usual at supper. She could barely eat, though roasted mutton with mint was usually one of her favorite dishes. She longed to run away with Lancelot, and see only Lancelot's face at her table. But Arthur would never let them flee in peace.

Lancelot was almost as frightened of being alone with Guinevere as she had been the first time she had gone to the queen's room. Guinevere was more beautiful than ever, with soft gray hair interwoven with the black. As soon as Lancelot was in the cherished room that night, she began to speak in a faltering voice.

"I have been unfaithful with Bagdemagus's daughter Elaine, who healed me. I love you dearly and I hope that you will forgive me."

Before she could say any more, Guinevere threw her arms around her and embraced her tightly. "You're back, you're well, you love me, nothing else matters." Guinevere kissed her passionately.

Guinevere's beloved scent was the same, her mouth was as sweet as ever. Lancelot wanted the kiss to last forever. Tears streamed from her eyes.

Finally, she pulled away to wipe her cheeks. "I thought you and all the court were gone forever, under a spell, with false people pretending to be you," she choked.

Guinevere sucked in her breath. She also had tears in her eyes. "Oh my poor love," she said, gathering Lancelot once more into her arms. She made love to Lancelot more ardently than before she had gone away, with no hint of reserve or restraint.

Lancelot was at the same time completely excited and completely comfortable, and marveled that such a thing could be. Guinevere's tongue drove her mad, but this madness was entirely pleasant.

She wept and held Guinevere tightly. The grail meant different things to everyone, no doubt, but for her the search began and ended with Guinevere. She moved down, touched Guinevere, and drank.

They slept with both arms and legs entwined, as if to say that no one could part them.

In the middle of the night they woke, and Guinevere began kissing Lancelot's shoulder, but the handsome warrior said, "I have something to tell you."

Guinevere shivered. "Nothing more, I beg you."

Lancelot held her hand. "But I must tell you that Bellangere tried to poison Gawaine in order to get revenge on me for killing Sangremore. Bellangere wanted the blame to fall on you."

Guinevere fell back against her pillow and closed her eyes. She was vindicated, not just saved with a suspicion hanging over her head. "I knew that a man must have done it," she said in a sharp voice.

"You were right, dearest," was all that Lancelot said. She pressed her lips to Guinevere's hair.

But Guinevere knew she could never forget that Lancelot had suspected her. "I fail to understand how anyone could have imagined that I would have poisoned Gawaine."

"No, of course you couldn't have. But please never speak slightingly of him again. He suffered when I was mad and did not recognize him. When you have defeated a worthy opponent, you should not belittle him."

Guinevere's stomach knotted. "And have I defeated him?"

"There could be no contest," Lancelot said, although her words suggested there had been one. "I love you, and as long as you love me, I'll never give encouragement to anyone else."

Lancelot began to make love to her. Guinevere felt tears beginning to swell in her eyes, but abandoned herself to Lancelot's embraces.

The next day Arthur sent for Lancelot to come to his room.

The room was the same as ever. One of Arthur's dogs, an Irish wolfhound pup, rolled on the floor and the king laughed.

Lancelot looked out of the window. Arthur's view showed more of the tilled fields and the town than some of the others did. She knew the king liked to look down on his people much better than on the forest, where the beasts might be indifferent to him.

"Lance, are you truly healed?" Arthur pressed her shoulders.

As always trying to keep from flinching at Guinevere's husband's touch, Lancelot replied, "I am."

"Nevertheless, you seem a little worn. Rest yourself." Arthur sat on a fine carved chair and indicated that Lancelot should sit on a similar one.

She sat down, but there was little of repose in her. Her muscles still were tense.

"It was Bellangere who poisoned the apples so he could kill Gawaine and blame Guinevere, because he was angry about Sangremore's death. He attacked me in the forest, just before I sank into whatever spell or madness came upon me. He is dead now," Lancelot told the king. She did not want to mention Bellangere's taunts about her madness.

"The traitor! Let his name be stricken from the list of my warriors forever!" cried Arthur, pounding his table with his fist. "Thank all the saints you survived." He smiled at Lancelot. "This is no time for anger. I am right glad that you have returned."

"This is my place," she said.

"Now what about the young lady who healed you? There are all sorts of rumors. I suppose she is not the woman Etaine who pretended to be Guinevere a few years ago?" Arthur asked in a tone of man-to-man congeniality and poured himself some ale. He motioned for Lancelot to pour some for herself, but she did not.

"She is not," Lancelot said briefly. "Her name is Elaine, and she is nothing like Etaine."

"Will you marry her?" He leaned closer to Lancelot. "Bagdemagus's daughter is not such a great match for you, but Gawaine told me that she is devoted to you. He said that you don't want to marry her, though, and that I shouldn't urge you to, but of course I will."

Lancelot felt herself flush. These questions were totally unexpected. Surely he knew why she would never marry. There was no room in her heart for anyone but Guinevere. "I have no plans to marry, my lord."

Arthur grimaced. "Now, now, don't talk to me with those formal 'my lords.' Save that for God. He may appreciate it more than I do. You aren't getting any younger. It's time you had children. You'll be sorry if you don't. Of course I know you want to stay here, and I want you to stay. But you could bring her to Camelot and live here. There's nothing to stop you. We'll welcome her, of course. Or any other girl you want to marry." Arthur drank some ale and lifted up his cup as if to toast a possible marriage.

What torture for Guinevere, Lancelot thought. "I will never marry. The Lady Elaine is a good woman, but I cannot marry her."

"Perhaps she's not quite good enough, eh?" Arthur asked with a sly smile. "You needn't be so stiff. You can talk about it with me."

Lancelot wanted to strike him, but she kept her voice formal. "No, my lord, I cannot. Please say no more about it. I am afraid that I am still a trifle unwell. May I have leave to rest?"

Arthur shook his head. "Still determined to speak purely, are you? Go and rest. We need you to be well."

Lancelot rested on a carved bench in Guinevere's room, with her head in Guinevere's lap. The queen stroked her hair and told her how sweet her face was from that angle. Lancelot was nearly dozing, and thinking about what they would be doing later that night.

"Have many people asked you about the grail yet?" Guinevere inquired. Her braids dangled over Lancelot's face and tickled her nose. "The more pious men all started talking about it after you left. Bors insisted on going in pursuit, and took young Percy with him, and Gareth tries looking for it when he is on his way back from rescuing widows or maidens or whatever he's doing. I suspect that some of the others sneak off and look for it, too. Men love this idea of chasing after some mystical thing."

"Why not?" Lancelot asked, not wanting to think about anything except Guinevere, but making an effort to do so. How pretty Guinevere's chin was, and the blue gown she wore matched her eyes. "I suppose they could be doing worse things-- or better, too, more practical. I don't imagine that anyone is looking for it in a peasant's hut."

"Of course they aren't. It does make me wonder whether I am giving Talwyn enough of a vision. Reading the Roman works. Will those sustain her?" Guinevere wrinkled her forehead.

Forced to think, Lancelot sat up beside her. "I don't know, and I often wonder whether we are giving the young warriors enough ideals. Defending the country and others who are in need of help, is that enough?"

"I don't know, you're the one who lives by doing that. Is it?" Guinevere looked as if she really wanted to know.

"In a way it is, but I would be very sad if I didn't have our love and I don't think I could keep on if I didn't have companions who were trying to do the same thing." Lancelot remembered what it had been like when she was mad and had imagined she would never see her friends again. Guinevere's cat jumped into her lap, and Lancelot was glad to hear its familiar purr.

Guinevere sounded less sure of herself than she had been not many months before. "I'm not certain of anything, except what is wrong. I'd like to try to put things right, but I don't want to chase grails. Do you? Did you begin to find the idea appealing?"

"Of the grail? It's a little tempting, especially because it's so vague." Lancelot tried to smile at herself. She ruffled the cat's fur. "It's so much easier to say that you are looking for that than to say that you want to feed all the poor or end all killing. What about you, love?"

Guinevere shook her head. The candlelight made the silver in her hair shine. "It may be enough of a grail to try to hold up my head, and be your lover. And to encourage other women who are brave enough to hold their heads up, too. There may be battles to keep Talwyn from being married off to someone she doesn't want. Arthur has strange ideas about suitability. He keeps mentioning sons of Bors and Bedwyr who are much too dull for her."

Remembering Elaine, Lancelot stiffened. "I must do something about Elaine. Her father may be trying to find a husband for her because he thinks that I got her with child. I must return there soon and see if she needs to get away. I did ask whether she wanted to enter a convent, but she declined. She may change her mind if her father tries to marry her off, though. I'm ashamed at how easy it is to put her out of my mind. It's only been a matter of days."

"I suppose I'm fortunate that you remembered me." Guinevere retreated into sarcasm. "Perhaps if Gawaine hadn't appeared it would have taken you several more months."

Lancelot looked into Guinevere's blue eyes. They were not the blue of the lakes or the sky, but their own dear color. "No, I never forgot you. I was looking for an excuse to go."

"That's a beautiful sentiment." Guinevere's tone was not entirely sweet and her gaze was not entirely warm.

Lancelot was even more abashed, but she clasped Guinevere's hands. "How can I say beautiful things when I'm thinking about how I wronged you? You can see that I'm here, instead of helping her out, as I probably should be."

"Yes, you should. She shouldn't be married off. Just come back to me." She pressed Lancelot's hand.

"There's no doubt about that." Lancelot returned the pressure and kissed her mouth. Although she thought she should go back to help Elaine, she made excuses to herself for staying with Guinevere a little longer. They had been apart so long, and surely Elaine's father couldn't marry her off yet

When Lancelot went to the stable for her morning ride, she saw Gawaine examining his horse's hooves.

"I should have him shod again before I go," Gawaine said.

"Off again so soon?" Lancelot raised her eyebrows.

"I've asked Arthur to send me off on a mission. I'm in no mood for court life," her friend said, patting his horse's neck. "But it seems to suit you. You're looking well."

"I feel well indeed." Lancelot grinned, unable to say more about her delight in Guinevere for fear of being overheard. "Will you be back for the Pentecost contests?"

Gawaine shook his head. "Not this year. I leave the honors to you."

"Does Arthur know you'll miss the contests?" she asked, incredulous that the king would allow him to be absent.

"No. I've planned a longer journey. But there's no need to tell him, is there?" Gawaine grinned.

Nevertheless, she felt that he wasn't so cheerful.

Elaine fell back to her old routine. Her father didn't speak much to her, but she didn't mind that. She wanted to be silent. She tried to regain her pleasure in her walks, now solitary as they had been before Lancelot. At night, and sometimes in the day, she wept.

One morning while she was telling the servants what to cook for supper, Bagdemagus bade her come to his great hall. The tic in his eye was moving faster than ever.

When they were alone, he said, "You might not be here for supper. I am sending you away. You have disgraced me."

Elaine could hardly believe what she heard. It felt as if a blow had struck her chest. "I'm sorry if I have disgraced you, Father, but how could you send me away? I've tried to be a good daughter."

His face reddened and his mouth tightened. "You're no daughter of mine. I had hoped that your father would be grateful to me for raising you, but I was wrong."

He was not her father? She trembled at his words. Surely they were just spoken in anger. He could not believe them. "There must be some mistake." Her voice faltered. "My mother would never have been untrue to you."

Bagdemagus yelled, "Of course my wife was never unfaithful to me! You aren't her daughter, so stop saying that you were." His face twitched more fiercely than she had ever seen.

She could hardly remain standing. "My mother was not my mother? It can't be true."

Looking at Elaine as if she were a rat hidden among the rushes on the floor, he raged on despite her shaking. "Your mother is the witch Morgan, and I have sent for her to take you back. Your bad blood has shown itself."

Reluctantly, she began to believe this unbelievable tale. Her head spun. She glanced at the hangings on the walls, the benches, the trestle tables. Would she never see them again? She had never known any other place. "But I look like my mother--like the Lady Elaine."

"As you know, my wife was a cousin of the witch's on her father's side, worse luck. She wanted a daughter and didn't have one, so I let her take you. I was a fool." He glared at her.

"Don't you care about me at all, after all these years?" Elaine begged. She wasn't so fond of any of his qualities, but she was used to him, and the thought of leaving her home terrified her.

"I have a son. I have no need for a daughter who is no daughter, who disgraces my name. Morgan, your lady witch mother, sent a messenger who said that she should be here today, or by tomorrow at the latest. Go get your things ready. You may take all of the clothes and little things I have given you over the years." He averted his gaze from her.

Sobbing, she ran to her room. Her mind was such a blur that she could hardly make out what he had said.

The Lady Morgan was her mother! She had liked the lady when she had met her, years before, and her mother--but she must not call her that anymore--had said that Morgan was no witch. But, however pleasant the Lady Morgan was--and she had been that, although formidable--she was not the one who had held Elaine when she was sick or the one who had taught her everything. Elaine did not want to leave the woods and marshes where she had walked with the woman who had raised her. She would have left them for Lancelot, but she did not want to go with anyone else.

Her mother was not her mother. Who was her father? That didn't matter.

After some time, she heard a horse ride into the courtyard, and went to the window. She saw the Lady Morgan ride up, and quickly darted away because she didn't want to be seen just yet.

Soon she opened her door, and she heard voices from the hall.

"How can I take her back to Tintagel?" the Lady Morgan was saying. "That would disgrace her far more than being with Lancelot. She'd be called a witch. It's better for her not to go anywhere with me. Let me send for Lancelot to take her away somewhere else."

"Take her away without marrying her? No doubt he'd like that. You have no shame, and neither does she!" Bagdemagus shouted.

Elaine rushed out of her room. The Lady Morgan didn't want her either. She ran to the stable and threw herself on her horse.

Elaine rode towards the bog. No one wanted her. Her mysterious brother might have, but he had never even told her his name, much less where to find him.

She rode as fast as she could, fast as a woman who has come from nowhere and has nowhere to go, who has only the wind to ride through. Nothing was behind her and nothing before her. She wished that the wind would carry her away to some crag, where she might find comfort with ravens and eagles.

Morgan frowned at the stubborn man. Why had her cousin married such a dolt? "You have given up too soon on Lancelot. He still might marry her. I hope he will be persuaded without having to be told who her father is, but if nothing else works, that might. He is the perfect husband for her." True, Lancelot was a woman--which of course she wouldn't tell Bagdemagus-- but what could be better than denying Arthur grandchildren? The handsome warrior would be gentle with Elaine.

An old serving man hurried into the hall.

"Lord Bagdemagus, the lady Elaine has ridden away in great haste," he said anxiously. "It isn't safe for her to ride so."

"What have you told her? Have you driven her away?" Morgan cried. "Where did she go?" she asked the serving man.

"Towards the bog, Lady."

Morgan ran from the hall, found her horse, and rode towards the bog.

She saw Elaine's horse galloping by the bog, where no horse should run. Waterfowl from the pond screamed and flew up.

Morgan called out, "Elaine!" All her love and fear went into her voice as she called again.

But Elaine rode on.

A bittern's large brown and white body, frozen still, blended into the reeds. When Elaine's horse came near, the bird suddenly flew up, and the horse threw its rider. Elaine fell into a pond.

Morgan galloped to the spot, leapt from her horse, rushed into the shallow pond, and pulled out her daughter's limp body. She wailed.

Morgan moaned like the wind, shrieked like the gulls she knew so well, howled like a wolf. She curled there, at last with a chance to hold her daughter.

She thought of the last time she had held her, a babe at her breast, and how her breasts had ached after she had to give the child away. They ached again at the memory.

The child of so much passion could not hold back from passion. Morgan castigated herself for not seeing that much sooner.

She managed to lift the poor body, pull it onto her horse, and carry it back to Bagdemagus's dun.

The wretched man came to the courtyard and wept at the sight of Elaine's body. "She was a good girl. I didn't mean to hurt her."

Morgan didn't want to hear anything he had to say. She had rather strike him dead. But she said, "We should send her to Camelot. Let Lancelot mourn her."

"I don't suppose the king will reward me for raising her now." Bagdemagus moaned, seeming to grieve over the loss of an imagined reward as much as that of the girl.

Holding back her rage, Morgan spoke in an icy tone. "No, he won't. Don't dare to tell him about her, or I shall tell him how you treated her in the end, and he'll be angry. It would be too cruel to tell him about her now--but not as cruel as what you would face. You have my curse, but no doubt you fear him more."

Shuddering, Bagdemagus turned away.

Morgan, with the help of his serving people, prepared the poor body. Then she accompanied Elaine's body in a cart to the river that flowed by Camelot. The body, still uncorrupted after the journey, she placed on a barge. It was strange to her that she so much wanted her daughter to be buried near Camelot, even though she could not visit the grave there because Arthur had exiled her.

When Morgan had bade farewell to the barge, she rode, not to her caer in Cornwall, but to the Convent of the Holy Mother in the woods.

As soon as she entered the convent, Morgan began weeping. Soon the abbess was by her side and put her arms around her.

"I shall take her to my quarters," the abbess told the other nuns. When they had reached the abbess's office, Morgan slumped against her.

"Elaine died," she sobbed. "Why her instead of me, why, why? I would have died to save her. Why?"

"Does there have to be a reason for these things? Just weep, that's all right." She stroked Morgan's hair, which had turned white in these few days. "Stay here as long as you want, and heal."

Morgan flung herself on the bare floor and pounded it. "Heal? You never bore a child. There is nothing more terrible than living after your child has died. I never even knew her, I just saw her a few times. She was the sweetest girl who ever was, the sweetest. I couldn't see her first steps, I couldn't be the one to talk to her when her first blood came, I wasn't the one who taught her about wild things. I could kill Arthur for calling me a witch so I didn't dare to raise her."

Then her tone changed. "Poor Arthur, he never even knew about her." Morgan wailed. She grieved for their lost love and the lost child of that love.

A groom from Camelot's stables brought the message that a man on a barge in the river wanted to see Lancelot.

"There's a woman's corpse in the barge, too," the boy ventured. The whole court, the pious and the appalled, the amused and the morbid, went down the hill with Lancelot to view it.

The king and queen both came to stand near the barge.

Seeing Elaine's pale body, Lancelot could hardly keep standing. She jumped on the barge, bent over, and kissed the cold cheek. She tried to take the stiff body in her arms.

"What happened?" she choked.

The wrinkled man who poled the barge said, "She was riding. She fell and hit her head, and died, that's all."

Lancelot exclaimed, "Can that be true? What really happened? Did she kill herself, or was she killed?" She still clasped the poor body.

"That's what I was told," the man said.

"Who told you that?" Lancelot asked. "Her father?"

"The Lady Morgan of Cornwall, who put her on this barge."

"What did she have to do with her?" Arthur asked, with the usual displeasure in his tone when Morgan's name was mentioned.

Impatient with the king for thinking only of his old grievance in the face of this tragedy, Lancelot spoke. "The Lady Morgan was her mother's cousin. The mother was related to the Duke Gorlois, Morgan's father."

Arthur leaned over the barge and looked at the girl.

"Pretty, but no great beauty," he said. "But of course she healed you, and that is why you were fond of her."

Lancelot made no reply. She cut off a lock of Elaine's hair and put it in the small pouch of treasures that she wore hanging from a piece of leather around her neck. With Peredur's help, Lancelot lifted Elaine's body from the barge.

No one spoke much until they had put Elaine's body on the bank.

Tears streamed down Guinevere's cheeks. "Poor, poor girl," she sobbed.

Lancelot loved Guinevere more than ever because the queen wept over Elaine.

After the funeral, Lancelot rode out to the old convent. Now the forest bluebells held no charm for her, nor did the birdsong cheer her. Mother Ninian must have anticipated her visit, for she was waiting in the oak grove where they sometimes walked.

The old nun opened her arms in a motherly embrace. "So, you have loved another woman and she has died."

Lancelot felt only a little surprised that the old seer seemed to know what had happened. "If you can see these things, why don't you warn me, that I may avoid them?" She was ready to be angry with anyone.

Ninian shook her head. "Would you have me be like Merlin, who gave people warnings they didn't understand? No one can see everything, and half-warnings are worse than nothing. They would only worry you. No one can live with knowledge of the future. And I did not see this. The Lady Morgan came here and told us."

"Elaine was so good, so gentle," Lancelot moaned. "And I hurt her. It's my fault that she is dead."

"You must never believe that." Ninian was firm. "You gave her happiness. Everyone must die."

But Elaine was the one who was dead. The blue sky seemed to mock Lancelot's pain. The new leaves on the oak trees promised a rebirth that would not come.

"Do you know how she died? Can you tell me? Did her father kill her because he was angry at her for being with me? Did she kill herself because I left her?" Lancelot did not want to hear, but she thought she must.

"I do know what happened to her," the old nun said, clasping Lancelot's shoulders. "It was not what you fear. Morgan saw Elaine's death. Elaine was riding by a bog. A bittern flew up, her horse threw her, and she fell into a pond and struck her head on a rock. That's all."

Lancelot sobbed. "I can't believe that it's no fault of mine. I think that if had been there, she would not have died."

"You can't think that way," Ninian scolded her. "You can't know everything. What should you have done, gotten attacked in a different part of the country so she never would have seen you?"

Lancelot would not be comforted. She pulled away from Ninian's embrace. "Why wasn't I there with her? Why do I always fail when it is most important?"

"Not so, not so," said the old woman, patting her shoulder.

Lancelot wept. No tears would ever be enough for sweet Elaine.

"Enough·water from your eyes. You should go to the nearby pond and swim," Ninian urged.

"How can I?" It seemed like too great a pleasure, something she did not deserve. She also thought of drowning.

"Of course you can swim." Ninian led her, holding her hand.

Thinking of Elaine's body riding down the river on the barge, Lancelot went into the water, still cold though it was a warm day for spring. She begged Elaine for forgiveness. She longed to drown, but of course she could not with the old nun watching on the bank. Was part of her really living in the depths of some pond with Elaine, as Elaine had said? Should she join her?

Lancelot stayed in the water a long time, and eventually started seeing the fish and hearing the spring frogs. A kingfisher hovered over the water, preparing to dive for a fish. It saw Lancelot and, giving its loud, rattling cry, flew off. An otter slid down a bank into the pond and swam its bouncing way across the water, even though it must have seen Lancelot. The closeness of the animal, going about its life as if she were not there, touched her. She knew that Elaine would have felt the same way. You are with me, I remember you, she thought. See the woods and the water with me, please.

She did not want to leave the water, but when she did she felt calmer.

She had left Elaine, but she must never abandon Guinevere. When Lancelot climbed out on the mossy bank, Ninian said, "Good, that's done. I urged you to swim while I was near because I feared that you might go in sometime by yourself, and stay there. The danger has passed for now."

True, Lancelot no longer thought of dying, but she saw that Elaine had been right in saying that she would follow always in Lancelot's tracks and that there was no escaping from her.

Talwyn watched Guinevere reading. When the queen lifted her head, the girl dared to speak.

"Lady Guinevere, is it true that women can feel passion for each other?"

Guinevere glared as she had never done before.

Talwyn winced.

"I cannot believe that you would ask me such a question. Never do so again."

Talwyn had never heard so little tenderness in the queen's voice.

"I think Galahad may be a woman." She blushed.

"Impossible!" Guinevere let her precious book drop to the floor. She paused, then picked up the book and put it gently on the table. "Where did you get such an idea?"

"Creirwy observed it."

"Did she? Creirwy is a clever girl." Guinevere sighed. "How dangerous for Galahad."

The queen did not add "and for Lancelot," but Talwyn understood that was also on Guinevere's mind.

"And what does that mean for you?" Guinevere scrutinized her.

Talwyn suddenly felt shy.

"I think I want Galahad, whatever I find out. But when women love each other, is there more than kissing? I feel passions, and I don't know that I can give my life to Galahad if she is a woman and there is no passion between women."

"You're a dear girl," Guinevere cried, embracing her. "I'm sorry that I didn't understand. Yes, there is passion. Very much."

Talwyn held back from the embrace. "Please don't tell anyone. It may just be a mistake."

"Of course I won't tell." Guinevere spoke with her for a long time and told her many things.

Lancelot, still holding her head down with grief over Elaine, walked past Camelot's lime-whitened chapel. Father Donatus rushed through the door and ran to her. Short of breath, the plump priest grabbed Lancelot by the shoulder, and whispered in her ear, "Gareth is lying on the chapel floor. I suppose he has prostrated himself in prayer, but it frightens me. Please help me speak with him."

"Certes!" Lancelot exclaimed with much concern, hurrying after him.

They found Gareth lying face down in front of the altar. The crucifix above it looked down on him.

The priest spoke in a gentle voice. "Gareth, are you well?"

The young man jumped up, much flustered. "Is there nowhere that I can pray?"

"Indeed there is, but I have never seen anything like this, at least not here at Camelot. I was worried about you," Father Donatus told him. "Please come to the sacristy. Do you mind if Lancelot comes with us?"

"I don't mind." Gareth looked pleadingly at Lancelot, as if she were someone who might speak the same language, which apparently the priest did not.

Father Donatus took them to the tiny room filled with finely embroidered robes, candles, and other holy things. The smell of incense permeated the air.

"Is something the matter?" Lancelot asked. She knew that Father Donatus was not a man who was eager to pry, and she had always been glad of it. He often asked her whether she wanted to be shriven, for she used to be before becoming Guinevere's lover, but he never chastised her because she refused.

Bowing his head, Gareth stared at the floor. "My thoughts are so sinful that I'm ashamed even to look at decent people. I wonder whether I should castrate myself."

The others both gasped in horror. Lancelot almost fell over.

Gareth continued in a mournful voice, "The gospel says, 'if your right eye offends you, pluck it out.'"

"Holy Angels!" Lancelot exclaimed, shaking her head. "The world is not full of Christians with their eyes plucked out, nor castrated ones. You must not take those words so literally."

"Of course not," Father Donatus hastily agreed. "Prayer and good companions should be sufficient. If women tempt you, just spend more time with the other warriors, especially those whose conduct is generally good."

Gareth sighed as if in agony, and Lancelot could see that the advice might not be adequate.

An oil lamp illuminated the young warrior's pale face, surrounded by gold-embroidered robes, giving him the air of a saint's image.

"But," said Gareth, "any man who looks at a woman with lust has already committed adultery with her in his heart."

"That is different from doing it in the flesh," the priest said, "and really much less grievous."

It occurred to Lancelot that it might not be women who Gareth was committing adultery with in his heart. She wanted to touch Gareth's arm, but she feared that might be an imposition on one so tormented. She tried to think of something in the gospels that might help him. "But if Mary Magdalene was forgiven, why not you? Or anyone?"

Gareth's face quickly turned contemptuous, as if he smelled something rotten. "That story must just mean that it's of no consequence what women do. They may not even have souls. Men have souls that can be destroyed."

Lancelot almost reeled.

The priest's eyebrows shot up. "Of course they have souls," he said. "The Church baptizes them, doesn't it?"

"Why not?" said Gareth. "It probably does no harm to baptize them, in case they do have souls. But I think that letting them take the other sacraments goes too far. Surely an example about a woman--and a whore, at that--is not appropriate for a man. None of the apostles were unchaste."

"How do you know that?" Lancelot asked. Surely some of them might have been before they became saints.

"Of course they would not have been allowed to be apostles if they were," Gareth said earnestly. "And the warriors of the round table should be just as pure."

"They are not priests," Father Donatus said to him, although that was abundantly obvious, "but if you are so troubled, you should marry."

Gareth sagged as if he had been hit. "Perhaps I must. I wonder whether it would help."

"Don't be too hasty," Lancelot told him. If perhaps he was inclined toward men, marriage might only bring grief to him and a wife.

Father Donatus frowned at her, as if to say that Lancelot was no good example in the matter of marriage.

"Do you think I shouldn't, Lord Lancelot?" the young man asked, giving her an inquiring look.

"I think you should do so only if you love a woman and she loves you," she replied.

The priest stepped between Lancelot and Gareth. "Most marriages are not made for such reasons, but are meant to bring children into the world and to help men be good," he admonished.

"Thank you for your advice," the young warrior said, bowing to them both.

Lancelot wondered what to say to him, and how. Not knowing how to broach the subject, she put it off.

21 Galahad's Quest

On the great mountain Yr Wyddfa in Gwynedd, far north and west of Camelot, Galahad rested by a stream whose banks were covered with not-yet-blooming heather. She could see snow at the top of the mountain.

Perhaps it is not so bad being a mountain, Galahad thought, looking at the lichened rocks and the soft plants bathed in the afternoon light. The mountain's life seemed quiet, but perhaps it was not. Galahad imagined having rocky limbs, covered with earth, with trees and flowers sprouting from them and streams running down the sides. Storms would wash away some of the soil and leave part of Galahad clear and bare. Grouse would scramble across Galahad, digging for bugs, and deer would nibble at roots. An occasional wolf would leap at a deer, and carry it back to her cubs. Ravens' calls would wake the mountain in the morning, and owls would fly through the mountain's dreams in the night.

Galahad could easily imagine Moses and Jesus going to mountains for prophecies, as the Lady of the Lake had peered into the waters. The mountains looked almost ready to speak. Or rather, they seemed to say that they had a message for anyone who could learn to read it.

Then Galahad's thoughts turned to wondering whether it ever would be possible to explore Talwyn's mountains and valleys.

The tranquility of the scene was disrupted by a large warrior in chain mail who galloped up to the slope where Galahad lay, as if to ride right over her. She rolled away in time to escape being trampled.

"Why did you do that?" Galahad exclaimed, but instead of replying, the man turned and charged again, with spear out to impale Galahad. Clearly not all warriors obeyed the rules of fighting taught at Camelot.

A sword hung from Galahad's baldric, but Galahad's spear was on her horse, which grazed some distance away. As the warrior bore down on Galahad, she turned aside, then lunged out and grabbed his spear, pulling the attacker off his horse.

He cried out in anger.

"Why must you attack me? Stop this madness," Galahad cried, attempting to sound calm though her heart beat faster than it ever had before and her breath came in great strangling gulps.

"I attack everyone who comes here," the man snarled, scrambling to his feet and reaching for his sword.

"Then I'll leave," Galahad said, but before that was possible, the warrior had attacked again, and Galahad had to draw her sword and fight off his blows.

The strange warrior aimed at her head as if he wanted to cut it clean off her body, but Galahad was able to cut his right arm. Yelling in pain, he dropped his sword.

"Can we stop this fight?" Galahad asked, panting, but then two other men in chain mail came riding across the ridge.

Help me!" the warrior called, and they galloped up. He laughed unpleasantly. "These are my kin. You'll be finished now."

"But why?" Galahad cried, just as perplexed as dismayed. "I have fought only to defend myself against this man's unprovoked attack," Galahad called out to the men who were bearing down.

"Wretch, he's our kin!" one of them yelled.

Galahad briefly prayed to be spared the fires of hell, but then another warrior who held a familiar shield emblazoned with a hawk and wore a familiar many-colored plaid cloak rode in from another direction.

"Hold on, Galahad!" Gawaine called, and his horse flew towards the attacking men.

There was a great clash of spears and swords, in which Galahad fought the warrior who had first attacked her, who had grabbed up his sword with his left hand, and Gawaine fought the other two. At the end of it, the three turned and fled, and Galahad rode off with Gawaine.

"Many thanks," Galahad gasped, when the breath to talk returned.

"I'm glad I was there," Gawaine replied gruffly. "You fought well, though."

"I suppose so." Galahad sighed, not amused by the narrow escape. Everything seemed a blur. Someone had wanted to kill her for no reason. Truly, men were mad. She was surprised that she had the strength left to climb back on her horse.

They came to a stream running down the mountain slope.

"It should be safe to camp here," Gawaine told Galahad. Thank all the gods he had come in time to save this decent young man. "Those men won't be in any shape to look for us, and they seemed to be marauders, without followers to back them up." He pulled out his flask of wine and drank deeply.

Galahad also drank from a flask.

"Do you have only water? Want some wine?" Gawaine asked, wondering how the young warrior could recover from the fight without a stronger drink.

"No, thank you." Galahad sprawled on the grass, which was just springing up this far up the mountain.

Poor young man. No doubt this was the first time anyone had tried to kill him, Gawaine thought. Remembering the first time he had faced a similar threat, so long ago, he splashed some water from the stream on his face.

"If I had been killed, no one would have known to tell my mother, because no one knows who she is." Galahad sighed. "I am not supposed to say what my family is. I have kin at Camelot, but they don't know it."

Gawaine groaned and shook his head. What was the matter with young people? "Why must all the young warriors have this desire for anonymity? Gareth hid in the kitchens, Percy pretends that he has no father though he has a good one, and Mordred won't say who his real mother is. Must you also live incognito? If you have kin, you should let them know. That man who attacked you had kin who helped him, and your kin would help you."

A foolish grin spread across Galahad's face. "I wish that Lancelot was my father."

Gawaine snorted and leaned back on a rock. "But you know that he is not." He was sure that Galahad could not believe that rumor.

Resting on an arm, Galahad admitted, "True, but I want to be just like Lancelot."

Gawaine suddenly looked at Galahad, then looked away. He recalled that Galahad, like Lancelot, never wrestled, and was unusually modest, too. Galahad might be a woman. He should have seen it sooner. "Perhaps you are like Lancelot."

Galahad drank some water and sighed. "Unfortunately, the lady I am in love with says she wants someone who is more like you than like Lancelot."

Gawaine smiled. Amusing, if Galahad was a woman. "I think you might better aim to be like Lancelot. I hope that Lancelot has advised you about wooing this lady."

Galahad picked up a rock and examined it. "No, I asked and he wouldn't tell me. He said I should ask Bors how he wooed his wife."

Gawaine silently laughed at the thought that he had guessed Galahad's secret and Lancelot had not. "Bors chose his wife because he thought she would be a good mother to his children. I don't think that's what you want."

Galahad moaned. "No, it's not. The lady I love is Talwyn, and she does not want children."

Stifling wild laughter, Gawaine stared at the rushing stream. Very good, if Galahad could not sire them. "Well, that's not exactly a cause for grief, is it?"

Galahad did not seem to wonder at this strange remark. "No, but how could I ask for her hand? I have no property, and all I can say for myself is that I have some unnamed noble kin." Galahad frowned.

Gawaine removed his boot to shake out a pebble. "Who is your mother, anyway? You can tell me. I'll keep your secret."

"I can't tell you her name, but I can tell you a riddle," Galahad said, wiping dirt off his--or was it her?--breeches. "If

Eve was made from part of Adam, does that mean Adam was her father?"

Gawaine choked. "Of course not. That would make their joining a horrible thing, not only to Christians but to all people."

"But they were of one flesh. Adam must have been her brother then, so their sin was not as great. I am the child of Eve." Galahad pulled a dried apple from her pack.

"Gods!" Gawaine dropped his boot. "Your mother was Morgan! I'd never heard that she had a child."

"I was raised in a convent by a wise old nun," Galahad said, munching the apple.

"Indeed?" Gawaine stared at the young warrior.

"So you see, I was saved by kin today, because you are my mother's cousin. You are related to my father, too."

Gawaine took a long look at Galahad. "Yes, it seems that I am." Galahad was Morgan's daughter. And about the right age to be his. Although her thin frame was nothing like his, she had reddish hair and merry blue eyes that looked much like his own. The old nun who had told him to search for a missing daughter had said that she had eyes like his. But Morgan apparently had told Galahad that she was Arthur's. Gawaine's head swam. He wanted to throw his arms around Galahad.

"I shouldn't have told you. You won't tell my father, will you?" Galahad said with a contrite voice.

Trying to recover, Gawaine smiled at Galahad. "I won't tell anyone."

"I don't want him to know. I don't ever want to be a king, for then I would have to kill people in wars," Galahad confided. "I may be lazy, but I much prefer riding about and seeing the world."

"Of course. I understand." Yes, she was truly his daughter, with no ambition to rule. Arthur and Morgan were both made of ambition. Gawaine's chest swelled with pride.

A herd of red deer came into plain sight, but Gawaine was looking at Galahad and scarcely noticed them, while Galahad was staring into the stream. Talking to Galahad seemed more important than killing a deer for their supper. Galahad's hair stood up in various places, and Gawaine longed to pat it down.

"So you grew up in a convent?"

"Yes. I was raised in a convent by this old nun--she was jolly, as well as wise--who taught me about the forest and another who taught me to fight, but my mother often visited there. Pardon me, all this couldn't interest you."

"No, it does, very much," Gawaine hastened to say. "After all, I don't know much about convents." He had never guessed that the place with many women where the old nun had told him his daughter lived might be a convent, not a brothel.

"No, I don't suppose you do." Galahad chuckled, then continued her confiding tone. "It worries me that Talwyn says she wants someone like you."

Gawaine tried not to smile too broadly at Galahad's obvious fear that Talwyn wanted a man's body. "She surely is a maiden, and is not thinking of these things as specifically as you are. She can't really mean what you imagine. I think she just means that she wants someone who jests more than Lancelot and tries to kiss her."

"She did say that she wanted someone who jests. She said that she thought I was more like you than like Lancelot." Galahad looked at Gawaine, as if trying to see whether he was insulted or complimented.

"And so you are like me, around the eyes a little. She is more observant than you believe." Gawaine had just noticed it himself. He wondered why he had not recognized the resemblance sooner. Probably because Galahad was skinny.

"What?" Galahad blinked. "Yes, of course you are my cousin."

"Don't be afraid of this lady," Gawaine advised in his gentlest voice, which he sensed was louder than other people's gentle voices. "Just try, and if she doesn't want you, you can love another." Thank all the gods he had turned down Arthur's suggestion that he marry Talwyn, or else his daughter would have hated him. He wanted to tell Galahad that Talwyn was fond of her, but how could he explain ever having such a personal conversation with Talwyn? And it wasn't certain that Talwyn would feel the same if she knew Galahad was a woman.

"I am afraid," Galahad admitted. "That's half the reason I went away."

"Running away from the girl you love is not the best way to catch her."

Unable to look at Galahad any further without giving away his delight in her, Gawaine suggested, "Why don't we eat something?" He took some yellow cheese and barley bannock out of his pack and urged Galahad to eat it.

The deer had moved away, and he was too full of joy to go in pursuit of them.

"Thanks. You're good to be so concerned about me. I'm glad I told you that we're kin. But I don't want to tell the king."

"No, you're right, don't tell him." Gawaine's voice was solicitous. He finally remembered to put his boot back on.

An evening fog began to rise up the side of the mountain, and he watched it more anxiously than usual, as if the mist might become so thick that it could hide the young warrior from him.

"It's so pretty in these mountains. That does cheer me."
Galahad said, taking a bite of cheese. "I was thinking earlier
about Moses and Jesus coming to the mountains for revelations,
but even without any great revelations the mountains are
wonderful."

"Yes," Gawaine replied, grinning about his own revelation,
"but if you'll recall, who the latter met was the devil. I hope
you won't think me such a bad companion."

Galahad laughed. "Not at all. The devil probably would be
less entertaining. I'm not interested in being handed kingdoms."
She took a large bite of the bannock.

"I've always thought it was puzzling that Jesus said, 'Get
thee behind me, Satan.' If I was standing on the ledge of a
mountain with the devil, I wouldn't want him to stand behind
me." This might be a clean enough jest for Galahad.

Galahad laughed, choking on her food.

Galahad swallowed. "I don't suppose I'll ever find the grail."
She sighed. "I wish I were better." She shook her head. "I try to
be good, but I'm afraid I'm not as good as Lancelot."

"Who is? You don't have to be perfect." He thought that
Galahad was perfect, but it would be too flowery to say so.
Galahad must know that Lancelot was a woman, but Gawaine
couldn't let on that he knew about either of them.

Gawaine remembered that he had thought that Lancelot was
as she was, loving women rather than men, because her mother
had been raped before her eyes. Could some man have done
Galahad an injury? "It may be good that you were raised in a
convent. I hope that you were not hurt when you were growing
up?"

"I fell off horses a few times, but that's not so bad." There
were no painful undertones in Galahad's voice suggesting
anything else.

"No, it's not." Gawaine sighed with relief.

"That wise nun--is she round bodied, with a gentle face and many wrinkles?" he asked.

"That sounds like Mother Ninian," Galahad replied.

"I met her once in the forest. She was a good teacher," Gawaine said.

"She has taught you, too? She also advises Lancelot," Galahad told him.

"Lancelot told me that."

Gawaine didn't mind that the nun had let him misunderstand and go on a mistaken quest. He appreciated his wonderful daughter all the more because she was so different from the sad, embittered, prostituted girl he had imagined.

Gawaine believed that Galahad was his daughter. But even if she was not, he accepted her as his daughter in his heart.

He thought that if he had not learned how to be Lancelot's friend, he would never have known how to be with Galahad.

The next day, they rode together through heather-covered mountains in the kind of terrain that Gawaine knew well and Galahad was seeing for the first time. Galahad paused to look at every stream and listen to every bird.

Gawaine watched Galahad as much as he could without being observed. He had never noticed before how well Galahad rode, what a fine voice she had, how pleasant her face was, though it was not exactly handsome. And that tiny beard-- perhaps Galahad was not as much a woman as Lancelot?

They rode along peacefully enough until a figure on horseback suddenly erupted from behind some rocks. It was a dark-haired girl of about fifteen. She wore a gown of good wool and an embroidered cloak, but her hair was tangled and her eyes showed fear.

"Please help me hide!" she exclaimed, gasping for breath.

"Of course we'll help you," Galahad said instantly.

"How many men are pursuing you?" Gawaine asked, thinking of tactics.

The girl hesitated. "I'm not sure. Two at least." She looked as if she might fly off again at any moment.

Smiling what he thought was a reassuring smile, Gawaine put his hand on the hilt of his sword. "Don't worry, then. We can easily kill them."

"No!" The girl reached out frantically as if to stop him. "It's my father, and the man to whom he betrothed me."

Tensed for a fight, Gawaine relaxed. His concern for her began to abate. "You shouldn't flee from your father, child. What's the matter? Is the man he betrothed you to evil?"

She shook her head, and looked all the more eager to depart. "No, Royth's just ordinary. But I love another, and I'm running to him."

Gawaine hesitated. "Are you sure that's wise?" he began to say, but Galahad interjected, "Don't ride off. We'll help you. What's your name?"

"Keri."

Gawaine sucked in his breath when he heard that her name was the same as that of his first wife, the one he had loved. "And who's your father? And who is the man you want to marry?"

Her horse pawed the ground, and clearly the girl was just as restless. "My father is King Maelgon."

Gawaine groaned. He had just been at the caer of Maelgon of Gwynedd, visiting that peevish king to ensure his continued allegiance to Arthur. He hadn't seen the girl there.

"I love Uwaine, son of King Uriens of Rheged," she continued. "My father wants me to marry Royth, a son of

Cador of Eburacum, because he is his father's eldest son, and wealthy, while Uwaine is King Uriens's youngest son, who won't inherit much. He wintered at my father's caer and we secretly pledged ourselves to each other."

"Why isn't he here fighting for you, then?" Gawaine asked, trying not to sound harsh. Uwaine was a warrior sworn to Arthur, but he was usually off somewhere in the West or the North.

"He broke his arm in a hunting accident. He cannot fight. But he's riding even now to meet me." Again, Keri surveyed the rocks around her and looked as if she wanted to flee.

"Why must these things depend on fighting?" Galahad exclaimed. "Anyone could be injured at a time when he is challenged."

"Maelgon is an important subject king of Arthur's," Gawaine began, but there was no point in further describing Maelgon because a large, gray-bearded man and a somewhat slimmer young one rode into view.

"Father!" Keri cried in a sinking voice.

"What do you mean by running away?" her father demanded, scrutinizing her with hawk-like eyes. "I came only with Royth so no one else would know that you had done such a thing. And what are you doing in such company? Gawaine, why are you here? There was a good reason why I didn't introduce my daughter to you. You've always said you'd never marry any of my daughters." Maelgon looked tense and ready to fight, as did the young man accompanying him. The king tried to ride up to his daughter, but Gawaine and Galahad blocked the way. Maelgon glared at them.

"I may not be spotless, but young Galahad is," Gawaine replied in a tone that was meant to be calming. "We have just encountered your daughter. Why must she seek help in escaping your orders?"

"She's just a foolish girl, too young to know what she thinks," Maelgon began.

"And therefore too young to marry," Galahad piped in.

Maelgon turned his glare on Galahad. "Royth here is a fine young man. I am not forcing my daughter to marry some brute, am I, Keri?"

"No, Father, but I want to marry Uwaine," she said, trembling a little but speaking boldly.

Her father and Royth glared at her. Gawaine noticed that there was no tenderness in Royth's face, though the young man was not bad-looking.

"Is there some great objection to Uwaine?" Gawaine asked, mindful that Galahad was watching him. "Is he cruel, or a wastrel?"

Maelgon's face grew redder. "Why must I answer to you? I'm within my rights in marrying my daughter to whom I choose. There's nothing the matter with Uwaine, but Royth will inherit much more."

"Must you sell your daughter to the highest bidder?" Gawaine demanded, surprising himself with his anger. "Do you want his gold so badly? You should help your child, not seek to profit from her." Did Maelgon have no idea how precious a daughter was? Although Gawaine had believed that Galahad was his daughter for only a short time, he shivered at the thought that he could have done such a thing to her.

"How dare you interfere with us!" exclaimed Royth, who had not tried to say one word to Keri.

But Maelgon just put his hand on his sword, and said, "I shall complain to King Arthur about this. You know that I have the right to take my daughter home. Come, Keri, you must obey me."

Keri just shook her head.

Gawaine looked at her, then at her father, and then at Galahad. "I would like to help Keri, but I don't know that we can, if her father can't be persuaded," he admitted.

Maelgon gloated at these words. "Come along, daughter," he said in a milder tone. "Royth and Uwaine are both fine young men. The only difference is that she thinks she prefers one of them. That's no reason to fight."

"Yes, it is," Galahad cried, advancing on Maelgon. "I won't let you take her." The young warrior drew her sword from its scabbard.

In an instant, Maelgon drew his sword, and Royth did likewise. They both attacked Galahad.

With the first swipe of his sword, Maelgon slightly cut Galahad's cheek. "You'll find that no man fights so fiercely as when he's fighting for his daughter," he snarled.

The flat side of Gawaine's sword knocked Maelgon off his horse, and Gawaine flung himself on the ground to fight him. "You fight the young one, I'll fight the older," he called to Galahad.

Keeping an eye on Galahad and seeing that she easily knocked Royth's sword out of his hand, Gawaine beat Maelgon into the ground and stood over him.

"Don't kill him, Gawaine!" Galahad cried out.

Recalled from his anger that Maelgon had cut Galahad, Gawaine put up his sword and demanded, "Go home with this young man, and leave your daughter to marry whom she wishes."

"Why, she's gone!" Maelgon exclaimed. "She didn't even stay to see whether I survived the fight."

They all looked at the place where Keri had been, and sure enough, only rocks and bushes were there.

"Don't pursue her," Gawaine demanded, continuing to speak as he had never dared speak to a king before. Well, he was a king's son himself.

Maelgon, bruised and bleeding from a cut on his head, staggered up, helped by Royth. "I shall complain to King Arthur. If you tarry in Gwynned, I'll have you seized and put in chains," he threatened in parting.

Gawaine and Galahad rode off in the direction that they thought Keri had taken.

Looking downhill at the trail below them, Galahad said, "There she is, and Uwaine is with her."

A handsome, brown-haired warrior with a bandaged right arm rode beside the girl.

"Why, he must have been there all the time, waiting in hiding. He's a damned coward," Gawaine grumbled.

"But his right arm is broken," Galahad protested.

"That wouldn't have kept me from a fight, if it was for a girl I loved."

"Or for any other reason, considering how much you like to fight," Galahad observed.

But Gawaine shook with indignation. Uwaine didn't deserve the brave girl who had run away for his sake.

They forced their horses to go faster until they caught up with the young couple.

"Your father is not much hurt, but he won't pursue you until he gets more men to help him," Galahad said to Keri.

"Thank you," she said, smiling at them, particularly Galahad.

"See that you marry her," Gawaine ordered Uwaine, with a notable lack of warmth.

"We're secretly married already," Keri told them, "and I am with child." She blushed a little. "I was afraid to tell my father that."

"Well, you don't have to ride so fast now. Just keep on at a steady pace. We'll watch and make sure that you aren't followed," Gawaine said, speaking only to Keri. Uwaine he dismissed as a poltroon.

Soon, Galahad and Gawaine were riding alone again on the mountain rocks.

"She's too young to be married and have a child!" Galahad exclaimed.

Gawaine nodded. He was used to seeing girls marry at that age, but now the thought that Galahad might have been married for years and have her arms full of children disturbed him. "Yes, she is, but there's no help for it. At least she's with a man she wants, and that may make her happy. I hope she survives the child-bearing. My first wife, who also was named Keri, died in childbed, as many women do. So did my second wife."

"I'm glad I don't have a life like that!" Galahad said with considerable fervor.

"I'm also glad that you don't," Gawaine replied, trying to keep his voice less fervent.

But Galahad brightened, put a cloth to her cheek, and said, "I have my first battle scar now. Isn't it splendid? Do you think it will last? Did I fight well?"

Gawaine surveyed the cut on Galahad's cheek. "Wonderful. You'll probably have a scratch. You fought bravely, and I'm proud of you. But if you fight every father who tries to marry his daughter to a man she doesn't like, I fear that your own life will be very short."

Galahad sighed.

"I know. I suppose I can't fight every injustice. I know that I don't fight as brilliantly as Lancelot. I'm glad you were with me this time."

"So am I," was all that Gawaine said. But that seemed too curt, so he added, "You are the bravest warrior in the world."

Galahad's mouth opened wide. "But Lancelot is the greatest warrior in the world."

"That's true. That's why you're even braver than Lancelot, because you are a good fighter, but not the greatest. Holding your seat at the round table is therefore even more of a challenge. It is a perilously held seat," Gawaine said, trying to convey what he meant without directly saying that he knew Galahad was a woman.

Galahad looked at Gawaine sheepishly. "Actually, ever since Lionel died in the tournament I have been thinking that I don't want to kill anyone. Would you think me a coward if I didn't spend my life as a fighter like you and Lancelot?"

In a voice that strove to keep out relief, Gawaine replied, "Of course not. You have good reasons. Fight or don't fight as you wish." He had no desire to see his daughter cut down in a fight.

Galahad's eyes widened. "I thought you would look down on a young man with a warrior's training who didn't want to fight. You were hard on Uwaine just now."

"Oh, no, you misjudge me. I would never think you a coward. I can see that you're very brave." He kept himself from saying, "Too much so."

They camped on another heather-covered mountain. To Gawaine, it seemed so fair that the heather might as well be blooming, though it would not for another month or so. The ground was cold and hard, but to Gawaine it felt better than the softest cushions. Being with Galahad was more wonderful than resting in the finest caer.

Twilight came, and they gathered sticks and built a fire.

After they had eaten stale bannock, Gawaine told a story about a woman who had rushed between her lover and a madman and thus saved her lover's life.

"What a woman!" Galahad said admiringly, brushing crumbs from her lap. Her face shone in the light from their small fire. An owl hooted.

"You know her, in fact. It was Guinevere."

"Queen Guinevere! I knew she was very clever, but I didn't know she was that brave."

"She loves Lancelot greatly. I hope that you will find a lady who loves you as much." And who isn't married to someone else, Gawaine thought. He tried to assume an innocent look, or at any rate as innocent a look as it was possible for him to assume. He looked at the sky and pretended to have a great interest in the stars.

He cautioned, "Be careful when you ride with Lancelot, for he still has many fears from the war and other horrors he has seen. Watch out for him."

"I had heard rumors that he was sometimes fearful, but I didn't believe it. Perhaps everyone is afraid of something. What are you afraid of, Gawaine?" Galahad dared to ask.

"Oh, of you, I suppose," Gawaine replied, laughing and cuffing the young warrior lightly on the shoulder. It was true. He feared that Galahad might not want him for a father, but would prefer to think herself Arthur's child.

Galahad howled at what seemed like a jest.

Gawaine slept fitfully that night, and dreamed of the day when he was seventeen, and had battled his way into a town at the head of the warband that supported his father, King Lot of Lothian, over Arthur for High King of Britain.

He had soon found his father raping a young girl, and inviting him to join in with the many men who were raping girls. In the dream, Gawaine saw the girl's face and heard her scream as clearly as he had so many years before. His father yelled at him, "I didn't know my son pissed squatting," because Gawaine wouldn't grab a girl.

He woke, remembering how he had left his father that very day to fight on Arthur's side. His brother Agravaine had stayed with Lot--and no doubt did what Lot was doing.

Some months later, Agravaine had followed Gawaine, and he had asked Arthur to make his brother welcome, which Arthur graciously had. But Gawaine was never sure why Agravaine had come--because he had missed his older brother? Because he had guessed that Arthur was going to win? Gawaine had doubted that it was for the same reason that he had.

Gawaine had drunk little on this journey with Galahad, but his head hurt with the memories. Sleep was impossible.

He remembered another, even crueler war. He had seen the burned Saxon town, the bodies of disemboweled women, and been distressed that Agravaine defended the men who raped and killed them. Gawaine even imagined that Agravaine might have done the same, if he had had the chance. Why did Agravaine have no heart?

Perhaps it was his fault for not getting Agravaine away from that other town long before. How could Agravaine not learn from his own father? Knowing how a man could get used to killing other men, Gawaine guessed that men could get used to women screaming and struggling, and even want it.

Lancelot had once thought ill of him for defending the use of camp followers. No doubt she still did. True, taking along camp followers was not pretty, but what he had seen seemed so much worse, and he was sure that warring men would do whatever they wanted to get women.

He scarcely noticed the dawn.

Galahad was clattering about, humming cheerfully, feeding and patting the horses.

Feeling a hundred years old, Gawaine pulled himself up and walked over to join Galahad.

"I can feed your horse, too, Gawaine. Why, you look grim as a ghost. Didn't you sleep? Are you ill? What's the matter?" Galahad's face wore a look of concern.

He saw that he had to tell Galahad the things that he least wanted to relate.

"Let's not ride off just now. Sit down and listen to me." He slumped down on a stone and declined the barley bannock that Galahad offered. Giving Galahad a chance to break fast, Gawaine thought about what he would say before he lost the nerve.

"Why so solemn?" Galahad asked, munching, looking around at the pipits that were calling not far from them and the hawk that soared overhead.

"It is well that you don't want to fight," Gawaine began, hearing how heavy his voice was, "for men too easily move from fighting to other things." He told the tale of how he had left his father's side and gone to Arthur's, a story that he had never told anyone else but Arthur and never would.

Galahad paled and dropped the bannock on the ground, but she said only, "It must have been hard to leave your father. I'm glad that my father isn't like that."

If he had been, he could never have dared to tell her.

"And you aren't, either," Galahad added.

Gawaine felt a pang of envy for Arthur, the first he had ever had, because Galahad believed that she was his daughter. But there was only so much that he could tell. "I have done many things in my life, but not like that." He wanted her to know that he was better than his father had been. It mattered more than anything that Galahad never judged him harshly.

"Of course not. I'm sure that none of King Arthur's men would have."

Galahad sounded just as innocent as Lancelot had been when young, which was good, in its way, but too dangerous.

"Some have." And he told about what had happened to the Saxon women, and said that some of Arthur's men, as well as the lesser kings' men, might have had a part in it. He also reminded Galahad that Sangremore had raped a Saxon thane's daughter.

Galahad's face finally was as sick as Gawaine felt, and it tore his heart to see it so. He wanted the expression in her blue eyes to always be merry.

"Stay away from warring men, Galahad," he added. "For if you do not do what they do, it might anger them."

Galahad nodded. "I see. You were right to tell me, but could we ride now? I'm aching to move."

So was he. Even more restless than the horses, they were soon away, galloping, and Gawaine wished that he could take his daughter to another world where such things never happened.

Eagles swooped in the air over the mountain passes, and they stopped to watch the majestic birds. Gawaine and Galahad made a relaxed journey, vaguely east, but it did not matter where. Gawaine pointed out all of the mountain wildflowers that Galahad did not know, and told how many of them were tinier versions of flowers that grew at lower elevations.

Galahad should see the hills of Lothian, Gawaine urged, and Galahad agreed.

Gawaine told stories, many of which had brave women in them and none had much of bedding. He told the tales about his life that he wanted Galahad to hear, such as the story of how Lancelot had saved him from the Green Warrior.

"You might have been foolish not to marry the Green Warrior's widow, Alais," Galahad suggested. "It sounds as if she was very fair and exceedingly fond of you."

"That might be true," Gawaine admitted. "Perhaps someday I'll go find out whether she has married again." He remembered Alais's warm embrace and, still more, her insistence on sharing the blame for lying with Gawaine, thus leaving herself at her husband's mercy. A fine woman, the only woman--except for Lancelot--who had ever been willing to give her life to save his. Yes, he wanted to see her. She had loved him. Perhaps it would not be so hard to love her, or even to marry her.

"At the time I last saw Alais, when I tried to save her from her brutal husband, but barely escaped with my life because Lancelot happened by, I was mad about another woman and had no wish to marry. It was Ragnal, who was a serving woman at Camelot. She died a year ago." He looked up to see whether Galahad thought it was odd to care about a serving woman. "Do you remember her?"

Galahad shook her head. "No, I'm afraid I never noticed her. I'm sorry you lost her."

Gawaine sighed. It was unlikely that a young warrior would have noticed a gray-haired serving woman, of course, but it saddened him. How little Galahad knew about him, and how little he knew about Galahad.

He wished he had seen Galahad as a child, the merry girl she must have been. Yes, he wanted children now more than ever.

At Gawaine's urging, Galahad repeated some of the tales that Mother Ninian had told, full of saints, goddesses, and wild creatures all speaking with each other.

Soon Gawaine and Galahad were trying to best each other at devising strange tales, such as how Cerridwen and a weasel resurrected St. John the Baptist--many people believed that weasels could revive the dead--but the characters always seemed to be clothed and fairly modest.

How had Galahad managed to pretend to be a man? Gawaine wondered. There must be many stories, and, because Galahad laughed easily, many jests. He wished that he could ask, but he feared that Galahad would be uneasy with him if she knew that he guessed her secret, but not that he was her father. Galahad might ride off sooner, and Gawaine longed to continue the journey.

One night Gawaine dreamed of the old nun. Smiling at him, she said, "The grail is not to be loved, but to love."

He woke with tears in his eyes.

When the two warriors from Camelot rose one dawn in a hillside camp, Galahad said, "Now that I have seen much of the West, I want to see Eburacum, go north to Hadrian's Wall, and see all that I can."

Gawaine turned away, trying not to sigh. Much as he wanted to stay with Galahad, he had been wondering whether Lancelot still was happy and whether her mind still was calm. "I have been away from Camelot far longer than I told Arthur I would be. I had better return. I hope you will return soon also." He forced himself to smile.

Galahad returned the smile. "Not too soon, I think. Many thanks for your lessons and for your good company."

The young warrior flung her arms around Gawaine. "I'm glad I told you that we are kin."

"So am I." Gawaine returned the embrace, brief as it had to be. "Enjoy your journey. And you might tell me where that convent is. Your Mother Ninian taught me a lesson once, and I'd like to thank her. Who knows, perhaps she'd teach me another one."

Galahad rode off to the tune of the skylarks' song.

As Gawaine went south alone, the skylarks did not sing as sweetly as they had when Galahad was there.

Gawaine thought he would tell Lancelot about Galahad. It would be amusing if he had guessed Galahad's secret and she had not. He would tease Lancelot about that, and show no mercy.

And he would tell her that he believed Galahad was his daughter. He did not have the courage to tell Galahad that he was likely her father, but perhaps Lancelot could find the words to tell her. He had no doubt that Lancelot would want to help him.

Riding through glens, Gawaine thought about the past, which he generally tried to keep as far away as possible.

He remembered meeting Keri, a pretty girl who laughed all the time. She had died and the baby boy was born dead, and as soon as the funeral was over, he had ridden home to weep on his mother's shoulder. Then there had been his second wife, who looked a little like Keri. He couldn't believe it when the midwife said that she, too, was dead, and the baby was still alive but weak.

He remembered that the midwife at his urging had tried to keep her alive. He had begged the tiny thing, "Fight, Girl," but she had not survived, and he had learned from the midwife's surprise at his grief that sometimes baby girls were allowed to die.

After that day he had thought at times about the missing daughter, and it seemed as if she should be there, and even more so after he had learned that he really had a missing daughter. Then, when his mother told him that he had had a sister whose life she had snuffed out in its first moments for fear that she would have a life of misery, Gawaine had thought about the missing sister, too, and it seemed as if she should also be there. Now perhaps they both had appeared, and he was glad that they were armed.

He shook his head, telling himself that he had learned more about women's troubles than he had ever wanted to know.

It eased his mind that Galahad liked women, not men.

Gawaine liked men very well and thought many were good companions, but he didn't want his daughter to marry one.

22 Drian's Tale

Drian strode down the streets of Eburacum, far north of any place she had ever been before. She surveyed the city's crumbling Roman buildings, fewer than half of which looked to be occupied. Her glance, always on the alert for some salable discard, darted amongst the rubble, although many other passersby must have scouted the place out over the years.

A beautiful lady approached her. Drian smiled--until she saw it was Cecilia.

"There you are, Lancelot. At last I've found you." Cecilia's eyes gleamed.

Drian backed off. "Lady, couldn't you see at that fighting contest that I'm not Lancelot?"

Beginning to run, Drian turned a corner--and encountered several of Cecelia's men, wearing her peacock badges.

A burly warrior grabbed her. "You're the coward who ran away from our lady's service."

Cecilia came around the corner. "Yes, he is. Take him to the villa where we're staying and hold him there. He won't escape again."

Drian cursed her luck. She walked to avoid being dragged by the brute, whose grip was like a fox holding a chicken. She had left her horse, with her harp tied to it, tethered far off. She had no intention of telling them where.

Galahad entered a tavern. She looked around carefully because she did not much like the company of drunken men, but she was hungry and was unsure where else to get a meal.

A serving woman batted her eyes at Galahad, and Galahad smiled back. No harm in just a smile. She ordered trout because meat might be who knows what, but fish were fish.

While she ate, Galahad heard some of the drinkers boasting.

"Lancelot of the Lake is supposed to be such a great warrior, but we took him easily this morning." The large man who spoke wore rusted chain mail and a tunic with an outlandish badge on it. He slopped some of his ale on the floor, which already had several pools on it.

"Sure, and I'm holding King Arthur in my cellar," sneered another drinker.

"No, this is really Lancelot. Lancelot of the Lightning Arm, hah! His arm wasn't so lightening swift today," the man with the badge said. "He just let us take him away. Mayhap my lady's so pretty that he doesn't much mind being her captive."

Galahad froze. Lancelot a captive! No lady was fair enough to make Lancelot forget Guinevere.

Galahad rose and strode over to the boaster. "I've seen Lancelot in fighting contests," she said. "I'll bet you a barrel of wine that your man isn't Lancelot."

"He is so!"

"Then take me to see him. I'll buy you a barrel if you're telling the truth."

"And you think I'll take your word for it that he's not, and buy you a barrel, even though I've never seen you before? I'm no fool." The man laughed.

"Oh no, you would pay no penalty if he's not Lancelot, but you would get the wine if he is." Galahad tried to give him her most winning smile. "You have nothing to lose."

"I'm no fool, but you must be one. But why shouldn't I take advantage of that?" The man gulped down his ale.

"Perhaps I am. Let's go before I change my mind," Galahad said.

The man with the strange badge led her to a villa that was old but looked solid, as did the walls of the outbuilding where they stopped. A short warrior in chain mail and a similar badge guarded an iron door.

"This young man will pay me well to see our prisoner," the warrior with rusty mail said.

"What about me?" The guard looked around to be sure that no one else was around. "He'll have to pay me, too. If our lady catches us, we'll both feel the whip."

"I'll give you a jar of the wine I'm getting," said the rusty-armored man. "Come on, let us in."

"Take a look inside, but be quick about it," the guard said, unlocking the door.

"Don't get any ideas, Lancelot," he called inside, drawing his sword and entering with them. "This man is just here for a look at you, though I don't think you're a sight worth paying for."

"Our lady thinks otherwise." The man in rusty mail chuckled coarsely.

The room had little furniture, but it couldn't be called a cell. Galahad stared at the person sitting on a stool in the corner. It wasn't Lancelot. But it was another woman dressed as a man. Galahad held back a gasp. The woman was about Lancelot's age and build, with a handsome face and short hair that was a dark brown, not black like Lancelot's. She wore a russet tunic that was made of good wool, but far from new.

The short-haired woman grinned. "Look at me all you like." She rose and turned about, as if on display. She might have recognized Galahad for what she was.

"That's not Lancelot," Galahad told the warriors. "Lancelot has much larger muscles. But I'll pay you for your trouble anyway." She pulled out of her pouch enough for a barrel of wine and then some. "Since he isn't Lancelot, you might as well let him go."

"Ha!" The man with the long-worn mail grabbed the money from her. "Our lady'd skin us alive. She fancies him for some reason."

"But she wouldn't want to be fooled when she finds out I'm not Lancelot," the woman in the russet tunic said. "She'd be in a temper then, and she'd probably make everyone around her feel her wrath."

"Not half the temper she'd be in if she found out we let you go," the guard replied.

While the warriors were looking at the woman--she really was as handsome as Lancelot--Galahad drew her dagger and hit the guard's head with its blunt end.

He crumbled to the ground, and his fellow warrior whirled around. "What the hell are you doing? You're in league with our prisoner." Drawing his sword, he advanced on Galahad, who jumped out of his reach.

The handsome woman grabbed the stool, crept up behind him, and hit him over the head.

As he fell, she said, "Amazing that such thick heads can crack so easily, isn't it?"

"Let's go. We have no time to waste." Galahad hurried out of the door. She was followed by the handsome woman, who took the guard's key, pulled the door shut behind them, and locked it.

She then put the key in her tunic. "For a keepsake," she said.

Galahad hurried to her horse, followed by her new companion. Galahad mounted, and the woman swung up behind her. "I have my own horse, tethered at the edge of town."

"Good. Direct me there."

Galahad made her horse hasten. She was proud that she had saved another woman. My, those arms around her felt warm.

"I'm Galahad, trained at Camelot," she said. "I know Lancelot, and you aren't he."

"You aren't he either." The woman laughed.

Galahad frowned. "Don't mention that."

"I'll keep the game as secret as you will, for many good reasons," the woman said. "I'm called Drian, my fine rescuer."

They reached Drian's horse, and she dismounted, sighing as she let go of Galahad.

Galahad started to ride away, but the handsome woman rode off with her.

"So you're Galahad," Drian said as they rode off. "May I call you Gal?"

"You may not!" Galahad snapped, eyeing Drian with suspicion. "What are you doing posing as Lancelot? Lancelot trained me, and I resent your impersonation."

Drian looked her in the eye.

"I'm not posing. A lady named Cecilia mistook me for Lancelot, and imprisoned me once because of it. I got off once before she found out what I am, but I thought I wouldn't succeed a second time. Lance is my friend, and would be glad you've helped me." She grinned. "I suppose she's proud of you."

Galahad gulped. Her voice became anxious. "Lancelot hasn't observed what you have. Please don't tell her."

"What, she doesn't know that she's trained a girl like herself?" Drian howled with laughter.

"I'm not a girl," Galahad snapped.

"I'm just as glad I won't have to make love to the not-so-kind lady Cecilia," Drian said, ignoring Galahad's irritation.

"What, would you have made love to her and let her know that Lancelot is a woman?" Galahad frowned and her face reddened.

Drian hooted. "How green are you? I wasn't going to take my clothes off. She might have guessed I was a woman, but she couldn't know for sure."

Galahad's eyes widened. "Make love without taking your clothes off? Why would you bother?"

Drian eyed her in an intensely personal way. "You've never made love to a woman, have you?"

"No." Galahad stared at her horse's mane. "But I don't think I'd want that Cecilia."

"No more did I. A more equal match is better. I'd rather spend the night with you than Cecilia anytime." The sky was reddening, but probably no more than Galahad's cheeks. "How about it, Gal?"

"There's a lady that I'm fond of in Camelot," Galahad said stiffly, trying not to look at Drian.

"That's a great many miles from here. Does she love you?"

Galahad hesitated, then said, "I'm not sure, but I really do like her."

Drian shook her head. "If that's your reason, all right. But if it's that I'm not high born enough for you, it's your loss, Gal."

Galahad flinched.

Drian added, "At least we might do what Lancelot and I did, which is not so bad."

"What is that? Don't tell me some unlikely story about Lancelot." Galahad's voice was full of suspicion.

"We slept in each others' arms without doing anything more."

Galahad gave Drian a sidelong glance. "Lancelot can perform many feats that I cannot, and that may be one of them."

Drian laughed. She touched the harp that was tied to her saddle. "Tonight I'll play the harp and sing to you. Has anyone ever sung just for you?"

"No. That would be splendid." Galahad thought of playing the pipes in return, but they were not so good for soft songs. The only one she knew she planned to play for Talwyn, and that, at least, she would save.

Drian woke in the middle of the night, warmed by the feel of Galahad in her arms. She kissed Galahad's cheek, but Galahad did not stir. She smelled horsey, but still delicious. The stars smiled down on them.

Galahad was sweet, and her looks were winsome if not handsome. But in a few days Galahad would doubtless go away.

Drian wouldn't tell Galahad about Lancelot's madness. Lancelot had seemed far better when Drian saw her walking with Elaine, and Lancelot could tell Galahad what she pleased.

Nor would Drian tell Lancelot about what she did with Galahad.

Galahad, like Lancelot, belonged to a world that was not Drian's. But Drian would keep the nobles' secrets as well as her own. She feared that their lives might be as perilous as hers.

After she and Drian had parted some days later, Galahad saw two warriors riding in the distance on the wind-swept moor. As they approached, it became clear that they were Bors and Percy. Not having seen anyone from Camelot except Gawaine in months, Galahad galloped up to them and greeted them with hurrahs.

"Have you found the grail?" Bors asked immediately, in a voice that sounded almost envious.

Galahad shook her head. "No, have you?"

"No," Percy replied, wiping the sweat from his grimy but handsome face. "But we're glad to meet up with you, because you are becoming famed for purity and we might find it if we travel with you." There was a hint of boasting in Percy's voice, suggesting that perhaps he was a little less pure than he had been a few months before.

Galahad mumbled that the idea that she could help bring them to the grail was nonsense. She was herself a bit less pure than she used to be. She regarded the yellow gorse.

"I think we should head for the forest. That's the most magical place," Percy said. "I mean the holiest," he added quickly when he saw Bors's look of reproach.

It was a hot day, so the others quickly agreed that the cool forest would be the best place to look. By evening, they were in a forest, and Percy warned Bors that it was better to sleep far away from Galahad because Galahad screamed loudly throughout the night.

Galahad noticed that although their conversation was pure, Bors and Percy were not nearly so modest as Gawaine, who always went off behind rocks.

When the two younger warriors were off together gathering firewood, Percy whispered to Galahad, "I wish I still were pure. I tried lying with a lady, and she laughed at me because I was not able to . . ." His voice trailed off and his face was red as an apple. "So don't be too eager to sin."

Galahad felt her cheeks flush. "That's too bad. Don't worry overmuch about it. I, too, have been with a woman, but it was good."

"Truly?" Percy looked at Galahad with interest. "Perhaps there's hope for me--when I marry. I won't try again until I do."

"No doubt that will be better," Galahad said.

"I pray that it will." Percy sighed.

Then they saw Bors, which ended the confidences, none too soon for Galahad.

The sun lingered in the sky and they didn't feel like sleeping. They sat in a beech grove where Bors told stories about the saints and assured the young warriors that nothing was more glorious than holy martyrdom.

Then came the most exquisite music they had ever heard, music produced not by nightingales, but by something like harps. They rose and walked through the trees to seek the source of the melody.

They came to a clearing that was even lighter than the rest of the still sunlit woods. There sat a small mud-and-wattle chapel with an overwhelming light pouring out through an open door, and with it the music.

"How wonderful!" Bors exclaimed. "We must go inside."

Bors and Percy started towards the chapel, but Galahad saw an old woman beckoning from behind an oak tree.

"First, I must speak with this crone and find out whether she needs anything," Galahad called out.

"If she does, let her come to the church and be given alms," Bors said. He entered the church, and Percy, after a backwards glance, followed him.

"We'd better take whatever chance of grace we have, because we might not get another," Percy said to Galahad.

The small, gray-eyed crone, who seemed to be the most ancient woman Galahad had ever seen, moved away and beckoned Galahad to follow her. With only the slightest hesitation, Galahad did, holding her horse by the reins. The way seemed too narrow for Galahad's horse, yet somehow the steed slipped through the bracken and brambles.

As they passed into a grove of hazel trees, the withered crone danced in front of Galahad and chanted, "Holy cup and holy grail, holy rant and holy rail, holy wine and holy ale, holy girl and holy male." She laughed. Then she chanted again, in a more solemn tone, "Holy laugh and holy wail, holy hill and holy dale, holy hawk and holy snail, everything is the holy grail."

Then she ran off into the forest and Galahad followed her.

Toward morning, a mist rose and she lost track of the crone. Galahad's mare had shied at the bank of a stream and she was trying to soothe her.

The white horse wobbled on her hooves, then steadied and shook her head so that her mane rippled. Galahad let out a joyful shout that was stronger in spirit than in elegance.

Here, in the mist, was the grail. Here, on the banks of a stream, was the grail. Here, on the hooves of the horse, was the grail. A fine rain began to drizzle, and Galahad pulled her cloak around her. But still the grail was present.

The crone appeared again, out of the mist, and Galahad again followed.

23 THE SCARRED WARRIOR

Guinevere had gone out with Cai to admire the garden and thus please the men who tended it. Yes, she said, the roses looked as if they would bloom well this year, and it would be good to plant more rosebushes. She praised the lilies as well.

She walked off by herself, looking out towards the forest, and wondering where in it Lancelot was. The day was fine, and she wished that they could be together. She wandered about on the grass near the horse pasture. She wanted to ride, but she planned only to ride her favorite horse around the pasture because she didn't want to ask any man to ride with her. Since the episode with the warriors from Dumnonia, Arthur had been all the more insistent that a number of men must accompany her. She pointed out that the warriors had only gotten themselves wounded when they confronted the Dumnonians, but she could not sway him.

She saw blackbirds squabbling. No doubt one male was fighting for territory with another male. It was rather amusing in birds, she thought, but not in men.

When she reached the stables, she saw that there was a great commotion, with grooms rushing around and Cassius the physician bending over someone who was lying on the floor.

There was no reason to think that it could be Lancelot, but Guinevere hurried over anyway and saw Mordred lying unconscious.

Cassius had taken off Mordred's tunic and was examining his left arm, which appeared to be broken. Guinevere saw that the young man was covered with terrible scars that looked years old, but she thought that he had never seen battle. He must have been beaten when he was still a boy. She gasped.

"Mordred fell from his horse, but he'll be well soon enough, I warrant, except for that arm, Lady Guinevere," said Cuall, the old stablemaster.

Mordred regained consciousness and, when he saw the group surrounding him, flew into a rage. "Why the fuck are you stripping me and examining me in front of all these onlookers?" he yelled at the physician. Then his gaze focused on Guinevere. "What are you staring at? Never seen a real man before?"

Even his crude speech could not erase her horror at seeing his scars. "Someone has hurt you dreadfully, Mordred," she said. Little as she liked him, she felt pity.

"Does that attract you?" he sneered, grabbing his tunic from a groom and trying to pull it over his head, which he could not manage with the broken arm. In his haste he nearly struck Cassius.

"No, you mistake my concern," she said, pulling away from the group, and most of the stablehands did the same. Mordred's serving man hurried over to help him.

"You probably want a younger man. I don't mistake that," Mordred said, although the physician and all of the stablehands looked aghast at his speech to the queen.

"May you heal your mind as well as your body," Guinevere said to him as she swept out of the stable. She put aside the thought of riding.

Guinevere felt the need to talk with someone, so she went to her room and found Luned, who was making a new gown for Guinevere. "Mordred fell from his horse and I saw Cassius examining him in the stable. He is covered with scars. He must have beaten brutally when he was a boy. Mordred's an unpleasant man, but I never guessed that he might have suffered so. He looks so much like Arthur that he really might be his son, although not by Morgan as he says. She has written me that he is not."

Luned put the gown carefully on the bed. "Of course he's the king's son, my lady. Anyone can see that unless they pretend not to. His mother must have been a serving woman who worked for a cruel family."

Guinevere shuddered, and thought about how her father had sent Gwynhwyfach away. "How can men treat their children so? Arthur should do something for him. I suppose I should ask him to, but I don't want to do anything that could give Mordred a chance at the throne."

"You can't, my lady!" Luned cried, turning pale. "Of course the king must know that Mordred's his son, but if he acknowledges him, Mordred might rule us all someday, and everyone from the highest to the lowest can see that he's cruel. All the servants fear him." She trembled.

"I suppose I won't say anything, then. But I fear I may be selfish in keeping silent about Mordred." Few things made Guinevere feel guilty, but failing to support Mordred in his claims to his father did.

"Why, my lady? You would surely be a much better ruler than Mordred," Luned insisted, folding her hands as if she prayed for Guinevere to rule.

"Hush," Guinevere said, smiling a little, and they stopped talking.

She decided to tell no one, not even Lancelot, about Mordred's scars.

Gareth made his horse gallop across a moor. Neither a kestrel hovering nor a grouse drumming caught his eye. Nothing so worldly could hold his interest, except what was forbidden. He tried to think of heavenly things, to envision angels appearing on the moor.

A group of men in chain mail pursuing a lady came into his view. Alone, he attacked the four men. Two men soon were lying dead on the ground, and the others, one terribly wounded, fled.

The lady let herself slip from her horse. "Thank you, noble lord! What a fighter you are!" she exclaimed admiringly.

Gareth dismounted. "It was only my duty. My lady, are you unhurt?"

She looked up into his eyes. She was tall, but of course not nearly as tall as he was. Her hazel eyes looked at him with what seemed close to adoration. Her brown hair, tangled by the wind, framed her face softly.

"I am safe because of you. My name is Lynnette. And what is yours, finest warrior in the world?"

Gareth nearly stammered. "I cannot claim to be that. That is Lancelot of the Lightning Arm, my teacher. I am Gareth ap Lot of Lothian and Orkney, a warrior of King Arthur's."

"Gareth of Lothian and Orkney." Her voice pronounced the words in a tone that sounded much sweeter than anyone else's. She put her hand on Gareth's.

Her touch was warm yet strong. She wore a fine perfume, and her scent tantalized Gareth. The look in her eyes, the smile on her lips intrigued him.

Gareth felt stirred, as if passion would be possible, a desire that he had never felt toward a woman before. He had done well, and finally the Lord had heard his prayer and had blessed him. Perhaps this woman even had a soul. Much affected, he said, "I hope that you are not sworn to anyone else, my lady. If you are not, I would like to seek your hand in marriage."

Lynnette let out a brief exclamation that seemed to be one of pleasure, but her eyes became apprehensive. "I am not betrothed, and I want to be yours, but you should not ask for me until you have touched me, Lord Gareth."

Gareth was stunned by this unmaidenly response. "We must be pure, if I am to show you true respect and love, my lady."

In reply, she threw her arms around his neck and kissed him. He trembled.

"Oh, my lady, aren't you a maiden?" he asked, excited but worried at the same time.

"I'm frightened, but I must let you know what I am," she said, taking his hand and guiding it below her waist.

He felt something large and hard.

"You're no lady!" Gareth screamed in a rage. He leapt on his horse and rode away as fast as he could.

When he had ridden away from the sight of Lynnette, he sobbed. His prayers had not been answered. He was truly cursed. Only demons came to torment him. What could be a more terrible demon than one who wore the clothes of the other sex to tempt poor mortals with weaknesses like his? He told himself that Lynnette could not have been human, and he thought that if had been a truly good Christian he should have killed her. Probably that was not what Father Donatus would say, but the priest did not understand how dreadful it was to have such temptations.

Ninian stood at Camelot's inner gate. She held the reins to her gray mare. "I need to speak with the king," she told a muscular guard young enough to be her grandson, if not her great-grandson. He looked amazed at such speech from an old nun.

"The king doesn't have a public audience today, but he will next week and you can come then," the guard told her, in a reassuring tone that indicated he thought she was doddering.

Just then, Lancelot came by.

"Let her in, she's a friend of mine," Lancelot told the guard, who bowed and let Ninian pass. "Mother Ninian, what are you doing here?" She threw her arms around Ninian as she always did, despite startled looks from the guard and other passersby.

"This time I have come to see the king," Ninian said, returning the handsome warrior's embrace.

Lancelot beckoned for a stablehand to tie up the mare and led Ninian into the caer. "Let me present you to him," she suggested.

"No, I'll go on my own," Ninian insisted, looking around the caer, which was too ostentatious for her taste. "Just point the way." Her visit was a test for Arthur, and Lancelot's presence would spoil the test. The king must decide on his own whether he would accept her help. He faced danger from his son, and only she could warn him, for only she could see the future.

"Very well," Lancelot said dubiously, explaining the way.

Ninian walked into the great hall, which was the largest she had ever seen. How had Merlin ever been comfortable in this place? His tastes had been much simpler when she had known him. Shields and torches hung from the walls, and a number of warriors were grouped around the fire. Arthur stood to one side, giving orders to an impeccably dressed, beardless man who must be his foster brother and seneschal, Cai.

The beardless man noticed her first. "A lady of religious disposition is seeking to talk with you," he said, smiling at her as she made her way towards the king. The guards watched her with little apparent concern. Their hands did not move to their weapons.

Arthur looked up.

"I am Ninian," she proclaimed. "I have come to help you. I was a friend of Merlin's." Indeed, she would not have come except that she knew Merlin would have wanted it.

Arthur regarded her warily, and she could tell that he recognized her as the one who many years ago had told him he had a child who was being raised in a brothel. She had not told him that the child was a boy. He scowled, surely not his usual expression on meeting a nun.

The king nodded coldly to her. "I do not need your help, Mother," he said. "Give her a donation for her convent and send her off courteously," he told Cai, and turned away.

"I need no assistance in leaving," Ninian said, departing without waiting for the donation. She had known that Arthur would reject her service, but she had to ask anyway.

As she rode her old mare into the forest, she came upon a warrior riding towards the caer. She recognized his face from a seeing she had had years before. He looked more than ever like Arthur.

"You're the poor little boy from the brothel," she said gently. "Are you well now?"

The man lunged at her with his spear, but she kicked her mare and disappeared among the oaks and bracken.

Mordred shook with rage, then he began to choke as if he would weep. Could he never escape the panderers, even though he had killed them? He wished he had killed the nun. Forcing tears away, he made horse gallop through the forest. Only fools wept. Fools like Lancelot who wept when travelers told of famines in distant lands. What good had those weepers ever done for Mordred? How could a strong woman like Guinevere love a man as soft as Lancelot?

The nun's words reminded him that there were people who had seen him in the brothel. He couldn't kill them all. It was best to try to gain the throne as soon as possible, before anyone could spread stories about him. After he was king, no one would dare.

Mordred befriended Accolon, a young and hot-spirited warrior from Rheged who fought exceedingly well. Accolon was brave but ugly, with a huge nose and flapping ears. He had once been wounded on a mission in Cornwall, and the Lady Morgan had been called in to heal him. He had told this tale privately to some of the other warriors, including Mordred, and made much of how beautiful the lady was, so that even though she was old enough to be his mother, he had begged for her love, but had been denied it. The warriors had warned him not to let a word of this adventure come to the king's ears, because he still might be jealous over his sister.

Mordred could see that Accolon would be a good tool.

Mordred rode with Accolon out in the forest, and, when they were hidden from any human eyes, pulled out a sword from his scabbard. "This is the king's sword," Mordred told him, and showed him the gleaming sword with its magnificently jeweled hilt. A huge amethyst shone in the pommel.

"God's breath, it looks just like it!" exclaimed Accolon, staring as if he had never seen a sword before. "But it cannot be."

"It is. I stole it, and replaced it with another that looks similar but is not quite so well made," Mordred boasted, smirking. He had bribed one of the guards to let him enter the High King's room, but he did not need to tell that to Accolon.

"Are you mad? He'll kill you." Accolon's eyes darted around, searching to see whether anyone was spying on them. He looked as if he wanted to flee.

"Oh no, good Accolon. You'll kill him, and thus win the love of his sister, who hates him." Mordred waved the sword in the air, as if wishing that the wind had a heart that could be split.

Accolon shuddered. "Kill the king? I'd be killed myself for such an act."

"You would not, because I am his son and would succeed him. I cannot challenge him because he would not fight me." He poured his voice like a soothing potion. "Come now, I know how the lady feels. She's my own mother. She has been lonely and is longing for some man to deliver her from exile. She would be eternally grateful to you for avenging what the king did to her." If he spoke of the witch Morgan, Accolon would be daft enough to believe anything.

"No matter what he did to her, it was a lifetime ago, before we were born, and I cannot just murder any man, much less my king," Accolon protested.

Mordred felt the sword's sharp blade with one of the fingers of his bandaged left arm and smiled at the thought of whom it might cut. "Of course you'd fight him, not just cut his throat. I understand that you are a noble warrior, with much honor. If he knows that you have his sword, he'll want to fight, I can assure you. And if he believes that you're fighting for her, he'll be so maddened that he'll be bound to lose. But it will be an honorable fight, not like a murder."

"Could it be true that she might love me? She would scarcely look at me. She just patted my hand, and said, 'Go off and heal, Accolon, there's a good boy.'" But Accolon's face showed that he was longing to be convinced.

Mordred slapped Accolon on the shoulder. "Why, she only wanted to fire you to love her more. That's why some women resist at first. And it worked, didn't it? You're mad for her, and will do this to show your love, won't you?"

Accolon did not immediately accept this cajoling, but Mordred wore him down easily enough.

"But the king still has the magic scabbard that keeps him from bleeding to death," Accolon objected. "It appears that you didn't steal that."

"There's no magic in the scabbard," Mordred assured him. Amazing how his father had convinced so many fools that he had magical powers. If only he, Mordred, could lay claim to some!

Lancelot was riding in the forest with Arthur and a few of his warriors, including Mordred, who always made her uneasy. Unlike anyone else, he gave her looks that suggested she was beneath contempt. The sun was hot, but forest trees shaded the party from Camelot. Lancelot wished she was alone. The men made so much noise that she could scarcely hear the birdsong.

A warrior in chain mail appeared from a beech grove.

Lancelot had started to pull her sword, then sheaved it when she saw it was only Accolon. "For the Virgin's sake, Accolon, you shouldn't rush up like that at a party that includes the king. I might have thought you were endangering him and attacked you," she chided him.

All of the warriors looked at Accolon coolly, but Arthur regarded him more indulgently.

"Arthur Pendragon, I have come to challenge you," Accolon called out, in the tone that warriors used at such moments, but generally to social equals.

"How dare you call the king 'Arthur' in such a tone, you cur's puppy?" Bedwyr growled. The warriors all growled similarly and pulled out their swords.

"What is this, Accolon? Are you drunk? Are you mad?" the king asked in a condescending tone, letting his hands rest on his horse's reins.

But Accolon did not seem rattled. He drew a sword whose jewels gleamed in the light. "I have your sword, Excalibur. It was taken from you for the sake of your sister, whom you dishonored. If you want it back, you must fight me for it." He was like a man enchanted with the power of what he was doing.

Arthur shook his fist and yelled, "I'll fight you, then, curse you!"

Lancelot interposed her horse between them. Worried because Accolon was a skilled fighter and twenty years younger than the king, she said, "No, my Lord Arthur, don't dignify this fool by fighting him. I shall fight him for you."

Glaring at Lancelot, Arthur exclaimed, "You will not! Out of my way. Only I shall fight for my sword."

So Lancelot had to rein in her horse.

Arthur swung down from his horse more vigorously than he had in years. "Fight me on the ground, with swords, and even though I use the weaker weapon, my own will come back to me."

Accolon dismounted, too. "I fight for your sister, whom I love," the young man proclaimed.

Arthur let out a shout and attacked.

The fight was bitter and the warriors watched anxiously. Accolon fought blindly, like a man drunk on his own power. He parried the king's first foray, but lashed back too quickly and missed his target. It was not long before Arthur struck a great blow to Accolon's chest, slashing through the mail and cutting him to the heart. The king retook his sword, and held it over his head, yelling in triumph.

His warriors rushed up to him and praised his prowess. Mordred lauded him most of all.

"Nobly struck, sire," Mordred said in a voice full of emotion. "You are the greatest fighter in the world as well as the greatest king."

On the ride back, Arthur did not speak to Lancelot.

When they returned to the caer, there was a great hue and cry, as everyone heard what had happened, and warriors, ladies, and serving people all tried to get close to their king and shout their praises of him and their congratulations on his victory.

After a little of the din had subsided and Arthur had gone off to change his clothes, Lancelot followed him down the passageway. "Are you displeased with me, sire? I wanted only to assist you."

"Or to unman me?" Arthur asked, turning towards Lancelot only slightly.

Lancelot was startled. "I had no such thought."

"Isn't it obvious that if I could not retrieve my own sword, you would seem to be the better man?" The king was looking middle-aged, with prominent wrinkles, and a little weary.

"Such a thought never occurred to me," Lancelot insisted. "I thought only of protecting you. A few years ago, when your sword was stolen, you asked me to retrieve it, and I did."

"That was a secret matter, and this was a public challenge," Arthur said, and his tone was not pleasant. "I wonder who stole the sword, for surely Accolon never came so near to my room. Could it have been the queen?"

Astounded, Lancelot leapt to defend Guinevere. "But what would the queen want with your sword? She has no use for it."

"I know now that she befriends my devilish sister, and perhaps she was part of this plot with Accolon." He looked into Lancelot's eyes, as if trying to find some evidence of plotting.

"She would never do such a thing. You do her wrong to suggest it," Lancelot insisted.

"I" his voice was bitter "do her wrong? Aren't you a trifle confused?" Then Arthur went into his room to dress, and Lancelot did not follow him.

Pentecost came soon. Lancelot's fighting was not her best, but nevertheless she won the individual contests and her side gained victory in the general fighting. She said it was because Gawaine had not yet returned from his mission to Gwynedd, although she carefully praised Bedwyr, who had led the other side of the fight.

Pentecost also was Arthur's chief day for hearing petitions, so after the contests, the great hall was crowded with petitioners of all ranks, as usual.

There was a clamor, and some guards brought in a gray-haired woman, dressed in a black gown in the style of the merchant class. Chains were fastened to her arms, and her legs were chained together so that she could barely walk.

Heads turned and many gasped at the sight. Lancelot's heart flooded with pity.

"Forgive me for bringing this woman here, sire," the chief guard said, "but she begged to bring her case to you, and the lord Cai said that I could."

"Poor, wretched woman, what is your tale?" the king asked.

She threw herself on her knees and folded her hands as if she were praying to the king, but her gaze was fixed on the floor. "I killed my husband, who was a wine merchant, majesty, and the magistrates found out. He beat me for years, and I poisoned his food." Her voice was choked with sobs. "I just couldn't bear it anymore, majesty. Please let me live. I'll do no harm. I've never injured anyone else. My sons and daughters will tell you."

Several young men and women who had come in with her spoke up at once saying, "She's always been so kind." "She won't hurt anyone." "Father was very hard on her. It frightened me how he beat her."

But Arthur looked at her with loathing. "I understand that your sons and daughters would grieve if they lost you as well as their father, but killing your husband is treason," he told her.

The woman moaned and sank to the floor, letting her face lie among the rushes that were spread there.

Guinevere spoke up in front of everyone. "Let me intercede for her, my Lord Arthur. Surely this woman is good and kind, and her husband was cruel. I beg you to show the world your gracious mercy, and pardon her."

Lancelot admired Guinevere's audacity in choosing this case as the one in which she would intercede.

Arthur stared at his wife as coldly as he had regarded the woman in chains. It was late May, but his voice was January. "You actually ask me to pardon a woman for murdering her own husband by stealth at his table? Does anyone join the queen in asking this strange boon?"

Everyone was silent. The only sound that could be heard was a dog yapping.

Then Lancelot spoke up. "The queen is right, my lord Arthur. Some husbands are brutal, and sometimes the only way the women can escape is to kill them. I have helped protect a few such women from punishment."

Many warriors gasped at her words.

Arthur's face looked as gray as the petitioner's. "Let this woman be released into the custody of her eldest son," he told the guards.

The woman and her family wept and exclaimed their thanks, but Arthur did not acknowledge them. He said, "Next petition."

Bedwyr drew Lancelot aside. "Are you completely mad?" he asked. "How could you join the queen in defending a woman who killed her husband, and say that you have helped other women who killed their husbands? Do you think Arthur will ever trust you again?"

"He should," Lancelot said simply.

But that night at supper, Arthur did not speak to Lancelot, and pretended not to hear her when she asked how he was. He spoke with icy courtesy to Guinevere.

Not able to leave things as they stood, Lancelot went to the king's room the next morning. When she entered, he gave only a nod, saying nothing, and turned away, scarcely looking at her. He was seated, but he did not invite Lancelot to sit in her usual chair. He continued to read a scroll in his hands.

She remained standing. Arthur had never treated her that way before. Miserable, she forced herself to speak. "If you don't trust me, then we should leave. I suppose we should have left long ago."

Arthur dropped the scroll. His eyes widened. "No, don't leave. Who said anything about your leaving?"

She kept her voice firm, though her heart was pounding. "I think that we should leave, and then you might be able to marry another woman. Surely you would be happier. No doubt a bishop would release you to do so." Lancelot had never before spoken so openly to him about her love for Guinevere. She said "we" because she had no intention of leaving without Guinevere. Although Guinevere showed no signs of wanting to depart, surely if Arthur said that Lancelot should go, the queen would change her mind.

"I don't want another wife. Whatever gave you such an idea?" The king sounded surprised, not angry.

"But even if there is no such lady now, perhaps there would be if we left. Perhaps I have injured you too much for you to trust me." Lancelot knew she should not speak of leaving without getting Guinevere's agreement first, but she felt too sad to want to stay.

Arthur leaned forward in his chair. "No, please don't leave. Of course I trust you. You are needed here. Promise that you won't leave."

Lancelot closed her eyes for a moment. The king couldn't know that she had been urging Guinevere to leave for a long time. "I can't promise that."

"I have been good to you, have I not?" Arthur demanded.

"You have, you have," she choked, feeling guilty. "But if you could believe that I would injure you, the ties between us must be wearing thin."

"I was just unnerved by that petitioner." The king never apologized, but now he seemed to be doing so. "Don't take it too seriously." Arthur reached out his hand as if to keep her from leaving. "I depend on you. You must not think of going. Having served me for so long, would you disgrace me in the eyes of the world?"

How could she bring dishonor on the king who had been so kind to her? And after all, how could she bear to leave the only place she knew and the only people who were familiar to her? Perhaps she didn't have to leave. Besides, Guinevere had never agreed to go.

"Very well, not now," she said reluctantly. "But tell me if you ever want me to go."

"I'll never want that," he told Lancelot. "You are the best of my warriors. You generally defeat even Gawaine in the contests."

"Very well." How much he still must love Guinevere, to want so much to keep her here even though she doesn't care about him, Lancelot thought. I'm glad she doesn't love him, but how sad for him.

Bowing her head slightly, she departed, eager to be alone, away from this painful talk. As she walked through the passageways, she thought that every stone in the walls was precious to her. She looked at the faces of a serving man, a young warrior, a stablehand. They all smiled at her. One of Arthur's wolfhounds came bounding up to her, and she patted it. She now loved Camelot nearly as much as Arthur did.

But she decided she would not go off with Arthur on a hunt planned for a few days hence. She had no wish to spend more time with him, even in the company of other warriors.

Mordred smiled at Agravaine and Gaheris over the ale they had given him. The Orkney clan always had fine ale in their rooms. At least Agravaine and Gaheris did. Mordred had never been invited to Gawaine's house.

"Everyone knows that Lancelot and Guinevere are lovers," Mordred said. "Of course, Lancelot is committing treason. If we catch them at it, the king will have to execute him, and punish Guinevere, too. I've procured a key to the queen's chamber."

Mordred could hardly keep the glee out of his voice. How good it was to have accomplices in his plan. Sinking back into his chair, he savored the ale as if it were the finest wine. He doubted that Arthur would kill Guinevere. He would send her away in exile, as he had Morgan, and Mordred would find her there. Guinevere would be grateful.

Agravaine shook his head and drank down his ale. "Unfortunately, Arthur won't execute Lancelot. And Lancelot might kill us. If he doesn't kill us when we burst in on them, he would later."

Mordred had anticipated this objection and had prepared an answer. "The room will be dark, of course. I plan to wear Arthur's clothes. If you wore Gawaine's clothes, you could pass for him in the dark. That way, it would be easy to get close enough to Lancelot to kill him. Even if he's angry at being interrupted, he'd not be likely to kill Gawaine." He chuckled.

"Killing Lancelot's not a bad idea," Agravaine agreed, looking around him as if someone could be spying on them. "But he's too popular. What if someone wants to avenge his death?"

"No one, not even kin, is allowed to avenge a man killed committing adultery with another man's wife," Mordred pointed out, pouring Agravaine more of his own ale, and doing the same for Gaheris, who stared open-mouthed like the fool he was. "Arthur might want to, but of course he wouldn't be in any position to punish men who salvaged his honor, certainly not kinsmen like you. Gawaine is the one who might break the law and avenge Lancelot. That's why it's a good idea that you kill him, because Gawaine won't hurt his own brother." And if Lancelot recognized him as Agravaine and killed him, Mordred himself might be safe.

In fact, Lancelot might kill all three younger brothers Lothian, and Mordred had no objection to that. Then there would be fewer legitimate kin who might possibly succeed Arthur. Of course, Gawaine would still be an obstacle.

Agravaine laughed unpleasantly. "Not a bad plan, is it?" he asked Gaheris, poking him in the ribs.

"How could we do such a thing to the High Queen?" Gaheris asked in a tone that was none too steady. "And Lancelot saved our lives during the war."

"How do you know the queen didn't try to poison Gawaine?" Mordred asked in a reasonable tone, putting out his hand to touch Gaheris's. "We have only the word of Lancelot--an admitted madman and a brute in his killing of Sangremore--to say that Bellangere tried to poison Gawaine. For all we know, Lancelot might have killed Bellangere as he did Sangremore."

"I never thought of that," Gaheris gasped, squinting as he tried to puzzle out an answer. "But won't Gawaine be angry at us if we kill Lancelot?"

Agravaine snorted. "He will, but it will be too late for him to do anything. I'm tired of the way he favors Lancelot. Aren't you?"

"Yes," Gaheris admitted, gulping down his ale as if it were the last in the world. "But I can't imagine barging into the queen's bed chamber. I'm going to get Gareth." He set down his drink and rushed out of the house.

"Stop!" Agravaine yelled at him, but Gaheris was gone. "That will wreck everything," he groaned. "Gareth will never agree."

Mordred patted his arm. "Don't worry," Mordred said. "Let me handle it. Including Gareth will give us the perfect cover."

"If he agrees." Agravaine shook his head.

"He will." Mordred smiled. "Keep drinking. You'll see."

Not long afterwards, Gareth burst in without knocking. Gaheris trailed behind him. Gareth waved his fist at Mordred and yelled at him. "How dare you accuse Lancelot of adultery! Lancelot would never betray the king."

"If that is true, come with us." Mordred smiled as if Gareth's words had been sweet. "You can ensure that we treat the queen with due respect. But I think you'll be disillusioned by what you find."

"I won't go, and neither will you." Gareth glared at Mordred.

"You're wrong, little brother." Agravaine pounded the table. "Mordred and I are going. The two of you can come with us or not."

"I can't let you do this! It's a sin to listen to scurrilous gossip. Shut your ears to it!" Gareth's hands formed fists.

"King Arthur's my own father!" Mordred cried, sounding as if he were close to weeping. "Everyone pretends that's not true, but I know it is. I can't bear seeing his honor defiled. I can't let it go on! I won't let it go on!"

Gareth's hands unclenched. "I see that you're distressed, but . . ."

"But nothing." Agravaine stood up. "We're all King Arthur's kin, and it's our duty to protect his honor. If you come, everyone will understand that's what we're doing."

"Perhaps we should wait until Gawaine returns," Gareth said.

Agravaine shook his head. "No one knows when that will be. Mordred's right. We need to act now. I'm going with him. Are you coming or not?"

"I'm going," Gaheris said. "We need to protect the king's honor."

"Shouldn't we ask the king first?" Gareth said.

"I've hinted as much to him," Mordred told them. He put his hand on Gareth's arm, but Gareth pulled away. "My father doesn't want us to do it when he's at Camelot. He's going on a hunting trip, and I'm sure that's the sign that we should act." Mordred doubted that Gareth would ask the king whether that was true.

"Oh." The pious youth sighed in apparent resignation. "I'll go with you then to assure the queen that our intentions were only the best."

"Bring your sword," Agravaine said. "We all need to be armed."

"I don't think we will, but it will do no harm to bring it anyway," Gareth replied, sighing.

"I am grateful to all of you," Mordred said. He smiled.

24 THE DISCOVERY

Lancelot lay in Guinevere's arms in the queen's soft bed. Although Lancelot had never liked to talk much after love-making, she thought it might be a time when Guinevere would listen to her. She rolled on her side and looked at Guinevere through the flickering candlelight. "I'm so weary of hiding our love. Arthur doesn't trust me any more, although he says he does. Can't we go away?"

Guinevere stroked Lancelot's hair. "Don't worry, love. We have each other."

Guinevere covered her with kisses, and Lancelot let herself dismiss her concerns.

The door crashed open, and men burst into the darkened room. Lancelot could not see who they were. Only a few beeswax candles glowed by the bed.

Lancelot's heart nearly stopped beating.

The early summer night was chilly, so Guinevere was wearing a bedgown, but Lancelot was naked. She jumped up, pulled on her breeches, and grabbed her sword, which hung on a nearby chair. She must protect Guinevere.

She could dimly see Gareth, with others following him.

Gareth howled. "Witch! Changeling! Monster!" he screamed, slashing at her with his sword. His eyes were like those of an attacking wolf.

"Gareth, stop," Lancelot demanded, blocking him with her sword. How had he come here? She didn't want to hurt him. His usually solemn face was so distorted that he seemed to be a different person entirely, a man gone mad.

"You're a demon with breasts! By God's will, I'll smite you down!" Gareth yelled. He lunged at her, aiming for the heart.

"I'm no demon, just Lancelot." He was the one who seemed possessed. She warded off the blow, but hesitated to strike back although Gareth continued trying to stab her. She just kept on blocking him, saying, "Gareth, Gareth, you must stop," but he persisted in trying to kill her. Perhaps she should wound his sword arm.

Slashing with his sword, another man threw himself at Lancelot. For a moment, Lancelot froze in horror, for it seemed to be Gawaine. How could he so betray their friendship? His face looked frankly brutal, contorted with a snarling expression she had never seen on it, not even in battle. For an instant, she wanted to die.

Then the man screamed, "You filthy sluts! You deserve to die."

She knew from his voice and his words that it must be Agravaine, and she was willing to kill him. Her veins almost burst with rage. She tried to strike out at him, but Gareth was in the way and she was not willing to kill the addled, pious youth.

Agravaine's sword, thrust over Gareth's shoulder, cut her left arm. Blood streamed from it, but in her agitation she felt nothing.

Gareth cried out, "You're bleeding! You're human!" He quickly turned to Agravaine and tried to block his sword. "You can't kill her, she's a human woman!"

But Agravaine was lunging forward, and his sword slashed into Gareth's chest.

Lancelot's sword cut Agravaine's neck, and he fell.

She looked down at the bodies at her feet. There was Gareth, his youth gone forever. And the other body, with staring eyes...

Lancelot reeled. Gawaine's body was lying before her and she held a bloody sword. She must have killed him. She knew not where she was or what had happened. She cried out. "No! Gawaine! I've killed Gawaine! I'm truly mad!" She turned her sword on herself.

Someone grabbed her arm. "Gawaine is alive. Gawaine is not here." The voice sounded like Guinevere's. "It's Agravaine, who attacked us. Gawaine never would have. Go, go, you must flee!"

A man's voice said, "Yes, you're mad, Lancelot. We'll lock you up and take you away so you don't harm anyone else."

She lowered her sword, as if to give it up.

"Flee, Lancelot, flee!" the woman's voice urged her. A woman shoved Lancelot's tunic and boots into her hands. "Go now!" The woman opened a door and almost pushed her through it.

Holding her things, Lancelot stumbled down a stairway that seemed familiar. The door closed behind her. She pulled on her tunic and her boots, then began to run. It was Guinevere's secret staircase. As soon as she was out in the courtyard she knew where she was.

She was mad. She had killed Gawaine. Who knows whom she might kill next? In her madness, she might even murder Guinevere. She must run far, far away from everyone. Almost blinded with tears, she rushed to the stable, waking astonished stablehands, saddled her horse, called for a guard to open the gates, and rode plunging down the hill and off towards the forest. The world had ended.

She had killed her best friend. She was worse than any of the men she had fought. Guinevere was better off without her.

But perhaps the woman--was it Guinevere?--had been right. Perhaps she had not killed Gawaine. No, that was a false hope.

Guinevere snatched her dagger from under her pillow. She faced Mordred and Gaheris.

"Don't try to follow Lancelot," she demanded. She was lost herself, she believed. Her only thought was to save Lancelot.

Gaheris slumped down by his brothers' bodies. "My brothers!" he moaned, as if unconscious of anyone else in the room.

Mordred faced Guinevere and lowered his sword. "What do I care about Lancelot? She's powerless now. Whoever would have guessed she's a woman? You have exotic tastes, my dear."

"Don't talk to me that way," Guinevere demanded.

"You're the one I want," Mordred said in an insinuating voice. "Wouldn't you like a real man for a change? If you're nice to me, I won't even tell anyone that Lancelot's a woman. Don't worry about Gaheris." He looked at the sobbing man, whose back was turned towards him, and made a gesture indicating that he could silence Gaheris forever.

"No more killing. Stay away from me!" Guinevere jabbed out with her dagger at Mordred, who was slowly advancing on her. At least she was distracting him from pursuing Lancelot.

"A spitfire, aren't you? I like that. I'll enjoy taming you," he said.

He came too close, and she cut his arm, but Mordred only laughed. "That madwoman can't protect you now. I'm your only hope. I can say that Agravaine and Gaheris planned to attack you, but poor Gareth wanted to stop them and asked me to help him. We can leave Lancelot out of it."

"You think I believe you'd be silent about Lancelot?" Guinevere's voice showed her scorn. "I'm not plotting with you."

"You're pretty in your bedgown." He coaxed her, as if she were a puppy that could be won over with a pat. "I'd like to try my father's wife. I'll be good to you."

"Stay away from me," she demanded, maintaining her hold on the weapon.

Cai and Bors burst through the open door.

"How dare you enter the queen's room!" Bors yelled at Mordred and Gaheris, menacing them with his sword.

"Are you hurt, Lady Guinevere?" Cai asked breathlessly, a sword in his hand.

"Lancelot was in bed with the queen," Mordred said calmly, as if no one held a weapon. He sheathed his sword. "We thought to tell the king about the treachery, but Lancelot has killed Gareth and Agravaine and fled through a secret passage in the wall." He gestured to the door, which Guinevere had not had chance to hide with the tapestry.

"Not so! They burst in and tried to rape me, and I have defended myself," Guinevere exclaimed, not expecting to be believed.

Mordred sneered. "What a tale! Who would rape the king's wife? Certainly not Gareth. And could she have killed two large warriors? And why is Lancelot's cloak lying near the bed?" he asked, pointing at it.

"Leave the queen's room at once!" demanded Cai. "We shall take care of this matter."

"Who listens to you, Cocksucker?" Mordred snapped. "You had better board up that door by the wall hanging, so Guinevere doesn't escape."

Gaheris simply fled the room, and Mordred more slowly followed. Bors ushered him out.

Cai looked at the bodies. "Put down your dagger, Gwen." She put it under her pillow. She began shaking, now that she did not have to hold off Mordred.

Cai looked at her with sympathy, all sarcasm for once gone. He patted her shoulder.

Bors returned.

"Have you gotten rid of them?" Cai asked. "Then get some help and carry Gareth to the chapel. And Agravaine too, I suppose."

They took away the bodies. Cai sent men down the secret passage, and told them to guard the outside door, which he had to do now that it was known, and ordered others to stand guard outside the queen's usual door. "And guard the queen better than you have this night!" he chided the guards.

He bade servants to clean up the blood on the floor.

Finally, Guinevere was alone and she felt a great emptiness. She thought she would never see Lancelot again.

Let Lancelot be safe, she prayed. Let her find herself again and be healed in the forest. Let her go back to Lesser Britain and live in peace.

The room had died. Where she had seen a kind of home, there was only cold stone. Her room had been reddened to a battlefield. She had been roused from her bed by an assault.

Her lover had been surprised naked, and forced to fight, and had become maddened.

Guinevere tore her hair. Lancelot, her woman of iron, had shattered like the most fragile glass.

What hope could there be? If only she could have left with Lancelot, but she had to hold back Mordred. Now Guinevere was guarded, locked in. She felt as if she were in chains. She longed to follow Lancelot. She would dive after Lancelot to the bottom of the sea, if only she could.

She slumped in her chair and laid her head down on the table.

She wished that she had died then, and did not have to live alone. She still had her dagger--but no, that would be cowardly. Lancelot should never have to hear that she had done such a thing.

As long as she could be defiant, she would live.

She saw that no room was safe, nor was any forest or mountain top. Safety is a dream we have, she thought.

Arthur would decide her fate. It was fruitless to wonder what that would be. What if he chose to execute her? She had said she loved Lancelot more than life, but was that true? Would she prove it? No, it was base to think of her own life when Lancelot rode off in madness.

Her prayers were for Lancelot rather than herself.

The only forgiveness Guinevere wanted was for urging Lancelot to stay at Camelot. She had put Lancelot to unbearable tests. Why had she failed to imagine how their affair would end, that they would be caught? She had betrayed Lancelot by keeping her. She should have driven Lancelot away, given her up like the mother who came before Solomon.

Other people loved Lancelot, though no others loved me, Guinevere thought. Lancelot is more lovable than I am. I should have left her for someone else to love. I asked more of her than I should have asked of anyone.

If I knew that our love would drive her mad, would I have embraced her anyway? In defying Arthur, I have risked my life and my sanity, but did I have any right to risk Lancelot's?

Guinevere finally went to bed, but she could not sleep. She wondered whether a great love was too much to ask of anyone.

25 Sorrow upon Sorrow

On a misty morning, Gawaine rode through the forest. He longed to see Camelot. He heard a party of men in the distance and recognized their voices. He hurried his horse, and came upon Arthur and a party of his warriors. They exchanged hearty greetings, clapping each other on the back as they usually did after weeks or months of separation.

"I killed a boar yesterday," Arthur boasted, indicating a huge beast that was being borne by huntsmen.

"Not bad for a man whose hair is turning gray," Gawaine teased, proud that he could speak to the king in a way that no one else could. He was also not above boasting because his own hair was still entirely red, although Arthur's had only a little gray. It was good to be home in familiar forests with his friends. It would be even better when Galahad returned.

The songs of thrushes filled the forest as harpers' music would fill the great hall at supper. Gawaine looked forward to eating roasted boar that night. But he was not so eager to tell

Arthur that he had angered Maelgon of Gwynedd by helping his daughter run away.

They rode together joyfully, swapping stories of long past hunts. When they approached Camelot, a single rider emerged from the great gate and moved down the hill towards them. It was Cai.

Gawaine stared at him. What trouble could have prompted Cai to hurry towards Arthur before they entered the gate?

Cai rode up to his foster brother. Wrinkles stood out on the seneschal's face.

"Grave news, Arthur," he said softly, but Gawaine could hear him.

Arthur's mouth tightened.

"The brothers Lothian broke into Guinevere's chamber last night." Cai's tone was flat. "They discovered Lancelot there. Lancelot has fled."

Gawaine's heart sank.

"What fools!" Arthur's face purpled. He glared towards the caer. "Is it possible to keep this quiet?"

Cai shook his head. "Mordred led them. He lives, and so does Gaheris." He turned to Gawaine. "I grieve to tell you. Gareth and Agravaine are dead."

"Not Gareth!" Gawaine moaned. He put his hands to his face. His head spun.

A man ran through the gate and made a mad dash to the party of returning warriors. It was Gaheris, screaming, "Gawaine! Gawaine! Our brothers are killed! Lancelot killed our brothers!"

Arthur shook, apparently with rage, but he moved closer to Gawaine and put a hand on his shoulder. "My poor cousin. I'm sorry for this terrible hurt. But keep that fool Gaheris away from me."

Gawaine dismounted, and Gaheris rushed up and flung his arms around him.

Gawaine returned the embrace. No matter how much of a fool Gaheris had been, he was his one remaining brother.

"Lancelot is a woman!" Gaheris screamed, loud enough for the whole party to hear. "The bitch killed our brothers!"

Gawaine shook him. "Hush. You're raving."

The warriors had been muttering, and now the sound of their muttering increased.

"Silence your brother, Gawaine," Arthur commanded. "He has gone mad."

Gaheris looked at Arthur. "We did this for you, Lord Arthur." His voice shook. "Lancelot and the queen were in bed together. They committed treason."

"And do you think acting without asking my leave is not treason? The damage you have done is incalculable." The king regarded Gaheris as if he had destroyed Camelot, and perhaps he had, Gawaine thought. "Tell no more deluded tales."

Unnoticed in the turmoil, Mordred approached. "All that he says is true. Lancelot is a woman. We saw her breasts." He smirked. "She has deceived us all."

"Silence!" Arthur thundered, glaring at Mordred. Arthur's hands clenched into fists. "How dare you take matters concerning the queen into your own hands instead of going to me."

"But, but, the outrage!" Gaheris stammered. "But our brothers are dead!" He began to sob.

"Come to my house," Gawaine said, taking his arm. "We can weep there." He handed the reins of his horse to one of the guards. Between his fears for Lancelot and his grief over his brothers, he could hardly walk, but he had to lead Gaheris.

"Let everyone behave in an orderly manner," Arthur ordered,

still mounted and leading the way back through the gate.

"Aren't you grateful that we found the traitors out, sire?" Mordred asked him.

"Wipe that smile off your face." Arthur's voice cut like a sword. "If Lancelot was not as he seemed, no one must speak of it, lest I be made sport of by the lesser kings. Can't you see that this insane raid on my wife damages me and threatens my power?"

"I had no intention of doing that," Mordred said meekly.

Then Gawaine walked out of earshot. Tears spilled down his face. "But what happened to Lancelot?" he asked Gaheris, dreading the answer. It would be too much to bear to lose Lancelot, too. "Was he hurt?"

"Not much, worse luck." Gaheris spat on the ground. "Lancelot's completely mad. When she killed Agravaine, she thought it was you and ran away raving."

"Gods!" Gawaine moaned. He must find poor Lancelot.

"We must take revenge on her!" Gaheris cried. "Revenge!"

"Have a drink, calm down. Lancelot's not a woman." Gawaine pulled out his flask and extended it to Gaheris. "Our brothers' deaths have unhinged you."

"Lancelot's a woman, by Lugh. I saw her body. She must be a witch to have defeated us all these many years," Gaheris insisted, taking his brother's flask and downing the wine in it. "We must avenge poor Gareth, who idolized the creature."

Gawaine led him into the house. "Rather, let us weep for our brothers."

Gaheris drank from Gawaine's flask. "We can get a group of men together and deal with her."

Gawaine drew back from him. How could Gaheris say such a thing about Lancelot? "What, rape her? Do you forget that

Lancelot has saved all of our lives? And, if Lancelot is a woman, I swore to the king that I would defend all women."

"Surely the king would let you off that oath this time," Gaheris begged.

"Stop this talk of revenge. You were a fool to try to take Lancelot in bed. Who wouldn't fight back then?" Gawaine slumped into a chair. He who was called Gawaine of the Matchless Strength felt almost too weak to stand.

"It was foolhardy," Gaheris admitted. "But admitting that does not bring them back. Our brothers, our poor brothers," he moaned.

And Gawaine moaned with him.

Gaheris flung himself on the bed and sobbed.

Pouring himself a cup of whatever drink was nearest, Gawaine thought of the boys who had grown up playing on the sands of the North Sea. All of them had looked up to him. Could he have led them better?

Even Agravaine had had his pleasant moments as a boy. They had dragged up strange masses of kelp from the sea together and examined them for creatures that might or might not be fit for the cooking pot, but always were full of interest. They had ridden for hours across the rocks of Orkney and over the hills of Lothian. Agravaine had never admitted being tired, even when he was nearly falling from his horse with exhaustion. They had practiced fighting with wooden swords, and even though Gawaine had always won, Agravaine had fought back gamely. When had the brave boy become a cruel man?

Angry as he was at Gaheris, Gawaine thought of the little boy who had trailed after him. When he had gone to Camelot, Gaheris had then followed the second brother, Agravaine, and Agravaine had been the only friend that he had had.

When Gareth was a little boy, he had looked up to Gaheris, and was the only person who had ever done so.

Doubtless it had been hard for Gaheris to come to Camelot and soon learn that Gawaine preferred to spend time with other warriors, particularly Lancelot, rather than with his brothers. He had always known that this behavior bothered Gaheris. And that had left Gaheris to Agravaine.

Then when Gareth arrived at Camelot and thought the sun rose and set on Lancelot, that perhaps had been more than Gaheris could endure.

Perhaps it was too much to expect Gaheris to be fair about the deaths of Agravaine and Gareth.

Little Gareth! Gawaine saw a child who had run after his horse when he returned home for brief visits to Lothian. "Don't go, Gawaine! Take me with you!"

He had laughed and called out, "When you're old enough!"

How could he write his mother the terrible news? It would be better to tell her in person, if Arthur would give him leave to go to Lothian. No, his mother was now still further away, in Orkney.

But there was someone else who needed his help first. Where had Lancelot gone? Was she indeed mad? The thought that she imagined she had killed him and had therefore descended to madness tormented him. He wanted to tear his hair out. He longed to ride off that moment and search for her, but how could he fail to see his brothers' bodies and learn more about what had happened from men who were not as distraught as Gaheris? And if he immediately went off to look for Lancelot, everyone would be certain that she was a woman. They would also believe she was his mistress, an assumption that would anger Lancelot.

Gawaine prayed to every god he could name that what had just happened to Lancelot never would happen to Galahad.

Camelot would never again be what it had been, Gawaine felt sure. How could Camelot be Camelot without Lancelot? Gods and goddesses, let her not harm herself in her madness. And let no one else harm her.

Arthur stormed off to his room. He had thought Lancelot was the most trustworthy of his warriors. Why hadn't Lancelot told him she was a woman?

Damn Guinevere, why couldn't she keep her hands off Lancelot?

Well, he himself had suggested that they lie together, but of course he had no idea that Lancelot was a woman. Why didn't Guinevere recoil when she learned the truth?

Which one of them had seduced the other?

Lancelot had deceived him. Perhaps she was not as simply good as he had imagined. Perhaps Lancelot had confused Guinevere, driven her away from her husband. Could it be that Guinevere was not his enemy, after all, and that Lancelot was? Were they both vile? Perhaps one of them was an innocent woman and the other was a fiend, but which was which?

He poured himself wine and mulled over these thoughts.

Mordred busied himself talking to the warriors, especially the young ones.

"Lancelot is a woman," he told most of them. "What kind of shame is that for us? You've been following a woman. What are you going to do about it? What do you think she deserves?"

The answer to that was generally the same, and very crudely put.

But when he spoke with the few pious young men who had admired Gareth, Mordred said, "Poor Gareth was so holy, almost a saint, and he trusted Lancelot. She killed him. It was heartbreaking to see it. She must be a witch, and he is a martyr. If King Arthur is truly Christian, he must avenge poor Gareth's martyrdom."

They assented, strongly, and Mordred could see that it would be easy for his followers and Gareth's to fight together.

Thinking of Gareth, Gawaine stalked angrily across the courtyard. A gentle rain splashing on him did not cheer him as it generally did, nor did the scent of honeycakes baking in the kitchens. One of Arthur's hounds bounded up to him, but he did not pat it as usual.

Bors crossed the cobbles and said, "A word with you, please."

"If you must," Gawaine grunted. He had just seen his brothers' bodies and had no desire to do anything but mourn— and go seeking Lancelot. How far had her madness gone? Would he be able to comfort her?

"Let us go to your house," Bors said. "It should be quiet there."

Gawaine agreed readily. Bors's house was always crowded with his many children. His own house felt empty now, and the sight of Gareth's clothes and arms saddened him.

They entered the house, with its familiar smell of ale. Some well-meaning person had brought Gareth's sword there, and Agravaine's, too, and they lay on the table. The sight wounded Gawaine as if the swords had stabbed him. Thank the gods Gaheris had gone off to his own house.

Bors's face twitched. "Mordred says that Lancelot is a woman," he gasped in a loud whisper. "Can that be true?"

Gawaine cursed, trying to make it brief for Bors's sake. "That filthy whoreson. It's true enough, but don't tell anyone else." He picked up Gareth's sword and shoved it into the table's wood.

"But why not speak of it?" Bors cried. "This proves that everything was innocent, and the queen should not be punished. Lancelot was just her friend and slept with her so she would not be lonely. We must tell Arthur that Lancelot is just a woman."

Gawaine tried to speak gently to the pure-minded warrior. "Gaheris told Arthur that, but he's been angry at Guinevere for years, and I fear he may punish her anyway."

"Even though she and Lancelot are innocent?" Bors crossed himself.

"Yes, even though they're innocent." They meant no harm, and he certainly wasn't going to explain to Bors how women might be lovers.

Bors crossed himself yet again. "So many things are happening that are beyond my ken. Lancelot running off, Guinevere held prisoner, Galahad disappearing..."

Gawaine froze. "What do you mean about Galahad?" He almost stopped breathing. He could not bear any more grief.

Bors hemmed and hawed. "I may be mistaken. Perhaps he's still a heedless youth. Young Percy and I met up with him not long ago, and we traveled to a forest, where we came to a wonderful chapel with exquisite music and an unearthly light. Percy and I went inside the chapel and prayed, and I thought Galahad came in behind us, though I didn't see him. We stayed there for many hours. Percy became restless, but I silently reproved him for impatience with the divine. At some point, we left the church, and Galahad wasn't there. Could he have been taken up to heaven?"

Gawaine's tense muscles relaxed. "Was Galahad's horse gone, too?"

"Why, yes." Bors nodded.

Gawaine's voice was restrained. He shouldn't laugh at Bors. "I doubt that the horse was taken to heaven, too."

"Of course not. There are no such things in heaven," said Bors indignantly.

"It sounds as if you were in the chapel a very long time. Galahad is just young and restless, as you said Percy was. He'll be all right," said Gawaine, in a calm tone. An afterworld without horses would be a poor one, he reckoned. "If anyone's a saint, it's Lancelot. Hadn't you thought of that?" He had just thought of the idea himself. He pulled Gareth's sword out of the wood.

Bors's face shone as if a beam of light had just poured through the window and enveloped him, although the day was gray and wet. "That explains everything!" he exclaimed. "I suppose she would have to be that or a witch, and with Lancelot, of course, that must mean sainthood." Then his face dimmed. "But she hasn't taken the holy sacrament in many years. Mordred says that proves she's a witch, because if she had taken the sacrament she'd have been struck by lightning."

"She couldn't be a witch," Gawaine replied, trying to keep the anger out of his voice. Of course Lancelot did not take the sacrament because she was an adulterer. Bors was only foolish, although Mordred was much worse. "Whoever heard of a virgin witch?"

Bors was not a worldly man, but he was worldly enough to think that Gawaine would know whether Lancelot was a virgin. He was unworldly enough not to imagine that Gawaine would say anything but the truth about the subject.

"Of course there couldn't be one," Bors agreed with considerable solemnity. "So she must be a saint."

Bors was easy to convince because he would rather hear good about people than bad, but unfortunately no one else would be, because most would rather imagine the worst.

"I suppose Arthur will send Guinevere to a convent," Bors said.

"What else can he do?" Gawaine agreed.

After Bors left, Gawaine went to the great hall. In a foul humor, he saw that young Clegis was sitting in the place at the table that was usually Galahad's.

"Don't sit in that place!" he yelled, and Clegis jumped up and stared at him. "No one but young Galahad can sit in that place."

Several warriors shook their heads, as if Gawaine was addled, perhaps drunk, after the deaths of his brothers.

If they believed he was drunk, then he would be drunk. Gawaine helped himself to some ale, but he downed only a little. No, it would not do to drink himself into a stupor.

Striding out into the courtyard, he headed for Lancelot's house. Someone might take the opportunity to steal Lancelot's few possessions. He would take them and bring her what she might need, if only he could find her.

Gawaine pushed open the door, which was unlocked, and saw that Lancelot's foes had already been there. The chairs and table had been smashed, apparently with an axe, and so had the bed. Lancelot's clothes and bedding had been strewn on the floor, and many men had pissed on them. The room reeked with the smell. Lancelot's chain mail, helmet, shield, and spear were nowhere to be seen, doubtless stolen.

His veins almost bursting with rage, Gawaine cursed loudly. He saw another pile of clothes in a corner. No, it was Catwal.

The serving man lay there, bruised and bleeding. Gawaine went down on his knees and turned him over. Catwal was unconscious, but still breathed.

Brutes! Beating a blind serving man because they could not get to Lancelot! If Gawaine discovered who had done it, they would long regret their savagery--but this was not the time for that. He must find a healer for Catwal.

26 QUEEN OF FIRE

The door of Guinevere's room opened, and Arthur appeared.
Guinevere tensed. However ravaged and desolate, this room was
her territory and she would defend it. Twilight had come, and
the room was full of shadows. She could imagine that Lancelot's
shadow was among them.

Arthur shut the door behind him.

"So, Guinevere." He wore a fine white tunic with red trim.
His gray eyes probed her. There was no hint of gentleness in
them or in his voice. Well, she had expected none.

She remained seated. Anticipating this interview, she had
dressed in one of her finest blue gowns. Her golden torque hung
around her neck, but she did not wear her crown.

The king paused, letting her wonder what he would say.
Standing, he towered over her. The only sound was the drip of
rain falling past the window. She waited.

Finally, Arthur broke the silence. His voice was calm and
patronizing, the tone of one in a superior position who might be
generous to an erring inferior. "I recall that you were a good

wife for many years, until you met that creature. No doubt she deceived you at first. I suppose that you have never been with another man after all. Do you repent of this folly?" His hand reached out to her.

Guinevere smiled, but without affection. Did he believe that she would let him embrace her again? His perfectly sculpted though lined face, his scent, everything repulsed her. After Lancelot's touches, anyone else's would be unbearable. "Certes, I have never been with another man. I have always known that Lancelot was a woman. All of my love is for Lancelot, and I shall never repent."

Arthur jerked back his hand. Her words angered him, as she knew they would. His face reddened. "So you are the one who corrupted Lancelot and made her a traitor to me."

"I seduced her, and I am glad of it." She let her pride show in her voice.

"Do you understand what this means?" he demanded, glaring at her. The wrinkles stood out on his face, but women still found it handsome. However, none could have failed to be chilled by the expression that was now in his eyes. Perhaps only captured Saxons had seen it. "If you send me away now, I will never speak to you again, and you will face death."

Guinevere had suspected she would, but she would rather die than crawl back to his bed. She kept her voice calm. She would never plead with him. "Don't try to touch me, or you will regret it. I learned from Lancelot how to kill a man if I have to." She was prepared to press his veins in a vulnerable spot if need be, though she had no wish to kill him. Fear belonged to the past, to the time when she had much to lose. Now there was only her life.

Arthur recoiled. "So you are the monster, and she was the innocent one."

Pulling away from Guinevere as if he had discovered she had leprosy, he looked at her with loathing.

She nodded. "Yes, I am the monster." It was a great relief to say that to him. If that was how men saw her, let them. Lancelot was her love, loving Lancelot was her life's meaning. She had no life without Lancelot. Being a queen depended on being Arthur's, so it was worthless.

He clenched his fists. "Be damned, then. You'll burn at dawn for this treason against your husband. No one shall talk to you before then."

Guinevere froze. How could he hate her enough to decree such a terrible death? He knew well that she had always feared fire. But she managed to keep some vestige of calm in her voice as she said, "Burn me, then, if that is the kind of king you are, if that is the kind of man you are."

The door thudded behind him.

Guinevere shuddered and slumped in her chair. Looking out of the window, she saw that the rain had ceased. There would be no impediment to the fire.

Her beeswax candles burned on her table. She reached out a finger to one, then drew it back quickly.

She worried about Talwyn's grief, and of course Lancelot's. She tried to distract herself from fear, but she could not bear to remember happier times. All she could do was pray for Lancelot.

Creirwy carried a trencher to Guinevere's door, but a round-faced guard stopped her and demanded it from her.

"Only the guards are allowed to see the queen. I'll give her that supper."

"What do you think I've got, some potion to make her small enough to slip through the keyhole? Or perhaps I've got Lancelot hidden under the mutton," Creirwy snapped. "Lady Guinevere may need a woman attending to her."

"Give me the trencher, Creirwy," he sighed. "It's orders. The queen's goin' to be burned at the stake in the mornin', and no one can see her 'til then."

Creirwy thrust the trencher into his hands. "May you be kept from all that cares about you when it's your turn to die." She spat at him.

He made a sign warding off evil with one hand while he took the trencher with the other.

Creirwy stormed off, not to Luned to commiserate, but to the house where the young ladies slept.

Felicia was weeping and Talwyn was saying, "If Queen Guinevere has to go into exile, I'll go with her, but surely the king will pardon her."

Wanting to box her genteel ears, Creirwy snapped, "Surely he won't. Lady Talwyn," she said with exaggerated politeness, "May I speak with you?"

Talwyn nodded and patted Felicia on the back, then slipped out to join Creirwy in the courtyard.

Creirwy felt no urge to mince words. "She's to be burned tomorrow at dawn."

"No!" Talwyn staggered as if she might faint.

Creirwy spared her no sympathy. "So, do you mean to use those fighting lessons to some purpose? I do. I'll save her, or die trying, more like."

"So will I," Talwyn asserted without hesitation.

Creirwy felt a moment of grudging respect for her.

Arthur stood poised to enter his chamber when Bors and his wife hurried up to him. Lionors threw herself on her knees and clasped her hands as if in prayer.

"Lord Arthur, I beg you. Hear a woman's pleas and let Lady Guinevere live," Lionors gasped. "She is a kind woman."

"Get off your knees, lady, and leave me be. You know nothing of vice." Disgusted at Lionors's emotional display, Arthur remembered the last time a woman went down on her knees to him, when Enid told about her abortion. Bors's wife had been too modest ever to speak much to the king, and she should remain silent.

Lionors did not rise. "Please, lord. In your noble heart, remember her service to you and have mercy on her."

"For the love of God, Arthur, spare Guinevere," Bors said, his hand on his wife's shoulder. "Forgive us our trespasses as we . . ."

"Take charge of your wife, Bors. Remove her from my presence. Guinevere will die as I decreed." Arthur swept into his room. How dare they question his judgment?

Guinevere heard pounding on her door. Let them leave her alone. She had no thoughts left for any man. No woman knocked that loudly. She patted the cat that curled in her lap. Grayse raised her head at the sound.

Guinevere might have wanted to see Talwyn, but that would have been too painful. She hoped the girl would stay in her room in the morning and not see the burning.

"Guinevere! Answer me!" Mordred's voice demanded.

"Be gone!" she responded, even more imperiously.

Mordred's voice insinuated its way through the strong door.

"Guinevere, I'll help you escape. I've wanted you so long. I'll take you to Londinium and make you my queen. I'll defeat the old man and succeed him soon enough. You can help me."

His message turned her stomach. Could he possibly think she was degraded enough to lie with her husband's son? "Be gone, you rotten adder. I'll go nowhere with you. Leave me to rest in peace."

"So loyal to my father? He'll burn you. Or to that strange bitch? She can't help you now. And neither will Gawaine. He's back, but he isn't running to save you, is he? I'm the only one who cares about you."

Gawaine back? No, he wouldn't save her, but perhaps he would look for Lancelot. Guinevere prayed he would.

"No answer?" Mordred kept on urging her. "There are warriors who will follow me. Come with me, and you'll be safe. Stay and you're dead."

"Go away, Mordred. I'd rather burn and kiss the devil." She rose and walked as far as she could from the door.

"Burn then, fool. I'll take your sister as my queen instead."

She heard his steps pounding away and hoped that Gwynhwyfach would never trust him.

The thought that Mordred was the only person to try to save her life made Guinevere want to weep, but she did not. Did she matter so little to the people she had known? She must think not of herself, but of Lancelot.

Perhaps Gawaine truly cared for Lancelot, even though she had killed Agravaine. Lancelot would not be alone, Guinevere hoped. But she knew Lancelot would not be willing to stay in this world if her beloved was burned at the stake.

Talwyn rapped on the door of her father's room, and Huw the serving man answered.

Talwyn darted in past him. "Da!" she cried out.

Her alarm roused Gryffyd. He leapt up from his chair. "Child! Are the Saxons pursuing you?" He flung an arm around her and looked about desperately for a sword.

Talwyn pulled two swords from under her cloak and gave one to her father. Huw gasped and moved back into a corner.

"No, the Saxons are going to burn Queen Guinevere! We must save her!" She gave Gryffyd the look of trust she had had as a child, long before war and madness.

"We will save her," he replied, straightening his shoulders and looking like the formidable warrior he had once been.

"My lord, you mustn't. The king has ordered it," Huw muttered in protest.

"What, is the king a Saxon? I'll take no orders from a savage king," Gryffyd shouted, and he followed Talwyn out of the room.

Gawaine had seen to it that Catwal was under a physician's care. As he left the physician's house, Bors ran up to him. "Arthur is going to burn Guinevere at the stake!"

Gawaine froze. "Impossible. He'd never do that."

Bors shook. "I fear he would. My wife and I begged him not to, but he turned us away. I have a letter that the queen put in my keeping, to give to Lancelot if any strange injury befell her. I've read it, and I think you should as well."

Gawaine grabbed the vellum and read the words on it. He trembled with rage. "Arthur has threatened her before. She has feared for her life since then. Gods, what manner of man have we followed?"

"We must plan, and Cai has said he will join our plan." Bors's countenance was as grim as it had been in the Saxon war. "My wife is sobbing her heart out, and I'm near doing that myself."

Lancelot rode deeper and deeper into the forest, which for once had no charms for her. Red fox and red deer drifted among the trees, but she looked through them as if they were shadows. She had bound up the wound in her arm. The wound bled only a little, but she seemed to bleed everywhere. Her heart had caved in.

Evening came, but despite her exhaustion she could not rest, except for her mare's sake. Bats fluttered past her, but she did not marvel at their flight. An owl hooted. It probably had a mate and was not as lonely as she would be forever.

Perhaps she had not killed Gawaine, but she was not sure. Her only certainty was that she was too mad to be Guinevere's lover-—or anyone's. And now that she was known to be a woman, she could never return to Camelot.

She heard sounds of weeping, the only thing that would have drawn her. She followed the sobs and came upon a copse where a young woman sat crumpled under an oak tree. As Lancelot drew close, she saw that the woman was Nimue.

Lancelot had little desire to speak with Nimue, or with anyone, but she could not ignore such sorrow, despite her own heavy heart. She dismounted and went over to her. "Nimue, why are you crying?" Lancelot asked in a low voice so as not to startle her. "Are you still grieving for Merlin?"

The tear-stained face turned up to her. "No, I was weeping for Queen Guinevere because the king is going to burn her. I have seen it. I was searching for you to save her, but it seemed that I would never find you."

"No, it can't be! He couldn't!" Lancelot nearly fell over.

"He will, at dawn." Nimue's hair was tangled and she had the wild look of a prophet.

"No!" Lancelot stumbled back to her mare and flung herself over its black flanks. "Run as you never have before, Raven girl," she murmured.

Riding furiously, Lancelot imagined flames turning Guinevere's legs to ashes, roasting her whole body, while she still defied all the laws of God and man.

Leaving two lovers to their deaths was too much to bear. And as a child, she had been unable to rescue her mother. She seemed doomed to keep failing to save the women she loved.

Flames burst in her head. She saw every fire that she had ever known, roasting hares, pigeons, sheep--fat dripping, the fire sizzling--Guinevere. Clothes igniting first, elegant gown, bringing fire to the rest of her body, hair in flames, singed with the dragon's fire.

If Lancelot had to, she would slay the dragon. The man she had served all her life was far different than she had believed. Nothing, not even madness, not even guilt, must keep her from saving Guinevere.

Guinevere sat watching her last moon and stars and thinking over her life. How lonely it would have been if she had never known Lancelot.

There was a gentle knock on her door. For an instant, she let herself imagine it might be Lancelot.

The door creaked open. She had not expected any more visitors--ever. Had Mordred bribed a guard to let him in?

Father Donatus entered. "My lady, I have come to shrive you. I demanded that the king allow me to do so." His voice was hoarse, as if he had the ague. Could he have been weeping? Even in the candlelight she could see his frown. Did he frown more at her sin, or her death sentence?

Guinevere shook her head. "Thank you, good father, but I cannot be shriven, for I shall never repent loving Lancelot."

The pallor on his face increased. "My lady! Consider! You will burn in the fires of hell!"

"Perhaps. And perhaps not." He looked so distressed that she wanted to comfort him. "Don't grieve, Father. There are things in this world, and I hope in the next, that you cannot understand. I believe there is mercy for those who love."

"I am not saying that you should not love Lancelot, my lady, but only that you should confess that you sinned," he pleaded.

Guinevere shook her head. "No, I have no regrets about loving. I must hold fast to my love for Lancelot and think about Lancelot to keep myself from hating the king, which I acknowledge is a sin."

"Yes, Lady Guinevere, you must purge hatred from your soul."

He argued further, but she resisted.

Finally, the priest pulled a small vial from the sleeve of his cassock.

"At least take this, my lady. It may help ease the pain of the flames in this world, if not the next."

"How kind of you!" Guinevere accepted the vial and was so moved that she almost consented to be shriven, just to ease his worries. But she still refused.

Gawaine burst into Arthur's room. "Don't tell me you're going to burn Guinevere!" he cried out.

The king remained seated and spoke coolly. "I'm afraid I must. It's a pity. This was treason, after all."

"Horseshit!" Gawaine yelled, shaking with anger. Rank meant nothing to him at the moment. "You practically ordered her to lie with me years ago, so you'd have an heir. Then you let her be with Lance. You didn't mind, as long as you thought Lance was a man."

The king retained his composure. A wolfhound pup nuzzled his knees, and he patted it. "Of course I gave her leave to lie with another man, but only so that she could bear a child. This perversion could never lead to that, so it was wrong."

Arthur seemed like a man of ice, quite unlike his usual hearty self. But then, how was a man who was going to burn his wife supposed to look? Gawaine felt a wave of revulsion. He wanted to be out in the forest looking for Lancelot, yet he knew that he had to save Guinevere first. He had to do what Lancelot would want him to do. But he was impatient at the delay.

"You care only because they were discovered. Exile Guinevere; don't kill her."

"What do you care about Guinevere?" Arthur twisted his ring. "You've always disliked her."

"What does it matter whether I dislike her? Do you think that because a woman doesn't smile at me, I'd let her be murdered?" He glared at Arthur.

"This isn't murder. She would be executed for her crimes."

"If everyone who committed adultery was executed, few of us would be left alive," Gawaine argued.

"I would pardon Lancelot, because of all the service she has done for me, but never Guinevere. Did you know that Lancelot was a woman?" Arthur added, in a conversational tone, beckoning for Gawaine to be seated and have some wine.

Gawaine remained standing. If Arthur was going to maintain this calm pose, he would have to try to do so, too. Reining himself in, he managed not to shout. "I've known it for a couple of years. What does that matter?"

The king's eyes widened and his jaw dropped open. "Did she tell you?" He scrutinized Gawaine's face.

Knowing that the king was really asking whether he was Lancelot's lover, Gawaine answered, "Not because she wanted to." It seemed mad to be chatting and storytelling at the moment, but perhaps a story might distract Arthur from his rage at Guinevere. "It is a simple tale. One evening, we were riding in the forest, and we came upon a young woman who was great with child and moaning in pain.

"Lance exclaimed, 'Are you about to give birth, my lady?' and the woman said, 'I am.'

"'You cannot do that alone in the forest, my lady,' Lancelot said, but the woman replied, 'I must. I couldn't stay where they know me.'

"'I know nothing about these things, but let me try to help you,' said Lance.

"'Go away!' the woman cried. 'I won't let any man touch me.'

"'I'm a woman,' Lance said, and I nearly fell off my horse. She swung down from her horse and told me, 'Gawaine, don't stop there staring. I have heard that midwives use hot water, so go fetch some water, build a fire, and then leave us.'

"I did as she bade me. Many hours later, when I returned, the mother was sleeping with her babe in her arms, and Lance looked weary. 'Thank the Holy Mother I don't have to do that,' she said. 'It looks more difficult than a battle.'

"And that's all there is to the story."

Arthur frowned. "That's the cleanest story I've ever heard you tell. Are you sure it's the true one?"

"Of course it is." Gawaine was pleased with the story because it was just what Lancelot would have said and done if such a thing had happened. He had no intention of telling about how he actually found out, because Lancelot refused to share a bed at an inn with him, a story that might have appealed to the king much more.

"Why, if you knew she was a woman, didn't you try to . . ."

"No, of course not, she's just an old friend," Gawaine said brusquely.

"But a very handsome one," Arthur insisted, sighing almost imperceptibly. "I suppose she's a virgin, then?"

"She surely is." Discussing Lancelot's body with another man, even to say that, was distasteful to him.

"Didn't you mind that she has defeated you in fighting contests?"

"Her skill has saved my life many times. How could I object to that? It doesn't matter now. You cannot burn Guinevere." He tried to keep from yelling. "That's all that matters."

"Why didn't you tell me about Lancelot?" The royal tone was aggrieved. Arthur frowned at him. "I have never harmed any woman."

"And so you must not harm Guinevere." Gawaine clenched and unclenched his fists. "Do you no longer want to be known as Arthur the Just? How can a king famed for his kindness and justice burn his wife?"

When Gawaine had mentioned Guinevere's name, Arthur's eyes had briefly held the look of a bear about to attack, but the king took a drink of wine and patted the dog again, as if to show his benevolence.

"I must burn her for justice sake, of course. It is the law that for a wife to commit adultery is treason against her husband, and how much greater is that treason if her husband is the king? It would be unjust if I did not apply the law to my own wife." He spoke almost solemnly, as if from his throne.

"You want to kill her!" Gawaine shook his fist in his cousin's royal face. "You hate the woman, I know you do. I won't follow a man who'd kill his wife, and if I go, I'll take others with me."

Arthur stared at him. He grabbed Gawaine's arm in a restraining manner. Gawaine did not resist. "Calm yourself, Gawaine. You don't know what you're saying. You are sworn to follow me. But I'll forgive you," the king added magnanimously.

Arthur turned to look out of the window, towards the dark farms and the town full of people who loved him. The rain had ended, leaving a cloudless, star-studded sky. "Strange about Lancelot. I'm a trifle sorry for her. The poor thing must never have had a man, but of course that was what she really wanted."

Gawaine grunted. "Lancelot loves Guinevere. Stop changing the subject."

Arthur shook his head. "Nonsense, they are only two women."

Gawaine thought not only of Lancelot and Guinevere, but of Galahad. So would men dismiss any love that his daughter would have. He couldn't help retorting, "What of it? Do you know so much less about lying with women than I thought you did?"

Arthur shook his head. "It seems that even the women we believe we know are strangers. What do women want?"

Exhaling, Gawaine tried to cool his temper and answer shrewdly. "I think I know, but do you?"

"Different women want different things, to be sure," Arthur said, throwing a stick for the dog, which bounded across the room.

"So far, so good," Gawaine said. Arthur's pose of playing with the dog angered him.

"Most of them want a good man to lie with, the best ones want children, and the worst ones want to rule over men," Arthur pronounced, pouring himself more wine. The dog returned the stick to him, and he threw it again.

Gawaine sighed with exasperation. "What women want is to be able to decide what they want."

Frowning, Arthur grumbled. "That's a foolish answer. To want to be able to decide what to want. That amounts to nothing. They just want their own way, all the time, whether it makes sense or not."

"It's not nothing, it's everything. No caers or jewels or even caresses are worth anything if you can't say who or what you want," Gawaine observed, speaking as if to a child. "You would be miserable if you didn't have that, and so would I, and so are they." He had learned something from Lancelot and Galahad, he reckoned.

Arthur just shook his head and said, "Some women might know what they want. But virgins can't." The dog brought him the stick, but he ignored it.

Gawaine seethed, his temples throbbing. His daughter did indeed know what she wanted. "Lancelot will know that she doesn't want Guinevere to burn. If Guinevere is burned, Lancelot will go so deep into madness that she'll never recover."

"Nonsense. She was so ashamed at what she did with Guinevere that she ran off without her. She never wants to see her again."

"That can't be true. Lancelot ran off because she had a fit of madness." Gawaine groaned. He couldn't bear to think that it was because she thought she had killed him.

Arthur looked out of the window at the contest field where men working as hastily as they could in the dark had just finished erecting the scaffold for the queen's incineration and the pile of sticks under it. The structure's outline was barely visible by the light of their torches.

The dog went off to lie in a corner.

"You don't understand all the wrong Guinevere has done to me," Arthur said, his face reddening. "Remember Enid? Before she because Gereint's wife, she was my mistress. She became with child, but Guinevere had her fiendish old woman end the pregnancy."

Gawaine stared at him. "Did Enid ask her to?"

"Yes, but that does not excuse it." His voice rising to a frenzied pitch, Arthur proclaimed, "Guinevere murdered my child. She claims she did not know it was mine, but she must have."

"I don't believe Guinevere would do that deliberately." So this was the source of Arthur's anger. Gawaine tried to calm him. "You've never gotten any woman with child. Sometimes women think they are with child when they are not. No doubt that happened with Enid. She fretted, and went to Guinevere's woman, who gave her something to bring on her courses. But there never was a child, Arthur."

"I think there was, and I will be avenged on Guinevere."

Gawaine's hands were curled fists but he forced himself to unclench them. He wanted to strike the face that was like his own.

"Even if you hate Guinevere, spare her for the sake of Lancelot, who has saved all our lives many times and has always served you well."

"Hah! Nothing could be more debauched, more degraded than what she and my wife have done." Arthur spat on the floor. "It's like something whores might do if there were no men around."

Gawaine's shook with rage. "Nothing Lancelot could do would ever be degraded or debauched. Nor Guinevere either."

"Defend Lancelot if you like." Arthur said magnanimously. "But leave Guinevere to me. She's my wife, and I have the right to do anything I want with her." Arthur pounded the table.

"No, you don't. You can't kill her." Gawaine pounded back at him.

"I am your sovereign. I have let you speak to me in a way I would never allow anyone else to speak. I have heard your arguments, but my mind is unchanged. If you have nothing more constructive to say, you can leave." Arthur nodded towards the door.

A rosy light was starting to appear in the sky.

"It's dawn," Arthur said, yawning. "I should see whether the guards have finished the pyre. They are nervous about executing the queen." A hint of cruelty stole into his eyes and his voice.

Gawaine had never seen a cruel look on Arthur's face before this night. Determination to fight, yes. Anger, yes. Implacability, yes. But not cruelty. Gawaine held back from shuddering.

"You have been trying to distract me, but I have distracted you." Arthur gave him a most unpleasant smile.

"I've always been cleverer than you are. If you had understood how unshakable my determination to execute Guinevere was, you might have broken into her room and rescued her."

Sickened, Gawaine pulled back. "Why, that's true, I would have."

"It is time," Arthur said, again looking out of the window. "They have already brought Guinevere out on the field. We must go down."

They saw Guinevere, dressed in a plain black gown, her hands bound, led by guards.

Where was Bors? He was supposed to come to the field and take Guinevere away. For Gawaine had not relied entirely on his powers of persuasion. As the better fighter, he should have been the one to save Guinevere--though perhaps she'd rather die--but Bors could not have been the one to try to convince or at least detain the king. He would only have tried prayer, and Arthur would have sent him away.

Gawaine's stomach sank. "This is mad. You can't do this to your wife."

"I can." Arthur's voice was grim. His face looked harder than it had in the Saxon War. "Come with me or stay here."

Gawaine felt desperate, as if his own life were threatened. He could not let Lancelot's sweetheart die. He pictured Lancelot mad as she had been at Bagdemagus's dun. Or taking her own life. "You once made me swear to defend all women. I have done only a spotty job of it, but now I recall that 'all women' includes Guinevere."

"You're not supposed to defend her against me! I'm her husband," Arthur said, scowling at him.

"Nevertheless, I am sworn to defend Guinevere," Gawaine repeated, "although I would do the same even if I had sworn no oath." He grabbed the king's arm, detaining him. He imagined what it would be like to be known as Gawaine the Cruel, the man who deposed Good King Arthur. And no one would believe that it was for Guinevere's sake, least of all Guinevere herself. Well, no, for Lancelot's sake. "I won't let you kill her. If that means taking power from you, I'll do it."

Arthur tried to shake off his arm but he could not. Turning red, he exclaimed. "You're mad! This is treason! You can't save her now. They've already lit the fire."

Gawaine turned his gaze to the window. The flames were indeed lit. He tightened his grasp and drew his dagger. "Stop them. Yell out of the window if you value your life."

Arthur cried out, "God's blood, someone is trying to take Guinevere down from the scaffold! And there is Lancelot riding to the field."

It was true. There was conflict among the men near Guinevere, and, in the distance, Lancelot was riding there to rescue her.

Gawaine dropped Arthur's arm.

"I shall do nothing about your actions. I can't afford to charge you with treason, too," the king said. "You're my heir, and I need you." He rushed downstairs.

Gawaine hurried after him, almost tripping over the wolfhound that had wakened and was bounding down the stairs. Lancelot was not mad, Lancelot would save Guinevere. Would he be too late to help Lancelot?

"Don't pursue Lancelot and Guinevere," Gawaine warned.

Arthur paused. "If I don't, will you promise to stay with me?"

Gawaine paused only an instant, and pushed past him. "Yes, for a time." He didn't say how long that time would be.

"They are safe, then--as long as you stand beside me."

So he would be hostage for Lancelot again, Gawaine thought as he hurtled down the stairs and through the door.

Wearing a fine black gown, Guinevere walked with her guards to the scaffold. Her wedding ring was no longer on her hand and her gold torque was no longer around her neck.

The pyre was to the west of the door she had left. She resented that because she could not see the final rays of the dawn, the last she would ever see. She did not want to turn her head because that might make her look afraid. She had not taken the potion that Father Donatus had given her because she did not want to appear drugged.

A muttering crowd watched her. Guinevere could not tell whether their noises meant the people disapproved of what she had done or of her punishment.

She saw swallows flying high over the caer. She would never hear birdsong again. Although she had not thought as much about such things as Lancelot did, she realized they had mattered to her. A crow cawed, and she was grateful to hear that sound at least.

The day promised to be fair, and Guinevere wanted to see it. She would never again see the full sun of midday, or the glowing sunset.

Guinevere suppressed a sob. She must be strong. She must die like a queen.

Should she look among the crowd for her ladies? No, she did not want to see people's faces, which might be unkind. Most of those gathered were men, and they might be leering at her because of the adultery. She hoped they did not know that Lancelot was a woman.

She prayed that Lancelot had recovered her senses and had gone on her way to Lesser Britain and to safety. Or that Gawaine had searched for and found her.

Father Donatus approached and tried to pray with Guinevere, but she refused. The priest paled when she spurned him. She was still determined to die without repenting her love for Lancelot. She held her head high, daring the spectators to watch her. She made no pleas, and was determined not to let the pain make her scream. She hoped that she could manage that.

After looking at the pile of faggots that would be used to burn her, Guinevere climbed the ladder of the scaffold. To her disgust, she saw that the executioner wore a dark hood. No doubt he was ashamed to show his face. No one would know who the man was who killed a queen. But it didn't matter, she thought. He could be any man. Strangely, he smelled faintly of perfume. Did he want to stifle the smell of burning flesh?

As he bound her to the stake, he whispered, "The ropes are loose enough so that you can slip out of them when the moment comes. I'll grab your hand when it's time." It was Cai's voice!

"No, don't," she whispered back, not daring to say more lest the spectators see her conversing with him. How many lives would be lost in a rescue?

"Bors, Gawaine, and I have planned to save you," Cai told her. "Of course we would not watch you burn. Never fear, I made sure that the wood was green. It won't burn fast."

She felt a thrill of hope. Bors and Cai had always been her friends. And Gawaine? Did he truly want to save her? Why hadn't he gone after Lancelot?

Guards lifted the torches that would light the wood. She waited for the sound of sizzling faggots, for the smoke.

In a moment, Cai had cut the ropes that bound her to the stake and was helping her down the ladder, past the pile of sticks. A guard struck him, shoving him into the fire. Cai's cloak burst into flames and he shouted in pain, trying to roll away from the pyre.

"No! It's Cai!" Guinevere screamed.

Instantly, two guards grabbed him and tried to beat the flames out.

Guinevere wanted to rush to him and help, but her hands were still bound behind her.

Men, both warriors and guards, surrounded Guinevere, but in the din she heard a shout, "Saxons! Vile Sea Wolves!" and saw Gryffyd and another warrior, this one visored, slashing out at them. The men around her began to fall. Bors rode a horse and tried to press through the crowd to her.

The guards succeeded in putting out the fire that had enveloped Cai.

Someone flew at one the guards, knocking him down, but he drew his sword and fought back. Soon his assailant was on the ground, blood gushing from the chest. The guard pulled open the visor, and Guinevere saw that it was Creirwy. She nearly reeled. Tears for the loyal Creirwy poured down her cheeks.

More bodies were falling around her. Gryffyd was down, but he had struck down many men around him. The warrior who fought beside him was suddenly close to Guinevere and reaching for her when a blow from behind knocked the would-be rescuer down. The visor flew open, and Guinevere saw who it was.

"Talwyn!" she howled, seeing blood pour from the girl's back, and wished she had died herself instead.

A black horse thundered up to Guinevere, seeming about to trample her, but Lancelot's arms pulled her up and they were off. Lancelot rained blows on the men who opposed them.

Guinevere slumped against her. Was this truly Lancelot, or had she fainted? Was this a dream, or a nightmare?

Lancelot felt a rage greater than she had felt in any other battle. She had never hated a Saxon as she hated the men who tried to burn Guinevere. She had heard of blood boiling, and had thought it was an exaggeration--until now, when hers surged hot in her veins. Her sword felt like part of her. She was a blade, cutting down any obstacles to Guinevere's freedom.

Crowds of people who had come to watch the execution screamed and ran to get out of the way of the fight.

Most of the men who thrust themselves around Lancelot's horse were her students, so she knew their weaknesses and was able to kill them easily. There was Camlach, who never could parry blows from the left, trying to get his hands on Guinevere, so Lancelot slashed his left side. Cildydd, who was slow, grabbed at her horse's reins, but she cut him down before his sword could come near her. Ergyriad, who was overconfident, jumped in front of Lancelot's horse and she rode right over him.

Kicking at the armed men with her hooves as she had been taught to do in battle, Raven carried Lancelot and Guinevere away.

27 To the Convent

Arthur and Gawaine finally reached the field. Gawaine saw
Lancelot ride off. "Don't let them pursue Lance, or I'll proclaim
myself king," he demanded.

"Don't pursue Lancelot," the king shouted. "Stop fighting."

Some of the older warriors, led by Bors, blocked the younger
men from pursuit. The battle had ended. It had lasted only a
short time.

Mordred stood over the bodies on the ground, and kicked
Creirwy's. "Slut," he sneered. "So Lancelot was training an army
of whores to fight the king's men."

Gasping at the sight of Talwyn's body, Gawaine bent over
her. "Gryffyd's daughter lives. Where's the surgeon?" He
cradled her head in his arms. He had thought that Cai and Bors
would get Guinevere away, and had no idea what Talwyn and
the serving woman were doing in chain mail. He begged the
gods to let Talwyn live, especially for Galahad's sake.

Mordred's look and tone were insolent. He made no pretense
of speaking as he usually did to the king. "Will you stop us from

pursuing the bitch Lancelot? Why? Is she your mistress? Perhaps you had them both together. I didn't know you had such exotic tastes."

Arthur struck him in the face. "You will not disobey my orders, or question them."

"Thank you for your gift to me, Father. It will always be remembered." Shaking with rage, Mordred did not strike back.

A guard bowed to Arthur. "Beg pardon, Lord Arthur, but you should know that the Lord Cai tried to help the queen and was burned by the fire. He's been carried off to his room."

"Not Cai!" Arthur moaned. "Why would he? Why all this concern for that cursed queen? May she rot to a hag!" He shook his fist.

Gawaine followed the men who carried Talwyn to the surgeon. All he could do at the moment was try to save her.

Creirwy lay on the hard ground, with men milling about her. Pain suffused her. It seemed more like the Christian hell than like Annwyn. But it might be that she was alive. She'd better not let them know. There were even worse deaths than being shoved into the earth while still breathing.

Luned's voice said, "Pick her up, Cathbad."

Arms held Creirwy not ungently, but the pain made her long to scream in protest. Still she kept silent.

She was being lifted onto a horse, then someone got up behind her and put his arm around her.

The stablehand Cathbad's voice said, "We'll be hanged for the horse."

His wife Luned protested, "No, it's the queen's, and the lord Cai will know it's what she'd have wanted. You'll return the horse after you've taken Creirwy to safety."

Then Creirwy was away, aching like one great wound. She lost consciousness, thinking she might never wake.

Creirwy was falling. She woke, and felt that she was being taken down from a horse and carried inside somewhere. She was put on a bed.

Fencha, Guinevere's former serving woman, bent over her, trying to ease Creiwy's body into something resembling comfort. Fencha had shrunk and looked as ancient as she probably was, but she smiled.

"There, child, they brought you to me. We couldn't get you down from the horse too easy. These old arms aren't so strong any more." The old woman was stroking the hair back from Creirwy's face.

Creirwy's eyes managed to open and she saw that they were in a hut with herbs hanging from the thatched roof. The scent from the herbs filled the air.

"There, dearie, you'll heal, you'll be safe," Fencha crooned, lifting a flask of wine to her lips.

Creirwy drank, then muttered, "Can't be. Our kind never gets saved. Only the nobles are."

"This once, you are. Rest, now, my girl." Fencha began to peel back her clothing to see to her wounds.

Lancelot and Guinevere sped through the forest, where Lancelot had concealed a horse that she had stolen along the way for the queen to ride. She clasped Guinevere tightly and helped her dismount. Then she cut her remaining bonds. The sight of Guinevere's hands tied with rope made Lancelot shake with rage. They glanced back to look for pursuers, but saw none.

Lancelot grabbed Guinevere's hands and kissed them again and again. "Poor, sweet hands," Lancelot said, choking.

The first thing Guinevere said was, "You're not mad, thank heaven." But tears streamed down her cheeks.

"Forgive me for leaving you. That was mad indeed." Lancelot choked.

"Too many lives lost. If only I had die instead. No one should have tried to save me." Guinevere's voice sounded hollow.

Lancelot, her body tense from the fight, could barely speak. "There was my mother. And Elaine. I couldn't let you die alone."

Guinevere clutched Lancelot's hand. "Talwyn died trying to save me. She'll never laugh again. Creirwy died, too, so young. And poor Gryffyd."

Lancelot moaned. She reeled more from this news than from the fight. She slumped onto her knees. "Not both girls! Oh, Holy Virgin, why did I ever train the girls to fight? How could they think they'd defeat men with years' more training?" She wanted to beat the ground with her fists.

Guinevere clasped Lancelot's hand. "It's not your fault. You could never have imagined that Arthur would try to burn me. You never thought that they would be killed."

"You were nearly killed, too, because in my madness I left you. You can never forgive me for all of this slaughter." Lancelot looked away.

"They would have killed you if you had stayed. I would have gone with you, but I felt I had to stay behind to distract Mordred. I never thought Arthur would go so far. I cannot bear to hear you berate yourself. Please do not." Guinevere leaned over Lancelot and put an arm around her.

Lancelot moaned. "You are far braver than I am."

"Cai disguised himself as an executioner and tried to save me," Guinevere told her.

"He was burned by the fire, but I don't know how badly."

Lancelot gasped. "Poor Cai! All men said that he was a poor fighter, but he was full of courage after all. May he be healed!"

"He said that he and Bors had planned to rescue me--and he said Gawaine did as well, though I did not see him." Guinevere's voice was different when she said Gawaine's name than when she named the others.

Lancelot clasped her tightly. "We did have friends after all." Some of her tears were now shed in gratitude. She had not killed Gawaine. Some men were truly friends.

"We should leave now," Guinevere said, looking at the trees as if they concealed Arthur's men.

"Agreed." Lancelot helped her mount and they rode on, away from Camelot.

After a long silence, Lancelot asked, "Shall we go to Lesser Britain?" She had no great desire to see her native land, only to escape.

"No! Arthur would follow us anywhere to salvage his honor," Guinevere warned. "We can stay at the Convent of the Holy Mother. The nuns there are our friends."

Lancelot thought of Mother Ninian and was relieved. There at least was a sensible plan, if they truly were not followed. "Will we endanger them?"

"I doubt it." Guinevere shook her head. "They can say they took me out of charity. Arthur won't attack a convent."

"But can I stay there?" How could a warrior live in a convent?

"Of course you can, Anna." Guinevere looked into her eyes. "No one will know that you have been Lancelot."

The words jolted Lancelot. She grabbed Raven's neck to keep from falling. She had not been Anna since she was a child. So she was to be Anna now. She had no idea how to be Anna.

"I should put aside my chain mail?" That sounded like cutting off her right arm. Why, if she could not use her arm to fight, that was almost the same thing.

"If you want to live with me," Guinevere said firmly, with a nod to accentuate her words. Queen or not, she still had a commanding air. "Arthur won't let us live openly as Guinevere and Lancelot, even in another country. What else can you do unless you leave Britain by yourself?"

Lancelot turned her gaze away. She missed her mail coat, her second skin. Could she make such a sacrifice, even for Guinevere?

"You want to still be a warrior, while I am no longer queen," Guinevere continued angrily, her eyes blazing. "Don't you understand how few choices we have? Can you still believe that Arthur is benevolent?" Guinevere trembled, perhaps with anger, and perhaps because of the terror she had been through.

Lancelot looked into those defiant blue eyes, the eyes of a woman who had almost been burned to death because of their love. "Let me be a woman, then. If you can stop being queen, I can stop being a warrior. It will be a struggle greater than the fiercest battle, but I won't leave you." The thought of wearing women's clothing and putting away her sword seemed like death. Being within four walls with Guinevere would be like being in a tomb together, but she would rather be so entombed than lose her.

"It won't be so bad being in a convent." Guinevere's voice was uncertain, however.

"Thy people shall be my people," Lancelot said, trying to smile.

"My people already are thy people, Anna," Guinevere replied, clasping Lancelot's hand. "You are a woman, too."

Clouds covered the sun, and rain began to drip on them as they rode to the convent. When they arrived, it was late at night. The plump and smiling sister porter answered Lancelot's knock on the old convent's heavy door.

"Oh, you've come. We thought you would. Please enter, Lady Guinevere, Lord Lancelot. Please rest here while I bring the abbess." She beamed at them as if they had come for some happy reason.

Shortly afterwards, the Abbess Perpetua entered the hall, passing the statue of the Virgin. Thinner and seemingly taller than ever, the abbess took Guinevere's hand. "Sister," she said. She extended the other hand to Lancelot. "Sister," she repeated.

Although she was stunned at that word, Lancelot went down on one knee like a proper warrior. The abbess gestured for her to rise. "No need for that. I've always known that you were a woman. Please rest and be comfortable here."

Lancelot was nearly weeping.

Guinevere sobbed, "Comfortable, no, never that again."

The abbess held onto her hand. "You must not say that."

Old Mother Ninian came in and put her arms around Lancelot, while the abbess talked with Guinevere.

"I should never have taught Talwyn and Creirwy to fight," Lancelot choked. "They died fighting for Guinevere."

"Why should you not have taught them?" Ninian asked, holding her tightly. "What would they have done otherwise? Creirwy might have been raped many times, and Talwyn might have been forced into a marriage she did not want and died in childbed. How can you know? Was it worse for them to die fighting?"

Lancelot would not be comforted so easily. "How do you know? Perhaps they would have had a good old age like you." She pulled away and looked at the beloved many-wrinkled face.

"Perhaps they would."

"And I am responsible that they did not."

"You do not ask whether you should have taught the young warriors to fight," Ninian reminded her.

"Perhaps not them either. My own students wanted Guinevere to be burned. I trained the men who tried to kill Guinevere. I killed some of my students." Her words choked at the memory. During the fight, she had not minded killing them, but now their deaths made her heart ache. Gawaine had said that Camlach and Cildydd were not really his sons, but what if they were? Perhaps she had killed more of Gawaine's flesh and blood. She staggered, clutching at Ninian's arm so she would not fall. "Why did I ever take up a sword? And why have I not perished by it?" Her voice faded into despair.

"You took up the sword to help women like your mother. You have done what you could. None of us can do more." Ninian embraced and patted her.

A brown-eyed nun appeared and put her arms around Guinevere.

"Oh, my childhood friend! It is so good to see you, Sister Valeria," exclaimed Guinevere. Then she moaned. "Do you know how many lives have been lost because of me? Even the life of a girl I raised as a daughter."

"No more will be lost defending you," Valeria said gently. "Your years out in the world have ended, and now you can rest and learn. Those who cared about you would have been glad that you could."

"Thank you, my friend." Guinevere rested her head on the nun's shoulder.

Then Sister Branwen came and embraced Lancelot and met Guinevere, and Maire the housekeeper told them that she had prepared rooms for them.

Lancelot realized that she had many friends in this place.

For that night and many others, Guinevere and Anna who had been Lancelot just lay in each other's arms and wept over the young women. When Guinevere woke up screaming "Talwyn!" Anna held her.

After a restless night, during which he had wakened only to drink himself back to sleep, Gawaine staggered to the great hall to break his fast.

Far fewer warriors than usual were partaking of the food.

Arthur approached him.

"Mordred went off in the night and took many of the younger warriors with him." The king's face was red with anger. "I shall declare all of them traitors."

Gawaine looked at him wearily. "He plans to fight you, then."

"Let him try!" Arthur stiffened, as if preparing for war.

Gawaine had never been less eager to fight for Arthur, but he reckoned he would.

Morgan stormed into the Abbess Perpetua's office. She wore a gown of the finest black stuff, far different from the abbess's black robes. Her entrance was so dramatic that the striped cat at the abbess's feet jumped up, though Perpetua maintained her dignity. How dare she be so calm? It mocked the tumult in Morgan's chest.

"Lancelot will be staying here?" demanded Morgan. "Then I must leave. How can I stay under the same roof as the one who betrayed my poor daughter and thus caused her death?"

The abbess sighed. "Dear Morgan, Lancelot has helped some of our sisters and she has come here in need. I cannot turn her away."

"Indeed." Morgan trembled with anger. Were their years of friendship nothing? Was it ever possible to trust a Christian? "You will kindly see that a novice brings food to my room, for I shall not leave it while Lancelot is here. I shall soon return to Tintagel. Do not tell them that I am here, for I have no wish to insult Guinevere. How dare Arthur try to kill her? I never thought he would sink so low."

"As you wish," the abbess replied, majestic as ever.

Morgan swept out of the room.

Talwyn woke in considerable pain, surprised at being alive and not entirely pleased. She was in Guinevere's bed. Strangely, the room looked the same as ever. The wall hangings, the scrolls. But the room felt as if its spirit was gone. Guinevere's cat hopped onto the bed, looked disappointed that Talwyn was not the queen, and mewed.

Gawaine entered the room and came to her bedside. "I'm glad that you are alive. You're a brave girl. Guinevere is safe. Lancelot rescued her."

Talwyn sighed with relief. "Thank God and the Holy Virgin."

The large warrior's face was solemn. "I must tell you that your father died," he said in a voice much softer than his normal one.

"I saw that." Talwyn groaned and turned her face to the wall.

"Gryffyd was a brave man," Gawaine continued. "And almost the only man sane enough to know that Guinevere had to be saved." He patted her hand.

"I don't much care whether I die, too," Talwyn mumbled. Who was there to care about her now?

"I hope that you will care," Gawaine responded. "When I was away in Gwynedd, I saw Galahad, and he loves you very much, as Lancelot does Guinevere. Will that comfort you a little?"

Tears streaming down her cheeks, she turned to Gawaine. False hopes would be unbearable. "I can never laugh again. Will Galahad love me if I can't?"

He smiled and the red beard on his chin bobbed. His blue eyes looked so kind. "You may be surprised. People can go through a great deal and still laugh."

He was wrong. That was just one of the things old people said.

He left, and Talwyn buried herself in her covers and wished she was buried in the earth.

Luned brought her a posset to drink. When Talwyn turned away from it, the serving woman said, "I have news that should cheer you more than this drink. Creirwy, like you, survived the battle. My husband took her to Fencha, who will care for her."

Talwyn wept tears of relief. "Thank you," she said. She might never see Creirwy again, but she would always admire the brave girl who had served Guinevere so well.

Gaheris cornered Gawaine while he was putting on his boots and challenged him. "I can't bear it that you did not love our brothers. Not even Gareth." His voice broke. "All you care about is Lancelot. If you don't take some action against Lancelot to avenge our brothers' deaths, I might as well go off and join Mordred. At least he was willing to punish the woman who killed them. Won't you do anything?"

Gawaine's heart filled with pity at the sight of Gaheris's distress. "It was Mordred's fault that they died. But if it will ease your grief, I shall do something." He had no wish to lose his last brother. Perhaps something less than a fight would satisfy Gaheris. Gawaine guessed that Lancelot might be at the convent she and Galahad had told him about, with the old nun who Lancelot had said would heal her if need be.

He was not just thinking of Gaheris. He wanted to see Lancelot again, if he could do so without endangering her, to let her know that he had tried to save Guinevere. She must not think that he had supported Arthur's brutality.

Anna walked slowly in the black robes of a nun. As she left the refectory, the sister porter brought her a sealed vellum message.

Who could know that she was in the convent? Anna wondered. She saw Gawaine's familiar hawk seal, heaved a sigh of relief, and broke it.

Noble Black Warrior,
The Red Warrior challenges you, at the request of his brother, Gaheris, to avenge the deaths of Gareth and Agravaine in a duel. I hope that you will choose gwyddbwyll pieces as your weapon. Meet me at the clearing in the forest ten miles from Camelot, at midday the day after tomorrow.
> *Gawaine ap Lot of Lothian and Orkney*

She nearly fell over. She had thought that no more blows could wound her, but she had been wrong. Gawaine wanted to fight her. She couldn't bear to look at the letter a second time.

Guinevere, also black-garbed, approached her. "You look ill. What is the matter? Who has guessed that we are here?" she asked anxiously.

"Gawaine is challenging me to a fight." Anna's voice was hollow--hollow as her chest felt.

Guinevere gasped. "Don't go. It won't be a fair fight. It must be a trap."

Anna flared up. Would Guinevere's animosity toward Gawaine never end? "Gawaine would never trap me. I must go."

Guinevere took hold of Anna's arm. "But he might kill you. You don't have to give him a chance. You didn't kill Gareth, and you had to kill Agravaine."

"He won't know that unless I tell him," Anna explained. But would he believe her?

Guinevere's tone was placating, but her grip on Anna's arm tightened. "But who knows what other men may follow him and try to do you harm, even if he does not?"

Anna shook her head. "I have to go, explain what happened, and tell him how sorry I am about their deaths."

"I should think you would have had enough of fighting," Guinevere sighed.

"I have," she said solemnly. "But I cannot fail to go if my friend requests it."

Anna avoided looking into Guinevere's eyes. She had no chain mail now, and she needed none. If Gawaine insisted on fighting, she would quickly let him win. If one of them had to die, it would not be Gawaine. Her only regret would be leaving Guinevere to live on alone.

Gawaine told Gaheris that he would leave Camelot early in the morning, but actually he left the night before, taking with him Bedwyr and Peredur as witnesses--and to help if there was trouble if any warriors followed them.

They arrived at the clearing in the woods and waited among the oak trees, where crows cawed at them. He wanted to fade into the trees and never return to Camelot. The time for quests had passed, and he was sorry for it.

Lancelot appeared among the trees. Her hair had turned entirely gray. She wore her old tunic and breeches.

She bowed to them, and they bowed in return. Her face was pale and there were dark circles under her eyes, as if she had not slept since rescuing Guinevere.

Seeing her so worn-looking pained him like a cut in a sword fight.

"I regret the deaths of Gareth and Agravaine," she said in a mournful tone. "I am sorry that you have had this terrible grief. But I did not kill Gareth, and I cannot fight you, for you have been my friend." Her voice choked on the last words.

"Fight you? Never! Not even if you had killed all of my brothers, if they attacked you," Gawaine cried, stretching out his arms as if to embrace her. His heart lightened at the thought that she had not killed Gareth. "I said that we should only have a match at gwyddbwyll. I used the names Black Warrior and Red Warrior, thinking you would understand that meant a game."

"Oh!" She shook as if she might fall, but she did not move closer. "I barely glanced at the letter. How good you are," she choked. She seemed to be on the verge of tears. "I did kill Camlach and Cildydd."

He nodded. "They tried to prevent you from saving Guinevere." Surely she would not want to weep--not in front of Bedwyr and Peredur.

"I challenge you to a board game," Gawaine said, trying to make his voice light and easy.

"I accept the challenge."

Some of the pain in her face faded away.

"I also have brought you chain mail, a helmet, a shield, and a spear because I thought you might have need of them. Your own were stolen, but I did the best I could." It was not necessary to tell her that men had wrecked her house and pissed on her clothing. He unloaded the things from his horse, and Lancelot loaded them onto hers.

"Many thanks. You are so kind," she said.

He brought his gwyddbwyll board forth from his saddlebag. "This will be a fierce but honorable battle, noble Black Warrior."

"Thank you, noble Red Warrior." Her voice was calmer now. "You might as well call me the Gray Warrior now." Only her eyebrows were still black.

He tried to grin. It was good that she could attempt a jest. He thought she still looked just as handsome with gray hair, but he did not say so.

They sat on stones and Gawaine spread the board on another stone. He put out the pieces, taking the red for himself, and Lancelot immediately took hold of the black queen.

"I would never have let Arthur kill the queen," Gawaine told her. "I would have done anything, even fought with him, to prevent it. Bors and I planned to save her. No doubt she has told you that Cai took the place of the executioner." He gave an inquiring look, as if asking whether she believed him, and she nodded.

"Cai told Guinevere that you opposed burning her." Lancelot's voice and hand shook as she said the word "burning." "Was he badly hurt?"

"By good fortune, he will recover. Even lying in his sickbed, he already jests about it, saying that no one at Camelot knows how to cook unless he supervises them. Gods, of course I tried to keep Guinevere from burning. How could I do otherwise?" Thank all the gods, Lancelot believed him.

"I'm grateful that you did that instead of looking for me." She smiled, although her smile was weary.

"I knew that was what you would want." He returned the smile. "Yet it frightened me greatly to hear that you had a spell of madness. You must fight the madness, even when terrible things happen. If I die someday and you go mad, my shade will never be at rest," he warned her.

She shuddered at the thought of his shade suffering and wandering.

The game proceeded. She soon captured two of his pieces.

"Actually, one red warrior struck the other," she told him.

Gawaine stared at her. "You mean that Agravaine killed Gareth?"

She nodded. "Gareth seemed maddened at seeing I was a woman. He must have thought I was a witch. He attacked me, but when Agravaine wounded me, Gareth turned to protect me, and Agravaine killed him by accident. Then I killed Agravaine, to defend myself and Guinevere. I remember it all now, but at the time, I lost my head and feared I had killed you."

"Great Daghdha's cauldron! How dare Gaheris and Mordred blame you for both deaths!" he yelled, almost knocking over the board game. How could his own brother have told such a terrible lie about their brothers' deaths?

"It all happened so quickly, and the room was dark. Gaheris may not have realized what happened. It happened because of me. I'm sorry," she said in a sorrowful voice, her large, brown eyes full of woe.

"Gaheris wants me to kill you," he growled.

"He's just grieving," she said soothingly. "Let's play the game."

"Yes. Gaheris might follow me. We may not have much time." Gawaine tried to lower his voice because he was not angry at her. He remembered that he had something else he wanted to tell her, although it was difficult in front of Bedwyr and Peredur, who certainly must be listening closely, especially after hearing that Agravaine had killed Gareth.

Gawaine picked up one of his game pieces. "This warrior has a fine daughter," he said, but he did not proceed with a bawdy story as might have at some other time.

She smiled. "I'm glad to hear that." She seemed to guess his meaning.

He had less pleasant news. Grimacing, he told her, "I'm sorry to say that some warriors beat Catwal because they were angry at you. He was sorely hurt."

"Not Catwal!" Lancelot groaned, putting her hands to her head. "Why must he suffer for what I have done? Guinevere says the serving people are always unjustly punished for our transgressions, and she is right."

Perhaps he should let her know how dangerous her situation was even if he didn't tell her about the pissing. "Many men are angry at you . . . "

Lancelot sighed. Her brow furrowed. "Gawaine, I know what men want to do to me. I have always known what they would do if they found out."

"Why don't you go to the coast and sail to Orkney? You'll be safe there. I'll let mother know that you didn't kill Gareth." He tried to speak in a voice that was too low for Bedwyr and Peredur to hear. "I'll follow you later." He surprised himself. He hadn't planned to say that he would go.

Her eyes widened with amazement. "Go to Orkney? No, I have no thought of doing such a thing. I'll never leave Guinevere."

"Of course not," Gawaine agreed. "She should go there, too. She would be safe. My mother and I would give her every honor and comfort for the rest of her life."

Lancelot shook her head. "Guinevere would never consent to live under your protection. She wants to stay in the convent, so that is what we will do."

Gawaine gasped. "You won't let her bury you in a convent?"

Lancelot looked him in the eye. "I shall go or stay wherever Guinevere chooses, now and always," she said gently but firmly.

He looked away. "Very well." Of course she would. He must have been mad to suggest otherwise. But surely Guinevere would come to her senses and realize that Lancelot couldn't be so confined.

Then Gaheris rode wildly into the clearing. He threw himself off his horse. "What are you doing? Why aren't you fighting?" he yelled at Gawaine.

"We are battling at gwyddbwyll," Gawaine said, casting a bitter look at him.

"You can't avenge our brothers with a board game!" Gaheris shrieked.

"I can. Just watch me." Gawaine's voice was full of contempt. He had no intention of saying what he had learned. Let Gaheris stew.

"It's indecent!" cried Gaheris. "If she loses, she must forfeit her life," he demanded. Bedwyr and Peredur took hold of his arms and bade him be silent.

"If you were playing gwyddbwyll for your life, you might better have sent Guinevere, who would always defeat me," Gawaine said.

"Yes," Lancelot said, "she would."

"We had best play hastily. Gaheris might have told others to follow him. It's your move, noble Black Warrior."

They played as quickly as the game possibly could be, and then the Black Warrior won.

"The black queen has vanquished the red king," said Gawaine, smiling. "How appropriate!"

"You helped her make it come out that way!" Gaheris yelled.

Of course that was true. It had taken all of their combined but limited skill at gwyddbwyll to make Lancelot win, and in that manner.

Gawaine was slow to pick up the gwyddbwyll set. It was hard to say a proper farewell in front of the other men.

"The red and the black squares in this game board cannot be severed, and neither can the friendship of the Black Warrior and the Red Warrior," he said.

Lancelot stared at the gwyddbwyll set. "Stay away from Mordred," she said in a voice that was not like her own.

"I'll stay away when he's in hell. He's trying to seize the throne from Arthur. I'm going to kill him," Gawaine almost shouted.

He began to put away the game pieces.

Her face paling, Lancelot vaulted onto Raven. "Farewell, friend," was all that she said.

Gawaine was about to reply when Gaheris tore away from Bedwyr and Peredur and grabbed his shoulder.

"You aren't going to let her get away, are you?" His eyes were frenzied, like those of a wounded animal.

"Stop this shit," complained Gawaine, trying to shake him off.

"Won't you fight her? Not even an exchange of blows?" Gaheris begged, clinging to him. His voice sounded as if he was in pain.

"No, I won't. She defeated me at the game, and that's more than enough, when she didn't even kill Gareth. Agravaine did.

Didn't you see what happened clearly, or did you lie to me? Did you try to persuade me to kill my best friend for no reason?" He shook off Gaheris and turned to say farewell, but the Black Warrior had disappeared into the trees. His heart sank.

"I saw her kill them! She was mad! Do you believe that crazy bitch's word over mine?" Gaheris protested, gesturing wildly with his arms.

"Indeed I do," Gawaine said coldly.

"Then I'm going to join Mordred." Gaheris turned abruptly away from him.

"Can you be such a fool as that?" Gawaine asked. "He's the one who is responsible for our brothers' deaths. Don't go."

But Gaheris mounted his horse and rode away.

Gawaine didn't have the heart to ride after him. He had lost his best friend--he might never see her again--so why not his last brother, too? He felt hollow, as if he had nothing left.

He knew where Lancelot was, but he could not send to see her again, for every communication with her could endanger her, make it more likely that those who wished her ill could find her. He had been worse than a fool to have risked seeing her. Such a risk must not be repeated.

Lancelot rode off, reeling. When Gawaine was gathering up the game pieces, she had seen blood welling up out of the gameboard's red squares, and the red warriors had been covered with gore. Fearing that Gawaine would die, she trembled. No, this must be a sign of returning madness, and so must her babbling about Mordred. Perhaps it was well that she would be shut up in a convent. She had to depart in haste so Gawaine would not see her confusion.

She felt bitterly alone at the thought of her friends riding back to Camelot without her. Indeed, she doubted that Bedwyr and Peredur were still her friends, for they had neither looked at her kindly nor spoken to her.

So had she always been alone, she told herself, and she had been foolish to believe otherwise. She was alone except for Guinevere. But wonderful as it was to have a great love, she wanted other friends, too.

Feeling wretched, she returned to the convent, where the Abbess Perpetua greeted her with open arms. Ninian laughed at the story of the gwyddbwyll game and chided her for imagining that Gawaine had wanted to fight her. Branwen smiled at her, and Maire had kept her dinner warm. And Guinevere was there.

Gawaine silently rode back through the forest. Never had a ride been sadder. He longed for the night, when he could shed the tears that welled up behind his eyes.

"I hope we'll never have to see Lancelot again," Bedwyr said. He pronounced her name with derision.

"Doubtless she'll return to her lands in Lesser Britain," Peredur said, no trace of sorrow in his voice. "I came only to prevent bloodshed. I have no wish that men should harm her, but I regret that she ever came to Camelot."

Gawaine almost fell from his horse. He suddenly realized that Bedwyr and Peredur had spoken not one word to Lancelot, and she had spoken not one word to them. Now he saw from their grim faces that they were disgusted that Lancelot was a woman--and, no doubt, that she had defeated them so many times in fighting contests.

"If she had never come to Camelot, all of us would have been long since dead, and so would Arthur," Gawaine retorted.

Bedwyr snorted. "If you wish to make a show of your own dishonor, so be it, but you will find that other men do not want to be reminded of theirs."

So it was dishonorable to have one's life saved by Lancelot! Gawaine's heart felt even heavier than it had before. He would have remonstrated further with them, but he knew that would not help. They would only believe--they probably believed already--that Lancelot was his mistress, and denials would be worse than useless.

Poor Lance! How could she bear to lose so much? And how could she endure living shut up in a convent? He hoped that Peredur's speculation that she would leave for her lands in Lesser Britain was correct.

When they returned to Camelot, several warriors ran up to them. "Did you fight Lancelot?" they asked Gawaine. "Gaheris told us you would."

"He slaughtered me at gwyddbwyll," he told them, silently cursing Gaheris for telling them that he was going to meet Lancelot. He would not admit to anyone but Arthur and Bors that Lancelot was a woman.

"Gwyddbwyll? You played a game with your brothers' killer? Didn't you want to fight a woman?" warriors clamored.

"Lancelot is not a woman, and he didn't kill Gareth," Gawaine said. "That's why I didn't fight him. Agravaine was trying to kill Lancelot, and slew Gareth instead."

No one appeared to believe him, though, except Bedwyr, Peredur, and Bors.

Gawaine cursed himself because the tale that he had played gwyddbwyll with Lancelot instead of fighting would only confirm the warriors' belief that Lancelot was a woman.

Alone in his room, he was too dispirited even to drink. He put Gareth's cloak on the chair where the young man used to sit.

When I was young, Gawaine thought, I wanted to be glorious, the most renowned warrior in the world. Then all too soon, I wanted only not to be a brute. Now I can no longer bear to be a man. Oh gods who have made me a man, if I am reborn, let me be a simple beast again, for they know fear, pain, and death, but not so many kinds of suffering. But are they so simple? A dog may break its heart when his master dies. There may be no way to keep a heart from breaking.

Mordred's warriors were gathered at a caer that was not many days' journey from Camelot. Mordred paced about the hill fort, which belonged to one of his followers, scarcely able to keep still. His passions were so fired that he had no need of wine.

His father had struck him publicly. His father must die. Mordred had done everything in his power to make himself a worthy son, had learned fighting skills and languages, had distinguished himself in fighting contests and in diplomacy with the Saxons, but nothing he did was good enough. He had unmasked those who betrayed his father, but his father cared more about the traitor Lancelot than about Mordred. King Arthur would pay for his indifference. Mordred would slay him. No one else could do the deed. Then he would take everything Arthur had. Camelot would be his own caer, and all the land would be his. The land needed a strong king, not an old, weak one who would let women make a fool of him.

He must not think of Guinevere.

She had scorned him, had failed to recognize his greatness. It was weak to care what a woman thought. She didn't matter.

Some warriors who had left the king to join him were balking, but Mordred found answers for them all, each according to his temperament. He sat by the fire in the caer's great hall, and the men came to him one by one.

"Can I really fight against King Arthur, whom I have sworn to serve?" Colles, the son of Arthur's former mistress, Gwyl, asked. He was pretty, like his mother, but dull. His usually blank face frowned with the effort of trying to think. "Are we all sinning by breaking our oaths to him?"

"Sinning? By leaving a man who raped his own sister?" Mordred replied in scandalized tones. "Rather, you are being pious and uprooting evil."

"Did he rape her? I never heard that. I thought she was an evil witch," Colles said dubiously, his eyes narrowing.

"She is, but who do you think made her evil? She's my own mother, and I know." Mordred patted him on the shoulder. These thoughts were too heavy for Colles's small brain. "And he abandoned your mother, didn't he?"

"He did," Colles admitted.

"And so you have a grievance against him, as I do for my mother," Mordred told him.

The young man went away nodding with satisfaction.

A little later Clegis came to the hall and said, "I admire Gawaine, and don't want to fight on the other side."

"Gawaine?" Why admire a man who clings so sentimentally to Arthur, though he could perhaps have snatched the throne himself? Mordred shook his head. "Didn't you know that he killed his own mother? How can you follow a man like that?"

"Killed his mother!" exclaimed young Clegis, staggering back. "I never even heard that the queen of Lothian was dead."

"News takes long to travel from Lothian," Mordred replied. "Especially when the messengers are killed."

"Why would he kill her? I thought he loved her dearly. Everyone says so."

"Exactly," said Mordred, sighing piously. "And he was jealous of her shameless doings with other men."

"What vile stories about the clan of Lothian. I have always respected them particularly," Clegis said. He began to turn as if ready to leave for Camelot.

Mordred touched his arm to restrain him. "You could hardly respect and love them more than I do." He spoke as if wounded and looked sadly into Clegis's eyes. "I am one of them. She was my mother, whom King Arthur deceived and wronged."

"His aunt? I thought it was his sister."

"It was both of them." Mordred sighed. "I am her youngest son. So Gawaine is my brother, and I know of what I speak. So were poor Gareth and Agravaine, who were murdered by the witch Lancelot." Mordred wiped his eyes.

"Are they truly your brothers? Then your grievance is great." Clegis clasped Mordred's arm and made no more show of leaving.

"I don't believe those tales about Gawaine killing his mother," said young Blioberis, who came to see Mordred later in the day. He was a little shrewder than the others, and his eyes scrutinized Mordred's face. "He is a great fighter, and it seems to me a good man also."

"Oh, he was the best." Mordred moaned. "Alas, poor Gawaine. Lancelot killed him in a duel, didn't you hear? If you want to avenge him, you should fight on my side, as Gaheris is."

"Lancelot killed Gawaine? How terrible!" Blioberis shuddered.

"What can you expect from a creature like that? She must hate all men. She has bewitched the king, and we must defeat him. I need your help." Mordred clasped his hand.

Still another young warrior, Gillimer, arrived later. Indeed, he usually rose late because he always managed to bed some wench before the night was through. "I heard that Lancelot killed Gawaine in a duel. I can't believe they'd fight each other. If he knew she was a woman, Gawaine wouldn't have fought her."

Mordred nodded. "Of course he wouldn't have. The bitch stabbed him to death in bed while he was sleeping."

Gillimer gasped, believing him.

Mordred did not confine his attentions to the men around him. He needed allies with warbands of their own. He sent messages to all of the lesser kings who might be discontented, especially Maelgon of Gwynedd, who was angry because Gawaine had helped his daughter elope. He needed the older man, who had the experience of battle that he lacked. Most of the warriors who had come with him had seen no more of battle than he had, but they were eager to prove themselves.

Nor did Mordred neglect the Saxons. He had forged friendships among their leaders, and now these might be put to use. He promised them more land, for they always wanted more.

He made his men practice with their weapons at all hours, and provided them with whores to cheer them.

For Gareth's followers, he secured a chaplain.

Although he was preparing for battle, Mordred found the time to ride to Londinium.

In a restored villa there, he entered the atrium of a woman who dressed in the style of a court lady except for a veil that covered her neck. He was not fooled.

"My lady." Mordred managed to keep almost all of the irony out of his voice.

"I have nothing to say to you, Lord Mordred," Gwynhwyfach said with a dignity that he found ludicrous. "Kindly leave."

"What, no gratitude for bringing you to the king? I'm the cause of all your good fortune and this fine house." He gestured around as if it were his. Can't expect gratitude from a whore. Her taste was good for a whore, though, he thought as he looked at the hangings on the wall.

"No gratitude. None." Her voice, as she said the word "gratitude," was even more ironic than his.

"Ah, how soon benefactors are forgotten, Lady Guinevere." He shook his head as if he were greatly disappointed.

"Don't call me Guinevere. Pray, leave."

"Such formality. You'd think I'd never touched you." He leered at her to indicate that he remembered her body well. "But I'm glad to see that you've acquired a little dignity, because you are Guinevere, or close enough for my purposes. Guinevere has run off with Lancelot, and you can be my queen. People will believe that you are Guinevere, or they'll pretend to. I'll defeat Arthur soon, and you can laugh at them from the throne. Just what every abandoned mistress dreams of, isn't it, my dear?"

Gwynhwyfach studied him quietly. In reflection, her face more strongly resembled her sister's.

"Very good. You have her look." Mordred gave her a smile of approval. How wise he had been to take the whore to Arthur.

Now that she had been to court, she could do a passable imitation of her sister.

"Indeed I do." Her voice now also resembled Guinevere's more closely. She stood straighter, appearing like her sister somewhat taller than actually she was.

"Lady Guinevere." He inclined his head slightly. "Come with me now. You must be seen with me."

"Of course, Lord Mordred."

They rode from the obscure neighborhood where Gwynhwyfach lived. Some of Mordred's men rode with them.

They came to a stone tower by the river that was guarded by the king's troops.

"Attention!" Mordred yelled at the garrison. "I am your new king. Even Queen Guinevere is with me. My father the king has fallen, killed by traitors. Accept me now, and give me command of the garrison."

The soldiers stared down from the gates and muttered among themselves. Some began to moan or weep at the news of Arthur's death. They evidently had not yet heard about the queen's near execution and escape.

"Let us in!" Gwynhwyfach demanded in Guinevere's voice. "Even now the traitors endanger our lives." She moved her horse to the gate.

They were allowed in, whereupon Gwynhwyfach flung herself off her horse and rushed to the man in the finest armor, the garrison commander.

"Save me! The king lives, and Mordred is the traitor, trying to force me to betray him!"

The soldiers immediately closed ranks around the small, dark-haired woman.

"Bitch!" Mordred yelled at her. "She's not Guinevere! She's just a whore."

"I'll never let you destroy the name of Guinevere," she cried out.

The guards attacked him, and he barely escaped. He never should have trusted a whore.

Arthur and Gawaine had been studying battle plans in the king's room, but Arthur rolled up the scroll and began to speak of other things. "So Maelgon of Gwynedd has joined Mordred. I hear that's your doing, Gawaine. Some foolishness about his daughter. That was very ill done, trifling with the daughter of an important ally."

Arthur knew full well that Keri had married Uwaine, son of Uriens of Rheged, but he and Gawaine had been much less cordial with each other since the morning when Guinevere escaped death.

Gawaine grumbled. "I only helped her escape with the man she had secretly married. The girl had no interest in me."

"I'm surprised that you'd admit that any woman didn't want you." Arthur tried to jest, but did not move his hearer.

"I have learned that not all do." He no longer cared what Arthur thought of him.

The king sighed, looking around the room as if trying to find something he had lost. Summer sunshine made patterns on the floor. "I have heard rumors that you fought a duel with Lancelot. Did you?"

"Of course not." He had not told Arthur about the meeting because he did not trust Arthur's intentions.

"I suspect that you know where Lancelot is." Arthur scrutinized his face.

"Indeed. She's on her way to Orkney, where my mother will give her protection." Gawaine spoke reluctantly, as if being forced to admit the truth.

"Orkney!" Arthur rapped the table with the scroll. "That's unbelievable. If she has sailed anywhere, it's to Lesser Britain, I'm sure of it. You're trying to put me off her track. You're not honest with me anymore."

Gawaine shrugged. "You can decide whether to believe me or not."

The king's forehead wrinkled. "You dare to speak to me like that because fortune is not favoring me. There is no one I can count on. Despite all the good I have done for Britain, I am alone. And I have no wife now."

Gawaine grunted. "No, you do not." And with good reason.

"Therefore, I might marry."

"No doubt the Church would give you some dispensation." He barely concealed his total lack of interest in the subject. Poor woman, whoever she was, to marry a man who had nearly burned his first wife.

Arthur began to smile, but there was no warmth in his face, where the wrinkles were now more pronounced. "I think that I shall marry Talwyn. She's pretty, she's pleasant. She would be a sweet change from Guinevere," he mused.

Gawaine shuddered. "Not Talwyn!"

"Why not?" the king demanded. "You turned her down. Now, hearing that I want her, do you want her after all? That's petty of you." He poured himself some wine, as he had with increasing frequency of late. Since Lancelot had saved Guinevere, Arthur had seldom been without a winecup.

Gawaine shook his head vigorously. "No, no, not for me. The girl's been so fond of Guinevere. She fought to save her. You can't think she'd want to marry the man who nearly killed her."

"Virgin's blood, do you think that Guinevere corrupted her, too?" He pronounced his wife's name like a curse.

"No, no, of course not," Gawaine hastened to say. "No doubt the girl is innocent. But young Galahad loves her. He told me that he means to marry her."

"Indeed." Arthur's tone became cold. He rapped the table with the scroll of battle plans. "Galahad is a young warrior of uncertain parentage--perhaps he was Merlin's bastard, or very likely Merlin just fancied that he was--and no fortune."

"In fact, Galahad is my son," Gawaine declared, letting the pride show in his voice. "He'll have a fine inheritance."

"Your son? And you've never spoken of it until now? I don't believe you. You're just trying to vex me. First you pretend that Lancelot is going to Orkney, and now you claim that Galahad is your son," Arthur said, scowling. "Surely any girl would rather be a queen than be married to a man of lower station. Any woman except my last queen." Ignoring a pup that was wagging its tail and looking up at him with adoring eyes, he imbibed more wine.

"I believe that Talwyn and Galahad have some sort of understanding," Gawaine explained, desperately grasping for an argument that might have some weight, though he feared this one would not. He clenched his fists, but left them by his side and tried to make his tone persuasive.

"You mean he's tumbled her." Arthur gulped down more wine.

"No!" He did not think it wise to suggest that Talwyn might not be a virgin. "She's a good girl. I mean that you should find someone else."

"What do you care?" Suspicion filled his voice and he eyed Gawaine as if he were an enemy. "What's your part in this? Galahad looks nothing like you, acts nothing like you. How could such a skinny, pious youth be your son? When you turned down Talwyn as a wife, did you take her as a mistress instead? That sounds more likely."

Gawaine slammed his fist on the table. "I did no such thing! I care about Galahad. And poor Talwyn's not healed from her wound. Just let her rest."

"What do you think I'm going to do, force her while she's weak? Such tender matters must wait until I've defeated that wretch Mordred." Finally, Arthur consented to pat the begging hound.

You've become a tyrant."

"Only to Guinevere, who much deserved it."

"It started with Guinevere. But it will never end." Gawaine could not look at Arthur any more.

As soon as he could manage to finish his interview with the king, Gawaine made haste to Talwyn's room. That is, Guinevere's room, where Talwyn now was recuperating. It was hard for him to be in that chamber. He could almost see Gareth and Agravaine lying dead on the floor.

He remembered how he had hesitated to kill Arthur, even when Guinevere's life was at stake. Lancelot would have killed Arthur. And Lancelot had killed Agravaine. Gawaine remembered how he had wanted to kill his own father, Lot, when Lot had led his men to rape a town's women. But Gawaine had refrained, and later his mother had killed Lot. Why do I leave the villains for the women to kill? Gawaine wondered. Is it because the men are my own flesh and blood, too close to kill, too close to cast away, too close to me?

Talwyn stirred restlessly in the queen's bed. Her wound ached, and she tried not to think of other, worse pain.

To Talwyn's surprise, Gawaine entered her room. Odder still, his air was almost timid. "Might I speak with you?"

She stared at him vacantly. "Yes, Lord Gawaine." No one could say anything that would interest her. Words were nothing. How strange it was that other people didn't see that. She looked beyond him at the hanging of women picking apples that covered much of a wall, but she barely noticed it.

The tall man shuffled awkwardly, and she tried to turn her attention to him.

"Are you healing?"

"The physician says I am," she replied indifferently. There was nothing to live for.

"You might be better off with Lancelot and Guinevere. Do you want to join them?"

The sound of the familiar names nearly made her choke. "Is it possible?" She had hoped...she had not dared to hope. "Did Lady Guinevere send for me? Do you know where they are?"

Gawaine nodded. "I believe I do. Are you fit to travel?"

She stared off again. Guinevere hadn't sent for her. Guinevere didn't want her. No one wanted her. "It doesn't matter. Nothing matters. You'll tell me what to do, or someone else will."

A wrinkle creased his forehead, but he looked worried rather than angry. "If you stay here the king will." His voice was sharper. "He has spoken of marrying you."

"Marry the king?" Talwyn spat out the words. She lurched forward so quickly that her wound felt torn. She let out a small cry of pain. "He has a queen."

"He had one. He wants another. He has thought of you."

"Queen Talwyn?" she almost shrieked. "Then I'd become Mad Talwyn indeed. I'd jump out of the window first. Where is Galahad? Doesn't he love me after all? Why isn't he here to help me?" Not thinking about modesty though she was wearing only a woolen bedgown, she swung her feet out of the bed.

"As I've said, Galahad does love you." Gawaine's voice softened. "It is better if you go to Lancelot and Guinevere now. They would never let anything happen that you did not want."

"I never want to see the king's face again. Yes, I'll go." She nodded vigorously.

"Will your wound permit you to travel? It would be better to leave as soon as possible," he said, anxiety in his voice.

She didn't know why he cared what happened to her, but she would take advantage of his offer. "I'll leave tomorrow, if you can arrange it. I don't want to stay under the king's roof," Talwyn proclaimed. She felt not a trace of indifference now.

The next morning was rainy, but she did not mind. All she wanted was to be gone from Camelot. She asked Luned to help her put on her chain mail, though its weight sorely hurt her back, because she thought that would disguise her amidst the many warriors--although there were fewer now. She did not want the king to discover that she was leaving and try to detain her.

She carried a pack of her clothes, and a basket in which the queen's cat was concealed. "Go to sleep, there's a good cat," she whispered. After one small mew, the aged cat made no sound.

When Talwyn went to the stables, she found that her horse had not been saddled by a groom. Instead, Gawaine was waiting for her, with her horse ready. Rain dripped from his red beard.

"I hope that you are well enough for this journey." He sounded surprisingly solicitous.

"As well as I'll ever be." She saw a life of hopelessness stretching out before her.

"It should be fairly safe. Mordred's troops are moving in the other direction. I wish I could accompany you, but I'm busy with battle plans. My man, Hywel, will ride with you, in case you become weak. He'll be here in a moment."

"Whatever you say. He can ride with me." She wanted only to be gone.

"Would you mind carrying a message for me?" he asked tentatively, looking at her as if he hardly dared to beg a favor.

"What, do you have a message for Lord Lancelot?" Surely he wouldn't have one for Guinevere.

Gawaine shook his head. "For Lancelot? No, only that I am a friend as always, but surely Lance knows that.

"The message is for someone else." Gawaine sounded almost shy, which amazed her. He did not look into her eyes, but pulled on his beard. "I think that someday you might meet a woman who will tell you that she is my daughter. If you do, please tell her that I loved her and am sorry that I didn't do more for her."

This message caught Talwyn's attention. A secret daughter! Perhaps there were some interesting things in the world after all. "But who is she and how shall I find her?"

Still evading her gaze, Gawaine looked over her horse as if seeing whether it was in shape for the ride. "I don't mean to charge you with looking for her. If no one ever tells you she is my daughter, don't worry. But I think that you may cross her path, and if you do, please tell her."

"Of course. What a strange message."

Then Hywel, who was as short as his master was tall, entered the stable and Gawaine changed his tone. "Do you have everything you need?" Gawaine asked her. "Did you pack your winter things as well as your summer things?"

She nodded again, astonished at his solicitude.

"Hywel, did you see that food was packed for the journey?" Gawaine asked. "We mustn't starve the Lady Talwyn."

"I was planning to starve her, but you stopped me just in time," Hywel grunted. "When have I ever forgotten about food, Lord Gawaine?" He looked out with less than great enthusiasm at the drizzling morning.

Just as Gawaine was helping Talwyn into the saddle, a horse clattered up over the cobblestones to the stable.

The breathless rider opened his visor.

"Lord Gawaine! You're still living!"

Gawaine gave the moon-faced young warrior a cool look. "Alive, indeed, Blioberis. How did the gatekeeper let you in so early? Are you tired of the fare in Mordred's camp? Do you expect the king to bid you well come?"

"Mordred said that Lancelot had killed you. I should have known it was a lie. Mordred is ruthless. I am returned to beg the king's pardon." Blioberis dismounted and bowed his head.

"So you have learned that Mordred lies. And horses have four legs and hens lay eggs. I will not forgive you unless the king does," Gawaine reproached him.

"Mordred's negotiating with the Saxons to join him in rebellion against the king! The king must fight before they come in force to join him!" cried Blioberis, so wild-eyed that he must be telling the truth. "I left because I won't fight beside Saxons."

"Saxons! That rotten whoreson!" Gawaine's face was redder than his beard. He shook his fist.

Talwyn shuddered. Saxons! She had thought her father's idea that the Saxons were still a danger was madness, but perhaps it was not. How many people would they murder?

Gawaine seemed to notice her shivering. "You should be off while you can, Talwyn," he advised. "Go on, and Godspeed."

She nodded and started to ride off. Then, leaving Gawaine's man, she turned her horse back to Gawaine, who was walking away from the stable. Remembering that he was going to war, she wanted to say a better farewell.

"Everyone loves you, Lord Gawaine," she told him.

"Thank you, Talwyn. That was very kind." He smiled for the first time that day.

"What a nice, fatherly man Lord Gawaine is," Talwyn said to his man as they rode down the hill.

Hywel lifted his eyebrows but made no reply.

Anna tried to enjoy the smell of the convent garden's white roses. They were so full they almost fell off their stems. She told herself, I am Anna. I am sitting in a garden, not riding through the forest. I must seem to be at least a little content because Guinevere is sitting beside me. She's alive, and nothing else should matter.

Anna longed to saddle her horse and ride away from the convent. She longed for people to stop calling her Anna.

Guinevere held her hand. Anna tried to concentrate on her lover's hand and stop remembering striking down her students and thinking of Talwyn's and Creiry's deaths.

The sister porter entered the garden. "There's a warrior to see you, Anna," the nun said.

"A warrior! Will I be called to fight? Dare I see him without my chain mail?" She looked down at her black robes, where her sword was hidden, and touched it. She wasn't sure whether she was frightened at the thought of a fight, or relieved.

"No fighting!" Guinevere exclaimed. "Has Arthur found us?"

"I don't think this one will want to fight," the nun said. "He looks as if he has been wounded recently."

Anna strode to the convent's massive door. She had not yet learned to walk in nun-like footsteps, and she didn't much want to. She couldn't allow the porter to let the warrior in until they knew who he was. Guinevere followed her.

There stood Talwyn, pale and leaning on the doorframe. She was thinner than she had been, and her eyes had lost their familiar luster.

"Talwyn!" Anna and Guinevere cried in unison. Guinevere threw her arms around the girl before Anna could do the same. They both held her. Anna felt as if a weight had lifted from her heart.

"We thought you were dead," Guinevere choked, tears streaming from her eyes.

"I'm well," Talwyn said, and collapsed.

They put her in a bed and cared for her. Guinevere refused to leave her side, even to sleep. She sat by the bed and held fast to the sleeping girl's hand.

The sister porter came bearing a mewing gray cat. The cat leapt out of her arms and ran to Guinevere.

"The stablehand said this cat was in a basket on the girl's horse," the nun told her.

"Grayse." Guinevere bent over and stroked the cat, which rubbed her ankles, then jumped in her lap and fell asleep.

Anna watched Guinevere and Talwyn with pleasure.

The next day, Talwyn ate a large bowl of porridge at Guinevere's coaxing.

Anna brought her watered wine.

"Why did you come here when you are so weak?" Guinevere asked the girl. "You should have waited until you were stronger."

Talwyn flushed. "I couldn't wait. The king wanted to marry me, but Gawaine saved me. I hate the king now."

"Marry you!" Guinevere gasped. She clasped both of Talwyn's hands. "How vile!" She shook with rage.

"King Arthur is a far worse man than I ever imagined, but I'm glad Gawaine saved you," Anna said, trying to smother her regrets that she might never see him again.

"Gawaine is a good man," Talwyn said, smiling.

"Yes, I suppose he is," Guinevere admitted.

Anna sighed with relief at finally hearing those words.

After her initial rage, Guinevere slumped in her chair. "Thank God and the Virgin that you are safe," she said. "If only Creirwy had lived, too."

"She did." Talwyn almost smiled. "Luned told me that Cathbad took her to Fencha."

Anna wept with joy, and held Guinevere, who did also.

Then Anna finally persuaded Guinevere to go off to her room and sleep. Anna took her chair beside Talwyn.

Fidgeting with the covers, Talwyn told Anna, "Mordred's fighting to overthrow the king. He's bringing Saxons with him." She shivered at the word "Saxons."

Anna exclaimed with horror and closed her eyes. Not war with the Saxons again!

"I don't like the king any more," Talwyn said, "but I hope Mordred doesn't win. They say the Saxons are brutal when they fight. What if they burn the countryside again?" Her voice faltered. "Is it true that they rape and kill all the women?"

A strangled sound came out of Anna's mouth. She turned her face away, and looked out of the window, at the peaceful scene of black-robed nuns walking in the garden. She had heard of Saxons attacking convents and raping all of the nuns.

She knew all too well that the British also had raped Saxon women, that British men raped British women, and so forth, but the thought of the Saxons was too much for her. "Mordred would bring the Saxons down on us?"

"I can fight if I have to." Talwyn tried to rise from the bed.

"No, dear, never again," Anna said, quieting her own demons for the moment and taking Talwyn's hand. "Rest and all will be well."

When Talwyn dozed off, Anna sat on the bare convent chair and wondered whether she could fight for the king who had nearly burned the woman she loved. But how could she not?

Sister Branwen came to take a turn sitting by Talwyn, and Anna went pacing through the passageways.

Thinking that Guinevere never would understand, Anna wrote a letter begging to be forgiven, took her sword and the chain mail that Gawaine had given her, and left while her lover still slept.

28 THE DEATH OF ARTHUR

Percy rode up breathlessly to his family's villa and could not help noticing that it looked shabby now that he had lived at Camelot, though his father had repaired a wall that had been tumbling down. His mother, father, and brother all rushed to greet him. All of them were grimy from working in the garden like peasants, he noted with dismay. His mother Olwen's brown braid was nearly undone. None of them wore clothes as fine as those at Camelot.

"I've been away looking for the Holy Grail, but now I've heard there's a war on. I'm going off to fight for King Arthur. Mordred, a warrior of the round table who claims to be the king's son, is attacking him with a band of rebellious warriors," Percy exclaimed, his words running together. "Will you come to fight for the king?" he asked his brother and his father. Surely such important news would bestir them.

Indeed, they all turned most gratifyingly pale.

"Why, I've never even learned to fight, except a few lessons from father. Of course I won't," said his brother, Illtud.

Percy tried not to show his disgust. "But you know how to fight," he said to his father, Aglovale, whose beard was now mostly gray.

"And I also know how not to fight," his father replied, brushing his dirty hands across his old brown breeches. "I have shed enough blood for Arthur."

"Were you wounded in the Saxon War?" Percy asked. "You never tell about it. Everyone but you tells war stories."

Aglovale grimaced. "I don't want to keep living in it. Stay home with us, son. You don't know how horrible it would be killing the other warriors you know."

"Stay home! Then I'd be less than a man," Percy replied in horror, wondering how his father could speak in such a way without shame.

"Don't you dare say that! You're insulting your father!" said Olwen, clasping Percy's arms as if he were still a little boy. "Won't you have the sense to stay here with us?"

"Won't you tell me to come back with my shield or on it, like the Spartan mothers?" Percy asked, amazed that she was so little impressed with his courage.

"No!" she exclaimed, her gray eyes flashing as if he were a bad boy. "I didn't bear you to die for King Arthur."

He shook her off. "Oh, mother," he sighed. If his father was hopeless, he couldn't expect his mother to be strong.

"Don't be a fool and die before you've had a chance to live," Illtud chimed in.

"There's nothing glorious about killing," their father said. "It's just ugly."

Why couldn't he have a noble-hearted family like other young warriors? Percy didn't have much of a temper, but he reckoned that he would be angry if he did. "Don't any of you understand how important it is to fight for a good king and defeat an evil pretender to the throne?"

Olwen changed her face and her voice so they were all sweetness. "Whatever you say, dear. But before you leave for the battle, you should go and see your old fisher king. He's dying alone."

Percy felt a pang of sorrow, but not enough to cool the fire in his blood to be off and fighting for King Arthur. "But why can't one of you go? I have to go to war. Won't you go see the fisher king for me?" he asked Aglovale.

Aglovale shook his head. "I'm too busy looking after the crops. You'll have to go yourself."

"Busy! But you aren't doing anything as important as fighting Mordred!" Percy's voice was becoming shrill. "Won't you go?" he asked his brother.

"No, he's your fisher king. I don't even know him," his brother said with a dismissive gesture.

"Can't you have compassion for a dying man even if you don't know him?" Percy asked, disgusted. "Surely you have enough compassion to go?" he asked his mother.

"I've never met the old man," Olwen said. "You're the one who'll have to go, or he'll die alone."

"What a family. You don't think of me at all," Percy complained, glowering at them. "I might have had a better farewell than this in almost any other family. For all you know, you'll never see me again. I'll go and see the fisher king first, then I'll go to Camlann field, where Mordred waits." He jumped on his horse and rode off through the woods to the river.

The old man's mud-daub hut was much as it had been years before, if a little more dilapidated. The fine smell of fish permeated the air, particularly in the summer heat. Percival took a last breath, then walked inside.

Strange how the holy caer of gold and silver wore this temporal disguise, he thought. It must be because the old man was the fisher king, who guarded a treasure that was worth far more than any earthly jewels.

When he entered, the old man moaned, "Oh, I'm dying. I'm in so much pain. Nobody ever comes to see me." He looked unwell--just as unwell as he had when Percy had first seen him a decade earlier.

"That's terrible," Percy commiserated. How dreadful to be dying. Well, if he went to battle he soon might be dying himself. "What can I do for you? Do you want some water?"

"That would be nice," the old man said. "The best water comes from the spring two miles away."

"I don't have time to go so far," Percy told him.

A few tears dripped from the old man's eyes.

"Don't weep. I'll do it." Percy picked up the rusty old tin pail, which looked even worse than it had when he was a boy, and hastened to get the water. Strange how the sacred vessel's disguise had aged, he thought. He carried it reverently. Perhaps it was even the grail.

When Percy returned, he gave the old man some water. Then he asked, "Is there anything else you want me to do?"

The old man moaned in heartrending fashion. "Stay with me while I die. I don't want to die alone."

"That would be terrible," Percy agreed. He wanted to ask how long it would be, then thought that would sound selfish and not at all soothing, so he sighed and sat down on the dirt floor next to the bed. No one, whether fisher king or fisherman, should have to die alone.

Guinevere wept on a bench in the convent garden. The abbess sat beside her. Ninian stood nearby.

None of them admired the marigolds or the roses. The abbess sent away a novice who had been gathering hyssop for a tincture for sore throats.

"I can't believe she went to fight for the king who nearly murdered me," Guinevere moaned. "Yes, yes, I know she felt she had to for Britain's sake, and God knows Mordred could not hold all parts of the country together, but I don't care anymore. It's all very well to be a queen and think of such things, but all I want now is for her to live--as Anna, Lancelot, or in any other guise, but only to live."

Guinevere felt that her life was all weeping now. She never used to weep, except when Lancelot went away after their fight and when she had heard that Lancelot was seriously ill. And she had wept bitterly only once when she was young, on the day long ago when she first met Lancelot, who found her sobbing in the forest near Camelot because her husband had asked her to lie with Gawaine to give the kingdom an heir.

Guinevere thought of all the times she had wanted to run away, but she had not told Lancelot because she had thought that if they did the king's men would follow and kill her woman warrior.

What if she had been wrong? Guinevere now wondered. Perhaps they had been destined to run away, and how much suffering they would have been spared if they had run and somehow escaped.

Like a river that has been held back and finally bursts through and escapes its banks, the flood of tears overcame and choked her.

Old Ninian stroked her hair and said, "Your Anna will live."

But she did not look into Guinevere's face. The abbess did, and told her, "If Ninian says she'll live, then it must be so. She rarely ventures to tell us what will happen. If she has seen it, then it is so. Anna will need you, my dear, and young Talwyn surely does, so you must regain your strength for them."

Supported by the nuns on either side, Guinevere gradually let her flood ebb.

When Guinevere was calm enough to see the flowers around her, another woman swept into the walled garden.

"Sister, thank the Goddess you are safe," Morgan said. "I had not thought Arthur would dare to injure you. May I embrace you?"

Stunned at seeing Morgan, white-haired but still beautifully regal, Guinevere rose to meet the embrace of the woman she had so wanted when she was a girl.

"Well met. How came you here?" she asked, noting that Morgan's embrace now meant nothing to her. She wanted none but Anna's.

"Some of the women from Avalon found refuge in this place. I have known Ninian ever since my childhood days of study there," Morgan said, exchanging a glance with the old nun. "I am made welcome here, and am glad that you came to this convent. I hear that your sweetheart has gone back to fight with Arthur. Perhaps you can find another here," she added in an ostensibly friendly tone.

"If she lives, she will return to me," Guinevere replied, trembling now more with anger than with fear. She could scarcely believe that she had once been young enough to long for this woman just because of her beauty and regal manner. Those green eyes were not warm like Anna's brown ones.

Ninian, her face like a mask, said quietly, "Perhaps this time we shall go to seek Anna rather than waiting for her to return. When we hear that the battle has ended, we shall take a barge down the river to bring her back."

"And Arthur?" Morgan asked, as if he were the only one who mattered.

Ninian gave her a strange look. "To be sure, we'll take him on the barge, too," in a tone that said they would never see him alive again.

Morgan winced as if struck and inhaled sharply. "No!" she cried out, but she met Ninian's eyes and apparently saw what she feared to see. Her knees buckled under her and she sank to the ground. The abbess put an arm around her.

Guinevere shuddered at the love and hate that Morgan held for the same man and was glad that the person she loved and the one she hated were different.

The battle had commenced. Gawaine could see the faces of the young warriors riding towards him. They were all too familiar. He positioned his horse to the right of Arthur's to guard him while he could.

He saw no Saxons. Arthur had moved before the Sea Wolves could join Mordred's forces. Very good. But Maelgon and his men had joined the rebellion, and that king rode near Mordred the cur. At least it didn't appear that any other lesser kings were with Mordred.

The day was fair, warm for battle, and the field was filled with meadowsweet and knapweed. Startled goldfinches flew up and away from the thundering riders.

Sweltering in his chain mail, Gawaine charged to meet the enemy, his old students. He had felt a fierce joy at times when he was fighting Saxons, but now his heart was heavy. There was no time for regrets.

Colles charged him, and Gawaine met the charge with all the power in him. Colles's spear shattered on Gawaine's shield, and he knocked the young man off his horse. The charging horses trampled Colles.

Gods, Gawaine didn't want to see what happened to the young warriors.

Gawaine saw that the others were not attacking him directly. They were waiting until noon, when they believed that his strength would fade, he realized, smiling grimly.

He saw Gaheris riding near Mordred. Gawaine ached to kill Mordred, but he was determined to keep his distance from Gaheris. He wanted to end this day without shedding his brother's blood.

The battle wore on. The sun blazed and Gawaine boiled in his own sweat.

At some distance from him, Arthur attacked Maelgon, who had broken his oath to the High King. Maelgon went down quickly.

Gawaine saw that Bors had been unhorsed, and rode towards him to help. Bors had lost his helmet. Gillimer, fine young Gillimer, held a sword over Bors's head and smashed it down, splitting Bors's skull. There was no time for the pious warrior to say a final prayer.

Yelling wildly, Gawaine shoved his spear into Gillimer's side. The young man's body tumbled from his horse, but Gawaine's pity was all for Bors. Tears stung his eyes.

Clegis's horse drew up against his. The young warrior leapt from his horse and landed behind Gawaine. He tried to slash Gawaine's neck with his sword, but Gawaine's elbow smashed into his stomach. Clegis dropped his sword. Gawaine turned and struggled with Clegis, who recovered enough to fight back. They wrestled, and Gawaine felt the young man's strength push against him. Clegis clawed at Gawaine's throat. With a sudden twist of his body, Gawaine knocked Clegis off his horse.

Gawaine's horse Sword, just as angry as he was, stomped on the young warrior, and Gawaine did not stop him, though he ended it quickly. Clegis's once handsome face was destroyed.

Lancelot would be glad they had not taught the young men too much about how a rider might turn on a man who leapt behind him, Gawaine thought, pausing an instant for breath because no warriors crowded around him. And Clegis had doubtless believed that Gawaine would have less strength now that it was after noon.

Like Lancelot, he had killed the men he had taught. The taste of death was in his mouth. There would be no generation to succeed his, it seemed. Except for Galahad and Percy, who thank the gods were not here.

At least he had not killed his brother. He looked around for Gaheris, though he wanted to stay clear of him.

The field was littered with bodies fallen among patches of fragrant meadowsweet and wild mint, whose scent was drowned in the smell of blood. Gawaine rode with Arthur for high ground, to see how many--in truth, how few--warriors still lived. As they rode up to a ridge, they saw Mordred, bending over a body in the muddy ground.

Mordred saw them and called, "Gawaine, your brother's dying. He wants to speak with you."

"Damned Mordred caused his death," Gawaine growled to Arthur, but he pushed his horse to go faster. He thought of the little brother who had tried to follow him everywhere, and forgave him everything.

Gawaine dismounted and went over to his brother.

Mordred stood back to give him space. Gawaine bent over and saw that Gaheris was already dead. He felt a searing pain in his back, and realized that he was killed also. Mother, Lance, Galahad, Galahad, Mother.

"Soft-hearted fool," sneered Mordred, pulling his sword from Gawaine's back.

"Fiend!" Filled with rage, Arthur flung himself off his horse and attacked Mordred.

But the young man had the advantage. After some bitter fighting, he pinned Arthur down on his back, holding him there with a sword through his left arm. Arthur's sword lay on the ground nearby. He gasped with pain.

"Deny paternity now," Mordred jeered. "Yes, I really am your son, but not by the witch. My dam was just some whore you had. She died when I was young. She was a frightened, cringing thing. I scarcely remember her face or her name, and I'm sure you wouldn't. I was raised by panderers, and they taught me all I know. They beat me and raped me and taught me to beat and rape--and kill. They hoped to gain money from me because they knew that I was yours, but I killed them when I was old enough. There was nothing to be gained by saying I was the son of one of the lowest born women you had had, so I thought I might as well say it was the highest born one."

"Holy Cross, what a way to be raised!" Arthur's stomach churned. If he had realized that it was his only son, not a daughter, who was being raised by panderers, he would have spared no effort to find him. "Forgive me, son, and I'll forgive you," he moaned.

"Never." Mordred's voice filled with bitter glee. "Don't waste your pity on me, you'll need it for yourself." He tore the embroidered scabbard from Arthur's body and threw it far. "You've always claimed you won't bleed to death while you wear this. Now you can see that you will. I hate you too much to just kill you outright. I'll cut out your heart, I'll cut off your balls." So intoxicated was he with this talk that he could hardly act on it.

But Arthur was not paralyzed with fear. He knew fighting too well to be without strategies. He whistled, and his horse reared up, about to crush Mordred with its hooves.

Mordred turned in time, pulled his sword out of Arthur's arm, and slashed it into the stallion's stomach. It fell with a cry. But Arthur leapt up, grabbed his sword, and lunged forward to attack his son.

He had the advantage for a few moments, and dealt a blow to Mordred's side. But Mordred managed to pull his sword from the horse's belly and strike a blow to Arthur's chest. Then Mordred collapsed.

Falling to his knees, Arthur looked down and saw that his son was dead. He couldn't bear the sight of Mordred's body, so like his own young self.

The baby boy he had dreamed of had attacked him now. Was there no way to escape fate?

Overwhelmed with pain, Arthur knew that he would die from his wound. He managed to stand and staggered down the hill towards the river until he fell.

Hadn't Mordred been a fine fighter? Hadn't he been brave? But Arthur could not imagine Mordred as a just king. Yet, if he had embraced Mordred, had trained him, could Mordred have learned to be different, to care about the people? If only Mordred had told him his true origins, a more believable story than the one he had devised. But how could Mordred have admitted that his mother had been a whore? If only Mordred were still alive and Arthur could make it up to him. Perhaps, if Mordred had had only a little love, he would have been able to change.

If Morgan had borne him a son, that boy would not have been like Mordred. Morgan. If only he could have kept her beside him. He should have forgiven her for exchanging foolish letters with Guinevere. He longed to see Morgan one more time and tell her he loved her. Tears formed in his eyes.

He grasped his sword and willed it to bring him to Morgan. But he did not move. He muttered enchantments. He begged the sword. He held the sword and called Morgan's name. But the sword's magic failed him. He wept.

Lancelot arrived in chain mail at a field full of corpses. She rode through the sea of bodies, nearly all of whom were warriors she recognized. It seemed that all of the grasses had turned red. There were no Saxon bodies.

Most of them were men she knew. Mostly Arthur's men, though not all had fought for him this time. She saw one dead familiar face after another dead familiar face. There were her students. Who had killed whom? Did it matter?

She could not stop for everyone. She wept when saw the bodies of Peredur and Bedwyr, with their sons beside them, but was relieved that she did not see Percy or Galahad. She hoped they had not fought.

She gasped when she saw Bors with his skull split open. Tears streamed down her cheeks and she made the sign of the cross over him. Two of his sons lay nearby.

Not all of the warriors were dead. Some were moaning in their last agonies. A few saw her and called out to her, but she knew there was little she could do for them, and she was searching for someone in particular.

A half mile further, she saw Gawaine's body, high on a ridge. She rode up and saw that he was slumped over his brother's body. A raven inspected the deep wound in Gawaine's back. Lancelot yelled, and the raven flew off with a bit of meat.

Lancelot turned Gawaine over, knelt by him, closed his eyes, wiped the mud from his face, and howled. She knew not how long she keened.

She closed his visor to keep the ravens and crows from taking his eyes and wrapped his body in her cloak to keep them off a while. She had thought she would not care so much if her body fed the crows, but she did mind if her friends' bodies did. She took off his jeweled rings and golden armrings and put them in her pouch to send to his mother, but one ring she put in the bag that she wore around her neck. She knew that if she did not take the fingerrings human scavengers would cut off his fingers for them.

It only took a moment to close Gaheris's visor also. A bird had already taken one of his eyes.

Nothing was worth this sacrifice, she thought. It no longer seemed important to keep Arthur on the throne or Mordred off it. For the first time she understood that every man of the thousands she had seen die, of the many she had killed, save for some friendless few, had meant this much to his kin. For we each have only a few who, in one way or another, are kin to us, she thought. Even Bellangere--unjust and brutal as he was-- even Bellangere's rage over losing Sangremore she could understand.

She began to sob again.

"Lance! Is that you?"

It was Arthur's voice.

"Lance! Help me! I'm wounded."

Reluctantly, she rose.

Just over the ridge lay Mordred's body. Arthur lay further down, by the riverbank, covered with blood.

She did not want to leave Gawaine's body to go to Arthur.

"Lance! Come!"

Reluctantly, she moved down the slope. She passed Mordred's body and scarcely glanced at it.

Lancelot saw there was a gaping wound in Arthur's side. She had served him for so many years. Surely she should feel something more for him. But he had tried to kill Guinevere. Lancelot felt a wave of revulsion.

Arthur smiled at her. How dare he smile?

He began a halting speech. "Lance. I'm not alone after all."

She froze. "You are dying." She felt--she felt numb. The wound in his side bled terribly. She made no fruitless attempts to bind it.

"Mordred killed me. He was my son, and I would to God that I hadn't killed him. He killed Gawaine, too."

Lancelot moaned. The unfeeling sun shone down on them.

"My son, I killed my son!"

"You tried to murder Guinevere." Lancelot's voice shook with hatred.

"Forgive me for that," Arthur begged.

"I cannot." Lancelot remembered seeing Guinevere tied to the stake, and the flames beginning.

"Please forgive me," Arthur's voice cracked. "I was wrong. Stay with me. You will stay with me until I'm gone?" He trembled with anxiety.

Lancelot paused. "I'll stay." She did not want to look at him or be with him. But perhaps she owed that much to any dying man or woman. "But I must bring Gawaine here so the scavengers do not violate his body."

"Don't leave me, Lance!" Arthur cried.

"I'll be back." She climbed back up the hill. The sight of Gawaine's body crushed her heart.

She caught hold of his shoulders, wrapped in her cloak, and dragged his body, as gently as she could, down near Arthur. Gawaine's shield she left. He would not need it now.

She sighed and sat down on the ground between Gawaine's body and the king.

"My heir is gone," Arthur moaned. "Everything is undone."

"Gawaine was far more than your heir." Lancelot could not keep the anger out of her voice.

"He was a good man. Hold my hand," he said, as if he could still command anyone to do anything.

"No." She pulled back. "I pity you, but do not ask for more."

"I shouldn't have tried to kill Guinevere. I was mad. You know what it is to be mad." He tried to coax her.

"You weren't mad, only angry and cruel." She tried to keep her voice calm since she was speaking to a dying man, but she shook with anger at the thought of Guinevere taken to the stake. "I am sorry that you are dying. I'll stay here so you won't die alone, but that's all I can do for you."

"You'd have done more for Gawaine," he said querulously.

"Gawaine deserved my friendship." She wondered whether she was speaking too harshly to a dying man.

Arthur groaned. "Even you have turned against me. So many deaths, so much bloodshed." His voice became weaker with every word. "I wanted my people to live, and live well. I did not want to see this day."

"I am sorry that you are dying. Perhaps you should think of God now, not of me." His pain touched her in spite of herself.

"There is nothing left for me." He choked, as if there were blood in his throat. "No wife, no son, no kingdom, no warriors. No life. Only this pain."

"Is it very bad?" Her voice softened. She didn't want him to suffer more.

"Yes." Arthur could barely speak. "Help me to end it." His voice faltered and cracked more each time he spoke. "I want to give my sword to the Lady of the Lake--you. Take it, and help me end this pain. It is more than I can bear."

Lancelot shuddered. "No! I cannot do that. I have known you too long."

Arthur groaned. "For God's sake, pity me and let this pain come to an end." The grass around him was steeped in blood. "Take my sword."

Lancelot had so often been afraid that she would be asked to kill Arthur, but she had never imagined that he would be the one to ask. Her voice faltered. "Must I? Then we are both damned."

"No man--or woman--was ever damned for following his king's commands."

"I doubt that," Lancelot said.

"I can't bear to die slowly."

"You would have burned Guinevere. That is a terrible death."

"Please, Lance." Arthur moaned. "Remember that I was a good king."

"For many years, you were," she admitted.

He seemed to her weak and brave, lonely and clinging, striving for dignity and pathetic, desperate and calculating, and entirely human. He looked at her, then shut his eyes.

Lancelot stabbed him through the heart.

She flung the sword that he had prized so much into the river. She sunk to her knees, put her head in her hands, and sobbed.

She felt that Arthur had raped her. How could a dying man rape? She didn't know, but she felt he had. He had guessed that she had wanted to kill him, and he had forced her to do it. She felt defiled, stained with blood that could never be washed away.

If she had been with Gawaine when he was dying--if only she could have said a final farewell and consoled him, but no, it was better that he had died quickly--he would have left her soul innocent. At least as innocent as it had been, which was not very. He would never have left her with horrible images to haunt her.

After some time had passed--she could not have said whether it was a few moments or many--some farmers came by, looking to see what had happened at the battle.

"There lies King Arthur," moaned one of them. "King Arthur is dead!"

Weeping, the men came to see the king.

Lancelot looked up, relieved by their presence. She was able to act the properly grieving warrior. Others cared, many of them would care. She nodded to them. "Yes, our king is dead. Come and say farewell to him." Formality seemed the greatest of blessings. She stood somberly and let them pay their reverence to him.

She had not been able to touch the king's body. She asked one of the men to put gold coins on his eyes, and the man seemed honored.

She opened Gawaine's visor and put coins on his eyes. No one would steal them now. She would guard him until she dropped.

She gave the men coins in payment to bury Bors, Peredur, and Bedwyr, and told them where they lay, about half a mile away, and what armor they wore--if it had not already been stolen. She described their faces and sizes in case it had.

The farmers departed, and she sat with the bodies.

Despite her sorrow over Gawaine, she felt relief that here was someone she could simply mourn without ugly memories.

With Arthur and Gawaine gone, she felt that she truly was no longer Lancelot.

The sound of a pack of curs barking made her wince, because they must be at the bodies. In a way, she almost envied them, because most of her own pack was gone.

She heard the faint sound of a voice. She wanted to believe it was Gawaine's, but she knew that was impossible. The voice came from higher on the ridge. She looked up the slope and saw that one of Mordred's hands moved slightly.

Not hurriedly, she walked up to him. She didn't want to see him or hear his voice.

"Mercy." Mordred's eyes were barely open. His wound bled terribly and his voice was broken. "I was afraid that my father would finish me off if he saw that I was still alive, but I heard your voice and thought that because you're a woman you'd have mercy and save me."

"You're wrong. Your father would have tried to save you, but I won't."

A terrible scream, like nothing she had ever uttered, came out of her mouth, and she plunged her sword into him. She struck again and again, not caring that he was dead. He had killed Gawaine. He had killed Arthur. He had started this whole bloody war and caused all these deaths. He had killed Gawaine. His resemblance to Arthur didn't bother her anymore. She didn't care whether he was Arthur's son.

Finally, she stopped and looked down at Mordred's torn body. She saw what she had done and was horrified at how far her fury had carried her.

Returning to her watch by Gawaine, she slumped onto the ground, too weary even to weep.

"I hate this fighting, I hate it," she sobbed. "Am I going mad? You look like my mother, so helpless. Well, you're both dead." Like the girl she had been, weeping alone in the forest beside her mother's body, again she was left with the dead.

She moaned. "I am so alone."

"Mother! Mother! Mother!" she screamed until her voice was gone.

The river beckoned her. She could wash off the blood. She could plunge in, with chain mail on, and never have to remember her bloody deeds again. Cold, clear, and innocent, the water pulled her, as if she were already caught in its currents.

She remembered lying in the water thinking of dying after Elaine did, and the words "I cannot abandon Guinevere" came back to her. She had abandoned Guinevere once, but she could hold back this time--yet how could Guinevere love such a killer?

Then the river seemed to turn red, and Lancelot thought that she had caused it. The blood of everyone she had ever killed was in that river. It seemed to her that not saving was the same as killing, and that, like her mother and Elaine, Gawaine, Bors, and the other warriors were dead because she had not saved them. And she saw everyone she had ever failed to save, and Saxons' children who had starved because their fathers were gone, and every hungry woman, man, and child whom she had not fed, and Gareth, who had so much wanted to do good. And the girl she had accidentally killed in the Saxon War.

Gawaine had said that if she went mad at his death, his shade would never rest. Surely if she took her own life, that also would keep his shade unquiet.

She looked back at the river and it was water again, not blood.

"Mother, mother, mother," she choked with the cracked whisper that remained of her voice.

The crows came down to the field, and she did not welcome them. She was busy keeping them off.

Her mare, Raven, stood nearby, a little nervous at all of the bodies. Lancelot pulled herself together enough to pat Raven and be glad she had not been driven off by scavenging men like the many abandoned horses. She realized that Gawaine's horse was gone, and hoped it had run free.

A mist settled over the river, leaving her in a world outside of time, sealed off with the dead.

29 AFTER THE BATTLE

Guinevere, Ninian, and Morgan were poled down the river on a barge.

The searchers made many false starts, approaching the mist-covered bank and looking for Anna, only to find corpses beside a small tree, which they had mistaken for a still standing warrior. At each stop, Guinevere insisted on searching every bit of foggy land again and again. She stumbled over bodies of men she had known, and once came close enough to hear the robbers who were stripping them. The stench of dead flesh sickened her to the core of her being. She felt like Orpheus without music, searching through hell for the one she loved.

Then the boat came to a place where the fog was thick, and Guinevere again leapt onto the bank, calling out, "Lancelot, Lancelot, Anna, Anna." Morgan and Ninian followed her.

Guinevere stumbled over another unseen body, and saw that it was Arthur's. Then she saw her lover kneeling beside Gawaine's body.

Hollow-eyed, Anna stared at her rescuers. Guinevere stared at her in return, horrified by the terrible look on her face and the blood that covered her.

Guinevere opened her arms and Anna clutched her as if Guinevere were a tree leaning over the bank that could keep her from being carried away in the current. At least Anna recognized her.

Morgan threw herself down beside Arthur's body and wailed.

After a time, Morgan helped the men who poled the barge lift Arthur's body on board to take it to a church for burial. They staggered with the difficulty, because stiffness had set in.

"Let us take Gawaine, too, and bury him somewhere in the forest. I don't want to bury him here," were the only words that Anna said.

Although Guinevere had not been fond of Arthur or Gawaine, their murdered bodies seemed pitiful to her, and she could imagine how much worse it was for her lover. Making her voice calm, Guinevere directed the proceedings. "Yes, of course we can take Gawaine, too. I understand Antigone, dear." She realized after she said this that Anna would not know this Greek play about a woman who gave her life to see that her brother was buried, but it didn't matter. Probably the only words that did were "I understand."

"Move Arthur a little, there," Guinevere said. He had tried to kill her, but she felt no triumph at surviving while he died.

Lifting Gawaine's larger and longer dead body was even harder work than carrying Arthur's, but it was done. The fog had cleared somewhat, and Guinevere saw Mordred's body. While they were placing Gawaine on the barge, Guinevere strayed up the slope to Mordred and waved away the crows that worked at his corpse.

If she had born a son, he might have had that face, now cut and distorted. Sucking in her breath, she realized that Lancelot--Anna--must have been the one who slashed his body so terribly. Arthur wouldn't have done that to his son, or to a man who looked so much like himself. She thought it hard that the father should be buried with great ceremony, while the bastard son lay unburied. Who had his mother been? For the sake of that nameless mother, she called the bargemen to quickly bury his remains, for that was all they were.

She returned to the barge where Anna sat in silence. "Let me clean you off a little, dear." Guinevere said, dipping a cloth into the river and wiping Anna's face. "Will you have a little water to drink?"

Ninian said, "I think perhaps some wine," and lifted a flask to Anna's lips.

Guinevere wiped the blood from Anna's hands.

As they departed, two ravens flew over them.

Ninian said, "See, their spirits have gone." Anna looked plainly unbelieving. Stroking Anna's hair, the old nun said, "You don't have to fight any more battles."

Guinevere did not see the bodies of the dead they passed as they went down the river. All she could see was the misery in Anna's face, which had lost all of its color. Anna's mouth was slack and her eyes seemed to stare at nothing. Could she go mad again from seeing this horror?

Guinevere could scarcely believe that Arthur was dead. She had wanted him gone, not dead. She no longer hated him, but hoped that if there were some future world he would find peace. What would happen to Britain? She would have no say in that now. All she had was Anna, poor dearest Anna. As for Gawaine, Guinevere found herself praying for him and wishing that he still lived.

Morgan went only part of the way on the barge, because it was not safe for her to go to a church. They put her off in a place in the forest where she had ordered servants who worked for the convent to bring her horse so that she could ride home. They buried Gawaine there, beside oak trees.

Ninian and Morgan said some of the old prayers for him.

Anna remained silent, scarcely present. It seemed as if she would have blown away if the plump old nun had not held her.

Morgan had said not a word to Anna. Watching Guinevere and Ninian minister to Anna, Morgan had glowered.

The Lady of Cornwall kissed her brother's forehead in parting, then turned to Anna and spoke in a bitter voice. "Lancelot knows nothing of love or grief. Poor Arthur didn't know that you killed our daughter. How could you leave Elaine?"

Anna turned even paler and trembled at learning that Elaine had been Arthur's daughter. Guinevere flung her arms around Anna, as if trying to ward off the blow that had already been delivered.

Ninian reproached Morgan. "You might be a little gentler. She's grieving. One doesn't have to lie with people or give birth to them in order to love them."

Morgan swung onto her horse, almost as gracefully as Anna could, and galloped deep into the forest.

"Never mind," the old nun said. "People are often cruel at funerals. Morgan just wishes that she had been the one with Arthur when he died."

"She couldn't wish it any more than I do." Anna shuddered, and Guinevere clasped her hand.

They went through the funeral at the abbey on Ynis Witrin, which once had been Avalon, in a blur of requiems. Guinevere felt heavy from the ugliness of the field of death, but did not weep. For one last moment, she was appearing as Arthur's queen, though she had no crown.

The monks and priests stared a little because Lancelot--she was wearing her chain mail and therefore was so called--was so obviously much more affected than Guinevere, but of course a queen was supposed to be dignified even at her husband's funeral. They probably thought that a runaway queen might show tears of repentance, however.

One wrinkled old monk told Guinevere, "Your calm courage in the face of this great sorrow is an inspiration to us all. The great king long ago told us what he wanted on his tombstone. 'Here lies Arthur, the Once and Future King.'"

She stared back. "He even thought of that," she observed, careful not to show what passed through her mind. She was appalled that he had lived his life always for public show. He had lived to become a legend, and perhaps he would have his wish.

"He wanted you to be buried with him, so you can tell the nuns at your convent to make arrangements for that when you die," the monk informed her.

"I shall not be buried with him," she replied, unable to hide the vehemence in her voice. When she saw the monk's startled face, she recalled herself. "Of course he did not know about my sin when he told you that. I must be buried at the convent where I renounce the world." She vowed that she would be buried in the forest, so no one could ever take her body to Arthur's tomb. Apparently he had thought he could part her from Lancelot in death if not in life.

The monks went off to themselves and appeared to be deep in conversation, then one returned to Guinevere and said, "A golden-haired lady came here to die of the ague just yesterday, and she said that the only man she had ever loved was King Arthur. Perhaps we should bury her with him."

"Perhaps," Guinevere said. She went to see the woman's body, and saw that it was Gwyl, Arthur's pleasantest mistress. She decided that Gwyl would like the idea, so she assented to it. "Ah, yes, she cherished a pure and hopeless love for him, so she is fitter to be buried with him than I am," Guinevere proclaimed, as if with regret.

The monks gave Guinevere and Lancelot small rooms, of course separate ones. Anna did not want to sleep on the pallet in her cell. She prayed for the many dead--some in particular--then slumped and drifted off while still kneeling. She was by the river again, and saw Arthur's wraith crying, "Follow me and die."

Then another wraith, tall and pale but still red-bearded, stood by the river's shore. "Live, live, live," he called out. "Remember the once and future quest. Think of the once and future jest. Life is but a jest, so it should end with laughter." A ghostly laugh echoed.

"Stay, stay," she begged, but Gawaine was gone.

After they had returned to the convent, Anna went off to her room and sobbed and would not leave it. Her hair had turned completely white, though her eyebrows still were black.

Guinevere's own hair was now entirely gray. She did not mind that now. She feared for Anna.

After three days of Anna's seclusion, Guinevere stood by her bed, took her hand, and appealed to her, "I am frightened. Is some of this grief at being in the convent? Arthur can no longer pursue us, so we don't have to live here. I don't care whether I call you Lancelot or Anna. I don't care whether you are a warrior or a nun, dress in chain mail or black robes, or whether we live in a convent, or in Lesser Britain, or anywhere else. I only want you to live."

Anna looked at her miserably and seemed to force herself to speak. Deep circles made her large eyes stand out from her pale face. "I am not Lancelot. I never want to fight again, and I don't care about the rest."

Choking back tears, Guinevere pressed her hand. "This indifference is most unlike you. I don't want to imprison you. I have envied you for having the freedom of a man, but I don't want to punish you for it now. I haven't wanted to pose as man and wife, but if that is what you need, we could."

Anna returned the pressure on her hand, but weakly. "If I should be punished it is not for having the freedom of a man, but for using it as they did." She closed her eyes. "I can't bear to talk about it. I love you dearly, but please let me be for a while."

"For how long?"

"I don't know."

Guinevere went to the abbess and Ninian, who were speaking in the abbess's office. They turned gentle faces to her, but Guinevere was not cheered. "What can I do? All she does is weep. She does not want to go outdoors. That is strange, for Lancelot--Anna."

"Let her grieve," Ninian said in a tone that suggested that she knew grief very well. "Let her stay in her room a few weeks if she wants."

"Weeks?" Guinevere gasped. Could she bear seeing this strange, pale Anna for so long?

The plump old nun nodded, her wrinkled face soft with compassion. "Yes. Then you and I will take her out, bit by bit, and make her walk in the forest, even if she does not seem to want to. That will revive her."

The abbess took Guinevere's hand and said, "You have been through terrible things, too. Come and talk with us whenever you want to, and we shall do what we can. Even queens can grieve."

Guinevere returned the pressure of the stately woman's hand. Ninian went off and brought Valeria, who spent many hours both listening to Guinevere and being quiet with her.

After some weeks, Guinevere saw Ninian in the garden and clutched her arm. Dead blooms rose from the flowers' stalks, and Ninian was cutting them off. The browned petals littering the ground reminded Guinevere of the field of the dead, and she shivered. But she felt she could speak to this old woman without shame. "Anna still doesn't want to kiss me. She says she cannot because her mind is so full of horrible things. Does she love me still?"

Ninian put an arm around her. "You should not doubt her. Of course she does."

"But why won't she let me comfort her?" Guinevere spoke reluctantly, hating to say what she feared. "Is she in love with someone who is dead? I can't compete with the dead, because a golden haze surrounds them and blurs every fault."

The nun shook her head. "Do not be jealous of the dead. She has always loved you more than anyone else. It is not love, but horror that has taken over her mind."

Lying in her hard convent bed, Anna did not even want to look out of the window at the thick forest, but stared at a blank wall. Sunlight streaming into the room seemed to mock her sorrow. When Ninian entered her room, Anna forced herself to turn her gaze to the old nun.

"I couldn't save Gawaine, nor any of my old companions," Anna moaned.

Ninian nodded. "That's right, you couldn't. Why think that you should?" Her voice was less gentle than usual. "They had to carry their own burdens as you have had to carry yours. In trying to save them, you nearly lost yourself. You must not play at being a saint any more. Or at being a man. Your disguise served its purpose, but after all, you didn't really want to be one."

Anna shuddered and wrapped the covers around her. "Far from it, and it's hard to believe that they did. When I was young, all I wanted was not to be a woman. Now all I want is not to be a man. But, even though I was an adulterer, I did want to be a saint."

"That's not such a good ambition, either," the nun admonished her, nevertheless stroking the hair from her forehead. "Why should everyone look to you for help? Aren't love and friendship enough? Fortunately, Guinevere doesn't see you with a halo, or she cared no more about your halo than you did about her crown."

"Can we go on and still love? I am so afraid. I keep dreaming that she has died, too." She put her hands over her face. She could still smell the rotten stench of the battlefield.

The old woman's voice sounded soothing. "I shouldn't tell you the future, but I shall. You and Guinevere will be together for many years. Now you must think of cheering her. She worries so about you. You must forget your suffering enough to remember hers."

Anna looked into the sweet, wrinkled face and wanted to believe. Did Ninian truly know the future, or was she just inventing tales to reassure her? Anna sighed.

"I shall try, but it's so hard. It's not just that my friends died--Lancelot died also."

"Then you must learn who Anna is," Ninian told her. "And who is Guinevere? Is she just a pretty woman who touches you, or just a former queen? Do you understand her?"

Anna shook her head. "Not her, or anyone."

"Don't you want to? Or are you so full of your own grief that you think nothing of hers? It's time that you did. Her husband nearly killed her because of her love for you." The old nun frowned.

Shamed by the reproach, Anne protested, "I have stayed alive only so as not to abandon her."

"Did you ever happen to think that Guinevere may have stayed alive only so as not to abandon you?"

Anna groaned. "I'm not worthy of her love."

"That's only another way of avoiding her." Ninian walked to the door. "You must learn to ask for her to help you. And she must admit that she needs your help also."

When Guinevere next came to Anna's room, Anna forced herself to look into her eyes. "Please help me," she said, feeling that the words hurt her mouth.

Guinevere trembled. "I will. Please help me, too." She took Anna's hands in hers.

So Anna let Guinevere and Ninian take her into the forest. She tried to smile a little at the squirrels that dashed about gathering nuts, but her heart felt as heavy as ever.

Then they walked to the nearest pond, and Anna wept when she saw it.

She had swum in the pond in other times. It looked so tranquil and innocent, not stained with blood.

Ninian said, "Why don't you both go in it?"

The summer was turning to autumn, but the air still held some warmth. A wren sang, only a part of its song, but sang nevertheless.

"Wouldn't that be dangerous?" Anna asked. "I might chance it, but how could I ever let Guinevere risk taking her clothes off in the forest?" The only time they had made love in the forest, years before, she had been so overcome that she hadn't thought about it.

"There is no danger for miles around," the old woman assured her. "Just this once, believe that I can cast a magic spell that will protect you. I'll keep watch on the path, but it isn't needed." She folded her arms and stood as if she were a guard at a caer's wall.

They undressed, and went into the water. Guinevere had never learned to swim, but she walked out to the deepest part where she could stand.

Anna swam a little, and Guinevere teased her, calling her by the names of many water creatures. She called her otter, and Anna wondered whether she could be like such a playful creature despite all of her killing. She had thought of herself as a wolf, never as an otter. Then when Anna came close, Guinevere embraced her.

They embraced in the water, and then on the mossy bank. Guinevere's body was softer than the moss.

Anna rested in Guinevere's arms. "I love you so. I can't believe that it's possible to feel this good again."

"I know that you have seen hell, and I have seen it, too," Guinevere said, holding her tight. "But the story that people can never return to the garden after they have lost their innocence is a lie. Sometimes we can find the way. What we can't do is stay there and be innocent always, and it's wrong to try."

Feeling downcast, Percy rode up to the old villa that he had called home. His mother, his brother, and his father came running out to meet him. All of them screamed and threw their arms about him, in such a tumult that it seemed almost like a battle. But then, he had never seen one.

"You're alive!" they screamed. "You're alive!"

"But I heard from a merchant I met on the road that King Arthur is dead." He could barely speak the words. He had not fought for his king, had not tried to save him! "What about Uncle Peredur?"

"He's dead, too, and so are nearly all of Arthur's other warriors," Aglovale said, and Percival could see that all of their eyes were red.

Percy found tears in his eyes for many reasons. "I missed the battle. I'm so ashamed. The fisher king kept saying that he was dying, and I couldn't leave the bed of a dying man. I must have sat there for days. Then finally he said that perhaps he wasn't going to die just now, and I could leave. But I missed fighting for King Arthur to stay with the fisher king! It's terrible. I've never been so ashamed." How had he dared imagine that the poor old man's life was worth as much as the king's?

"Your fisher king has saved you!" Olwen exclaimed with delight, embracing him.

"You don't understand. I'll be ashamed all of my life," Percy moaned.

There was a faint grin on Aglovale's face. "But you'll have a life."

"Why didn't any of you care about the old man? You live so near that I'd think you'd visit him," Percy demanded.

"Don't be a goose, Percy," Illtud chided. "Of course we visit him, and any of us could have gone this time. But it was your turn to go."

Percy was nearly speechless. His own family had deceived him! "You kept me from fighting."

"It wasn't us, it was you," Aglovale said, giving him one of his warmest smiles. "You decided that you cared more about comforting the fisher king than about killing for King Arthur."

Percy groaned. He had lost his honor, and they didn't even care. "Did any of the other warriors survive?"

"Lancelot did, and sent me a message," his father told him.

Percy felt stirrings of joy at that. "Good news. And he's kind enough to forgive me for missing the battle."

Olwen clung to his arm. "No doubt. I hope that he'll come to visit us again. But don't be disappointed if you find that he's changed from the way you remember him."

Aglovale and Olwen laughed heartily at that, and Percy shook his head again over his strange family.

30 LIFE AFTER DEATH

Guinevere entered the abbess's study. A cat raised its head in sleepy greeting, but Guinevere refrained from patting it, for she had a grave matter to discuss.

"Holy Mother, will you shrive me?" she asked. For an abbess could hear the confessions of her sisters, and though Guinevere had taken no vows, she was surely under the woman's care.

"I will," said the abbess in a tone of the utmost gravity.

So Guinevere knelt down and confessed all the years of love for Lancelot as she never had to a priest. Bowing her head was easy, for she did not want to look into the nun's eyes. At some parts of the telling, she trembled. What if the abbess would not forgive her?

When she had finished her account, she dared to look up.

"You loved Anna dearly, did you not?" the older woman asked, her face and tone solemn.

"Far more than my own life," Guinevere assured her.

"In your case, that is no exaggeration." The abbess nodded.

"Your husband had mistresses, did he not? He did not grieve overly because you turned from him?"

"Since the beginning of our marriage, he lay with other women. I did not care. I was relieved. He never minded my lying with Lancelot until the last couple of years, when he was angry with me." She then confessed her other hidden sin, her years of taking the potion to prevent childbearing. She also told of helping Enid.

The abbess forgave her, and said nothing about ending her loving.

"I love Anna still," Guinevere made bold to say.

The abbess nodded. "I know. You would not be the only one within these walls to love another who is here. I think such love is unchaste only if it keeps one from loving God and this community. Take care that it does not," she admonished.

Guinevere almost wept with gratitude, but her lifetime habit of restraint stayed with her. "Indeed, I give prayers of thanks for Anna every day. I have always seen her as my greatest blessing, not as a temptation. I am sure that loving her has made me a better person. And I can never say how much your good community has meant to me. You have saved us, body and soul."

There was a knowing look on the abbess's face. Her hands remained folded in her lap. "So now you can tell Anna that I will shrive her also. That's what you truly wanted, isn't it? She longs for absolution more than you did, I think. But you came to me first because you wanted to learn whether I would tell her to stop loving you. Never fear."

Guinevere felt her cheeks grow hot. "You see much, Reverend Mother. Yes, I will tell her. She will be glad."

The old abbess nodded. "Guinevere, I have plans for you. I want to train you to take my place when I die." She sounded as if she thought her own death was of far less concern than the convent's future. "I think you could rule this convent well--if the nuns chose you, that is. Would you be willing?"

Guinevere gasped. "Of course I would! You would trust a sinner like me?"

"Don't boast about your sins to me." The abbess continued to speak in her voice of command. "I am thinking about your capabilities. Perhaps the Lord sent you here for a reason. But don't become proud again too soon. It might do you good to be humble for a while." Although her voice was stern, she touched Guinevere's hand for an instant.

Guinevere bowed her head and tried to keep her voice steady. "I shall do whatever you say, Holy Mother." She backed out of the room as if she were leaving her sovereign.

Anna was shriven, and wept for joy for hours, but she still feared that her past sins weighed down her soul too much for heaven.

She felt the strangeness of long skirts constricting her legs and a veil on her head, though no longer having to bind her breasts was an unspeakable relief. The robes seemed awkward, but they were much lighter than chain mail. Standing in Guinevere's room, she slipped out of them, carefully putting aside the dagger she carried concealed in the folds of her garment. It was a relief that no one called her out to fight, but she could never quite believe that it was true.

She feared that Guinevere would no longer want her when she was Anna, dressed in long skirts, even though Guinevere had said she would.

Guinevere reached out to embrace and reassure her. She kissed Anna passionately, and Anna glowed with warmth. Away from the king and the court, Guinevere's affection seemed to grow greater than ever, and she was almost never angry. They still made love in Guinevere's room, perhaps because they had always done so.

Her room was not as plain as Anna's, but very simple compared with what Guinevere had had at Camelot. One green embroidered covering lay on the bed and one hanging with a forest design hung on the wall. Both were gifts from the abbess.

While Guinevere combed Anna's white hair, Anne turned, looked in her eyes, and said, "I was afraid that you loved only Lancelot. Didn't you love the victories at fighting contests, the fame?"

Guinevere took Anna's face in her hands. "So I did love Lancelot, as Lancelot was a part of you, but I knew that that was only one aspect. Did you love me because I was a queen, and could command many to do my bidding?"

"No, of course not. Is my having been Lancelot as little to you as your having been a queen is to me?" Joy suffused her. She felt as if she were floating on air.

"Yes, just as little. What matters is that we are together. You still taste just as sweet." And she kissed the neck that had been Lancelot's.

Anna rubbed her cheek against Guinevere's. It was a relief that she no longer had to scrape her cheeks every morning so they would look more like a man's, but the years of so doing had made the skin rough.

One day a messenger brought a letter from Cai. Anna eagerly broke the seal and unfolded the vellum. She held the letter so Guinevere could read along with her.

Dear Lancelot and Guinevere,

I am glad that you have survived.

So have I, though they tried to roast me, and, insulting to relate, without herbs or other seasoning. Therefore, I was not in the great battle, and I am glad of it. I am thankful that Dinadan, who is dear to me, was far away trying to persuade lesser kings to fight for Arthur and is now safely returned.

I miss Arthur. One does not like to admit this about one's foster brother, but he really was a great man, although he did some wrong as well, as I suppose most great men do.

The people are afraid without Arthur. Some of them are so afraid that they have asked me to protect them. I am in command of Camelot and will do what I can for the people around here, but I certainly shall not compete with the lords in other parts of Britain. Let them fight it out.

In his last will and testament, which he wrote just before he went out to battle Mordred, Arthur divided all of his personal wealth (which was not that great, because he was always building) among "my good sister, Morgan of Cornwall, my good foster brother, Caius, and my good cousin, Gawaine of Lothian and Orkney. I proclaim that my wife, Guinevere, was not guilty of the charges falsely brought against her by the traitor Mordred." Thus he tried to place the blame for nearly burning her on Mordred, absolving himself.

Gawaine also made a will before the battle. He left half of what he had to Lancelot, and the other half, I am not sure why, to Galahad. (I hope that Galahad will return from his quest. If some other warrior had left so much to a young man, I would be suspicious, but surely Gawaine was interested only in women.) I assume that you do not want property in Lothian, and I shall correspond with people there about it for you if you wish. I see that you told him your name, because he asked me to help him write two wills, one saying Lancelot and the other saying Anna.

He told me to use the one that was most fitting at the time. Anna is a pleasant name, though not as elegant as Lancelot.

I suggest that we use the will saying Anna, because Queen Morgause might find it less strange that her son would leave an inheritance to a woman she never heard of than to the warrior who she must have heard killed two of his brothers.

No one knows that you are a woman. All of those who heard it must have died in the battle, except for Dinadan and me, who saw it all along but never told you we knew. I have said that you entered a monastery in Lesser Britain, and everyone believes it.

Catwal has recovered and is my serving man now. I should have stolen him from you years ago.

I wish you and Guinevere both well.

The thought of Lancelot in a convent amuses me. Do the nuns swoon over you?

I have changed my name to Constantine, because it has a more royal sound, and people think of Cai only as the seneschal. Dinadan calls himself my empress but says that he will leave me if I start seeing visions of crosses in the sky.

Caius now Constantine,
Lord of the kitchen and now of Camelot

Glad he had survived, they smiled at his signature.

Then the messenger told them that he had also brought Guinevere's favorite horse, and Guinevere exclaimed with joy and dashed out of the convent door to welcome the mare.

Anna wrote thanking Cai for his assistance, and sending her warmest regards and what money she had to Catwal. She said that all of her share of Gawaine's estate should be used to help destitute women. And Guinevere wrote that all of her jewels should be sold to provide for the widows of the battle of

Camlann, Lionors first among them. She grieved at the thought of Bors's widow raising their large flock alone.

Anna sat at the long refectory table, at the left hand of Guinevere, who was placed at the left hand of the abbess. The oldest nun, Ninian, sat at the abbess's right.

A new tapestry of the Last Supper, with the Blessed Virgin and Magdalene included, hung on the wall across from the old hanging depicting the miracle of the loaves and the fishes.

Anna watched everything with great interest. The food was simpler than it had been at the round table, but the table manners were certainly better. There was no shouting or throwing of food.

The conversation was also better. The nuns talked about books, both Christian and not. They said that there were women who wrote, that a library in distant Alexandria had held books by women, but the Romans had destroyed it.

Anna thought she should read more so she could understand the conversations better, but she was not much inclined to do so. To Anna's amazement, women who were Christian and a few women who still had a belief in the old religion, or at least parts of it, lived together and seemed for the most part to respect each other. A few others, like Guinevere, appeared to care more about books than prayers.

Some nuns were quieter and spent more time in chapel. Some fasted often. Anna remembered that at one time she would have found those nuns the most congenial. Guinevere found them the least congenial.

It was true that some nuns became a little testy about theology, for some worried about heretics within Christianity as well as old believers.

"It's almost Samhein," Ninian proclaimed, as if that were still a feast she celebrated.

Sister Branwen made the sign of the cross. "That is a pagan feast. Marking the seasons is a pagan practice. Only events in the gospels should be celebrated."

Ninian grinned. "Well, where do the gospels tell about the Trinity? And a strange Trinity it is, with a Father and Son and no mother."

Branwen and a number of other nuns gasped and crossed themselves.

"Enough of your jests, Ninian," said the abbess gently. "She is only testing your faith," she told the others.

"They have no sense of humor," Ninian grumbled.

Covering the awkward silence, old Sister Darerca told one of her stories about having known Saint Brigid of Kildare. "No doubt we'll always have a warm hearth here, for she told me that I would have the blessing of her holy fires for all the rest of my life."

Ninian stopped eating her salmon. "If you're making up stories, you might as well call the goddess Brighid by her true name, and not make her one of your saints. Goddess of the flames she is indeed, and what is Kildare but an oak grove?"

Darerca snapped back, "I should know my own mentor, shouldn't I? Sure, she was named after your pagan goddess, but she was so pure that she pulled her own eyes out of her head rather than marry."

"I find it more wonderful that she put them back in again," Ninian retorted, oblivious to the muttering of the many nuns who were indignant to hear her cast doubt on one of their favorite saints.

"It is a mystery. What would life be without mystery?" the abbess said, unshakable in her calm.

"Some convents have a rule of constant silence, and I have heard that Rome thinks that all convents should," said sweet-faced Sister Fidelia, looking around as if asking whether others thought such a rule likely to spread.

The abbess scoffed. "Surely men in far-off Rome could never tell us what to do."

"Perhaps we should spend more hours in prayer," one sister ventured.

"We should instead read more, for reading is prayer," another replied.

Of course there were also the usual disputes over Pelagius and Augustine and the rules of the Irish Church versus the British Church. The nuns even debated whether priests should have tonsures, though Anna could not see why the women should have any interest in that.

Anna went off to Guinevere's room to complain about the spats among the nuns. When she entered, Guinevere put down a scroll that she had been studying by the light of her candles. Even in the convent, she still had fine beeswax tapers.

"This place is like a cauldron," Anna told Guinevere. "I thought it would be peaceful, and in a way it is, but these women fight about theology as if their lives depended on it."

"Like a slur on one's honor?" Guinevere asked in a sarcastic tone.

"Well, yes. There is just as much gossip here as at Camelot, and there are just as many quarrels." Anna sighed. "The only difference is that there is no drunkenness, no one is pressing anyone to go to bed if they do not want to, and no one comes to blows."

"Yes, those are the only differences," said Guinevere, giving Anna a disgusted look.

Anna set out plates of food at Samhein for her friends who had died during the year (except for Bors, whose ghost would be scandalized by it), though she knew that only Branwen's fondness for her kept her from starting a great uproar about this pagan ritual. Anna smiled at the thought of Gawaine's shade visiting the convent, but she reckoned that if it went anywhere, it would more likely go to Lothian, where Queen Morgause no doubt had set out supper for all four of her dead sons.

After Anna had set the platters of wheaten bread and apples at the empty places, Branwen put an arm around her shoulder.

"No doubt all of your friends will be resurrected and will dwell in peace," she said.

Ninian smiled enigmatically, saying, "They will live on in some form, no doubt, because nothing is ever lost, and even the rains that dry go back to the heavens and fall again."

Anna noticed that Guinevere seemed to talk more familiarly with Sister Valeria than anyone else, although Valeria was clearly close to Sister Fidelia, who had the best voice both speaking and singing. But Valeria was entirely too pretty.

One day Anna saw Guinevere and Valeria laughing and chatting in the passageway with their arms around each other's shoulders. Anna bristled and glared at them.

Guinevere laughed at her. "What ails you?"

Valeria also laughed. "I have loved dear Gwen all my life. We used to sleep together when we were girls."

Anna stalked off and Guinevere followed her to her room.

"What is the matter?" Guinevere asked, still full of mirth. Her cheeks were rosy--could it be from blushing? But Guinevere never blushed. "Valeria has been my dear friend ever since childhood. She was the first woman I lay with, when I was on my way to Camelot to marry Arthur, but she has been with Fidelia ever since she joined the convent."

Anna's stomach muscles tightened. Arthur was no longer, but now she had to speak with a woman who had once been with Guinevere. She scrutinized Guinevere's face. "And how do you feel about her now? I'm jealous," she complained.

Guinevere scoffed. "I don't whether to laugh or to yell at you. You have a great deal of gall. How many have flirted with you? I don't want anyone but you, fool that you are." She put her arms around Anna, who accepted her kiss in a chastened manner.

Anna found that she did not miss Camelot's dogs so much because the convent was full of cats, who ran about as they pleased. One white cat in particular liked to jump in her lap and go to sleep. And sometimes in the middle of a solemn reading at supper, when the nuns were listening to noble words, a cat would suddenly wake up, stare at some feline apparition, and run tearing across the refectory, much to the amusement of nearly, but not quite, everyone.

Anna went often to the chapel, where she could hear the old hymns her mother had loved without feeling that she was being untrue to Guinevere. She did not partake of the sacrament.

One evening in her room, Guinevere asked, "Why don't you take the sacrament, now that you no longer need to fear that we are committing adultery?"

Sighing, Anna shook her head. "So many doubts have been opened to me. I shall never know what to believe, so I shall not do what the believers do."

"I take the sacraments, as I have always done," Guinevere said, taking off her veil. "No doubt much of what the priests say is true, but I don't worry about the details."

Used to Guinevere's practical attitude toward religion, Anna did not chide her.

"You seem relaxed here, more so than at the court," Anna said, not adding that even at her most relaxed Guinevere had an air of authority.

Guinevere pressed her hand. "I thrive on the reading. I almost wish that I gone to the convent much sooner, instead of marrying. But my father would have said the convent was for the younger daughters of large families, not for the only daughters of kings. Besides, then I never would have met you." She kissed Anna's lips, and Anna returned the kiss.

Guinevere pulled back and scrutinized Anna's face. "All the guilt you felt toward Arthur drove me mad." Her voice had an edge to it. "Why feel guilty, unless you really believed that he owned me, and I had no right to love anyone but the man my father chose for me?"

Anna thought she had more reasons for guilt than Guinevere realized, but she was not ready to talk about how Arthur had died. She did not want to think about him. The horror of his death obscured the memory of his life. She put a hand on Guinevere's shoulder. "That wasn't the reason for my guilt. Until he sentenced you to burn, I believed that he loved you as I did, and must be as heartbroken as I would be if you broke off with me. He sometimes spoke against you, but I thought that was from wounded love. How could anyone not love you?"

Making a sharp, disgusted sound, Guinevere wrinkled her nose. "He certainly never loved me. He liked me when he thought I was fond of him, but did not love in the way you mean. I don't think men can."

"No, he clearly didn't love you, but that doesn't mean that a man couldn't love. They are only human, after all, and can learn that as I could learn to fight. But I am very glad that I'm with you." Anna kissed her and stroked Guinevere's beautiful, thick, silver hair.

Anna walked or rode out in the woods every day, early and late, while the more prayerful nuns were on their knees. Whether she saw a mouse or a badger, an owl or a goldfinch, it delighted her. She was amazed that after seeing so much death she could still feel joy.

Sometimes Ninian rode with her, for she also enjoyed the woods. And of course, Guinevere also liked to ride, and did.

One day, as Anna and Ninian strolled to the pond to look for migrating geese and other waterfowl, the old woman asked how she liked nun's clothes.

Looking down at her black skirt, Anna spoke wistfully. "To tell the truth, I miss the chain mail. I know that I am wearing a great many robes, but I feel naked without it." She touched her skirt, which felt flimsy.

The old nun laughed and the wrinkles danced across her face. "My poor turtle has lost her shell. Truly, you are the only woman in the world who ever has felt or ever will feel naked in nun's garb. Perhaps sometimes you could wear chain mail under the black robes. It would show through just a little bit."

Anne laughed with her, then started sobbing. "Gawaine would have laughed so at that. I cannot laugh again with a light heart. Mordred has murdered laughter."

"That he has not," Ninian scolded, shaking a finger at her as if she were a child. "Murdered laughter! Who could ever do such a thing? Don't give him so much power. He was not a devil. Would Gawaine want you never to laugh? Wouldn't he pound you on the back and try to jest with you? How do you know his ghost isn't trying to get you to laugh even this very moment?"

Tears dripped down Anna's cheeks. Ninian's words only made her sadder. "You know he isn't doing anything of the kind. He's just dead."

A swan swam near the shore where they stood, but it did not cheer Anna.

"You have always prayed to your mother, as if you believed she heard you," Ninian said.

"I was so young, I had to believe that," Anna admitted, tossing a bit of bread to the swan. "And perhaps I still do. Besides, she seemed so saintly. I could hardly pray to Gawaine. Even praying to Elaine seems farfetched, though I often ask her to forgive me."

The nun grabbed her by the shoulders. "Well, speak to them, then, don't call it prayer. They are indeed living if you remember them, and think of what they would have said."

"Dead, all dead." Anne sobbed. "Nearly all of the court is dead."

"Guinevere is alive," Ninian replied, gently but firmly, rubbing Anna's cheeks with a white linen cloth. "You must be brave to live after Camelot. Mourn indeed, but to grasp life's joy, we must never be too solemn to be the fool. It's a good jest that the world's greatest warrior was a woman! It's an even better one that the world's greatest warrior has retired to a convent! You and Guinevere don't have to hide your love as much here as you did at Camelot. Do you hear me, it's hilarious. You can still jest about these things, as if your friends heard you, and you should."

A pair of mallards flew up quacking, circled the pond, and settled down on the water again.

"Thinking of Gawaine should bring you peace," the old nun said. "You don't believe that a just God would send Gawaine to hell, do you?"

"No!" Anna gasped, tripping and nearly falling into the pond in her indignation. "I would never believe that he is in any such place."

"And was he any less of a sinner than you are?" Ninian asked.

"No," Anna admitted. Perhaps more of one, she thought but did not want to say.

Ninian grabbed hold of her hands. "Then you won't go to hell either, will you?"

Anna swayed, almost collapsing with a surge of relief. "I suppose not." She had worried so much about hell ever since she and Guinevere had first loved each other that she could scarcely believe that her fear could be gone.

"So Gawaine has given you hope?" Ninian smiled one of her smiles that brought summer to winter.

"Yes, the old sinner, he has." Anna smiled, then recoiled. "Don't tell me his death served a purpose because it took away my fear of hell. I don't want peace at that price. There was no excuse for his death."

Ninian looked deep into Anna's eyes. "You would not agree that anyone should die to save you or others?"

"To die to save a life, yes, that's acceptable, though I wouldn't want anyone to die to save mine. But to die to comfort or console someone else, no, of course I would never accept that."

Ninian raised her eyebrows. "Don't say that too loudly in the convent."

Understanding her meaning, Anna paused, then said, "But I don't accept it. I don't want anyone to suffer for me."

"I won't tell you that Gawaine's death was God's will, that it was just, or that it was his destiny, only that it is," Ninian said. "It has happened, and nothing can change that. I agree with you that it must be the life that matters, not the death. Remember the life."

Anna hugged her tightly. "I do. Then, if you would, please throw some food onto my plate at supper sometimes, in memory of Gawaine, who used to say I didn't eat enough."

That night at supper, Ninian tossed a trout onto Anna's plate. The other nuns stared speechless. Anna laughed and cried, as did Guinevere, recognizing the gesture and trying to sympathize with her.

Priests visited the convent, of course for Mass, and then they joined the nuns for a meal in the refectory. At one such meal breaking fast after Mass, Anna sat still and uncomfortable while a thin, sharp-nosed, young priest talked about the tragedy of the death of King Arthur. She had insisted on sitting far down the table, away from Guinevere, because the priest was there.

Anna kept her left hand under the table, because not many nuns were missing two fingers on their left hands.

"Our great king was brought down by treachery," the priest intoned in a nasal voice. "Earthly kingdoms, even the greatest, are fragile."

"Even one evil man can bring down a great kingdom," he proclaimed, looking with narrow eyes at Guinevere. "Such a one was Lancelot. He betrayed his king and killed many of his companions, even the great Gawaine of the Matchless Strength, who fought him because Lancelot killed his brothers."

Anna gasped, jumped up, and ran from the refectory. Could people possibly believe that she had killed Gawaine?

She rushed to her room, threw herself on her bed, and wept, and soon Guinevere came to join her.

"I told the priest that you were a kinswoman of Gawaine's and he had distressed you by referring to his death," she said, taking Anna in her arms. "And the abbess said that I had repented and was living a life of atonement, so he should not talk about Arthur's court any more. Because she far outranks him, he bowed his head in submission."

"The world knows that I'm an adulterer and a traitor," Anna sobbed on Guinevere's shoulder, "and that I killed some of my fellow warriors. But saying that I killed my best friend, too, is just too much. All I did was defeat him in a board game. Will the ignominy never end?"

Guinevere wiped away her tears. "You'll at least be remembered for saving many lives. There's nothing you can do about the tales that will be spread. Anyone who knew you knows you would never have killed any friend, much less Gawaine, and it's not believable that he would have tried to kill you either."

Anna did not stop weeping. "Of course he wouldn't have." She looked into Guinevere's eyes. "But I did kill Arthur."

Guinevere jumped back as if she had been struck. "I can't believe it!" she exclaimed. "You wouldn't have, except if you had to, to save my life."

"I did," Anna choked, no longer weeping but looking at the white-washed wall. "Mordred had given him a mortal wound, and he couldn't bear the pain. He asked me to end his life." Would Guinevere find her repulsive now?

Guinevere pressed Anna's hands tightly and exclaimed, "The wretch! He wanted you to suffer even more."

"That's true," Anna said, more quietly, daring to look at her again. Guinevere's eyes were wide with amazement, not disgust at what Anna had done.

"He wanted the death of Arthur to be the end of everything." Guinevere frowned.

"He wanted me to never be able to . . ." Anna felt her face grow hot.

"To love me again. Well, he didn't succeed." Guinevere pressed Anna to her bosom. "It's just as well that no one knows this," she added. "You may think it would have been worse to have killed Gawaine than to have killed Arthur, and I agree with you, but other people would not. Let us put out the story that Bedwyr died after Arthur and was the last person to see Arthur alive. He was Arthur's first warrior, so people would like to hear that he was the last one also. It's so symmetrical."

"If we can do that, can't we put out a different story about Gawaine's death, such as the true one?" Anna ventured.

"We can, but men love stories about men killing their best friends, so I doubt that we can change it," Guinevere told her, stroking her white hair.

Sunlight poured in the window, and Anna marveled that Guinevere still loved her.

"You neither hate me for killing your husband nor are pleased that I did?" She had so longed to ask Guinevere outright whether she wanted her to kill Arthur, but she had dreaded the answer.

Guinevere cried out. "I spent a year keeping you from killing him, to protect you from harm. Have you no idea how he treated me in the last year of his life? He learned that I had helped a girl to prevent bearing a baby that was his. I didn't know it was his until afterwards, but Arthur didn't believe me and he hated me for it."

Anna gasped and gripped the bedstead.

"He did all that he could to make me miserable. He threatened to have me killed in an apparent accident, and though I didn't believe it, I was never easy after that."

Anna grabbed Guinevere's hands. "Holy virgin! That's horrible. Why didn't you tell me? We should have left immediately."

"I didn't dare tell you, for fear that you would attack him and be killed. And Arthur threatened to pursue and kill you if we ran off. That's why I wouldn't go. I feared him, but I couldn't show it." Guinevere's voice trembled as it seldom did.

The fear in Guinevere's tone wounded Anna's heart. "You were afraid for a year or more and I didn't see it." Tears formed in her eyes. "He tried to poison my mind against you, and God help me, he did do damage. Forgive me."

"I do." Guinevere put an arm around her.

Guinevere told Anna a great deal, and Anna embraced her again and again and blamed herself for not seeing what had been hidden. She had imagined that Guinevere might be a murderous wife, while instead she had been a persecuted one.

Guinevere told the reason why she had been sobbing when they first met, because Arthur had urged her to lie with Gawaine to conceive a child, and that was why she had so disliked Gawaine. "After my first burst of anger, I saw that it was all Arthur's idea," she said, "but Gawaine I could snub, and Arthur I could not."

Anna pressed her tightly. "How awful! Why didn't you tell me?"

"You were so proud to serve a good king. I didn't want to disillusion you. And you couldn't have taken me away without risking your life," Guinevere told her.

In the days after that, Anna told her all of the parts of her life that she had left out in previous tellings, the adventures that were just a little too dangerous, the things that people had said that she hadn't wanted to repeat, and even the time that she had slept in Drian's arms--not when she was ill, but earlier, when it was a substitute for lying with her in another way.

When all was told, Guinevere smiled and said, "Your tales are all very innocent. I'd have forgiven you for far more--in fact, anything."

"It is better not to have too much to forgive, but I'd have forgiven you anything, too," Anna assured her.

"And done so in noble suffering that would have been unendurable," teased Guinevere.

Anna smiled a little in return. "Am I really that bad?"

"Yes, you are." Guinevere tousled her hair.

In the night, Anna woke and could not return to sleep. She felt Guinevere touch her forehead.

"What thoughts now, dearest?" Guinevere asked her.

"Above all, I'm glad that you're safe, and angry that I didn't see you were in danger." She held Guinevere tightly.

"But there is more," Guinevere prodded her.

Anna sighed. "I thought I was helping to build a lasting peace, or at least a lasting kingdom. But the king was not as good as I believed, and the peace did not last. Nor did the kingdom."

"No, it did not." Guinevere sat up. "Perhaps it is my fault because I did not bear an heir. But who knows whether I would have had a son, whether the son would have been wise, or whether he would have been able to defeat challengers and keep the throne? Who knows how long he would have lived? We can never know these things. You have done what you have done. You have saved lives, you have been part of things that were good. You have tried to change the world. Who can say more? Who can do more than try?"

"We have both tried." Anna clasped her hand. And so did others at Camelot, she thought. She did not have to say that, because Guinevere knew it. How strange it was to live after Camelot.

Talwyn lingered in her bed and only sometimes ventured downstairs, although her wound was healed. Guinevere gently prodded her to get up, but Talwyn said she wasn't well enough. She cared about nothing.

Old Mother Ninian joked with Talwyn, but no jests moved her.

Once when Anna visited her room, Talwyn ventured, "Perhaps I could become a warrior. But I should swear an oath to someone. Now that I have shown that I can fight, can I swear an oath to you?"

Anna shuddered and reached out her arms, as if to shield her. "No! I no longer believe in fighting, so I cannot accept such an oath."

"But I would not be like men. I would be different from them, as you are," Talwyn protested, tossing her head.

"Different? Perhaps, but not different enough. Women, too, can learn to be brutal." Her eyes evaded Talwyn's.

"You could never have been brutal, and I wouldn't be, either," Talwyn insisted, almost rising out of the bed.

"No wolf in the forest would do to its kind what I have done to mine," Anna replied in a solemn voice. "If you must swear an oath, go to Camelot when you are strong enough and ask Dinadan or Cai. I suppose they would accept it."

But Talwyn decided that perhaps being a warrior wasn't worth getting up for after all, and she stayed in bed. She cared not whether the sun poured in through the window or the rain splashed in the garden. She had no life anymore.

31 GALAHAD

Morgan looked out towards the sea, but she did not see the water, or the gulls that flew over it. An oystercatcher landed on a rock near her, but she scarcely noticed it.

When she looked down at the water, she saw Elaine's poor frail body lying in the pond. The rocks invited her. Why live when her child was dead?

"Mother!"

She found herself in Galahad's arms, clinging to her remaining child. She had not seen Galahad coming down the rock causeway to her caer.

"You're alive, you're back." She touched the homely face as if it were the most beautiful that she had ever seen.

Galahad kissed her.

"I have heard that my father died." Galahad's voice and face were solemn.

Morgan paused, then said, "Yes, your father died." She trembled. "I can hardly bear to say it, but your sister died, too." Great tearing sobs shook her, and Galahad cried also.

They sat on the rocks and watched the crashing waves, gulls keening while Morgan told the tale of Elaine's death.

"She loved, and her lover left her. Then her foster father wanted to cast her out, and sent for me. She must have heard us talking, and went riding so fast that her horse threw her and killed her."

Galahad's eyes filled with rage. Her hand clutched the hilt of her sword. "Who was this lover? I'll fight and kill him."

Morgan saw her mistake. "No, you won't, you mustn't."

"I will. I swe . . ."

"Don't swear," Morgan interrupted. "You don't understand. It was Lancelot. Of course you won't fight her. I know you're fond of her. I have been angry at Lancelot, but she was ill when she met your sister and I don't think she meant to hurt her."

"Lancelot!" Galahad gasped. "How could she? She's never cared about anyone but Queen Guinevere." Subdued, Galahad wept. "No, I can't fight her. She's alive, then? I worried about her."

"She is." Then Morgan explained that Lancelot had gone mad for a time, and Elaine had healed her. She admitted that it might have been Elaine who had asked Lancelot to love her. She was a little ashamed of raging at Lancelot, but she didn't tell about that.

Her voice full of regret, she gazed out over the sea. "Perhaps I should have sent Elaine to Guinevere when her foster mother died, rather than leaving her in that lonely place. But I was afraid that Arthur would find out who Elaine was if she went to Camelot, and I didn't want her to be married to some man who was trying to gain favor with him. Nor could I bear to think of Arthur seeing more of her than I could."

"Poor Elaine," said Galahad again, rubbing her eyes, "but I am glad to know that Lancelot is alive."

Morgan felt a pang in her heart, but she reminded herself that Galahad after all had known Lancelot much longer than Elaine.

"I have heard rumors that she was, but I didn't know for sure. Did any other warriors of Arthur's survive?" Galahad asked.

"As far as I know, only Cai, who never went to the battle."

Galahad asked hesitantly, "Gawaine died, then?"

Morgan's hands flew up to her mouth at the mention of that name. Why him, in particular? "Yes, we buried him."

Galahad began to weep again in great choking sobs. "I know I shouldn't say this, but I liked him even better than my father."

Morgan took Galahad's hand and looked at her daughter's tear-stained face. Perhaps she should tell what she had never revealed. "That is impossible."

Galahad pulled her hand away. "It's not. Will you make me speak in pieties? I did like him better."

Morgan stroked Galahad's red hair. "Gawaine was your father."

The surf crashed below them. Galahad stared at her. "Why didn't you tell me? Why did you tell me it was King Arthur? I wish I could have told Gawaine. I wish he had known." Then Galahad paused a moment and exclaimed, "I think he did!"

"He couldn't have," said Morgan patiently. What a foolish fancy her daughter had.

"Yes, he knew as soon as I told him you were my mother."

"You weren't supposed to tell anyone," she said, but her chiding was only half-hearted. Keeping the secret no longer mattered, for she no longer wanted Galahad to try for Arthur's throne. She had lost one daughter and had no wish to risk the other one.

Galahad was half crying, half laughing. "As soon as I told him that you were my mother, he began to be kinder than ever to me. And when I said I feared I wouldn't be able to marry the girl I loved because I had no known kin, Gawaine told me I could say that he was my father. Oh, he knew. I'm glad, but I wish I had known then, too."

Morgan waited while Galahad laughed and wept. When Galahad stopped, and just looked at her inquiringly, she began to speak. "Don't be angry at me, child, I couldn't bear for you to turn from me. Elaine really was Arthur's daughter. You are not her twin, as I told you, but were born a year and some months later. After I gave her away to my cousin, I wept constantly, and thought of her all the time. I could not take her back, because my cousin also loved her desperately. I wanted to have another child.

"There was another reason, too, I must admit," Morgan added. Why not tell Galahad all? "I was disappointed that she was a daughter and most likely could not rule after Arthur. I wanted another chance to have a son, and say that it was Arthur's."

"You wanted me to be a son," said Galahad in a heartbroken voice, looking down at the rocks. More tears dripped down her cheeks.

"Yes, but I would have loved you no matter what you were like, dear one." She took Galahad's hand again, and Galahad let her. "So, I sent a message asking Gawaine to come and stay with me a while. I liked him well enough, though with no great passion. He was Arthur's cousin as well as mine, so it wouldn't have seemed strange if the child looked a little like him. I didn't tell him about Elaine, or about you either. Then I took you to the convent, as you know, and that was a place where I could visit you, much more often than I could visit Bagdemagus's dun and see Elaine. And you always knew that I was your mother."

"I am glad of that." Galahad embraced her, and Morgan could breathe again. Her daughter was not angry at her.

"I could not have endured it otherwise. Not a second time." She clung to Galahad. When had she ever clung to anyone before? She wondered. Perhaps never. "So when I saw what your disposition was like, I did not discourage you from dressing like a boy and acting like one."

"No, I'm very glad you let me. I always wanted to." Galahad held her tighter.

The gulls' cries now sounded happier to Morgan. She stroked Galahad's hair.

"By that time, I had heard enough reports of Guinevere to think that she could be a great queen, so I thought of your ruling only if she could not. And of your perhaps succeeding her after she died. But now I hope by all that's holy that you do not want to try to rule." Morgan shuddered. "You would have to fight for it and I could not bear to risk losing you in some terrible battle. The sight of the dead from the battle of Camlan will stay with me always." She clutched at Galahad and looked into her blue eyes.

Galahad sighed with relief. "I would not fight to be a king, no matter what you wanted, so I'm glad that we are in accord."

They looked at each other, as if they were just becoming acquainted, and knew that they were.

Morgan wondered how she had ever borne a child who was so homely--and so gentle-hearted. So little like herself. She was just as glad that she didn't have to deal with a daughter who was as proud and fierce as she was. "My seal girl," she said caressingly, not adding that Gawaine had called her by that name many years before.

After a short time, Galahad ventured, "I can understand why you were angry at Arthur, but you had no reason to be angry at Gawaine.

"I still wish you had let me know."

Morgan shook her head. "I knew you would never have pretended to be Arthur's son if you didn't believe that he was your father."

Galahad shrank back on the rocks. "No, of course not"

Morgan trembled a little at seeing her child pull away from her. No one else could have made her tremble. "Like Arthur, Gawaine never thought about whether there might be a child. Why should I have cared what he might have felt if he had known? He undoubtedly fathered others, too. I had no idea that it would matter to you. I never knew my father because King Uther killed him before I was old enough. It never seemed to bother you overmuch that Arthur didn't know. You never said you wanted to tell him."

Galahad's eyes widened. "Why, that would have been like claiming a throne. I didn't want to be like Mordred. Telling Gawaine would have been entirely different. I would have told him just because I liked him. If it had been a man I didn't like so much, I wouldn't have wanted to tell. But Gawaine must have thought I was his son. If I had known, I might have told him the truth, that I was his daughter. He might have understood." Galahad sighed.

"That's hardly likely, dear. How could a man understand such a thing?" Morgan kissed Galahad's cheek. "I'm sorry if I made mistakes, but you're alive, you're alive, you're alive!"

"So are you, thank whatever god or goddess," said Galahad.

They looked at the sea, and the crashing waves held no menace, but the promise of more years to know each other.

"Are you still so fond of the girl you told me about when you went off on your quest?" Morgan asked. When Galahad nodded vigorously, she had to say that Talwyn had been wounded, but was safe, and tell where she was. Morgan held her daughter while she sobbed again.

After a time, Galahad walked to her horse and, much to Morgan's astonishment, took down a set of northern pipes and went by the sea to play a wail of mourning.

Morgan went to the kitchen to bid the cooks to make a fine meal for Galahad. When she returned, she saw a strange sight.

As Galahad sat there with her pipes, a raven swooped down in the sky before her. It dove and tumbled again and again, as if it were going to fall, then caught itself, seemingly at the last moment. Galahad laughed. Then the raven landed on a rock not far from the young warrior, cocked its head in a comical way, and hopped to a closer rock and a still closer one.

Galahad smiled at the bird.

Morgan walked out towards her again, and the raven flew further away, but not too far.

"Did you see that bird? It came so close to me."

"It's probably one of the two that have been flying close in recent weeks," Morgan said, pointing to another raven in the sky. "This one, which isn't quite as large, flies often close to me. And the larger bird seems to have taken a fancy to you."

Anna walked in the woods. The bare trees and sunless sky did not sadden her. She had seen a fox earlier in the day, so her thoughts turned to the vixen.

A figure in breeches appeared before her on the path. Tensing, Anna put her hand in the place where her sword should have been.

But the newcomer called out to her, "Lance, is it really you?"

It was Drian, as handsome as ever, with a little gray in her hair, leading a fine chestnut mare.

Anna threw her arms around her friend. "Drian! I've never had a chance to thank you for saving my life."

"I'm not used to being hugged by a nun. Should I kiss you?" Drian did not wait for an answer, but kissed Anna most impiously on the lips.

"I have taken no vows. I just wear these clothes, and call myself Sister Anna."

"And live in a convent. No doubt you cause quite a stir there. What a lot of women!" Drian pretended to be nuns swooning over Anna.

Anna laughed and led her along the path. "You're still the same as ever. I'm glad to see you. How did you come to these parts?"

Drian grinned and ran her fingers through her hair. "Why, to see whether you were alive, of course. I heard that nearly all of the warriors of the round table were killed in King Arthur's last battle, but some said that Lancelot wasn't in it. People said that the queen had gone to this convent, so I guessed that you might be here, too. I'm glad you're looking sound, if a little feminine."

Much of Anna's happiness faded at the memory of Camlann. "It was a terrible battle. I didn't arrive until it was over, and I saw Arthur die." She couldn't bring herself to add what her part in that had been.

Drian spoke up in a teasing voice. "And, if you were gone, I thought I'd comfort the beautiful widow. Perhaps Guinevere would have decided she liked me after all."

Anna stared, then laughed. "You're still incorrigible."

"And was the young warrior called Galahad in this terrible battle?"

"No, I think he was still away on a quest, thank the Virgin. So you've met him, and decided that not all men are bad?"

Drian roared with laughter. "If all young men were like him, I'd like them very much."

Anna saw no reason for merriment. "Too many died. I regret the deaths even of those who weren't so good."

Drian's laughter abruptly ceased. "Did your friend Gawaine die?"

Tears formed in Anna's eyes. "Yes. I found his body, and helped to bury him." She could say no more. How could Drian, who had disliked Gawaine, care?

Drian put an arm around her. "I'm sorry. If he kept your secret, he was a true friend."

"He was," Anna choked.

"I'll compose a song about him. There are many others, but this will be different."

"Not about the fighting," Anna said. "About how he could jest."

"About his jesting," Drian agreed, wiping the tears off Anna's cheeks. "Speaking of jests, how did they get you in those clothes? Why don't you put on some breeches?"

"That would look a little strange when I'm living in a convent. I don't care anymore. Another life, another disguise." She made a dismissive gesture to show that all such worldly things were behind her.

"Don't care, indeed! I wouldn't let anybody put me in a skirt."

Anna laughed. "Surely no one would try." She tried to picture Drian in a skirt and failed.

"But can I greet the wondrous Guinevere? Don't worry, I doubt that I can steal her from you, but I'd certainly like to try." Drian winked.

Choking back laughter, Anna said, "Very well, you can, but I'm not sure she'll like you any better than she ever did."

"I'm not suitable for her, am I?"

"You are a little different. She has lived only in caers and convents." Anna wished that those two had never met before, or at least that Drian had not openly flirted with her in front of Guinevere. It would be good if Guinevere could like Drian now.

Just walking beside Drian made the sky seem less gray. Even the air was not so cold. Jackdaws' cries seemed as pleasant as the songs of other birds.

They came to the convent gate and tied up Drian's mare. Anna brought her friend to the great oaken convent door. The sister porter giggled at Drian's winks.

"Perhaps I should live here myself," Drian said.

Anna couldn't restrain her laughter. "I hardly think so, especially if you won't give up your breeches."

"Oh, I'd take them off often, every time I was asked to."

Stifling a laugh, Anna said, "Hush. Guinevere is probably in the library."

She led Drian to the library, where nuns were reading and copying manuscripts, then to the table where Guinevere was perusing a faded scroll.

Guinevere looked up and stared.

"Guinevere, do you remember Drian?"

Drian grinned at Guinevere and devoured her with her eyes.

Guinevere smiled and rose from the table. "Of course I remember Drian. I thank you very much for saving Lancelot's life." She inclined her head and extended her hand.

Drian seized the hand and kissed it. "Thank you, most gracious highness, still the fairest lady in Britain."

Guinevere took back her hand. "I am queen no longer. The sisters are trying to read and copy manuscripts, so we should be quiet. But perhaps you could play for us all later? I think the abbess would permit us to hear a harper. With suitable songs, of course."

"Of course, nothing bawdy," Drian promised. "I've never had a chance to play at a convent. It would be a great honor."

"Best confine your playing to the harp," Guinevere said with the faintest of smiles. She resumed her seat. "I am indeed glad to see you. I know that Anna has always had a fondness for rogues."

"I think you may be the greatest rogue of all, Lady Guinevere." Drian bowed as if presenting a great compliment.

Anna barely managed to hold back laughter, and could see that Guinevere was doing the same.

"For many years, I have been composing verses," Guinevere said. "I cannot own that they are mine, but perhaps if I told you some, you might sing them."

"I would be honored." Drian's smile was genuine.

Anna guided Drian out of the library, past the nuns who were surreptitiously staring up from their books and scrolls.

As they emerged into the courtyard, Drian laughed. "God's eyebrow, Lance! This is too funny. You're the feminine one. She's the one who should have been the warrior, and you should have been the lady."

"Nonsense, there is no such thing between us. Feminine, indeed! I have been the greatest warrior in the world." Anna was irritated, especially because she had to stand there in those black robes.

Drian just kept guffawing until they were in the convent garden. A blue tit flew across a bed of faded plants.

They sat on a bench.

"Sorry if I've embarrassed you. I'm just not cut out for a convent."

"No, you certainly are not." She tried, somewhat unsuccessfully, to be cool. Seeing that Drian was the same as ever made her happy. "Where will you go now? I hope you aren't still stealing jewels."

"No, I'm too old for that." Drian shook her handsome head. "I need a quieter way to live. I've heard that Cai is lord of Camelot now. Do you think he'd let me live there, as long as I don't steal anything?"

"No doubt he would. I'm sure he'd find you entertaining." Yes, Cai would be amused.

"Can I say that I'm your friend?"

"Of course, as long as you don't then jest about how feminine I am."

"I don't know whether I can resist that, dear sister nun. What a pity you aren't wearing clothes that show your legs a bit more," said Drian, nudging her in the ribs.

"Well, visit me sometimes, but not too often," Anna told her. "I'm afraid that Guinevere will fall in love with you if she sees too much of you."

"She's not the one I'd try to seduce," Drian replied, looking into her eyes.

Anna's tone became more serious. "Guinevere is everything to me, now more than ever."

"I know, that's the only reason I'm looking elsewhere," said Drian, kissing her on the mouth.

Anna put her arms around her and pressed her tight.

"You saved me when Bellangere attacked me. I owe my life to you. How can I ever thank you?"

Drian stroked her cheek with weather-worn but gentle hands. "I won't even try to answer that one. I'm glad you're well."

Another letter arrived from Cai, now Constantine.

Dear Lady Guinevere, or is it Sister Guinevere?

You were my foster sister-in-law, so I suppose that in either case Sister Guinevere is the correct form of address.

Soldiers from the garrison of Londinium tell the tale that Mordred tried to force you to marry him, but you escaped to their garrison, locked yourself in the Tower, and did not depart until you heard that Mordred was dead. No doubt it was your sister, Gwynhwyfach.

Apparently she is living a quiet life in Londinium now. The soldiers say she was the purest lady imaginable when she stayed in their garrison and called herself Queen Guinevere.

Cai, now Constantine

Guinevere rejoiced that her sister had not trusted Mordred and had escaped from him, but she sighed over the impossibility of being close to Gwynhwyfach.

Talwyn barricaded herself in a plain convent bed with no draperies around it. She felt too dispirited to go and rest under the bare trees in the garden, which even in the brown, damp winter was fairer than the convent room. However, Guinevere had found some pretty things to brighten it up for her. Cai, now Constantine, had sent a few of their favorite coverlets, hangings, and gowns, entirely unbidden--somehow he had known what their favorites were. Or perhaps the serving women knew and chose them.

With only a slight knock, Galahad walked through the door and shut it.

Talwyn pulled up the covers. She wore only her woolen bedgown. Her delight in seeing Galahad was dimmed by the thought of how bedraggled she must look, for she had been desultory in combing her hair.

She tried to sound indignant, though her heart beat fast. Galahad's face was browner, but Galahad otherwise looked not much different. "What do you mean by walking in this way? I haven't seen you in a year, and you walk into my room as if you belonged here. I can't believe that I'm not safe even in the convent. How did the nuns ever let you come in here? Go to the room for visitors and wait for me to come and see you. I don't want any man to see me like this, not even you."

Galahad bowed to her and did not leave. A rare ray of winter sun lit the young warrior's red hair. "Pardon me. I just arrived, and I have heard that you had been wounded. I couldn't bear to stay away, or even to wait for you to come to the visitors' room. I had to come and see you. You look to be healed. Are you?"

"Yes, it doesn't hurt much now." Talwyn pulled the covers up even further, but she felt less embarrassed. If Galahad truly cared about her, her looks at the moment would not matter. But nevertheless she wished that she was wearing a pretty gown and her hair was combed.

"I'm sorry that your father died." Galahad spoke quietly and touched Talwyn's arm.

"Thank you." Talwyn tried to hold back tears. At least Galahad did not say, as some people at Camelot had, that it was just as well because he was mad. Or tell her like some of the nuns that it was because God had wanted him.

"My father died, also." The light in Galahad's blue eyes faded. "And so did my sister."

Poor Galahad! Talwyn reached out and clasped the young warrior's hand. "That's terrible. The sister who pretended to be a man?"

"No, she didn't. I'm the one who does that." Galahad looked at her inquiringly.

Talwyn nearly jumped at hearing these words. The subject had been much on her mind. "Is it possible? You look more like a man than Lancelot does."

"I'm not a man, though. Once you said that nothing I could tell you would make any difference in how you felt about me. Is that still true?" Galahad's voice quavered ever so slightly.

"Probably. But now I don't know what to believe. You'll have to drop your breeches and show me." Talwyn grinned. Far from embarrassment, she felt as if she were playing some pleasant game.

"What a thing to say after you haven't seen me for a year. 'Drop your breeches.' I'm too shy." Galahad nevertheless returned the grin and appeared to be holding back laughter.

"If you don't, I'll touch you. I must know." She laughed.

"Is that supposed to be a threat? Go on, Talwyn, do your worst." Galahad leered with delight and moved closer to her.

"You shameless thing!" She touched Galahad's leather breeches, but pulled her hand away quickly. The verdict was unmistakable. "You are a woman!"

"You didn't touch me for long," Galahad whined in a voice like a child wanting another cake.

Talwyn laughed again and, pretending to be coy, pulled her hair over her face, then smoothed it back again.

"You'll have to kiss me for a while first. You're just as bad as a man."

"Of course I want to kiss you. I'm just jesting." Galahad sat on the bed with her, and they hugged and kissed, laughed and jested, and touched in other ways as well.

The convent's bell rang, and its sound was joyous, but no more than they were.

Talwyn felt warmer than ever before. But was Galahad truly pledged to her? "You said that your sister dressed as a man so that she could marry a woman. Have you done that?"

"No. I only intended to. And I still do, unless you still object to marriage." Galahad wrapped her arms around Talwyn.

"Where's the need for it," Talwyn asked, "if you'll let me dress like a man, too, and go on quests with you?"

"How frightful! A woman dressing like a man. How could I ever permit such a thing? Of course you can, who's to say you can't?" She eyed Talwyn wickedly. "But it will be a little harder to conceal your shape than mine."

"You're terrible! Have you at least been true to me?" Talwyn asked, running her fingers through Galahad's red hair.

"Almost." Galahad nibbled Talwyn's neck, hiding her own face.

"That's not so bad when I wouldn't make any promises, but you must do better in the future," Talwyn admonished, and Galahad assured her that she would, and said that after all they would be traveling together.

The next morning, many kisses and other touches later, they dressed.

"I can't bear to see you cover yourself up," Galahad groaned.

"It won't be for long," Talwyn assured her. "I am also attached to the sight of you," she said, nuzzling Galahad's shoulder.

While Galahad pulled on her tunic, Talwyn asked, "Who gave you that pleasant face, anyway? Who were your parents?"

"My mother is the Lady Morgan of Cornwall." Galahad said this a little tentatively, as if Talwyn might object.

"The notorious Lady Morgan! How exciting!" Talwyn exclaimed, delighted until she thought that Galahad's father must be King Arthur. She tried to keep her face from showing what she thought of that.

"And my father was Gawaine."

Talwyn smiled. "How wonderful!" He would have been a good father-in-law. And--and he knew it! She remembered Gawaine telling her that she might someday meet a daughter of his. He must have known about Galahad. That's why he had been so concerned about Talwyn. "I have a message for you. Gawaine asked me, if I ever met a woman who was his daughter, to tell her that he loved her and wished he had done more for her. He knew I loved you. That's why he gave me the message."

Galahad grabbed Talwyn's arm. "Are you sure?" Her eyes were wide. "He knew that I was a woman? He knew that I loved you, and he cared about me nonetheless?"

Talwyn nodded. "Indeed he did. Your father told me several times that you loved me. He warned me that the king wanted to marry me, and helped me flee so I could marry you. Your father arranged your marriage!"

"So he did!" Galahad laughed and cried, and Talwyn held her. "Why didn't he tell me that he was my father?" Galahad asked, still sniffling. "Or that he knew I was a woman?"

"Perhaps he thought that your mother had the right to tell you what she wanted, and he didn't want to contradict her." Talwyn did not truly think that this was so. She thought it likely that Gawaine had imagined that Galahad would rather believe she was King Arthur's child, and hadn't wanted to see her disappointed to learn that she was not. But Talwyn did not want to say that, because she thought Galahad would brood about it for years and be sad. She was a little surprised that Galahad seemed readily to accept the unlikely story of Gawaine believing in the mother's right to tell whatever she wanted about the father, true or false.

Talwyn thought about how Galahad had said that night that she had loved her for years and been afraid of being rejected for being a woman, and that Lancelot had been afraid of Guinevere for the same reason. Talwyn thought that Gawaine had also been afraid that Galahad wouldn't love him as a father, and she marveled at how afraid people were of those they love. As for herself, she might have been bold enough to tell Galahad how she felt if she had known that Galahad was a woman, but she had been sure that it would be foolish to declare her love too readily when she thought that Galahad was a man.

Waiting for Ninian to accompany her into the forest, Anna paced around the convent garden. The winter sun had already replaced the dawn, and she longed to be away among the trees-- not the garden apple trees, but the wilder oaks and beeches. She could see her breath when she exhaled with impatience.

The sister porter entered the garden and told her she had a visitor, "a young warrior called Galahad."

"Oh, send him here!"

She nearly leapt at the door when Galahad appeared.

Galahad looked much the same as before, but glowed in the chilly morning air. Here was someone else who, like Drian, was familiar, unchanged, and Lancelot rejoiced at the thought. She flung her arms around the young warrior.

"Lord Lancelot!" Galahad exclaimed, returning her embrace.

"I'm called Anna, or Sister Anna, now, although I have taken no vows," she explained, clasping Galahad's shoulders. "How good it is to see you. Talwyn is here."

Galahad's smile was even wider than Anna had expected. "I know. I've seen her. I wanted to see you for a moment alone. I traveled North and West. It was wonderful. But I missed the great battle, and now King Arthur is dead." Galahad sighed.

"Thank all the saints you were not here, or you would have perished like the others," said Anna, embracing Galahad again. "I'm glad to have a moment to speak with you alone. There are some things I'd rather not tell a woman."

She could not look into Galahad's earnest blue eyes. Her voice lost its joy and became toneless. "You were right to ponder giving up fighting after Lionel's death. I hope that you have decided that you don't want to be a warrior anymore, or at least won't fight battles, now that the men of the round table have killed each other."

Anna forced herself to continue. She looked at the ground, not at her young friend. "Gawaine once said to me that he could see no point in getting fond of women only to see them die in childbed. If I could, I would tell him that I see no point in being friends with men, only to see them dead on a battlefield.

"I did not find him alive," she said, her voice trembling, "but I was with Arthur when he died. I sat with both of their bodies. Mordred had stabbed Gawaine in the back, and when I came upon his body I saw a raven flying away with flesh from the wound. I took off Gawaine's gold and jewels so the battlefield scavengers would not cut off his fingers or arms to get them, as they did to so many others. I saved the jewels to send to his mother. Then we took him and buried him. So that is what comes of this glorious fighting and dying bravely, one lies there powerless and has one's body nearly abused at the end." Tears dripped down her cheeks.

But there was more that Anna needed to tell someone, and could not bring herself to tell Guinevere. She stared at a flowerless rosebush. "Then, after the king died, Mordred called out and I learned that he was still alive. He begged for mercy, but I killed him and slashed the body many times, like some mad brute. I can scarcely believe I did that." She slumped onto a stone bench, exhausted from telling her tale.

She looked up and saw that Galahad had paled. The young warrior sat on the bench beside her and hugged her tightly. Then Galahad burst into tears, in a quantity that surprised Lancelot, and she had to soothe Galahad.

After some time had passed, Galahad spoke. "If you wanted to persuade me to keep from fighting in battles, you have succeeded. I can't imagine you slashing corpses, but if you could I could. Have you recovered from these terrible things?"

"As much as I can."

A raven landed in a nearby bare apple tree and called loudly. It moved its head from side to side as if it were trying to understand the conversation.

Galahad managed to smile. "That raven has followed me ever since I visited my mother at Tintagel. Whenever I walk outdoors, it flies with me. It amuses me when I am sad, and calls out when other riders come near. Isn't that strange?"

Anna nodded. "Yes, but there is something very likable about that bird. I had thought I would never like the sight of a raven again, but yet I do."

The raven made a sound, as if answering her.

"This raven eats its meat from the table," Galahad said. "I have never seen him worry a corpse."

Thinking that she had imposed too much of her own pain on Galahad, Anna forced herself to speak of other things. "So will you marry Talwyn?"

This question made Galahad grin.

"She does not want to marry. She thinks I could be a tyrant, especially if I went off on quests without her."

Anna nodded again. "Guinevere does not want us to go off and live together, with me pretending to be the husband. So we shall live here, in this community."

"We have solved the problem in a different way," Galahad said. "You are both dressed as women, and we shall both dress as men, and go on quests together."

Anna frowned a little. "But even so, you should marry her."

Galahad shrugged. "I'm convinced, but you'll have to persuade Talwyn. I'll get her."

When Galahad returned to the winter garden, Guinevere as well as Talwyn accompanied the young warrior. Talwyn had more color in her face than she had since coming to the convent, and this was the first time she had summoned the energy to walk to the garden. Anna rejoiced to see the girl break her long self-imposed exile in her room.

It was good that Talwyn had brightened on seeing see Galahad, but the orphaned girl needed someone to talk sense to her. Stern as a parent, Anna spoke to Talwyn. "You really must marry Galahad if you want to go off with him. What if he gets you with child?"

Talwyn giggled. "I wouldn't mind causing a little scandal."

Then Ninian hurried out to join them. She shivered at the cold, but her smile was enough to warm the others gathered there, or even the whole community of nuns.

"Dear Mother Ninian," Galahad said, embracing her.

The plump old nun hugged Galahad.

"Why, how did you know Mother Ninian?" asked Anna.

Ninian beamed and clasped the young warrior's hand. "I raised Galahad here. What do you think of my handiwork?"

Looking a little nervous, but also proud, Galahad launched into an explanation. "My mother was the Lady Morgan of Cornwall."

Her eyes widening, Guinevere gasped. "So Arthur had a son after all! There's so much she didn't tell us."

Galahad hesitated and regarded the bare ground. "She did have a child by King Arthur, but it wasn't me. My sister was Elaine."

Anna shuddered. Would she lose Galahad's friendship? "I now know that Elaine was Morgan's child. Your mother told me." She didn't say in what manner Morgan had spoken. "I wronged Elaine. Please forgive me." She bowed her head.

"Of course I do," said Galahad, clasping her hand.

Anna felt overwhelmed with gratitude. Tears formed in her eyes. "Many thanks," she choked. "The horrible thing is that I would have been more careful of Elaine if I had known that she was the daughter of a man who I believed was my friend. And if that's the case, I never should have touched her anyway. Poor Elaine."

There were tears on Guinevere's face. "Morgan never trusted me. I wish she had let me take care of Elaine when her foster mother died, and then Elaine would still be alive and perhaps would have found someone who could return her love. I would have protected her."

"You're a good foster mother," Talwyn said, putting a hand on her shoulder.

"It's strange to think that the one who might have been kindest to Elaine was her stepmother, but I think it's true," Galahad mused.

Anna was not eager to keep talking about Elaine. "But what about you? You said you weren't Arthur's child?" she asked Galahad.

Galahad colored red as her hair. "My mother had always told me that my father was Arthur, but when I returned, she told me that my father was truly Gawaine, and I was glad to hear it because I liked him."

"Why, that's wonderful," Anna exclaimed, hugging Galahad. "What a perfect son for Gawaine! I wish he had known that."

Galahad grinned. "He did, at the end. I was the only one left ignorant."

"It's clear why your mother told you that you were Arthur's," said Guinevere, a little testily. She tossed her head, letting her veil float in the breeze.

Must Guinevere think about the succession to Arthur? Anna sighed inwardly. Surely those concerns were now behind them.

As if anxious to repair any damage, Galahad quickly said, "Please don't think that she plotted against you. She thought you would be a good ruler."

"Of course she didn't plot," Guinevere said, too sweetly. Her smile did not look genuine.

Anna spoke up to prevent these two from quarreling. "Imagine Gawaine's son being raised in a convent."

Talwyn's eyes and mouth were so full of mirth that it seemed as if not only they, but every part of her body, was laughing.

"Lord Lancelot, I mean Sister Anna, Galahad fooled even you. Galahad is not anyone's son."

Reeling, Anna stared at Galahad. She looked at the young warrior from head to toes. Her gaze fixed on the cheeks, on which there was no stubble, despite the tiny beard on Galahad's chin. "What? It can't be."

Galahad was half blushing, half laughing. "But it is. I look a little more like a man than you do, but I am a woman."

Anna's legs nearly crumpled under her. How could she not have guessed?

"My mother thought that it would be wise to take advantage of my seeming sex, and I agreed," Galahad went on. "It is much easier to be a king than a queen, as I am sure you'll agree, Queen Guinevere."

"Of course it is," laughed Guinevere, truly smiling at Galahad now.

"And even if I never tried to become a king, I thought life would be much easier for a man than for a witch's daughter. I'm sorry that I deceived you, Lord Lancelot--Anna. There never was a sister who dressed like a man, only me."

"But why didn't you tell me? Surely you knew I'd keep your secret." Anna was mystified. How could Galahad have kept the truth from her?

Galahad looked at the bare flowerbeds. "My mother made me swear not to. I now suppose that it was because she thought she might have disagreements with Queen Guinevere, and didn't want her to know about me because I might be a possible rival for the throne. I'm glad to be out of all such plans, and I'm even happier that my mother has abandoned them, too. Also, I never thought of myself as a woman. I'm not much like my mother, am I?" They all nodded in agreement. "I never met a woman who was like me until I met you, and so I never wanted to be one. Now it doesn't seem so bad."

Galahad turned her gaze to Talwyn. "Fortunately, although Talwyn did not guess my sex at first, she didn't care when she found out."

"No, I didn't, but now I think it's nice that you are a woman, more or less." Talwyn pressed Galahad's arm and giggled.

"And I am glad that you are Gawaine's child," Anna said, embracing Galahad again.

Then, in front of all of them, Talwyn tried to tickle Galahad in the side, and Galahad pretended to fence with her hand to keep her off, and they were both dueling with their bare arms and chortling.

"You see," the old nun said to Anna, "Mordred did not kill laughter. And even though Arthur and many other people you have known have met tragic ends, not everyone has to."

Galahad's raven made a loud sound that might have been laughter.

When Galahad and Talwyn prepared to leave, they spoke with Anna alone in the garden, where the first shoots of snowdrops and crocuses were breaking through the earth. A rosy dawn was dissolving into yellow sun.

Talwyn, like Galahad, wore a man's breeches and tunic.

"We don't like to leave you to spend your life confined in a convent," Galahad told Anna as they walked along the well-marked paths while the nuns prayed in the chapel. Galahad's raven perched on her shoulder.

Seeing the anxiety in Galahad's blue eyes, Anna smiled. "If I am confined, who is confining me? Neither father, nor brother, nor husband, nor lord. Neither the civil law nor the Church law. I am living among friends, with the woman who is more to me than any other. Don't worry about me."

"But we do," cried Talwyn, grabbing her arm. "You can't have changed that much. You always liked to travel. We have decided that you can travel with us whenever you want."

"Yes, we would like that," Galahad said, and her raven flew from her shoulder to Anna's, perched there, and cawed.

Anna laughed--not at her young friends, but at the bird. "Perhaps I shall at times, by and by, but just now I want to spend all my days with Guinevere, and I am certain that you want to be alone together. I won't be lonely. I am planning to visit my friend Aglovale's family."

"Greet Percy if you see him before I do," Galahad said.

"Indeed I shall. And I am sure I'll have visits from my friend, Drian, which won't be dull." Anna grinned. "I believe you have met Drian?"

"I have," Galahad said, blushing.

"Who's Drian?" Talwyn asked.

"I'll tell you later," Galahad said, pressing her hand.

The morning sun was rising higher in the sky. "You should leave while the day is ahead of you," Anna said. "I am grateful for your concern." She embraced them, and the raven flew from her shoulder back to Galahad's.

"I have to see Lady Guinevere one more time," Talwyn said, hurrying back into the convent.

Anna and Galahad went to ready the horses.

Galahad and Talwyn visited Morgan at Tintagel, but they were been summoned by an urgent message from Cai--now Constantine--to come to Camelot. Queen Morgause of Lothian and Orkney had sent word that she was on her way there and expected to see Galahad. Galahad felt much curiosity. She remembered seeing that queen from a distance, but of course the queen had not noticed her.

Spring made the journey to Camelot pleasant, with its clumps of violets growing by the streams and bluebells in the woods. Galahad's raven flew with them, sometimes perching on her shoulder. Talwyn wore her chain mail, though it was a trifle tight. Galahad worried that Talwyn looked too pretty to be convincing in the guise of a man. And poor Talwyn was not used to binding her breasts, which were much larger than Galahad's. Galahad could see that she looked uncomfortable, squirming as if rebelling against the binding.

Galahad tried to teach Talwyn the songs of different birds, but Talwyn didn't try very hard to learn.

"I like my little bird best," she said, grabbing at Galahad.

"Warriors are not supposed to be grabbing at each other, at least not when they are out riding," Galahad told her.

They laughed loudly because they were both nervous at going back to the caer that held too many memories.

Talwyn had not wanted to go. "What am I supposed to say?" she had asked. "'Here's the spot where I was wounded, and here's where Creirwy was struck down? My father was killed over there? This is the place where the stake was put to burn Queen Guinevere?' I suppose you'll want to know all that."

Galahad had shuddered. "I don't want to put you in any more pain, but I don't want to be parted from you even for a little while."

Talwyn hadn't wanted to be parted either, so she traveled with Galahad.

There were only two guards at the gate and a sprinkling of guards in the courtyard, far fewer than in King Arthur's day.

Galahad had thought that only ghosts would welcome them, but by the time their horses were stabled by the lone stablehand, Constantine and Dinadan had come to the courtyard. The two greeted them and talked so rapidly that she did not have a chance to feel lonely.

"Wait 'til you meet her highness, queen of Lothian and Orkney," Dinadan said. His dark brown hair had not yet turned gray. "She arrived last week and she's been ordering us around ever since. I don't think she's grasped the fact that Cai is lord of this place now."

"I have to be respectful to her. She's my foster brother's aunt. Do you think you could manage to be respectful to her, too?" Constantine had grown a mustache, but he grumbled in a way that made it seem as if everything were the same as ever.

"I do respect her, in fact I adore her," Dinadan insisted, rolling his eyes. "It is especially sweet how she says that there aren't any real men in the world anymore, now that Gawaine has died--except for her dear Lamorak. Dear Lamorak must be heartbroken at staying in Lothian alone for a while."

"Let me take you to her, or she'll have my head," Constantine commanded, taking Talwyn's arm. "She's staying in Arthur's old room. She would have stayed in Guinevere's, except of course that Gareth and Agravaine died there."

First they went to the rooms that had been Guinevere's, and Talwyn changed into one of her old gowns.

It was more than a little strange going to Arthur's room, where they had never been. They had seen his tapestries, because those had been sent to Tintagel, and Morgan had hung them in her great hall. Lesser hangings did not quite fill the spaces.

White-haired Queen Morgause stood tall and erect, dressed in magnificent gold-embroidered black robes. She immediately swooped at Galahad.

"Dear grandson," she exclaimed, hugging Galahad.

Galahad pulled back a little. How could Queen Morgause know that she was Gawaine's child?

"Of course I knew the moment I learned about dear Gawaine's will that you must be his son," Morgause explained, gazing at Galahad as if she were the most fascinating person in the world. "You do have his eyes."

"It's true, Gawaine's my father," Galahad said, relieved that she knew. "And the Lady Morgan of Cornwall is my mother."

"Good for her! I never appreciated her enough, but of course I didn't know that she had borne Gawaine a son," said Morgause fondly, embracing Galahad again. "I am astonished that he never told me."

"No doubt he meant to." Galahad did not say how recently Gawaine himself had learned.

"He sent me a strange letter before he went out to battle," Morgause said. "All he said was, 'I love you, mother. Lancelot did not kill my brother Gareth, and killed Agravaine only because of an unprovoked attack. If Guinevere and Lancelot ever come to your lands for protection, please give it to them.' That was an odd farewell."

Galahad smiled. "He was always concerned about his friends."

"Hmpf. And who is this young lady?" Queen Morgause asked, looking over Talwyn.

"This is my wife, Talwyn." Like a proud husband, Galahad put an arm around Talwyn.

"Greetings, Queen Morgause," said Talwyn, cheerfully but not shyly, curtseying.

Morgause's gaze went to Talwyn's belly. "Are you carrying a child yet?"

Talwyn giggled. "Not yet."

Morgause gave Galahad a look that was sterner than it had been. "Gawaine's wives both had babies after nine months. You don't look much like him, more's the pity, but I hope you will keep up the tradition. Keep plowing the field, Galahad."

Galahad burst out laughing, but Talwyn did not. Galahad noted that Queen Morgause neglected to mention that Gawaine's wives had both died in giving birth, and the babies had died, too.

Morgause frowned. "Can you tell me how Gawaine died? I can't believe that Lancelot killed him in a duel, as the stories say."

Galahad felt a small flash of pain, as she always did when she thought of her father's death. "No, Mordred stabbed him in the back when he was bending over Gaheris, as Gaheris lay dead."

Morgause groaned and put her hands over her face. "Gaheris wasn't worth it."

Galahad silently agreed, but thought it was a bit hard for Gaheris's mother to say so.

Morgause wiped her eyes, which had tears dripping from them. "I knew it must be something like that. No one ever could have defeated Gawaine in a fight."

Galahad had seen Lancelot defeat Gawaine in contests a number of times, but she said nothing and was thankful that Talwyn didn't contradict her grandmother.

"Lancelot, Guinevere, and my mother buried him," Galahad said.

"Do you know where he's buried? Cai didn't know," Morgause asked eagerly, grasping Galahad's hand.

"Yes, Lancelot showed me, so I can take you there if you like. I have not been to the battlefield to see where Gaheris died." She hoped that the queen had no desire to see it either.

"Of course I want to see where Gawaine is buried," Morgause said. "I don't want to go to the place where my sons were killed." Then she pursed her lips and her voice became indignant. "Some conniving woman managed to persuade Gawaine to mention her in his will and is trying to take part of your inheritance. But I won't give her a thing, dear."

"She's not conniving," Galahad said, suppressing a laugh. "Indeed, she's already said that her share should go to the poor. I think you should let the will be administered the way my father wanted it to be."

"Don't you believe that she'll give it to the poor," Morgause replied, shaking her handsome head. "And if Gawaine had really cared about her, he would have married her."

"Perhaps she wouldn't have wanted to marry him," Talwyn said with irritation, although it was obvious that these words would anger the queen.

"Nonsense. Any woman would have wanted to marry Gawaine," Galahad's grandmother snapped. "Galahad, your wife is impertinent. Be a man, dear. Don't let her."

Galahad couldn't help but laugh. She said what she hadn't planned to say. "In truth, Queen Morgause, I'm your granddaughter."

The Queen of Lothian and Orkney pulled away and sank into a chair. Her face sagged, showing more wrinkles than had been apparent before. "Gawaine had no son, then." Her voice sounded old.

Peering at Galahad, the queen studied her face, then cast her gaze down Galahad's body.

Galahad flinched. How foolish she had been to imagine that she might have the queen's love.

Morgause rose from the chair. "Dear Gawaine was so manly that I shouldn't be surprised if his daughter is, too. I understand wanting to be a man, Galahad dear. Anyone with any spirit would." She embraced Galahad again.

Galahad smiled, amused, relieved, and pleased. She knew that being dear Gawaine's only known surviving child was the reason that she was acceptable.

Morgause assumed a commanding air. "Of course, you'll have to have the child yourself, then."

"Child!" Galahad jumped back.

"To continue the line, dear. But so many fine warriors have died! Where will you ever find a man who is good breeding stock?" the queen sighed.

Galahad recovered a little. "There's always Lancelot," she suggested.

Morgause nodded. "That's true. I've heard he's horribly pious, so I don't think he'd be entertaining, but he'll do for the purpose."

Talwyn gave Galahad a sly smile. "Will you promise that you'll do with Lancelot only what will get you with child? I won't be jealous then."

"Only that and nothing else," Galahad assured her, not meeting her gaze.

Morgause gave Talwyn a dismissive look. "Galahad dear, if you let your wife speak so freely, people might guess that you aren't a man."

Galahad saw the expression on Talwyn's face and knew that Talwyn might never dress like a woman again, no matter how uncomfortable breast-binding was.

Galahad's raven flew in through the window and perched on Galahad's shoulder.

Queen Morgause gasped.

"He's wild but tame," Galahad assured her. "He flew with me from Tintagel. He likes to stay nearby."

"Of course he does." Morgause had turned pale. The bird flew to her shoulder. Tears formed in her eyes. She sank down in the nearest chair.

Galahad reached over to touch her arm.

"Don't worry over me, Galahad," her grandmother said. "At times I see things other people do not." The raven flew to her hand and she smiled at it. "I'm right glad this raven accompanies you."

When Galahad and Talwyn strolled back into the courtyard, they heard a few bars of harp music.

"Welcome to Camelot, Galahad," said the harper, who looked familiar.

"Drian! Greetings. I didn't expect to find you here." Galahad felt her face flush.

"I come here at times to amuse the Lord Constantine."

"Talwyn, may I present Drian the harper, an old friend of Lancelot's. Drian, this is my lady wife, Talwyn." Galahad spoke quickly, before Drian could make any more familiar greeting.

Drian made a sweeping bow to Talwyn, "I am honored, fair lady."

"And I am glad to meet you." Talwyn smiled, clearly recognizing Drian for what she was. "How many of us are there, I wonder?"

"Now I also have a wife, though she does not come to Camelot." Drian's eyes twinkled. "I believe you know her. Her name is Creirwy."

Talwyn clapped her hands. "Oh, how splendid. She's well, then? Please tell her how glad I am to hear it."

Looking to make sure no one was near, Drian replied, "I've always had a weakness for women warriors."

Galahad frowned.

Percy saw a nun ride up to his father's holding. He had never seen a nun ride astride before, and that black horse, which was somehow familiar, seemed a strange mount for her.

His father hurried to greet the nun, who swung down from her horse like a man and embraced him.

Who ever heard of a nun behaving like that? Percy stared.

The nun turned to him and said, "Greetings, Percy. I'm right glad to see you."

He flung himself on his knees at her feet. Lancelot was a woman, a nun! It was a miracle, the greatest miracle he had ever been privileged to witness.

"You are a saint!" he cried, filled with awe.

"No, I'm not." Lancelot backed off. "Get up, Percy. I'm just a woman. Nuns have given me refuge and I call myself Sister Anna, but I'm not truly holy."

But Percy was not to be swayed. He remained kneeling. Of course she was too modest to admit she was a saint. "You are a saint, come to live among us sinners. Please bless me."

"No, no, get up off your knees," Lancelot insisted, her voice full of distress.

Percy's father was choking as if he was attempting not to laugh. He always tried to spoil solemn moments.

"I won't get up until you tell me what to do with my life. Should I enter a monastery? Can I marry and still be holy? Please tell me." Percy looked beseechingly at her.

The saint who had been Lancelot sighed. "Very well, I'll tell you what you should do. Never fight in a battle. And listen more often to your parents, who are wiser than you think."

Aglovale smiled broadly. "Thank you, my friend."

Disappointed, Percy sank back on his heels.

But he nodded, "Holy Sister Anna, I promise never to fight in battles. May I fight to defend women?"

The holy woman put one of her blessed hands on his shoulder. "I suppose so. But you should fight as little as possible and try to find other ways to help them if you can."

Percy began to stand, but he remembered that he had another question. "And can I marry someday?"

"Of course, if you love truly," she said.

Her smile seemed almost maternal and he wondered why he had never noticed that before. Perhaps he had not had the grace to see it.

He couldn't wait to see his friend Galahad and tell him the astounding fact that Lancelot was a woman.

In the spring, Guinevere was eager to ride out with Anna and learn the flowers and bird songs. Anna suspected that Guinevere was moved primarily by concern for her lover rather than by birdsong, but still it was a joy to be with her there in the green world.

They raced their horses and laughed, not caring who won. Guinevere's mare was a head swifter.

"What is winning?" Guinevere asked.

"I never heard of such a word," Anna answered her.

Then they tumbled on the grass, calling each other 'Guincelot' and 'Lanevere,' their old pet names.

In the evening, the women talked about their days, with Fidelia reciting the poetry she had read that day, and Branwen telling her new theories about the meaning of the gospels. Guinevere talked about her idea of a city of women, in which women could do any work they wanted. Ninian told tales in which Christian saints and older gods and goddesses had adventures together, and not too many nuns seemed to take offense. Fidelia and Valeria sang duets, although Fidelia had much the better voice. Darerca told about long-ago battles of words and arms between women and men in Ireland, but Anna told no tales of fighting. Instead, she told about the red deer she had seen that day, and what the deer had said to her. A cat purred in her lap.

She began to realize how much she liked the sound of Fidelia's voice reading poetry, and the sharpness of Branwen's mind. Anna was even growing used to Valeria, despite that nun's old tie to Guinevere. The abbess's diplomacy when the women quarreled also impressed Anna. She choked with laughter at Ninian's jests, and began to feel that she was not alone. She had companions, and did not even have to fight for the privilege.

When the abbess died, Guinevere wept. But she could hardly conceal her pride when the nuns elected her the abbess's successor. Some of the nuns objected that she was insufficiently pious, but others pointed out that she would be the best suited to contesting with the bishops.

One sister was bold enough to ask Guinevere whether she preferred the convent to marriage. Guinevere pursed her lips in a smile. "Yes, my dear, I do. But my marriage was different from most. I remained a virgin throughout it. That is why there were no children."

"Why, you are a saint, then," exclaimed the nun. "And perhaps King Arthur was, too."

"That would be quite an exaggeration," Guinevere replied. "I was just willful. A willful virgin." She laughed to herself.

Anna let herself become more and more a creature of the wild woods. Though the nuns were pleasant, she felt more akin to the wild beings. She sometimes thought she might have lost her ties to human life altogether if Guinevere were not here. If she had never met Guinevere, she might have become a saint--by good fortune, she met Guinevere, and was spared that fate.

At Anna's urging, no one told novices new to the convent about her past, but of course they know that Guinevere had been a queen.

Once a novice asked Anna, "You have known the Abbess Guinevere for a long time, haven't you?"

Anna smiled and said, "Yes."

"Pardon me for asking, but there are rumors that when she was married to King Arthur, she had a sinful liaison with another man. That couldn't be true, could it?"

"No, it couldn't," Anna said with a twinkle in her eye. "She never would have touched another man."

Anna rode alone. The very moss on the trees was not as green when Guinevere was not with her. Guinevere remained at the convent, which she did increasingly of late. There were so many reasons. Sick novices, visiting priests, newly arrived books. Today there was an old book that one of the convent's patrons had willed to the nuns, and Guinevere had immersed herself in its pages.

A wren sang and its song's sweetness pierced Anna. The notes trilled up and down. Anna spotted red mushrooms, beautiful but poisonous. It had rained the day before, but there was little mud. The sun shone as much as it could through the dense trees.

Screams drowned the wren's song. Anna made her horse race down the road til she turned a bend and saw a man carrying off a girl.

Anna's arm was stiff, for she was three score and ten, but she grabbed a dagger from her skirts and flew at the man.

He stared at her in amazement, which gave her time to come close enough to slash deeply into his sword arm. Now he was the one who screamed.

"An old nun! The legend is true!"

Anna pulled the girl from his horse to hers. "It is true." Anna spoke in her military officer's voice. "Go from here and never come back. Tell everyone you see that the ghost of an old nun still haunts this forest and protects all women."

"Will you help me bind up my wound?" he asked.

"No! Be gone!" Anna yelled.

He rode off quickly enough.

The girl Anna had saved gasped, "Thank you, sister." She crossed herself. "My father is a mile or so down the road. He tried to fight off that man, but the wretch unhorsed him."

"I'll take you to your father," Anna said, heading in the direction from which the girl had come.

"Everyone has heard the tale about the old nun who rescues women, but I hadn't believed it could be true." The girl's voice still shook.

"It is," Anna told her.

Anna's muscles ached. But she knew that Guinevere would rub a soothing potion on them that night. All was well because she was still with Guinevere.

THE END

ACKNOWLEDGMENTS

I express my gratitude to the writer whose story about Lancelot as a woman I read as a college freshman. I have searched for many years to find the story or the writer but have not been able to do so. That story inspired this book, and I have drawn on aspects of it, such as Lancelot's friendship with Gawaine.

I want to thank many people, especially Sherwood Smith, who has given me years of encouragement while I wrote these books, and Katherine V. Forrest, for a wonderful review of *Lancelot: Her Story.*

I thank all the friends who read the manuscript, especially Tricia Lootens, who read several early drafts, and Ken Louden, who read a very early draft when he was dying. I thank Betty Jean Steinshouer for reading more than one draft and for the considerable work she put into designing the books. I thank Virginia Cerello, Russell Cox, Liz Quinn, Victoria Stanhope, and Stephanie Wynn for reading the manuscript. I thank Amy Hamilton for helping me find the wonderful listserv ARTHURNET and for her encouragement of my writing.

I thank Viable Paradise for providing a great environment for writers, and everyone at VP XV, especially those who provided comments, including Stephanie Charette and LaShawn Wanak. I am particularly grateful for comments from Debra Doyle and Jim MacDonald, and to Debra for her editing.

I want to thank the wonderful friends and family who have given me emotional support over the years: Lois and Nancy Brown, Ned Cabot Sr., Suzie Carrigan, Tacie Dejanikus, Beth Eldridge, Colleen Flannery, Daniele Flannery, John S. Flannery, Carolyn Gage, Barbara Gardien, Julie Gerard Harris, Alice Henry, Marlene Howell, Jackie Hutchinson, Edward P. Jones, Sue Lenaerts, Vickie Leonard, Elizabeth Lytle, Colise Medved, Trudy Portewig, Luanne Schinzel, John Schmitz, Delores Smith, Liz Trapnell, and Judith Witherow. Above all, I am grateful to my wonderful mother, Joan Flannery Douglas, who always gave me love and encouraged me.

I am also grateful for the kindness of Mary Frances Moriarty, who has been like a second mother to me; Jim Bethea, who was my first unrelated male friend; Tom Field, a King Arthur who reigned with genius and compassion; Dean Ahearn, who was a true knight, loyal and excellent in all he did; and Lissa Fried, the bravest knight of all.

ABOUT THE AUTHOR

Carol Anne Douglas is a lifelong student of Arthurian and Shakespearian lore. Please review this volume and its prequel, *Lancelot: Her Story* on Amazon and Goodreads, and subscribe to her blog at **CarolAnneDouglas.com**

Proof

Made in the USA
Charleston, SC
02 November 2016